Ya'acov's WELL

NINA PECK

Ark House Press
PO Box 1722, Port Orchard, WA 98366 USA
PO Box 1321, Mona Vale NSW 1660 Australia
PO Box 318 334, West Harbour, Auckland 0661 New Zealand
arkhousepress.com

Cataloguing in Publication Data:
Title: Ya'acov's Well
ISBN: 9780648173458 (pbk.)
Subjects: Fiction
Other Authors/Contributors: Peck, Nina

Design by initiateagency.com

Contents

"To the one who believes in Me, it is just as the Scripture has said: 'Streams of living water will flow from within him.'" John 7:38 NIV

Dedicated to all women who relate to Mara bat Mal'akhiy. And to my own Shemu'el. I'm so glad you're still with me!

John 4
Luke 7
Luke 9:51-56
Acts 8

Key Characters:

Mara bat Mal'akhiy – this is her story
Mal'akhiy ben Yehudah – Mara's father
Yehudah – Mara's grandfather
Pinchas – Mara's grandmother
Dawid ben Mal'akhiy – Mara's older brother, a jeweler
Shemu'el ben Aharon – Dawid's closest friend, a shepherd from Sychar
Zimra bat Eli – Mara's close friend
Yelsaventa bat Yehu – Mara's wealthy friend from Sebaste
Levi ben Yehu – Yelsaventa's older brother
Amitai ben Yonatan – eldest son of the Samaritan High Priest
Micah ben Yosef – cavalry officer, turned merchant
Keren ben Yasriel – banker from Sychar
Naftali – mystery man – half Roman, half Samaritan
Eber ben Natan – runaway Jew, idol worshipper
Shimrit – cobbler from Sebaste
Kerah – lady of the night

Historical Characters:
Herod Archelaus – ethnarch of Judaea
Glaphyra – Herod Archelaus' Persian wife, former Queen of Mauretania
Yonatan – High Priest of the Samaritans
Yeshua – the Jewish Messiah
Philippos – the Evangelist
Cephas – Peter, the disciple of Yeshua
Yochanan – John, the beloved disciple
Shim'on the Magician – Simon Magnus – sorcerer in Acts 8

Chapter 1

A.D. 1, Sychar, Samaria, Roman province of Judaea

The scorching desert sun beat down on the group of travellers as they made their way through the hill country of Samaria – Shomron, the locals called it.

The russet earth, a stark contrast to the sky's vibrant blue, seemed to stretch on for miles, broken only by the puffs of green shrubs along the horizon.

A tall, dark man in his middle age cut a stately figure, climbing up the crags with the ease of a man many years his junior. His Roman tunic, neatly belted at the waist, clearly illustrated the world he lived in, but his tidily manicured beard showed that he was, first and foremost, a Samaritan.

Mal'akhiy ben Yehudah was proud of his heritage, proud to be what had once been one of the greatest races on this earth. He was, after all, flesh and blood of the great Israelites – a descendant of King Dawid, the Giant Slayer, and of Shelomoh, the Wise.

The Romans might rule every corner of the known world, but this harsh, desert hill country was not for the faint of heart and even after years of oppression from the Persians, the Medes, the Romans and of course, the Jews, the people of Shomron remained strong.

At Mal'akhiy's side walked a tousle-headed youth, perhaps sixteen years of age, without a trace of a beard yet gracing his smooth face. The boy, Mal'akhiy's youngest son, bore the name of the great Israelite king of old – Dawid.

Mal'akhiy smiled as he studied him. Dawid was everything a Samaritan boy should be – tall, well muscled and strong. His dark eyes gleamed with life. Dawid was Mal'akhiy's pride and joy.

Ahead of them ran a girl, laughing delightedly at the hot wind, blowing in from the Judaean desert to the south, rippling through her long hair. She loved the freedom of the mountains.

Mal'akhiy ben Yehudah watched his daughter as she ran. Eleven years old. Where had the time gone? How was it that his baby, his little girl, was nearly grown up already? He watched, silent in captivated awe, as the willowy child danced before him.

Mal'akhiy could still visualize her as the baby she had once been, not so very long ago it felt, the last of his offspring. He could still recall how it felt to hold her with her soft, baby skin and cooing cries, tight to his chest.

His oldest boy, El Jirah, was nearing twenty-seven years old now, had long since married and given him grandchildren. A girl, Maacah, had followed him, then Omri, a prized son, named after a long dead king of their people, then another girl, Rahal.

Dawid was his youngest son. They had thought that he would be the last, that five children would be all they'd ever have. Ado, Mal'akhiy's wife, was considered too old to carry more children. But Mara was a surprise, bringing with her a new financial strain and a sickness that lingered in her mother. Yet Mal'akhiy loved the child. Mara was his greatest treasure, but also his most tearing pain.

On a summer's day, after an easy labour, their delicate little girl had entered the world. She had hardly cried, giving just a little whimper, then falling into a contented sleep.

From her first few hours alive, Mara had been stunning. Such delicate features, such long eyelashes and thick, dark hair.

"She'll grow up to be a beauty, this one," people had said after seeing her in the days following her birth. She had been, by far, the prettiest newborn anyone had ever seen.

Like all babies, Mara had begun life with big, blue eyes, but like the rest of Mal'akhiy and Ado's children, they did not remain. Her eyes turned fiery golden within weeks.

"So unusual," the midwife had said, returning to visit the mother and baby. "There's something about this child. She is such a rare flower. You must name her something to turn the evil eye's attention from her, or surely she will suffer."

And so, they had named her Mara, meaning bitterness.

Little Mara had never been bitter, Mal'akhiy thought, as they continued their hike up through the hill country. She'd always been such a joyful, vivacious, little creature, full of life and fun and laughter.

Mara was the sort of person everyone just liked automatically. And yet, to Mal'akhiy, she represented both pain and beauty. But mostly pain.

Even after Mara was born, Ado had been weak. She had slipped from this life into death only four, short years after their baby's birth. Though he knew deep down it was unreasonable, Mal'akhiy couldn't help blaming the child dancing through the mountain grass for his deepest loss.

Ado wouldn't have died if Mara hadn't been born. He could have afforded the medicine to save his beloved wife if the child hadn't existed. The family could have remained in their hometown of Sychar, wouldn't have had to move to Sebaste, the great Romanised city at Samaria's heart, chasing the money that evaded them.

In some strange way, it was Mal'akhiy who had become bitter, though the name belonged to his child.

Winding their way up through the hilly valleys, Mal'akhiy found his eyes drawn, yet again, to his youngest. As she danced her way along the dusty paths, all Mal'akhiy could see was Ado as a girl. Mara was her very image. It broke his heart. How could he despise this child?

Mara's lush, dark hair flowed over her shoulders, framing her delicately boned, youthful face. Her skin was smooth, her features near-perfect.

As Mal'akhiy watched her, golden eyes flecked with fire gazed back at him. As always, they appeared full of laughter and ready for a challenge. He shook his head, rueful and filled with a deep-seated pain.

She was a stubborn one, this daughter of his. For all her good qualities, Mal'akhiy knew his wife, God rest her soul, had spoilt her as a little one. She had been too ill to do otherwise. And Mal'akhiy himself had pretty much left her to grow up on her own. It was too painful otherwise...

The result? Mal'akhiy knew he was reaping it now. Mara was oh-so sure of what she wanted at all times, oh-so confident and driven.

"Come Abba, we are nearly there! Hurry!" Mara called out over her shoulder, enthusiasm lighting her face. Mal'akhiy grunted. Always in a hurry, she was. And she loved him, despite his lack of open affection for her.

"I am coming, my daughter. Sychar isn't going anywhere. It will be there when we arrive whether we rush or not," he said. He tried to be firm with her, not to let her run away with her own desires. She didn't deserve that much freedom.

Mara had caused Mal'akhiy's greatest sorrow and for that he could not forgive her, nor for the relative poverty she had forced them into. And yet...

Tender, heart-breaking fatherly love filled him as he watched her, scurrying away up the crags, picking up her long skirts as she went, her sweet, little feet displayed for all the world to see. How could she know

4

the tumult of molten feelings – agony and affection – that she caused within her Abba?

Mal'akhiy wasn't ready for this time to be over. As much as he resented what she had brought, he still loved her, wanted her in his life. He wasn't ready for his little girl to be a woman, for her to be grown up and gone. But that time was approaching all too fast for his liking.

It wouldn't be long now, he knew, before the young men started coming and asking about her. Mara would be twelve in a few weeks – marriageable age in this Roman world.

Even though Mal'akhiy had little wealth to offer as dowry, there was no doubt that Mara's beauty would attract many admirers. Just like her mother had at that age.

Mal'akhiy could well remember the first time he saw the young woman who would become his wife, through an open window in an upstairs room. He and the other young men had often come to gaze upon Ado bat Ezra, undoubtedly the prettiest girl in all of Sychar. And somehow, it had been Mal'akhiy who had caught her eye, who had secured her hand. Still, all these years later, he couldn't help but wonder how he had been so blessed.

And now, their youngest daughter, Mara, was following in her mother's footsteps. Despite her youth, she was already the recipient of much admiration from the young men of their people.

And she encouraged them. A girlish laugh, a lingering gaze, a quiet whisper.

Mal'akhiy wasn't sure whether this was intentional, or an innocent, accidental by-product of her beauty and personality.

He knew he should probably address it with his girl, teach her the proper way to behave, but he didn't know how to. Talking with his youngest had always been difficult. He had avoided it when she was young, and now, in so many ways, it was too late. How he wished Ado was still around. She should have been the one to teach their child how

5

to be an honourable woman.

As they rounded the last hill, the narrow pass widened into the thick, dirt paths they were used to – no Roman roads this far out into the provinces. That was the one thing Mal'akhiy sorely missed about Sebaste when they were away.

On their left swelled Mount Ebal, green and flourishing; on their right soared the heights of Mount Gerizim, the mountain upon which their forefathers had worshipped.

Their ancestor, Yoheshu'a, had established a temple to Yahweh up on the mountain. But that was long gone now. The Jews, once the brothers of their people, had destroyed it just over one hundred years before. Mal'akhiy could remember exploring its ruins as a boy.

Soon, the family passed by the ruins of Shechem, another old town forged by their ancestors and destroyed by the Jews. It was hard to imagine that the crumbling blocks of golden sandstone had once housed families just like theirs. All too soon, the desert reclaimed what was abandoned as her own.

In the distance now, they could see the faint outline of their destination – Sychar. It was shimmering in the heat haze, but one could easily pick out its towers and the silhouettes of the square, flat-roofed buildings.

Ahead, Mara squealed in girlish excitement.

"Come on! Come on!" She begged, golden eyes flashing, taking her father and brother by one hand each, pulling them forward. Dawid, five years older than his sister, pulled his hand away, laughing at her exuberance. He was a good boy, Dawid, Mal'akhiy thought, watching. He had brought no pain to the family.

"We'll get there just as fast without your pulling me, Mara!" Dawid said firmly, unwilling to take his younger sister's bossing. "Besides, you have to remember, Abba and I are both looking forward to seeing our grandparents and all our friends. We don't want to hold things up either."

"You can't possibly be as excited as I am," Mara countered defiantly, her face full of cheek. "Or you'd be running as I have been!"

The faint view of Sychar's jumble of houses and mighty, columned, official buildings became ever clearer as they approached.

It changed from a silhouette into concise buildings, doorways, streets and people. Now they could see the marketplace at the centre of town and the forum, swaying palm trees outlining it all. Every part of the view looked like home.

Mal'akhiy and his family had lived there until Mara was five years old, when his work as a stonemason had taken him away to Sebaste. The long walk between the two cities was always worth it, just to feel the streets of home beneath his feet, and the arms of those he held dear about him. His children loved it here in Sychar as well.

Mara set off at a run, closing the distance between herself and town as fast as she possibly could. Her long hair billowed out behind her, her happy laughter carrying on the breeze.

Up ahead, Mal'akhiy could see his parents, older than he remembered, but otherwise unchanged, standing on their doorstep, just off the main street. Both of them stood, arms outstretched as Mara rushed into them.

"Savta! Saba!" She cried, hugging first her grandmother, then her grandfather, tightly. They hugged her back, eyes bright with joy.

"How you've grown Mara!" Her Saba, Yehudah said, a smile on his whiskered, old face. "I will no longer be able to call you my Little Flower soon!" He continued, a little wistfully.

He met Mal'akhiy's gaze over Mara's head. It was too soon. None of them were ready for their little girl to be a fully grown woman.

Mal'akhiy nodded his agreement. "She will be of marriageable age next month!"

Yehudah shook his head. "No! It can't be that already. It seems only yesterday she was a baby in your sweet wife's arms," he said. Mal'akhiy just smiled, not letting on to his own, very similar thoughts, or the underlying, much more angry musings he tried to hard to quell. *It should be Ado here, not this child who has robbed my life of joy, stolen my happiness.* Being home in Sychar always brought back the rawest of aches. It was here that his wife was buried, just outside the city's boundaries.

Unaware of his son's agony, Yehudah turned his attentions to his tall grandson. "Dawid! A true man now!"

Dawid grinned and embraced his grandparents. "We've missed you very much Saba and Savta."

His Savta, Pinchas, put her sun-spotted hand up to his cheek and patted it gently.

"We've missed you too, dear boy! As we always do," she said tenderly. "Come now, let us go inside!" She urged. "You've had a long journey, let's get you all settled."

Pinchas ushered them on into the courtyard of their house. The outer wall sealed in their little sanctuary, with its small garden and pillared terrace. Within that lay the two-levelled home they all loved so much. Nothing had changed in years, Mal'akhiy thought. Since he was a boy, even. The same white wash on the sandy walls, the same tall palms towering over the garden... It was good to be home. And it was good to have his youngest two right here beside him.

Chapter II.

A.D. 1, Sychar, Samaria, Roman province of Judaea

M ara bat Mal'akhiy was a clever girl. She always got her own way. Her Abba and her older siblings had always let her do as she liked – it was easier than trying to teach her, or mould her. Besides, she knew, all too well, the way to make people think her ideas were their own.

Whenever she was staying with her grandparents, Mara always managed to convince them to let her sleep out on their flat, open roof, wrapped up in thick blankets woven by her Savta. She loved to lie looking up at the stars, which always glowed so brightly here, away from the big-city lights.

She was glad that her grandparents' house scraped the very limits of Sychar, where the wind rustled the leaves of the olive trees outside and the cooing call of the birds echoed through the narrow streets.

As Mara settled down to sleep, she could hear the night-life of the town drawing to a close, ready to turn in for their rest, as well.

There were mostly family homes in this area, but in the distance, she could hear the sounds of laughter and music coming from the taverns off forum. The tapestry of sounds wove mental images of her childhood here.

Eventually, she would fall asleep, only to awaken as the first, golden rays of sunlight tiptoed their way over the horizon and up onto her face. Their warmth and light would welcome her to a new day whenever she was at Sychar, for it was almost always sunny.

This morning was no exception. Mara lay back, snuggled deep into the folds of her blankets, content to listen as the day commenced in the street down below.

The birds had been awake long since and now the shepherds and stock tenders were heading out of town and up into the hills. The melancholy strains of their flutes and the strums of their harps trailed behind them, mixing with the jingling of the sheep bells.

Merchants were heading into the town, to the market in the forum and all around the general populace were preparing for the day.

Across the street, a housewife was singing at the top of her lungs and another yelling for her to hush her loud mouth. A smile slipped its way across Mara's lips. There was no place like home.

Scrambling down from the roof, Mara made her way to where her grandmother was preparing bread in the open-air kitchen.

Most modern homes in Samaria were Roman-style and had the kitchen within the home, but Mara's grandmother had always insisted that this was the one old custom she would cling to.

Pinchas' mother and her grandmother before had had their ovens out in the yard and she herself had learnt to cook that way. Her cooking was fine the way it was – why should she change just based on a fashion?! – Pinchas would insist.

As Mara descended into the yard, her Savta was, as she expected, already hard at work over the big, round, stone oven. Pinchas had her long, greyed hair tied back in a large, demurely coloured scarf. A big smile bloomed on her kind face as she spotted her youngest grandchild.

"Sleep well, my lovey?" She asked, offering her cheek to Mara.

Mara kissed it exuberantly.

"I certainly did Savta. Have I ever mentioned that I love it here?!" She asked.

"Only every time you're with us!" Her grandmother laughed.

Mara breathed in deeply, enjoying the mixture of smells. Pinchas' kitchen always wafted beautiful aromas of cinnamon, saffron, caraway and cumin and as they filled her lungs, they filled her heart with happiness too.

Pinchas set Mara to work, preparing the dough to be rolled out into the large, flat, unleavened bread she would soon cook over the fire.

Mara obediently got on with her task, looking longingly out through the gate at the edge of the courtyard as she did. She wanted more than anything to escape out into the streets and rush out to Ya'acov's Well.

But her Grandmother wasn't ready to relinquish her quite yet. She sat her down at the table, and handed her a few dates – her favourite treat.

Pinchas ran her fingers through Mara's thick hair and then, reaching for her fine-toothed bone comb, began brushing it through.

"You've blossomed overnight my Flower, haven't you?" She said a little wistfully, pulling out a bottle of perfumed oil and brushing it through Mara's locks. The scent of mountain blossoms swirled around them.

Mara lent back into her Savta, enjoying the sweet moment. She'd missed things like this since her Imah had died and her sisters had married and moved away.

"I'm almost all grown up Savta! Next time you see me, I'll be a grown lady," she giggled, batting her eyelashes. Pinchas smiled, but inside she held back a sigh. If only the girl before her, right on the verge of womanhood, realized how much she would one day miss this time, perhaps she would not be so eager for it to pass.

Mara was tall for her age – already past Pinchas herself in height, willowy and becoming shapely. She had often been mistaken for older than her eleven-nearly-twelve years. How long now until the child within her was all gone?

Pinchas said nothing as she finished off Mara's hair, braiding two of the front-most pieces into a multi-faceted crown encircling her hairline. The rest was left to flow free. She handed her granddaughter her bronze mirror and Mara gazed at her reflection.

"You look just like your Imah," Pinchas said softly. Mara turned back to face her Savta and smiled somewhat shyly.

"Oh no, Savta, that could never be true. One thing I remember is how beautiful my Imah was, and I look nothing like that," she said, looking down as she spoke.

Mara couldn't remember much of her mother now. She could still see a flickering image of her, stunning despite her illness. But that flickering image almost seemed to Mara a stranger. Her heart ached as she considered what she had lost.

Pinchas shook her head slowly.

"You are her very image Mara. I truly hope you grow to become a good, faithful woman just as she was. Become her image-bearer in every way, child," she urged, tenderly. Mara smiled and got to her feet. She was finished being sentimental.

"May I go out to the Well, Savta? Do we need water?"

Pinchas swallowed. She wasn't quite so ready to get over her emotion.

"I suppose we do. Off you go then, but don't be too long." She waved Mara over to where her water jars and the long rope with the leather water skin lay. Mara had just begun to gather these up when Dawid came strolling through, rubbing sleep from his eyes.

"Off to the well, Mara?" He asked, yawning. "Can I join you?"

Mara grinned at her brother, eyes twinkling with mischief.

"If you do all the heavy carrying, of course you can!" She offloaded the heavy jar to him and led the way out into the street. Pinchas watched her two youngest grandchildren recede into the distance. Times were changing, she felt. That much was for certain.

* * *

Spending time with Dawid was something Mara had always loved. They had always been the best of friends. He alone of her siblings truly understood her and loved her deeply. Other than her grandparents, Dawid was the only one whose affections Mara was totally sure of.

Dawid knew Mara in the same way he knew himself and she knew him likewise. In a bond only siblings can share, their souls were bare to one another.

The two of them, despite their closeness, couldn't have been more different. Mara was impetuous, bold, outgoing, passionate... everything her brother was not. In turn, Dawid was quiet, steady, reliable and serious.

However, their shared memories of growing up fed into a tightly woven web of shared feelings, thoughts, fears and longings. It almost seemed that they could know what the other would be thinking without even a word passing between them.

As they headed out to Ya'acov's Well on that bright, sunny morning, weaving their way through the people of Sychar, the two of them knew each other's truest contentment and felt glad for one another. Both of them loved this town as the home of their hearts, and missed it desperately when they were away.

People waved and shouted their greetings as Mal'akhiy's two children passed by, but no one stopped to chat, so busy were they about their days.

Sychar was the political centre of the region and the home to many important people - not only political leaders, but also the high priest of their people, as the synagogue where they worshipped was at Sychar's heart.

Mara could see its many columned frontage from the street as they passed by, as well as the row of fastidiously robed priests making their way in. A little bubble of admiration escaped her lips at the beautiful fabrics their robes were crafted from– shining whites, reds and gold trims.

She stopped to watch a moment, but Dawid pulled her on impatiently.

"Let's go, Mara!" He urged. "Shemu'el will just be taking his flocks out of town now to water them before the day begins. We might catch him at the well if we hurry!"

Mara sighed and rolled her eyes playfully, but she followed him all the same.

Shemu'el was her brother's closest friend from childhood. Dawid always spent the majority of their time in Sychar in his presence. Shemu'el was as tall as Dawid and dark, tanned by his many hours spent in the sun. He was a shepherd by trade, having been left a nice lot of healthy sheep by an elderly uncle who loved him dearly.

Shepherds weren't known as being of good character. Most shepherds were in the trade because they couldn't get reputable work in the town. With Shemu'el, it was different. He did the work because he genuinely loved the outdoors and his motley flock.

Shemu'el was an honourable young man about a year older than Dawid. Mara couldn't help thinking that in some ways, he seemed *much* older, with his slightly serious face and his deep thinking ways. He was, however, always ready for some hilarity and had a most recognizable and infectious laugh.

Sure enough, when they made it to the well, a little way out of town near an overgrown, shady olive grove, Shemu'el was there with his flock. Shem grinned and waved as he saw the two figures approaching.

"Dawid! Mara! How good to see you both!" He called out. Dawid clasped his arm in greeting, before embracing his friend.

"We're glad to be back home for a while!" He said. "How are things with you?"

Shemu'el smiled, friendly crinkles forming around his eyes. Mara noticed he had a shadowy growth of facial hair across his face now – that was new.

"Things are well. Yahweh is good to me," he said.

He turned to hug Mara warmly.

"My, how you've grown since last I saw you," he said, surprised. Mara wasn't sure whether to feel flattered or offended.

"I wasn't so very much a child last time I was here, was I?" She asked, batting her eyelashes in half-offense, deeming this the best reaction. Dawid laughed at her indignation.

"You most definitely were, little sister. All of a sudden you've sprouted! You're almost a full-grown woman now," he teased, eyes bright. Mara swatted at him with her hands, rolling her eyes.

"I wish everyone would stop talking about me like I'm a fruit tree or something! My, you've sprouted, little bat-Mal'akhiy!" She mock-pouted, hands on her slim hips. She couldn't help but notice Shemu'el blushing a little and hurriedly changing the subject. Clearly, it was too strange to him for the three of them to be talking about growing up. Mara agreed.

As children, it had always been Shemu'el and Dawid trotting off to do things and little Mara trailing in their wake. She'd always wanted to be included and would beg Dawid to let her come with them. He'd always tell her to go home and she would cry. The tears would always been the point at which Shemu'el would tell him to let her come.

Shem had always had a soft spot for Mara. She glanced over at him, already deep in conversation with Dawid about something or other.

He was an adult now and here she was, on the very verge of adulthood herself. Would everything be different now? Would they remain friends? Or would that also change, along with the rest of Mara's world?

Proper young ladies weren't supposed to have male friends. Or go outside the house without an escort. Or dance in the streets... or have opinions. They were supposed to just stay home and weave mats, or help with the housework - even in their modern Romanised world! Mara wasn't sure she was ready for such a life! Not that her father would notice whether she behaved properly or not, she thought miserably. She was almost invisible to him.

Whilst Mara was still deep in thought, Dawid and Shemu'el drew up water from the well, watering Shemu'el's sheep and filling Pinchas' water jars. They splashed some of the icy water onto Mara, making her squeal and splash them back, but the water fight didn't last long.

Sitting on the well's edge, Mara listened to her brother and Shem talk, but her mind wasn't on their words. She was deep in thought. *What it would be like to be seen, not as a girl to be dismissed or teased mercilessly, but as a woman to be sought after, desired, loved, and cherished?*

What would it feel like to have handsome young men chasing after her the way they'd chased her big sisters once, before they got married and settled down with children? To have poems written to her, songs sung about her, gifts given to her? To feel desired. Wanted.

Subconsciously, she began to play with her hair, patting the coil her Savta had earlier made across the crown of her head and tucking long strands behind her ears.

Mara hoped she looked beautiful, that any young men they might chance to meet on the way back through Sychar would take notice of her.

"Hey, Mara! I'm talking to you!" Dawid's voice and clod of dirt thrown at her feet jolted her back to reality. She looked up and saw him standing with Shemu'el, a few paces from the well.

"Finished preening?" Dawid teased with a wink far too roguish for his humble personality, Mara felt.

She shot him a warning glance. He knew how she hated to be made fun of, especially in front of others. He grinned his most winning smile and shrugged an apology. "I'm going with Shemu'el and the flock. Will you be okay to take the water jar back to town by yourself?"

Mara nodded pertly.

"I'll be fine. I'll tell Abba where you've gone – he'll expect you back by evening," she replied, hefting the water jar up onto her shoulder.

She watched Shemu'el gathering his sheep all around himself in the long, tawny grass, numbering each of them. The two young men waved to her as they set off into the foothills of Mount Ebal, to the east. Mara waved back and began to make her way towards town.

The water jar was heavier than she had first realized, so she stopped for a little rest in a patch of wild flowers, near the edge of town. The vibrant colours of the blooms caught her eye and she couldn't resist picking some and tucking them into the braid gracing her brow.

She also picked a few more in a bunch for her Savta, knowing how much her grandmother loved the flowers that grew wild around these parts. The people of Shomron were intensely proud of their "promised land" and all it bore.

The town was bustling as Mara made her way back through, the water jar perched high on her head. It was mid-morning now and everyone was busy going about their days. Mara enjoyed walking through the streets, listening to people calling out to one another, or singing as they went.

Despite her heavy burden, she felt light and happy as she went along, carefully weaving her way around pot-holes and animal mess in the road.

Outside the synagogue, Mara paused once again. Seeing people go in and out, dressed in their best clothes, ready to make offerings or to pray about significant matters, was something she'd always loved to observe.

She watched a young couple making their way in, the young woman, hair elaborately coiled into the nape of her neck, with hands clasped through the man's arm. The woman looked up at the man so adoringly that Mara felt her heart flip with an intense longing.

She leaned up against a wall opposite, watching as the two of them stopped outside to talk to a handsome young man, with a distinctively curved nose and dark eyes, thickly lashed. He was fairly tall and well muscled under his Roman tunic, dark curls of hair falling across his

17

strong forehead. Mara watched him a little too intently, noticing more new feelings wash through her. This was the sort of man she had always dreamed of marrying.

As she watched, he looked across the street and their eyes met. In that instant, Mara felt a cold shock run through her, leaving her cheeks aflame. She saw a small smile cross the boy's lips, but that was all she saw before she turned and hurried away, embarrassed.

How had she allowed herself to be caught staring? Mara felt humiliated. She rushed all the way back to her grandparents' home, trying not to slosh the water from her jar as she went. The moment she reached the outer courtyard, she flung herself around the bend, out of sight from the street. She panted to catch her breath, not realizing she'd been holding it so long.

Pinchas appeared out of the home itself.

"Oh, good, Mara, you've returned. Where is Dawid? Out with Shemu'el, I suppose?" She asked. Mara nodded, hoping her cheeks were not still aflame. She didn't want her Savta to ask any awkward questions.

"Yes, he said to let you know he would be home by sunset."

She maneuvered the pottery jar into the house and hurried off before her grandmother could ask her anything else.

The roof felt nice and cool as Mara settled into a spot under the brightly coloured awning. The day had begun to heat up, but the breeze blowing off the mountains cooled her flaming cheeks.

She felt strange. This was the first day she'd ever really considered that her childhood was almost over. Everyone had been talking about it.

Before she knew it now, she would be of marriageable age and, she hoped, betrothed and well on her way to being a rich, married matron with a fancy house and many servants. It was the first day she'd ever really looked at a man and considered him a prospective suitor. It was silly, she knew, but the thought had hit her before she could help it.

Mara watched the people walking down below in the streets and tried to imagine each of their stories. At some point or another, each of them had married and moved on to the next stage of life. How many of them, she wondered, had married for love? Had that slight woman with the protruding belly, nearing her time of birth?

Mara studied the sad expression on her sallow face and decided she could not have.

What about that man wrangling the camels down the high street? Perhaps he was not yet married, for he still looked fairly young, she decided. She hoped he would find happiness, as she herself longed to.

Why is it that God gives some of us wonderfully happy marriages, and others, hopeless ones? Mara pulled her knees up to her chin as she thought. *And why does He end happy marriages like my parents' one, with death?*

She bit her lip, unable to answer her own questions and not thinking to take them either to her Creator, or to someone older, wiser, who might know the answers.

Mara didn't like asking people questions. It made her feel inferior. Her preferred method was to act as though she had all the answers she could desire already.

If only she did... Mara continued to chew her lip, deep in thought once again. For as long as she could remember, she'd had deep-seated doubts, secret, unanswered longings she didn't know how to handle.

It seemed to Mara that she was the only one in their community who could see how fickle they were. Some of their people worshipped their God devoutly, whilst others served power, money, foreign gods, or Rome much more highly. No one else seemed to care that their lives were essentially meaningless.

Why was it that her Imah had died, after living out her days entirely devotedly? Why was it that, despite her Abba's deep, complex love for her, Mara had always longed for a different life? A richer one. One where she was someone. Why couldn't she just be content? Why was she always so unhappy, deep down?

The sun was high in the sky, beating down with scorching intensity on the mud brick roof. As sweat began to trickle down Mara's spine, she left her post and descended into the cool interior of the house.

Pinchas had finished preparing the midday meal of olives and flat wheels of bread and they all sat around, eating and talking. Mara loved these peaceful times Sychar provided – no work to be done, no rushing to have everything ready for guests, or classes, or meetings.

Later, as the sun began its downwards passage to the horizon, Mara begged leave from her Savta once more and made her way out into the hills beyond Sychar.

She just wanted to walk, to let the wind breathe life into her. It was a hot wind now, filling her with sunshine inside. She felt much better for the good food and her grandparents' company. Her inner worries always fled in their presence.

Her feet lead her back to her favourite place – Ya'acov's Well. The well had been built many centuries before by the very first Israelite – Ya'acov himself. The stories of his life – his war with his twin brother Esau, his wrestling with God, his twelve sons and his two wives – one he adored, one he was tricked into marrying, had always intrigued Mara. There was such history in that place. Such mystery.

As she came to the well, she saw Dawid in the distance, heading her way. She ran to meet him.

"Did you have a good day?" She asked, cheerfully. Dawid nodded, wrapping a lanky arm around her shoulders.

"I always have a good time when I'm out with Shem. He's such a thinker, Mara. I'm sure he considers Yahweh all the time and thinks about His word constantly." Dawid shook his head in amazement. "I wish I was as good a man as he is. He has a heart after God's own, I am sure of it."

Mara laughed.

"Surely he doesn't think of Yahweh constantly, Dawid. How boring!" Dawid shook his head again, this time in denial of her words.

"Not at all. The way Shemu'el speaks, he truly knows our Creator and genuinely loves Him. Shem insists that we shouldn't worship any god but Yahweh and that He is a good God to our people. We just need to turn our hearts back to Him and follow Him in all we do."

"Then he sounds like a Jew!" Mara muttered in muted irritation. She didn't want to talk about religion. She'd already wasted too much of her day contemplating such things.

"He's much better than a Jew, Mara," Dawid continued. "None of those silly rules, none of the nonsense outside of the Law of Moses."

Mara rolled her big, golden eyes.

"Can't we talk about something else?"

Dawid hugged her tighter, chuckling affectionately.

"Am I boring you with my talk of religion, little sister? These things too lofty for your pretty little head?"

"Hey! Don't be so rude!" Mara griped. "What a thing to say. I can understand them well enough, I just don't see any use in discussing them all the time."

Dawid down looked at her, surprise crossing his slightly sunburnt face.

"Really, Mara? Can there be anything worth discussing more than this?" He asked. Mara wrinkled her nose and ignored his question, hoping he'd get the silent hint and change the topic.

"Well, surely even you can't deny that Shemu'el is a good man and that he seeks Yahweh with all his heart."

"Can you speak of nothing else but Shemu'el?" Mara asked impatiently, rolling her eyes again. Dawid ignored her words.

"You'd do well to marry a man like him one day," he said. At last,

Mara's desired topic had come up, but definitely not in her desired way. She laughed.

"Marry Shemu'el? You can't be serious!" She said, unable to keep a slight measure of scorn from her voice.

Dawid looked surprised again.

"Why ever not? He's a good man and he could provide well for a wife."

Mara pulled a face.

"Oh really, Dawid! There's more to marriage than that. He's not handsome at all and he has no wealth to speak of. What kind of marriage would it be? Besides, he only thinks of me as a child, as your baby sister."

Dawid frowned and pulled his arm away from her.

"I thought more of you Mara. Do you really think that's all that matters in a marriage? And besides, how do you know he only sees you as a child? He speaks highly of you, though now I hear what you think of him, I'm not quite sure why he would."

Mara sensed her brother was starting to anger and put a placatory hand on his arm.

"Really, Dawid, there's no need to get defensive. I'm just ambitious, that's all," she said, seeking to sooth his ruffled feathers. "I want to marry someone with status. Someone who will make me someone by default. Someone who has standing with Rome and who is favoured by Herod in Sebaste, or with our leaders here. I want to be someone and have the opportunity to be known. Shemu'el is a good man, but he can hardly offer me that."

Dawid shook his head ruefully and slung his arm back over Mara's shoulder.

"You're too young to make such decisions for yourself. You need to wait, or let Father arrange your marriage to a good man of our social standing. Right now, your judgement is clouded by youth."

Mara tried not to bristle at his well intended, but condescending words. "Oh, because you're so mature yourself!" She muttered under her breath. "And as if Abba cares who I marry, as long as I'm someone else's problem."

They were walking through the streets of town now, so she kept her voice low, not wanting to be overheard. Sychar was famous for its gossiping culture.

"I'm old enough to know my mind, at least and I know that I want to marry a man with wealth and reputation. I want to be someone, to be known as the richest, most beautiful, most desirable woman in the whole of Shomron and that will not change. I can tell you that."

Dawid said nothing, keeping his thoughts of her immaturity to himself.

As they passed through a group of young maidens, perhaps a few years Mara's senior, all pretty, with flowers woven into their hair, one of them smiled up at him and batted her eyelashes.

He turned away, a little embarrassed, but Mara had already seen. At once her grumpy mood lifted and she giggled.

"Oooh, Dawid. The girls can see that the most handsome man in town is my brother. And you could have anyone you choose," she teased. Dawid was about to deny it when he looked up and saw all the girls now smiling at him and waving over their shoulders.

He laughed.

"And you know what, Mara? I want none of them. I want a good wife who loves Yahweh and who will help me with my work. Besides, how can I afford a wife yet? I've not finished my apprenticeship."

Mara grinned as her imagination cast an image of a small, thin girl with big eyes leaning over Dawid's work bench, helping him select jewels. Any girl would be proud to marry the good-looking young jeweller's apprentice.

She wiggled her eyebrows at him and took his hand, pulling him along the street with her. The group of girls who had been watching them all turned away, disappointed. Clearly, the handsome boy was already taken. If only they had known the beautiful young woman was just his sister...

"Let's not talk about it anymore. I'm tired of all the discussion on growing up. Clearly neither of us are ready to marry, so I don't know why we're worrying about it yet. Let's just be content to enjoy our time here, away from all the cares and worries of Sebaste," she urged. Dawid grinned, a boy once more.

"You're right Mara. There's no need to get caught up in all of that yet. Come on, I'll race you back to Saba and Savta's!"

In that moment, Mara was perfectly happy. Tomorrow night would be the feast at the New Moon – the reason for their trip to Sychar – and all was right in the world.

Chapter III.

A.D. 1, Sebaste, Samaria, Roman province of Judaea

All too soon, the New Moon had come and gone and so had their time in Sychar. As always, Mara found their return to Sebaste to be bittersweet. She missed the calm, traditional pace of things and all her loved ones in Sychar, but still, it was nice to be back in charge of her daily life, sleeping in her own room and with her friends nearby.

Besides, as much as she adored Sychar, Sebaste was a far more modern city, complete with all of the comforts Romanisation had to offer. It was well known to be one of the most fantastic cities in all of the empire, thanks to Herod the Great, father of the current tetrarch, Herod Archelaus.

Sychar, situated in between the two mountains – Gerizim and Ebal – was a relatively arid region. Sebaste, however, built as the original City of Kings, was a lush, rich and most coveted area. The envy of all Palestine, some called it. Sebaste was a city of which to be proud. Herod's ostentatious palace, widely rumoured to be even more magnificent than Emperor Augustus' own palace in Rome itself, was the city's crown jewel.

It had been late the night before, long after sundown, when Mal'akhiy and his two youngest children had made it home.

Their two slaves, Achsah and Abihud, the door-slave, welcomed them home with water for washing and a good meal.

Soon after daybreak, Mal'akhiy and Dawid had both rushed off to their day's toil, leaving Mara home alone with the slaves to sort out the home after their absence.

Mara always loved the feeling of being in charge of the house and getting to give orders to the slaves. She couldn't remember a time when Achsah and Abihud hadn't been in her family's service.

Mal'akhiy had bought Achsah as a nursemaid for Mara soon after his wife had died. Nowadays, her role was more of a housekeeper and although she was getting on in years, she was still very capable.

Mal'akhiy was kept busy with his work as a stone mason. Sebaste was, after all, a Roman town in the midst of a sand-swept landscape and the intricate Persian carvings the city was forged upon were always in the need of repair. Now that Dawid had begun his apprenticeship to the master jeweller, Mara found the house very quiet.

She knew she should be thankful - the slaves were another luxury not everyone could afford. In fact, they couldn't really afford the slaves. If Achsah and Abihud hadn't been purchased in days of better finances, they wouldn't be here now.

Achsah was one of the things Mara missed most when she was away from their town house. The woman was of strong stock Canaanite, diligent and hardworking. She never shirked at tasks and never held back from sharing her opinion where she thought it might be welcome.

She was a part of the family really, although Mal'akhiy expected his children to still treat her as the servant she was.

Generally, Mara stuck to this principle, but sometimes, she couldn't resist making Achsah her confidante.

Of course, she had friends about the city, but as the unmarried girls' lives mainly existed around gossip and weaving, she never felt able to whisper her secrets into any of their ears.

Achsah was different – she, essentially, lived to keep her mouth shut, Mara figured. Besides, without a mother, Mara longed to hear the advice of an older woman, even if she was of far inferior rank and the advice was rarely actually taken.

"Achsah?" Mara bellowed from the top balcony of their home. "Have you seen my green palla?"

Down at the bottom of the garden, where she had been hanging washing over the bushes, Achsah put a hand on her back as she straightened, expression disapproving.

"Miss Mara! Does the entire neighborhood need to hear your requests? In case you hadn't remembered, this house joins directly onto other homes, and I'm sure they don't care even a little about your green scarf," she said sternly. But her eyes were twinkling under the little curls cut across her brow - the latest fashion, she had assured Mara.

Mara sighed and came running down the stairs two at a time.

"Well, have you seen it?" She asked upon alighting in the courtyard. Achsah shook her head, turning back to the laundry basket.

"You should keep better track of your things," she replied primly. Mara pouted, her pretty face clouding. Achsah gave her a look which clearly said spoilt child.

"I've been invited to a party at Hadassah's this afternoon, and I want to wear that with my white linen stola," Mara moaned, exasperated.

Achsah just shrugged.

"I'm sorry, I haven't seen it. Have you tried in the kitchen? You left some things draped over the bench last night when you came in."

Mara rushed to the kitchen. The scarf lay in a limp sea-green puddle and Mara snatched it up, delighted. Satisfied that her success at the party was assured, she skipped happily back up to her room.

Getting ready for parties – even simple garden parties like the one she was heading to now – was something Mara took very seriously. Earlier that morning, she had washed in the big ceremonial water jar in the courtyard – no time to visit the baths today.

Up in her room, she settled on her bed and set about her beauty routine. Using her bronze mirror, Mara applied make-up to her face, staining her lips red and painting her eyelids in a shimmery hue of muted green. It matched her green scarf perfectly.

She added dark cat's eyes of kohl. This was her favourite style of eye make up – it made her feel mysterious and grown up.

Mara summoned Achsah to style her hair, deciding to wear it half up, half down, ornamented with beaded slides throughout. She examined herself critically in the mirror before she left. Her fine-boned, angular face was lovely in all its adornment and she felt pretty. Splashing some perfumed oil onto her wrists and at her neck, she dashed from the room.

Mara knew she really should wait for someone to escort her to the party, as it was a few streets away and it was unseemly for an unmarried girl of her age and social standing to wander out alone. But she was eager to go and had no inclination to wait for her father or Dawid to return home. Taking care that Achsah wasn't looking, she slipped past Abihud and out the front gate.

Making her way through the streets of Sebaste, Mara was aware that she was the subject of many interested gazes, but ignored them all. She had once overheard her Abba telling her grandparents how people watched her, how she seemed to have power over people's gazes, but she didn't really care.

Mara was not overly tall, but her slender, willowy frame made her appear rather lengthy. Her skin was not as olivey as many of her people, nor was she too pale.

She was not heavy in the slightest, yet she had blossomed into womanly curves beyond her years.

Her hair, so thick and luxurious, drew the eye. Adorned as she was, exotic and enchanting, with her fire-golden eyes blazing happily, Mara was the picture of beauty.

And what she was not physically, she was by way of personality. Her quick, musical laugh and winning smile were enough to brand her permanently onto any man's memory, young though she was.

The power of her own charm and beauty was not something Mara had fully discovered yet. All she knew was that people seemed to find her attractive and she liked it.

As she walked, a boy called out to her across the street, but she ignored him, pretending to be intent on Herod's palace, towering in the distance.

The city of Sebaste had once been the city of the kings of Israel — they had called it Shomron, though outsiders referred to it as Samaria. It had been a city to rival the Jews' Jerusalem back then. The ruins of the old Samaria were still there, underneath a temple built by the ethnarch Herod, for the Roman Emperor.

The great kingdom of the Israelites had come to a sudden end when the Assyrians had arrived, taking the majority of their people into exile. The Jewish prophets had claimed it was a judgement; that their God, Yahweh, was angry with their people for turning their backs on His ways.

Later on, Alexander of the Greeks had come in and turned Samaria into a town for his Macedonian veterans. The enormous rounded towers, positioned all around the city, were built by these Macedonians as protection.

An Hasmonean king had utterly destroyed Samaria again about a hundred years before Mara's birth, only to see it rebuilt by his successor. It seemed this city was to be eternal.

Following that destruction, Herod the Great, vassal-King of Judaea under the Roman emperor, took control and transformed Samaria into what it now was — a bustling Roman city in the middle of a Jewish world.

Herod had once supported Emperor Caesar Augustus' opposition and, eager to regain the new emperor's favour, renamed Samaria in favour of him – Sebaste was born.

The columned *cardo*, the north-south Roman road through the heart of Sebaste, down which Mara now walked, was Herod's doing, as was the *decomanus maximus* – the east, west columned street and the forum, built at the two roads' meeting point.

He had also built a large basilica, a theatre and brought water into the city via an underground aqueduct. It was his doing, also, that Sebaste was surrounded by high walls - over four kilometres long, divided up by the gates and the towers built by the Macedonians long before.

The original Herod had died when Mara was little and the city of Sebaste was given over to his son, Herod Archelaus. Only a few short years ago, when the Romans had made Judaea into a proper province, Sebaste had become a sort of centre of Roman government. The local soldiers that had once been part of Herod's personal army became auxiliary troops to the mighty Roman war machine. Through and through, this was a true Roman city now.

As Mara neared the hippodrome, she turned off the *cardo* onto a small side street. Her friend's home was on the corner of the narrow lane.

Hadassah's family was wealthier than Mara's and, as such, their home was much larger. It was built with even more Roman grandeur, complete with its own private bathing facilities.

When Mara arrived, she was welcomed into the inner garden of the home, where several tall, brightly coloured tents had been erected.

A shining red head of curls poked out from the largest tent and Hadassah's dark eyes smiled up at Mara.

"Oh, Mara! I'm so glad you've made it! Come in, and join us. We're telling love fortunes," she giggled, in her little-girlish lisping voice, beckoning Mara on into their colourful booths.

Mara slipped her way inside, finding five other girls of about their age seated on cushions, strings of brightly coloured beads in their hands. The sunshine shining through the tent's colourful fabric gave the girls a glow of vibrant purple and red and set them awash with blue.

Hadassah patted the cushion beside her and Mara sat down. She looked over at the other girls, all adorned in splendid colours, with jewels and beads in their hair and about their necks. She recognized several of them. Her closest friend, Zimra bat Eli, was amongst their number.

Half of the girls present were tall, mature fourteen year olds, betrothed already, or soon to be. Hadassah, Mara, and Zimra were the younger ones.

Hadassah and Mara both looked older than their age, whereas Zimra was small and slightly frail looking. She had pale, nearly green eyes which stuck out from her face a little, appearing a bit too large for her slight features. She was a good, kind girl and Mara loved her despite her lack of beauty.

"So, who's to marry who then?" Mara asked, referring to the game the girls were playing with the beads strung through their fingers.

"Yelsaventa is to marry a Roman soldier!" Hadassah exclaimed with another giggle. "She got the red bead and she saw a handsome Roman in her dream last night. It has to be a sign." The girls all squealed and squeezed at Yelsaventa's hands. She was the oldest of their number, already engaged, but definitely not above their girlish games.

"I'd much prefer him to marrying that old man my Father has chosen," she sniffed and all the girls laughed sympathetically.

"Who wouldn't?!" Mara added, eyes twinkling. She shot Yelsaventa an understanding look though. To be betrothed to an old man, no matter how rich, was no girl's precious dream.

"At least he's a good man," Zimra said gently.

Yelsaventa shrugged. "I shan't be badly off at all. Besides, he'll probably die soon and leave me with a nice little fortune. Or I shall just take on young lovers," she added waving a hand airily, as if that were nothing at all.

"Yelsaventa, you won't!" Zimra said, shocked, her eyes widening so that they almost filled her small, sallow face. Yelsaventa laughed wickedly.

"Why shouldn't I? Don't I deserve to be happy?" She tossed her dark hair. "But enough of that. Let's do someone else's fortune. Mara?"

Yelsaventa had an air of commanding authority about her and all the girls nodded obediently. The beads were threaded through fingers once more.

Once everyone had a section of the beads, they all began to sing the little song that went with the game.

"Beads of fortune,

beads that know,

tell me where my heart should go,

tell me who will be my own,

bring me joy and not woe."

As they sang, they shuffled the beads around their circle, dancing them between their lithe fingers. The bead that ended between the fingers of the girl they were singing for indicated whom she would marry. It was a green bead between Mara's fingers when they finished singing. All the girls shrieked again.

"A relative! Someone here's sibling!" Hadassah exclaimed, enthralled. "Oh Mara, that is exciting! Who could it be?"

"Not me," Zimra giggled. "I only have sisters."

"Me too," put in another girl, named Sarah.

"And my brothers are all married or away in the army," Hadassah put in. "It must be Mirayam, or Yelsaventa!"

Mara laughed at that.

"But both of those families will be looking for girl of much higher birth. I'm not rich enough for any of them to want me," she said, shaking her head.

Yelsaventa raised a perfectly defined eyebrow.

"To marry, perhaps. But as a lover, they'd not care at all what your background is. They'd only care for looks and spirit then," she said, winking slyly.

"Really, Yelsaventa!" Zimra said, eyes reproachful now. "You shouldn't say things like that, even in jest. It isn't right."

"Who said I was joking?" The older girl asked. She looked very serious, Mara thought, as her heart began to thump with unconsidered possibilities. Could it be that a man would ever want her as a lover? No! It never could!

"And who says Mara would want to be someone's lover anyway?" Mirayam, a tall, thin girl, put in. "Lighten up, Zimra!"

"Let's talk about something else," Mara said, feeling rather uncomfortable. "What have you all been doing whilst I was in Sychar?"

"Nothing at all interesting," Hadassah pouted. "Whenever Herod is away and the Roman staff with him, nothing interesting seems to go on around here. There haven't even been races at the hippodrome or anything on at the theatre!" She said, frowning in mock petulance.

"Oh, well I, for one, am glad," Mara said with a smile. "I'd hate to think I'd have missed out."

The rest of the afternoon was passed frivolously; talking, eating fancy delicacies made by Hadassah's family's houseslaves and giggling. Eventually, evening was coming and the girls set off together for their respective homes.

As they began to head out, Yelsaventa grasped Mara's arm gently, pulling her aside. A conspiratorial smile on her elegant face, she beckoned Mara close.

"Mara, don't say anything to the others, but I wondered if you might like to join Hadassah at my family's townhouse tomorrow, for the day? I've only invited the two of you, as I think the three of us will get on best without the others," she said, rolling her eyes as if to indicate "the others" poor status. "Do say you'll come!" She entreated.

Mara felt flattered, as well as a little offended on behalf of the other girls. But all the same, the oldest, richest and most sophisticated of all her friends thought her mature? The flattery won out.

"Of course, I'd love to come. Thank you! What time should I arrive?"

Yelsaventa gave a practiced, charming smile.

"Oh good! Any time after midmorning – I do so value my sleep, don't you?"

Chapter IV.

A.D. 1, Sebaste, Samaria, Roman province of Judaea

Mara stood nervously outside the door to Yelsaventa's family's large town house the next morning. She hesitated, unsure whether to knock.

As she'd made her way there, past the Temple of Augustus on the hill, she had considered her father's words from the night before.

"Mara, you are a good girl deep down and an innocent one. Make sure these girls don't make you old before your time."

She remembered how offended she had been by his insinuations of her naivety. But now, she couldn't help wondering if there was some truth in what he said. Yelsaventa was only two years Mara's senior and yet they seemed worlds apart.

She was always smiling these knowing smiles and saying things none of the rest of their friends understood, or otherwise were completely shocked at.

Mal'akhiy had described Yelsaventa's family as "progressive", although a better term was probably "Romanized". They had strayed far from the traditions of their people, even further than most of the people dwelling in Sebaste.

It made Mara laugh to consider how shocked the people of Sychar would be by many of the things Sebasteans now considered normal.

She took a deep breath to steady herself and tossed her hair with confidence she didn't really possess. Why shouldn't she visit her friend? So what if her family's ideas were progressive? Maybe she could learn something from them. Maybe they all could.

After all, being like the people who ruled them might not be such a bad idea. If their own God could desert them so entirely, why shouldn't they desert His rules as well? The Romans ruled the world now. Surely, doing things their way was a wise move.

Mara reached out a hand and knocked firmly on the brightly painted door. She hoped whoever opened it wouldn't be shocked that she had come without an escort.

A tall, pale skinned man with thinning hair the colour of straw and a somewhat sullen expression answered her knock. He certainly didn't show any signs of shock.

"Miss Yelsaventa is through in the peristylium," he said in strangely accented Latin, guiding Mara through the big, high-roofed atrium and out into the garden.

Yelsaventa was sitting on a bench there, brushing her hair. When she saw Mara, she jumped to her feet and rushed to greet her.

Mara felt a little uncomfortable, unsure of what to do – Yelsaventa had never hugged her before – but she reciprocated the embrace and smiled warmly at her hostess.

"I'm so glad you're the first to arrive, Mara," Yelsaventa said, shooing the slave away with a flick of her hand.

"I wanted to talk with you before Hadassah arrived. I want to get to know you, but she talks so much it is hard to get a word in edgeways!" She finished in a conspiratorial tone.

Mara smiled again, feeling a little flattered. Yelsaventa wanted to get to know her? Yelsaventa seemed so very glamorous – she was, after all, one of the very highest young maidens of their social strata!

"I didn't want to be late," was all Mara said. Yelsaventa offered her cat-like smile once more. She grabbed Mara's hand and pulled her over to the bench where she had been sitting.

Handing her the discarded hairbrush – Mara could see now that it was beautifully carved from ivory! – Yelsaventa bid her continue the brushing. Mara settled to her task, trying hard not to pull at the older girl's thick hair.

"So what did you think of Alberich?" Yelsaventa asked over her shoulder. "Our door slave."

Mara wasn't too sure what she was *supposed* to think.

"He's very impressive looking," she hesitated. "So pale skinned and such light hair." Her response was obviously the correct one, for Yelsaventa nodded approvingly.

"Isn't he just?! He's from a Germanic tribe. My Abba saw him when he was at a slave market in Ephesus and brought him back for us. He thinks slaves from far off lands make a house seem more sophisticated and exotic," she confided.

Once again, Mara wasn't entirely sure what the acceptable response would be, so she just made sounds of agreement and nodded vigorously.

This seemed to satisfy Yelsaventa for she settled back quietly to allow Mara to continue her brushing. Once Mara had brushed right through it, her hostess called out for her slave girl, a tawny African named Ere, to come and style it for the day.

While Ere worked, Yelsaventa chattered on as if the slave wasn't even there, completely ignoring her existence.

"So Mara, tell me something of yourself," she urged, eyes bright with curiosity. "Who is Mara bat Mal'akhiy really, other than a pretty face?"

Mara shrugged, feeling, for the third time this morning, completely unsure of the acceptable response. "You already know all about me Yelsaventa," she replied, shrugging shyly. "Youngest of six children,

Imah dead, originally from Sychar..."

"No, no, no!" Yelsaventa interrupted with the same brisk wave of her hand she'd earlier used to dismiss the door slave. "I want you to tell me something you think. What your heart's greatest desire is. That sort of thing."

Mara gave a nervous giggle.

"To tell the truth, my greatest dream is that one day I will marry a wealthy man of standing and will be the envy of all who see me," she spoke honestly. Yelsaventa beamed and reached for her hand.

"You see, Mara. I knew you were the kind of girl I would like. I knew we could be true friends," she said. "I can help you achieve that."

"I've been watching you for a while now," she confessed, a slightly coy look on her pretty features. "I see so much potential in you and no one to guide it. You are a real beauty, Mara, but you need refining in order for men of class or standing to notice you. I can give you that."

Her smile deepened and she leaned close to Mara, completely disregarding the slave attempting to style her hair.

She was so close now that Mara could smell her spicy, exotic and altogether grown-up perfume. "I've decided to take you under my wing, to make you my little pet. What do you say to that?" Her gaze was both triumphant and magnanimous, as if she expected Mara to be completely overcome with awe and gratitude at her generous offer.

In expected fashion, Mara gasped before she could stop herself. She was beyond delighted and excited at the prospect. Yelsaventa's very own friend? And her shadow also? What opportunities and new worlds that would open up to her!

"You are very kind Yelsaventa! Thank you!" She breathed reverently. Yelsaventa put out her cheek for Mara to kiss it.

"Think nothing of it, Mara. I wish only to help a girl blossom into a woman that the world will not soon forget."

* * *

From that day forward, Mara was never far from her new mentor's side. Yelsaventa was as good as her word and took Mara entirely under her wing.

She spent long days teaching Mara how to style her hair in the current Roman fashion, (although, as a province far from the empire's heart, they were probably months behind) and how to apply make up in the most sophisticated fashion.

Mara was taught how to walk with swaying hips, how to laugh in an attractive manner and how to bat her eyelashes, or to look through them at a man.

Mara was taught to sing and to play the lyre. She was dressed up in Yelsaventa's old clothing – which, in reality was all still very new – and showed how to style them correctly.

For the first few weeks, Yelsaventa kept Mara very much to herself and to her slave girl, Ere. She said she wanted to surprise Sebaste with her new companion when she was ready.

Mara found it both exciting and rather tedious being kept away from the outside world in such a manner. She hardly had time for her chores at home during the day. Her other friends were being entirely neglected as well. But she adored the transformation Yelsaventa was achieving.

Yelsaventa took Mara to her family's private baths, where Mara was plucked, pulled and fleeced of all her "unsightly" hair, as Yelsaventa said no man in his right mind would like a woman with hairy legs or underarms. Even her eyebrows were done away with to a degree, until they were as imposing and deliberate as Yelsaventa's own.

Her skin ached after all the torturous hair removal, but a soak in the hot pool – Yelsaventa called it the caldarium – washed away all the aches, along with any inhibitions Mara had previously had about what Yelsaventa was doing with her.

As she lay back in the warm water, staring at the frescoed wall, she took in the images before her, the mural of dolphins leaping in bold, blue waves. How she longed to be like one of those dolphins, free, happy and filled with the simple joy of living. The warm water washing over her skin made her sleepy, relaxed.

Yelsaventa laughed softly at Mara's contented face. She could see how much the younger girl was enjoying the experience. "I'll take you for a massage next," she promised. "Then we'll go and have our skin softened with mud from the Salt Sea. You'll feel like an entirely new woman."

Mara let her long hair float out behind her in the water.

"I already am," she murmured softly.

Yelsaventa nodded.

"Yes and soon I'm going to introduce you to the world and they will see what a fine, accomplished and beautiful young lady you are. They'll see you as you truly are Mara, as you've been made with the opportunities given you. I can't wait!"

Excitement filled Mara at the prospect. Going out into society at Yelsaventa's side? She knew this meant they might attend parties, might meet new people. Perhaps, just perhaps, her future husband would be at one of the gatherings she would soon be attending. As her skin was massaged with the mud and sluiced clean by the bath slaves, Mara began to imagine a future for herself.

Later that night, as she sat Samaritan-style at the table with her Abba and Dawid for the evening meal, they both looked at her curiously.

"There's something different about you, Mara," Dawid said hesitantly. "Your face looks different and your skin..." his voice trailed off, unable to finish his thought. Mara beamed.

"You noticed Dawid! Yelsaventa and I have been trying a new beauty regime and I'm so pleased with it. I think it makes me look far more mature, don't you?"

Mal'akhiy reached across and brushed his youngest's forehead, wishing she would not bid away her youthful, innocent beauty so fast.

"My daughter, you don't need any beauty regime to make you

beautiful. You're beautiful simply because you are you!" He said softly, meeting her eyes with his own, trying to push the truth of his words home to her. But Mara merely laughed.

"Oh Abba, aren't you sweet?!" She said, squeezing his hand and issuing this condescendingly worded compliment with her usual, kind spirit.

There was something in the compliment that Mal'akhiy did not like. The words didn't belong to his daughter. They were assuredly from someone else. And this suddenly affected "grown up" attitude wasn't Mara's either. But somehow, he saw that they would soon be stuck with it. He wondered if there was anything he could possibly do.

The next day, Mara was all set to attend a formal dinner at Yelsaventa's family's home. It was to be mainly officials and people of political roles attending and Yelsaventa had requested Mara's presence as a companion for the evening.

She wanted to introduce Mara to some handsome young officials and her own intended – an older lawyer who originated from Rome itself.

The girls had been anticipating the dinner for several weeks now, preparing their outfits with care and discussing the etiquette one must employ when speaking to such high standing members of the community. Yelsaventa also encouraged Mara to use her womanly charms to her advantage.

"Perhaps one of the men in attendance will be just the sort of man you've always dreamed of," she had said, sending little thrills of excitement tingling down Mara's spine. Maybe it would be so!

The two girls saw in the day of the party with a lengthy trip to the baths. Mara loved this particular Roman custom more than any other. The feeling of soaking in the water and scraping away all the accumulated filth of the outside world... The massages and the facial treatments... It was glorious.

They spent a long time primping and preening with Yelsaventa's maid, Ere, on hand to assist. Yelsaventa was determined that both she and Mara would be as fashionable as possible, dressed in the most sophisticatedly Roman apparel one could source in Judaea.

She had chosen for them the softest of Egyptian cotton tunics, in the style of a peplos. Mara thought the loose, long tunic which fastened with broaches over the shoulders, was far more beautiful than the baggy, sacklike garments she usually wore. She could grow accustomed to this type of dress.

Next, Ere styled their thick locks into intricately woven styles at the nape of their slender necks, coiled up in the Greek style. Yelsaventa looked in her mirror and gave a satisfied nod, after checking Mara's appearance, she smiled and said magnanimously:

"Well Mara, I hope you feel beautiful. I wanted to give you a taste of what it is like to feel like a real lady for once. And maybe, just maybe, you will catch the eye of one of the young officers. I know, with me in the room, that may not happen, but it will give you a chance for certain. One of them I've already spurned may find you most attractive – you really do look quite lovely."

The proud nature of these words went right over Mara's head - she felt only gratitude to the older girl. Twirling and dancing around the room, she laughed and replied:

"Oh, I'm content only to attend! I've no interest in finding a suitor yet anyhow – I just want to be a part of society, and come to understand it first!"

Yelsaventa laughed in a slightly condescending way.

"Oh Mara! You say that now, but just wait till you meet the men in question. I am sure your head will be entirely turned."

* * *

Yelsaventa's words came true for Mara, although not in the way she'd intended. It was early evening when the meal was to commence, before the sunset had painted the sky. They were going to eat in the inner garden of the home and Yelsaventa was determined the two of them would make their grand entrance after all the guests had arrived.

They sat excitedly in Yelsaventa's room, sending Ere down to check of the progress at regular intervals. Eventually, Yelsaventa decided that the moment was right and the two of them descended the stairs, down into the garden.

The sight that met them took Mara's breath away. The garden path had been lit with many torches, all burning the beautifully scented, beeswax candles Yelsaventa's mother, Chavvah, favoured.

Swathes of brightly coloured, almost transparent fabrics, the likes of which Mara had never seen, were draped between the torch stands, making a pathway into the main gathering area; more bright torches, surrounded by exotically coloured cloths and oriental cushions.

Musicians played soft, haunting music in a corner, tambourine and lyre taking the lead.

"It has to be magic," Mara breathed to herself.

A collection of various guests were reclining, Roman-style, on the couches. Most of them were men, but a few also had their wives with them, all bedecked in the finest of clothing. Mara could see a few faces she recognized from the forum, as well as Yelsaventa's mother, Chavvah and father, Yehu, whom most people just referred to as the Patron.

She also spotted Yelsaventa's older brother, Levi. The moment Mara's eyes alighted on his fair-skinned face, framed by dark, tousled hair and a roguish smile, she found she couldn't look away. He had, in a mere instant, captured her heart.

Mara had seen Levi before, from a distance, or in other rooms of the house, but she had never really met him. She knew he was about Dawid's age and was never really around the family home if he could help it – always out in society, seducing ladies and bringing men into business partnerships, or so Yelsaventa had reported.

Never before when she had looked at him had Mara felt this pounding in her heart, the shaking in her knees, or the little thrills running races up and down her spine. It had only taken an instant and yet Mara, reckless with youth, knew she would never be the same again. In that moment, seeing him as she did now, she felt she'd fallen head over heels in love.

Something kept her from wanting to step forward, from following Yelsaventa on into the gathering. She had a strange sense that if she were to make another move, there would be no going back to her childhood; that the next step she took would carry her on, into her future.

Levi looked up at that very moment. The way his gaze met hers, the fire Mara felt ignite deep inside, convinced her that his attraction to her was every bit as strong as what she felt for him. His dark eyes flashed as they held her golden ones. The man next to him noticed Mara as well, she could feel it, but her eyes couldn't move from Levi's face and though the other man spoke to him, his eyes never left hers either.

For the first time in her life, Mara felt as though she and another were the only ones in the room. It seemed that the very air she now breathed was different - brighter, more life giving. Her bones felt stronger, her body quivering, as if she was being born into a new kind of life. It was as if she'd never truly experienced anything before that moment.

"May I present my daughter, Yelsaventa, and her companion Mara bat Mal'akhiy."

The Patron's voice interrupted the moment and Mara took her eyes from Levi's face to step into her future, to follow Yelsaventa down into the company. Yelsaventa walked proud and tall and she gained many appreciative gazes, but it was Mara – though smaller and clearly younger – that captured the attention of the gathering. She could feel it as she walked. She could feel the power she wielded. She felt invincible.

Yelsaventa lead her across the room and found an empty couch for them to recline on. Mara's heart continued to pound as she lowered herself down beside the older girl. The eyes of the guests had never left them.

"By Jupiter, Patron, your daughter is a fair maiden! As is her companion!" A portly looking Roman official from across the circle piped up. The Patron inclined his head graciously and nodded.

"Thank you, Marcus Venturius Betto. I am a blessed man." With a swift wave of his hand, he moved the conversation on to other matters and the two girls were left to blend into the mix of party-goers.

Mara couldn't help but feel overwhelmed by the new sights and sounds surrounding her. And more than anything else, by the new feelings taking over her body.

Opposite her, she could still see Levi's dark eyes flashing, not leaving her for a moment. He held her captive with his gaze, not allowing her to see anything else around her. She was his prisoner. And she loved it.

"So, Mara, what do you think?" Yelsaventa whispered over her shoulder, to where Mara was pressed up behind her.

"It is beautiful," Mara returned, forcing herself to drag her eyes around to face her friend. "I've never seen anything like this!"

Yelsaventa laughed under her breath.

"That's not what I meant, silly! I meant the men. See any you like? A lot of them have noticed you," she said, wiggling her eyebrows suggestively.

Mara's heart pounded, but she merely shrugged, trying her hardest to look nonchalant. She was well aware that, as much as Yelsaventa regarded her as a friend, she was a pet project and certainly not a prospective match for her brother.

"I suppose so. There are many handsome men here," was all she said.

Yelsaventa giggled.

"Oh yes, there certainly are! What do you think of that big soldier sitting over by my brother? I think he's ever so handsome. He's an officer in the Ala I Sebasternorum – our cavalry in the Roman army. He's usually stationed at Caesarea, but he's in Sebaste on leave!" She finished conspiratorially. Mara glanced over in the appropriate direction, eyes alighting briefly on an immense man, cutting an imposing figure in his armour, but the soldier could not draw her gaze from Levi.

"Very impressive," Mara breathed softly, but she couldn't make her words ring sincerely.

Yelsaventa didn't seem to notice.

"Oh! He's looking over at us! How do I look, Mara?!" She squeaked, twirling a finger through a tendril of hair softly framing her face.

"You look like a goddess," Mara replied wistfully. "He'd be a fool not to notice you." And she would be a fool to think Levi would pay her any more attention than just that simple, flirtatious game of eye holding. There would be no more to this and somehow, she would have to free her heart from chains which, in those few short moments, had become very heavy.

The rest of the evening seemed to dance right past Mara, just out of her reach. She couldn't quite grasp it, enjoy it, be part of it. It was elusive and over before she quite realized it had begun. Guests were leaving and she and Yelsaventa were being shepherded off to bed by Chavvah.

Ere was undoing their elaborate hairstyles and they were slipping into cool, cotton shifts, lying down to sleep. But sleep didn't come – that too eluded Mara.

Somewhere in this house, Levi was also sleeping. Mara prayed desperately to whatever deity she thought might listen, that he might just dream of her.

Chapter V.

A.D. 2, Sebaste, Samaria, Roman province of Judaea

Mara was unhappy. She felt listless and restless and miserable. Ever since the party at Yelsaventa's family's home, she had not been the same. She could do almost nothing without thinking of Levi.

It seemed strange to her that so much could change in so little time. All that had seemed important to her before no long seemed to matter.

All that mattered now was that Levi ben Yehu was her greatest thought, dream and desire and she was certain she'd never have him. He'd probably already forgotten that she even existed.

Mara was desperate to return to Yelsaventa's house, if only to see him for a moment – perhaps just a glimpse of him would help her through the day. But Yelsaventa was unwell after the night of frivolity and hadn't been able to receive visitors since.

Zimra and Hadassah had come to visit Mara and had noticed her sadness, but she didn't feel she could confide in them. Hadassah couldn't keep a secret if she tried and Zimra was too much of a good girl. She would never understand.

Good daughters weren't supposed to fall head-over-heels in love with men they could not have. Indeed, good girls weren't supposed to fall in love at all – they were supposed to just marry whoever their family picked for them.

But head-over-heels Mara had fallen and there was no going back. Even Mal'akhiy noticed how unusually Mara was behaving, but he just attributed it to her concern for Yelsaventa in her illness and he asked no questions. He couldn't possibly have guessed what was really ailing her.

It was almost a week after the party when Yelsaventa was finally well enough to receive anyone and sent Ere to summon Mara to her home. Mara got up from her weaving at once and eagerly made her way towards the door.

"Mara, why do you feel you have to obey that girl's every whim?" Mal'akhiy asked from where he was reading a scroll in the bright, natural light of the upstairs balcony, a slight frown playing on his lips.

"I don't!" Mara called back over her shoulder. "But she's my friend and she's been very sick. I want to see for myself how she is." Tossing her hair defiantly, she rushed out of the house before he could stop her. Her father didn't even attempt to.

Yelsaventa was looking paler than usual when Mara arrived, but her eyes were bright with excitement. "Mara! I have the most wonderful news for you!" She exclaimed, grabbing the younger girl's hands and pulling her down on the couch beside her, the moment she entered the room.

"What is it?!" Mara asked, heart beginning to hammer. It couldn't be. Could it?!

"A man has asked after you! Asked whether you are betrothed or promised to anyone!" Yelsaventa announced delightedly. "Isn't that magical?"

Mara's hands were all shaky and her mouth felt suddenly dry. Could it really be all she'd dreamed for? Could it really be that Levi had asked after her? Could it -

"It was that soldier I pointed out to you!"

Yelsaventa's words were like icy water running down Mara's spine.

"Remember him? The one who sat by my brother at the party. Micah ben Yosef. The one who serves in the cavalry."

Mara nodded slowly.

"Yes, I remember him," she stuttered. The big soldier, though handsome, was not the man who haunted Mara's every moment, waking or sleeping.

"You don't seem very happy about it."

Yelsaventa's face was pouting now. "I thought you'd be over-joyed. He's an excellent match for you, Mara, I don't think you'd possibly do better. I was delighted when Levi told me he'd asked about you. I felt all my hard work had paid off."

"Levi told you?" Mara spoke the words softly, breathlessly. Somehow the fact that it was Levi who'd put the question forward changed everything.

Imagination running wild, she found herself wondering, had Levi potentially asked, as if for someone else, but really for himself?

Yelsaventa nodded impatiently.

"Yes, yes. He said that Micah was very curious about you. No one's ever seen you before in our circles and you intrigued them all. I shouldn't be surprised if Micah attempts to contact you before he returns to his unit in Capernaum." She smiled proudly. "I think I did well with you, Mara. I'm very pleased with myself."

"And I'm very grateful for all you've done." Mara replied. She couldn't keep her heart from dreaming now.

* * *

Micah did not contact Mara, much to Yelsaventa's surprised distaste and to Mara's secret delight. Surely, if the man had truly been interested in knowing about her, he would have sought her by now.

But if it wasn't really he who had asked, then it was perfect.

Yelsaventa, however, justified the snub to her "creation" by stating that he must have been called back to his unit in Caesarea in a hurry.

It was several weeks since the dinner party had occurred now and Mara had yet to see Levi. She longed to, so very much. She'd suggested to Yelsaventa many times that they might go down to the forum for a walk, hoping she might spot him there, but Yelsaventa had been unwilling.

Finally, almost a full moon later, Mara was just leaving the Patron's home one evening when there he was. He was sitting at the top of the stairs in the grand entrance hall, leaning back, a slight, devastatingly handsome grin playing on his lips. Her heart took up its pounding the instant she saw him and she froze, unable to move, unable to turn away.

He wore his thick, black hair long and it fell enchantingly into his dark eyes as he began to speak.

"Hello, Mara. I've been wondering when I might see you again," he said huskily. He knew her name. He'd wondered about her.

Levi got up and descended the stairs towards her, leaving her feeling dizzy with anticipation. Would he talk to her more?

"I'm often here with your sister," she replied softly, looking up at him through her dark eyelashes. "I'm surprised you haven't seen me."

She wanted to memorize every aspect of his handsome face, every line, every scar, like the long jagged one that ran along his cheekbone. It did nothing to detract from his looks. In fact, Mara thought, it make him still more beautiful.

He grinned lazily again and came right down beside her. He was much taller than her, making her feel small, delicate, even protected. The clenching in her stomach she had begun to associate with Levi ben Yehu took hold of her.

"I know," was all he said. He gazed at her for a while, in silence. She felt like his eyes were boring right through her, that he was seeing right into her soul.

"It was worth the wait," he finally said, that lazy grinning still dancing across his lips. Mara laughed gently, still looking up at him through her eyelashes.

"I'm not sure that's true. I've been longing -" she left off, face coy, realizing she'd said more than she'd intended. She wasn't entirely disappointed though. Now he knew what she was thinking and she'd see for certain what he thought about her.

"Longing for what?" He asked, eyes sparkling. Mara shook her head and turned away, her own eyes dancing in return. She began to slip away. *Better leave him curious and wanting more, than bored and wanting less.*

She walked past him, turning back only once, a soft smile full of unspoken words playing across her lips. She saw the wonder on his face, the enchantment he was trying so desperately to hide behind a mask of bravado. He wasn't fooling her. She might have been young, but she saw it all. She knew. Levi ben Yehu would be hers, and she, Mara bat Mal'akhiy would be his. It was meant to be.

Chapter VI.

A.D. 2, Sebaste, Samaria, Roman province of Judaea

It began on the marbled entrance way in the Patron's lavish home, but after that meeting on the stairs, Mara saw much of Levi. He seemed to appear wherever she went – out on the streets when she was walking, or in the forum and basilica, often when she was visiting Yelsaventa as well.

Mara orchestrated none of these meetings deliberately, unless one was to count her subtle manipulation of Levi himself.

She was always friendly, always caring, yet never open. She kept a veil of mystery about her, trying never to let him know too much of her at once. Yelsaventa had taught her well how to play the game of flirtation and Mara was mastering the art, though she wasn't sure Yelsaventa had intended it to be used on her own older brother.

Mara wondered idly how Yelsaventa would feel if she figured out how exactly Mara was employing her new found skills... She was fairly certain she wouldn't be pleased, but she was also fairly sure that her friend had suspected nothing – thus far.

* * *

Something had changed in his sister. Dawid was sure of it. Mara hadn't been her usual self for weeks now. First she had been so overwhelmingly sad… Then she had become unexplainably happy…

He wasn't at all sure what to make of it. He mentioned it to their father, who had just dismissed it with a shake of his head and a tired sigh.

"All girls get like this when they come of age, Dawid," he had said rubbing his stubbly chin. He needed to go to the baths soon, Mal'akhiy had mused to himself, not paying much attention to what his son was saying.

Dawid frowned. He couldn't help but worry. Mara was behaving secretively and she'd never been secretive before, not with him at least. She'd always told Dawid everything that was in her mind, or playing upon her heart. And now, hardly a word.

It was this new friend of hers, Yelsaventa, who had caused the change, Dawid was sure of it. He had never liked the Patron's haughty daughter - too opinionated, too sophisticated in her manner and too desirous of attention.

Yes, she was a pretty girl, though never in Mara's league and she could be amusing, but her humour was always laced with spite, her stories always glorifying herself over others. It saddened Dawid to realize that little by little, Mara was becoming just like her.

As Dawid worked that morning in the workshop, crafting a fine piece of jewellery for a very rich woman to wear, he considered his sister's situation over and over again. Mara was so young, so without anyone to guide her.

He and their older siblings had tried, but they were no replacement for a mother. And as for their father, Mal'akhiy always remained as distant from Mara as he possibly could. Pausing in his thoughts, Dawid focused intently as he set a tiny blue gemstone into the silver he was skillfully molding. Soon, this would be a necklace of the very latest fashion.

Dawid had tried to raise this topic with Mara earlier that morning, but she had just laughed and told him to get back to work, that he was making assumptions. He didn't know the thoughts that passed through Mara's head, so why should he try to?

Mara has no idea about the real world. Thoughts crystallized in his mind as he worked. *She thinks she's so mature, so grown up and that she's got everything all under control. But she doesn't. She can't see that her dreams of a good marriage and a prosperous future depend on more than marrying a handsome, wealthy man.*

Frustrated, he turned from his work. "So stupid!" He muttered under his breath. "One day, you'll discover the world isn't what you think and a beautiful young girl like you is only a token in a rich man's game."

He remembered his father's words from the last time they had discussed this matter, when Mara was spending the night, yet again, at the Patron's lavish home.

"Dawid, she has no understanding of men, aside from how to turn their eye. She's only a child. She doesn't even truly know how to be a woman yet. She doesn't know the way men think, doesn't see that they will use her, that she has no control over her own destiny, as she thinks she does."

He remembered his father's sad eyes and weary, old face.

"You'll always look out for her, won't you, my son? I know I haven't been the best father to her, it is too difficult for me, but still, I don't want to see her hurt. I fear she will be, if she continues down this path on which she's started. She has my own willfulness in her. I've caused much of this, I know, with my neglect of the girl. She is seeking love, but I'm too old a man to start now."

Heart aching, Dawid had vowed to his father on the God of their ancestors, that he would look out for his sister.

"If only I'd never brought the family here from Sychar," Mal'akhiy had sighed. "Maybe she wouldn't have become so strong-willed, so sure of what she wants. I could have married her off to a good, respectable boy like your friend, Shemu'el and we could have been done with it. But she has far greater aspirations than that now and I don't have it in me to break her."

Dawid recalled his own words in response.

"But Abba, this is a harsh world to a young woman. If you don't break her now, break her willfulness and her immaturity, another surely will in the future. And another will break her far worse!"

Mal'akhiy had only shaken his head.

"I don't have it in me, Dawid. I can't do it. Though she pains me so deeply, still I love her too much!"

As Dawid got back to his work now, he couldn't help but wonder, perhaps their father's love had blinded him – perhaps he didn't love her enough. Dawid had seen the way men looked at Mara in the streets of Sebaste – and the way she encouraged their gazes.

She was fast becoming the most beautiful woman Dawid had ever seen; even though she was his sister, he knew there was no denying it. There were many beautiful women amongst their people, but Mara was special. Different.

The defined cheekbones, the delicate collarbones, the slender, yet shapely frame. The hair, the smile, the personality, the laugh. Mara was almost goddess status.

Dawid shook his head, fingers working swiftly as he continued to incorporate the gems into the silver. Mara thought she understood men so well, he could see that. She thought she had them under her control. But that couldn't be further from the truth.

The men she seemed to favour were men with influence and power, men who would rule a woman, make her miserable. Even a woman like Mara. This was not a woman's world. Dawid only hoped he could help her see that before she made some terrible mistake.

* * *

"Mara! Mara! Have you heard? There are going to be races at the hippodrome In a few weeks!"

Mara's morning had begun with Hadassah's excited voice ringing through the entrance hall of her home and it hadn't dulled down since. In two weeks, it would be the Roman festival of Ludi – a celebration of the goddess of love, Venus. Being a Romanized town, Sebaste would be following the Ludi tradition of chariot races and three days of public holiday.

All the local chariot factions had new blood brought in for the racing season to begin and everyone who was anyone was going to be there, no matter what god they worshipped.

The greatest excitement was, however, that some new charioteers had been brought in from as far across the Empire as Gaul and Nubia.

Mara was delighted when the Patron had invited her to attend with his family and to sit in their box. The prospect of spending an entire day in Levi's presence elated her, far more than the thought of the races themselves.

Yelsaventa was less looking forward to the event, as her betrothed – Ira ben Kershon – would be present and she would be expected to play the part of a good fiancee. Ira wasn't unkind, but he was old, older even than Yelsaventa's own father, at forty five, and held very little appeal to the spirited, fourteen year old Yelsaventa.

"I wish I was a man and then I wouldn't have my fate decided for me," she had grumbled to Mara the day before. "I would choose whom I marry and wouldn't be sold off to the highest bidder for my family's advantage."

Mara had sighed and held her friend's hand.

"I'm sure Ira will take good care of you. And it could certainly worse – he could be poor as well as old!" The two girls giggled for a bit and Yelsaventa began to cheer up.

"There is one more positive I can think of," she said pulling a face. "I'll be able to take lovers if I wish. If we lived in a Jewish city, I'd be in trouble, but not here in Sebaste. Ha. I can do what I want and no one need know. No one would even care – so long as I was discreet."

Inside, Mara felt a little shocked at the notion, but kept a nonchalant expression on her face. She'd heard Yelsaventa talk of such things before and it was beginning to sound less terrible each time she heard it.

Why shouldn't Yelsaventa be happy? This marriage was, after all, only for her family's benefit and it would hurt no one for her to have secret affairs, surely.

Lost in thought, Mara didn't notice the sly smile that had crept onto Yelsaventa's face, or the gleam in her dark eyes.

"Speaking of lovers, I've noticed you have eyes for only one man," Yelsaventa teased. "My brother adores you, Mara."

Mara felt a horrified blush of shock taking over her features. Was she really so obvious? She hadn't realised Yelsaventa was privy to her little intrigue with Levi, though she should have known – Yelsaventa made it her business to notice everything. Yelsaventa laughed.

"Oh, you innocent little thing! He's asked me to give you this," she said, wiggling her precise eyebrows and holding out a little scrap of paper. Mara grabbed for it, heart pounding.

Seeing you at the hippodrome is all I can think about. Save me a seat next to you.

Mara felt her hands trembling as she looked at the Latin words Levi had written in a bold, thick hand.

He must truly love her, she thought, cradling the scrap of paper like a tiny, fledgling bird. Perhaps he was even considering asking her father for her hand...

Yelsaventa looked over her shoulder, reading it.

"My brother will certainly make a good first lover for you, Mara," she said conversationally. "He is experienced and he will be kind."

Mara looked up at the older girl, confused. A first lover? Surely, that wasn't what Levi had intended. He was falling in love with her, she was sure of it. She wanted him to love her, to marry her, she wanted to be his wife...

Yelsaventa saw her expression and began to laugh in a quietly mocking manner, her face condescendingly sweet.

"Oh, my poor little Mara. Surely, you didn't think him in love with you, or anything of that nature? Even if he was, he would never be permitted to marry a commoner like you! My Abba and Imah want for him to marry a girl with a fortune – not their daughter's poor companion!"

The words cut Mara to the heart and her eyes pricked with tears. She refused to let them flow, refused to let Yelsaventa see what a fool she had been, how she'd lost herself in love over a man who had never wanted her as anything more than a lover. She was no more than a pretty face, a lovely figure to Levi ben Yehu. She could see it now.

"No, I didn't think he would. I was just surprised he'd think of the hippodrome as an ideal place for such an intrigue," Mara lied. "I mean, I'd rather not see my reputation in tatters!" She finished with a high pitched laugh. Inwardly, she was reeling with hurt, but she was determined Yelsaventa would mock her no more.

"Good." Yelsaventa looked pleased to hear this. Then her tone changed. "I'd have hated to see you really fall in love with Levi, Mara. Love does no one any good, especially not us women. We can use men to get what we want, but in a world where all decisions are made for us, what other power do we have? At least, that's what my sister says," she finished, suddenly looking as young, naive and hurt by the world as Mara felt.

That night, Mara cried herself to sleep, tucked deep into the folds of her mother's blankets.

"Oh Imah, I wish you were still here!" She whispered through her tears.

She had been so stupid, to fall in love with a man like Levi and to think he might truly love her in return. Such a foolish girl, just as Dawid had said.

No one could ever know, she was determined of that! Least of all Levi. He would not know she had fallen in helpless, desperate, childish love with him. No, if he had thought she was interested in him as a lover, then that was what she would become – his secret lover.

If that was the only way she could have him, it would have to do. Her feelings for him had changed now, after all her crying. Something of the real Mara had died when she realized the truth of her situation.

Perhaps love isn't even real, she mused to herself as she drifted off to sleep in the wee hours of the morning.

Perhaps Yelsaventa is right, the only power we have in this world is to use our charm to get from men what we want. Love isn't real and neither is true happiness.

No one will know what a fool I was. Levi will think I knew his true intentions all along and as for everyone else – they will never know anything about it.

Chapter VII.

A.D. 2, Sebaste, Samaria, Roman province of Judaea

The festival of Ludi was born on a bright, sunny day. The streets of Sebaste were all abuzz, as the people prepared for the drama of the races and the delightful three days of public holiday.

Mara felt none of it. She felt dead inside. Her first love had been ripped from her tender, bleeding heart and she was not sure she'd ever feel alright again.

Mal'akhiy noticed his daughter's melancholy as they sat down to break their fast.

"What is the matter, Little One?" He asked her gruffly. "Are you unwell?"

Mara looked up at him, her eyes tired and surrounded by dark, sad circles. She looked, in that instant, so very young and yet, so very old as well. She was too tired to even be surprised that her Abba had paid her this small attention.

"I'm fine Abba," she replied. "I just slept badly. And it is warm today. But I'll be fine as the day goes on, I'm sure." She went back to slowly eating her bowl of creamy yoghurt, drizzled with fresh honey.

Mal'akhiy wasn't convinced.

"I'm not sure I should let you go with the Patron and his family today, Mara," he said slowly. "I don't want you collapsing in the heat, or anything like that..."

Mara sat bolt upright, eyes wide with horror. Not go! That would be terrible! That would make Levi think she was scared and she certainly didn't want that!

"Oh no, Abba! I'll be fine," she said hastily. "I'll be sitting in the Patron's box, out of the sun and I'm sure they'll see to it that I'm alright. Besides, I don't want to disappoint Yelsaventa – and she will be very disappointed if I don't come!"

Her father frowned, not convinced.

"It's also a religious occasion, Mara. It is to honour a Roman goddess. You know how I feel about that..."

Mara snorted. "Abba, I don't think Yahweh even cares about what we do anymore – He's long since abandoned us as our God," she said, flippantly.

"You mustn't talk like that, Mara!" Dawid said, horrified.

"Why?" Mara rolled her eyes. "If He really does care, why is life the way it is for his people? Why-"

Mal'akhiy raised his hands, cutting off Mara's tirade. He could see the fire rising in her eyes. He sighed resignedly.

"Alright Mara, if you want to go that much, I won't stop you."

He looked across at his daughter and wondered what was going on in her mind. Could it really be that only a few months earlier she had been running through the hills towards Sychar for the New Moon festival? Mal'akhiy wished, for what felt like the millionth time, that they had never left.

* * *

Mara would never forget that day at the hippodrome. The

thunderstorm of emotions that swept through her were unlike any she'd experienced before.

She had awoken miserable, stiff and tired after her restless night. After breakfast and her conversation with Mal'akhiy, she had prepared herself for the races up in her room, layering on make-up to cover her tired skin and thick, black strokes of kohl to hide the redness of her eyes.

Mara fluctuated between feeling angry with herself for being so foolish as to fall head-over-heels in love with a man like Levi – a man, she ought to have known would never return her love - and feeling sad that a man could not just simply love a woman and desire to marry her, in this strange world.

Mara had, somewhere along the journey, forgotten that all she had going for her was her looks and her personality. She wasn't wealthy. She didn't have a good family line. She was a nobody, a stray picked up as a rich girl's amusement, her pet project.

As she brushed stroke after fiercely abrupt stroke through her hair, Mara determined never to let another person have the upper hand in her life again – never again to be humiliated internally in such a way.

Her hands worked fast, weaving her hair into numerous braids, forming a ring around the crown of her head, curls cascading loose down her back, to her waist.

Her heart raced as, in her determination, she vowed that she would not let what had happened hold her back.

This day would be the day where she, Mara, proved to herself and anyone who dared watch, that she was the ruler of her own destiny. She was no one's pet, no one's lover, no one's subordinate. No man, no woman, no god. *No one.*

Mara looked in her polished bronze mirror and was shocked at the woman that looked back at her. She was made up in the same way she was whenever she attended parties with Yelsaventa, but today, she looked different. There was a new boldness in her eyes, a new coldness in her heart. Her dreams may have been shattered, but she could piece them together in a new, better, more formidable way. The new Mara was here.

* * *

As Mara made her way through the streets towards the Patron's home, she felt buoyed along by the excitement of the crowd, heading towards the hippodrome.

The public holiday and the prospect of the races were what lifted the mood for most people, but Mara, stalking along determinedly, was carried by her own ambitions.

She had a vibrant blue palla draped around her shoulders, over her hair and she held it across her face, trying to avoid attention. Sticking close to the city walls towering above, she made her way to the Patron's home.

The excitement levels rose to a frenzy the closer to the hippodrome one became. Yelsaventa chattered away excitedly to Mara as they made their way out to the gilded litter that would carry them to the venue.

"I hear the Blues have an incredibly handsome charioteer from Gaul! I can hardly wait to see for myself!"

Mara wasn't sure she'd ever seen Yelsaventa so animated, so childlike in her enthusiasm.

For the first time ever, Mara felt the older of the two, trapped into her new-found and much disliked, world-wisdom, like a sparrow in a cage. But unlike the sparrow, there was no going back to freedom for her, that much was certain. She could, at least, reshape the prison that was her world. That much she would ensure.

Resplendent in his citizen's toga – a rare thing this far into Judaea - the Patron handed his wife Chavvah, Yelsaventa and Mara up into the litter. He gave Mara a small smile. He was greying around the temples now, but still, Patron Yehu was a handsome man, with all the good looks his son had inherited.

Mara's heart gave a twinge at the thought. At least Levi himself was not present – he wouldn't be joining them until later.

Mara watched as the slaves, arms bulging, strained to lift the litter and begin the short walk to the hippodrome.

The Patron and his party could have easily made the journey on foot, but it was all about keeping up appearances and staying out of the dust and grime that coated of the streets. Even with the modern aqueduct and sewage system, the region's heat did not make for clean roads.

Chavvah insisted that the rich, red curtains of the litter be drawn and they were cocooned away in their comfortably cushioned world until they arrived at the racing arena's gates.

The hippodrome was enormous. Mara hadn't ever been to the races before and was completely in awe as they made their way up through the crowds of people and on into the arena's best seating.

The tall pillars supporting the structure were seemed to lean in towards her as she looked up. The roar of the crowds, the size of the space, the heat of the day; it all began to get to her.

The pungent smell of many sweaty people crowded together, of the horses housed below and the excitement carrying on the air all filled her lungs as she took deep, gasping breaths.

Yelsaventa clutched at her arm, obviously a little overwhelmed as well and, secretly grateful, Mara leaned in against her.

"Can you believe this place, Mara?!" Yelsaventa shouted into her ear, attempting to make herself heard over the din of the masses below. "Isn't it incredible?" Mara had to agree that it was.

They were in the Patron's box now – a comfortably cool, tiled and pillared room, with slaves bringing refreshments and waving palm frond fans. Mara could even smell the sweet, heady scent of the flowers arranged over the box's arched entrance.

The seating, near the front of the balcony, was only a short fall from the track below and they could see everything clearly.

Rising up above them on all sides were row upon row of tiered seating, filled with colourfully dressed men and women of all rank, race and station. Music played loudly over the crowd.

The Patron's box was at the very centre of the hippodrome, surrounded on all sides by other boxes. From here, they had the very best view of events.

Down at the trackside, Mara could spot the stalls where the horses were kept prior to their races and at the two ends of the track she could see posts and altars.

"Why are there altars there?" Mara asked curiously.

"That is the most dangerous part of the track – chariots often wreck there," the Patron answered with lazy authority, from where he now reclined in the centre of the room. "The altars there are to the Greek god Taraxippus – the disturber of horses."

Mara looked closer and could see statues of other gods also lining the rim of the race track. She giggled a little, thinking how strange some of them looked. The Greek and Roman gods, or even the other gods of her own land all seemed a bit strange to her. Mara wasn't sure whether she even considered them real. How could anything so funny looking be powerful?!

Her Abba had brought her up to believe in Yahweh – the God of the Samaritans and the Jews – but she didn't know if she believed in Him either. She'd never admitted this to anyone and wasn't sure she ever would.

Enjoying, for the first time, the fact that Levi wasn't around, Mara found herself able to pay attention to the proceedings in the hippodrome.

The races began. First came numerous races by novelty charioteers - children driving ponies and the like. Then began the more serious races. As the day was drawing to a close, came the races everyone had been looking forward to – the ones featuring the champions from the other provinces – from the horse farms of Rome.

"Oh, look, Abba! They're starting!" Yelsaventa called excitedly. Looking down, Mara could see that, sure enough, four differently coloured chariots were making their way down onto the track.

People up higher in the stands roared, standing to their feet and clapping as their favourite teams made their way around to the starting position.

"Oh Mara! There's that charioteer, the Gaulish one!" Yelsaventa squeaked, clutching at Mara's hand, as the Blue's chariot thundered by.

Mara gazed down at the man Yelsaventa referred to. He was dark haired, but pale skinned – far paler than anyone Mara had ever seen, (with the exception of the Germanic door slave in the Patron's home).

The charioteer's dark hair was pulled back from his face, flowing out long from under his helmet and his beard clipped close. His face was streaked with blue war paint and his bare chest had strange blue ink markings, all over it.

"Look at his tattoos! My, doesn't he look fearsome!" Chavvah exclaimed from the other side of the Patron. The woman's usually refined voice was almost girlish in her excitement. Mara looked down. Chavvah was right, he did.

As he went past, the Gaul glanced up at their box and Mara's eyes caught his for just a moment.

With that glance, Mara knew the man below her was suffering the same pain she was. His dark eyes had carried a silent desperation she understood all too well.

He was a slave – a prisoner to circumstance – just as she herself was. And he was every bit as determined as she was to fight it, to become the conqueror, instead of the conquered.

Suddenly Mara was on her feet, cheering along with the rest. She wanted, beyond all else in that moment, for the tattooed Gaul to win. She wanted him to succeed, for then, she felt, there would be some hope for herself as well.

"It's a quadriga race," the Patron was explaining with an air of authority to anyone who might listen. "Four horses. These charioteers need to be the most skilled of all."

Mara prayed to Taraxippus that the Gaulish Blue might be spared, that he might be numbered amongst the most skilled, that he might make it out alive and might win.

The trumpet announcing the start of the race blew and in a burst of colour and a roar from the crowd, they were off.

The four, rickety-looking chariots began to blaze a trail through the sand of the arena. The crowds bellowed and Mara could hear her own voice joining them. The intensity of the moment was a powerful, almost spiritual force.

Up this close, Mara could smell the scent of the horses sweat as they galloped, see the whites of their eyes blaring. This was a fight for survival. All four of the charioteers were skilled, making it around the first obelisk unscathed. But then things began to heat up.

The red charioteer had out his whip and wasn't just using it on his horses, but also across the back of the green charioteer ahead of him.

The green charioteer was screaming and writhing, crying out in pain, Mara could see that from his open mouth, but his eyes never left the track, nor did he lose his hold of the reins bound tightly to his body.

Yellow and blue were pressed up together, in front of green. Mara watched as the Gaul shoved his horses right up against the next obelisk, turning as tightly as possible. He was out in front now.

The frenzied mood of the crowd only grew as the laps continued. The horses galloped wildly and their drivers became almost animal themselves, whipping each other, ramming hard into the opposition basket chariots.

Blood was drawn from the green's back and he was limp, only kept standing by the lacings fastening him to his chariot. But still his horses ran.

The final lap arrived. Yellow was ahead, with blue close on his heels.

"Blue! Blue! Blue!" The crowd began to chant and Yelsaventa joined them. Mara had run out of sound now, but she pressed up as close as she could to the railing, willing the Gaul on.

Yellow cut him off on the final corner. There was only the straight left to go. Surely, he couldn't make it.

As the crowd looked on, screaming with mad excitement, the blue charioteer called to his horses. Suddenly, they were away, as if they'd never run before.

On they edged, neck and neck with the yellow chariot. And then, ahead, over the line. Winner!

"Se-ver-a! Se-ver-a!" The crowd now chanted the name of the Blues charioteer. He had done it. Mara collapsed back, suddenly exhausted, into the cushioned seat. She had invested so much, emotionally, in that race. And he had won, just as Mara knew she would. It had been a sign. As the Gaul had overcome, so would she.

The charioteers slowed their paces, bringing their horses down to a trot. The Green's charioteer was cut from his chariot and carried away on a stretcher. The wreath was brought, presented to Severa.

Mara stood back up with all the crowd, cheering as he made his victory lap. As he neared their box, his eyes met hers once more and he nodded at her, almost imperceptibly. Then, with all his might, he threw the wreath up into their box and straight to Mara's hands.

Squealing excitedly, Yelsaventa grabbed it from Mara's grasp, dancing around in delight.

"He threw his winning wreath to me!" She cried almost hysterically, as the others in the box clustered around her.

Mara knew different though. The entire time Severa rolled past, his eyes never left hers and somehow she knew he understood. "You can win freedom too," his eyes were telling her. The wreath had been for her.

"My, my," spoke a soft voice in her ear. "Someone's captured the charioteer's interest." Mara looked up to see Levi, good-looking as ever in his Roman-style tunic, right by her side, his dark curls glistening as if he just come from the baths. The musky scent of his perfumed oil made her dizzy. Sandalwood. Her heart hammered under his gaze.

"Yes, Yelsaventa is very excited to receive the wreath," she said somewhat sardonically, but just as quietly, breaking his gaze, and looking away. She wasn't ready for this. Levi laughed, delighted by her show of spirit.

"Mara, don't pretend with me. We both know that wreath was never intended for my sister," he whispered. "That charioteer picked the prettiest woman in the crowd, the most enchanting Venus he'd ever seen and gave it to you." His breath was hot against her ear, yet it sent shivers down her spine.

No matter what Yelsaventa had said. No matter what Mal'akhiy had, or Dawid. No matter what she'd told herself.

Levi loved her.

Mara could feel it with all that she was. He wanted her for his very own, not as his mistress.

It was as tangible to her in that moment as anything had ever been. His scent intoxicated her. But she wasn't going to go back on her decisions. She couldn't. They could never truly be married – his family would never allow it. She wasn't going to let life ruin her, crush her spirit. She would still rise above this.

She looked over at the coriander wreath now adorning Yelsaventa's head and remembered the charioteer's fierce eyes. Mara was a fighter, just like he was. She would fight. She could do what she wanted. She could use even these strong, deep feelings to her advantage. Couldn't she?

As the day wore on, sitting in the same confined space as Levi grew harder and harder. It was as if his presence was burning into her. Mara longed for him to take her in his arms and hold her tight, to whisper of his love to her, to kiss her.

But instead, she sat by his side, watching race after race in the presence of his family, Yelsaventa's betrothed and other guests of the Patron.

Some of the other young men present tried to talk to her and whilst she replied politely, she hardly cared. Mara didn't want some other young man, she wanted Levi ben Yehu.

Slaves brought around trays of grapes and fresh fruit, but Mara couldn't eat.

Part way through the afternoon, after the lunch had been removed, Yelsaventa cast a sly look across at Levi and Mara, before getting to her feet.

"Come on Mara, I need to use the latrine. I want you to accompany me!" She urged in her pompous voice. Mara got up obediently and followed Yelsaventa out of the box. They walked a little way along the huge, shaded corridor and then Yelsaventa stopped.

"Alright Mara, wait here. Levi will come soon, I'm sure of it!" She said giggling and wiggling her eyebrows.

Mara flushed. What should she do? She knew that if she was in Levi's arms all her resolve would disappear and she would be helpless, at his mercy. She didn't want that.

But she didn't want to look like a child in front of Yelsaventa, or worse, appear that way in Levi's eyes.

She stood, frozen to the spot. A few minutes later, Yelsaventa headed back to the box alone.

Still Mara waited. There was no one else around – everyone was still watching the races, or down at the betting office on the ground floor.

If she just left now and went home, no one would be any the wiser. She'd just tell them later that she'd become disoriented and gotten lost. Or perhaps Levi would just think he'd looked for her in the wrong place.

But Mara lingered too long in her indecision. Before she knew it, there he was, walking towards her, his chiseled face bearing that cheerful smirk she'd come to know so well.

Her heart hammered and her mouth became dry with nervous thirst. It was too late now. She should have left while she had the chance.

He looked like a god in a Roman frescoe. She couldn't turn away. His eyes were fixed on her face with such an intensity under the grin. She was mesmerized.

"Oh Mara," he murmured, as he grew near. "You look so beautiful today. You've been driving me crazy this entire time." He was so close now and she began to feel light-headed. Suddenly, she was in his arms, his hands in her thick hair. "I couldn't bear to be without you another moment."

Mara was falling, falling, falling. She had to get out, had to stop this before it was too late.

"Levi, we can't be seen like this. Your reputation – and mine -" he stopped her in her speech, a finger pressed up against her soft, red lips.

"Will hardly be spoilt. I am one of the most eligible bachelors in Sebaste, Mara, surely you know that. And you are the most beautiful girl in this city. How would our being caught together spoil either of our reputations?" His lips brushed her ear, his eyes boring into her soul.

"I -" she began, but before she could continue, he was pushing her down into the stairwell, out of sight and his lips were pressed against hers. She could think of nothing else.

He filled her existence. All she knew was Levi. After a moment - or was it a lifetime? - he pulled away. He looked deep into her eyes, a look more vulnerable than she'd ever seen him wear covering his face. Suddenly he looked as young and lost as she felt.

"I've never felt feelings like this before Mara," he confided into her hair. "I must have you. Somehow, one day, I will make you my wife. But for now -" his lips met hers once more and she was carried away in a time of overwhelming senses. So this was what love and desire tasted of.

"Mara?! Mara!"

It was Dawid's voice, full of horror and outrage, that roused Mara from the dream-like state she'd entered into, in Levi's arms. The voice was below her, coming from the bottom of the stairwell.

Crying out, she began to pull herself from Levi's embrace, only moments before Dawid reached them, pushing her still further away.

Trembling with rage, Dawid launched for the other boy, his face flaming with righteous indignation. A fist connected with Levi's handsome jaw, sending him sprawling.

"How dare you touch my sister?!" Dawid snarled, readying himself to renew his assault. Mara shrieked and ran between then.

"No Dawid! Leave him alone!" She cried, but he flung her aside.

"You will pay for your actions!" Dawid shouted, as Levi got to his feet, wiping blood from his nose.

"It is you that will pay," he said, his voice icy. "You will pay for striking me. And as for your sister, I love her. I want to make her my wife, you fool." He rubbed his jaw, red from impact.

He started towards Mara, but Dawid pulled her away.

"You arrogant, rich pig!" Dawid returned. "You think you can just grab whatever you like and make it your own. But my sister is not some common slave girl for you to have your fun with. If you ever so much as look at her again, you will suffer. You will never have her, Levi ben Yehu. Never. My father will never let you see her again."

He began to drag Mara away, crying and straining, but Dawid was far too strong for her.

"We will see Dawid ben Mal'akhiy, we will see. But never forget, I never lose. I always get what I want, and Mara is mine." Levi shouted at their retreating backs.

Mara looked back and saw that other members of Levi's family had come out of the box to see what all the noise was about.

Her tear-streaked face, Dawid's red hot rage and Levi's bloody face was what greeted them. For the last time, Mara's eyes met Yelsaventa's and then, she was gone. It was over.

Chapter VIII.

A.D. 2, Sychar, Samaria, Roman province of Judaea

Mal'akhiy ben Yehudah wasted no time. The third day of the Ludi festival, he packed Mara off to Sychar. He had to get her out, to get her away from the malicious tongues of Sebaste, from the vipers of the upper crust. And away from that boy.

Mal'akhiy ached. He was deeply disappointed in his daughter, but no more than he was in himself. How could he have thought his young daughter, only just twelve years old, was mature enough to handle herself in an environment such as that provided by the Patron's family? They were well known as being too Romanised. And everyone knew what that meant.

He should have known. Should have intervened. Should have...

He peered into his daughter's room. She was face down on her bed, silent. After all the tears she had shed, all the shouting and screaming of yesterday, she was exhausted. Resigned. And Mal'akhiy wasn't sure he liked this any better.

The morning was dull and grey. Achsah sat beside Mara's bed, tearfully packing her things into a satchel, ready to go. The slave woman was crying. They were all lamenting for what had been lost.

Mal'khiy swallowed hard. His precious daughter.

She had been so innocent and now some spoilt, young boy had ruined that. Mal'akhiy's only consolation was that he had sent Dawid to check on Mara's health and had interrupted the situation before things got any worse.

"Why did you do it, Mara?" He had asked his tear-stained daughter when she arrived home, and Dawid, still trembling with anger, had explained the dark situation.

"Why shouldn't I have, Abba?" She had asked, eyes dark with resentment. "What trouble will Levi get into over this? None! And all because he is a man. But now you will punish me simply for being a woman and for having a man finding me attractive."

Mal'akhiy tore at his hair, remembering his own reply.

"I'm not intending to punish you, Mara, I'm trying to protect you. I want to save your reputation and help you to gain a good future for yourself. And as for the boy, he should be punished, for taking advantage of one as young and innocent as you, my girl."

Mara had scoffed in a way that saw her face twisted into some horrible form of worldly maturity.

"I'm not so young and innocent as you think, Abba."

It had broken his heart.

Dawid had wanted to go out at once and demand Levi ben Yehu pay the bride price and make amends for what he had done to his little sister. Mal'akhiy sighed bitterly. It would have been no use. There was no way the Patron's family would have allowed such a marriage, no matter how progressive they were. There was nothing to be done, no repairs to be made. The only solution was to flee.

The journey through the foothills towards Sychar was so different from the last time they had made it. This time, there was no dancing, no laughing and no singing from his daughter. Mara was a silent, solemn, broken stranger. He hardly even knew her. If he had ever know the girl at all.

* * *

Sychar was no longer the joyful place Mara remembered. Walking down the main street towards her grandparents' home – a walk which had always brought her incredible joy before – she felt nothing but sadness.

She felt alone. Deserted. Isolated. Desolate. She knew, deep down, she was none of those things.

She wasn't dying. No one had died. This wasn't the world's end. But, somehow, it felt like it may as well have been.

Mara had lost all she'd really cared about – her status as Yelsaventa's friend, the older girl's influence, her new identity as a young woman of society and worst of all, she'd lost Levi entirely. Now she knew he could never be her husband, nor even her lover.

Mara's heart felt cold as she thought back over the night before the races and how she'd vowed to come out on top in this. She thought of the Gaulish charioteer and the look he'd given her, how he'd urged her to beat the odds.

Dawid had told her that Severa died during the next day's races. Somehow, Mara felt like she'd failed them both.

Pinchas welcomed her granddaughter with open arms when she and Mal'akhiy arrived at their home. Mara couldn't find it in herself to return the embrace and stood, cold and aloof in her grandmother's arms. Having heard nothing of what had gone on, Pinchas was surprised and hurt.

"Imah, I've brought Mara here as I need her out of Sebaste for a while," Mal'akhiy began, trying delicately to explain the situation. He couldn't bring himself to say the words, to admit out loud that his precious child was fallen.

"You might as well tell them straight, Abba," Mara said emotionlessly. "Dawid caught a rich man kissing me and I'm being sent away because he cannot marry me." She raised her head and met her shocked grandparents' eyes with a cold, fiery gaze. "Abba has brought me here so there won't be a scandal."

Unsure of what to say next, they all just stood in silence. After what felt like an eternity, Pinchas began to rattle around in the cupboards.

"Will you be staying for dinner, Mal'akhiy?" She asked her son, trying her best to act as if nothing had happened. Her unnaturally high voice was the only thing that gave her emotion away. Mal'akhiy shook his head.

"No, I have to get back. Abba, may I talk to you outside, please?" He asked, turning to Yehudah, who nodded and followed Mal'akhiy out of the room.

And just like that, Mara's life changed. Her Abba was going to leave and she was set to remain in Sychar for her foreseeable future. Wallowing in self-pity, she slipped past her Savta and climbed the ladder up to her favourite place of solitude – the open roof.

The evening air was mercifully cool and Mara wrapped her arms around her knees. The breeze blew around her, carrying Sychar's familiar, comforting scent of spices, cooking and desert blooms. From below, her grandfather's voice drifted up to her.

"How will you find her a respectable husband now, Mal'akhiy? Will the young man in question make the happening known?" He sounded anxious and a twinge of what felt almost like regret rushed through Mara. She was sorry for causing her family pain. She heard her father sigh as well, filled with sadness, weariness.

"No, I don't think he will. It's in his own interests to pretend it never happened. A rich boy like him doesn't want anyone making accusations about him molesting a girl. He will also want a good marriage one day." Mal'akhiy sighed again. Mara could picture him running his hands through his thinning, dark hair, as he always did when he was upset.

"Mara is a beautiful girl. I don't think I'll have any trouble finding her a husband. My only fear is now she will seek to return to this Levi. She tells me she loves him – though I can hardly think she knows what love really is. Not that I've made any effort to show her." Her father's voice caught on a sob.

Mara snorted softly to herself, eyes pricking with tears. No, she didn't know what love really was. She longed to run down into her Abba's arms, to tell him all – to tell him what a fool she'd been and how she'd been deceived, to beg him to comfort her – but her pride would not let her. She couldn't do it. And she knew he'd never come to her. All her life, she'd brought Mal'akhiy nothing but sadness, but what she'd done now was the worst of all.

"Take care of her for me?" Mal'akhiy's voice pleaded with Yehudah. "Keep her out of trouble and bring the flower of life and joy and health and happiness back into her cheeks? I've missed my daughter." She could hear the raw emotion in his voice and she blinked hard, trying to keep her tears back.

"I'll do my best, Mal'akhiy." Yehudah's voice was gruff, husky with pain and Mara ached for them both. What had she done?

Later that night, after Mal'akhiy had gone and following the evening meal, Mara went back up to the roof and just sat in silence. The people of Sychar went on about their lives all around her – men heading to evening meetings at the synagogue, families walking home from meals with friends, children scurrying, dogs barking. None of them were aware of the broken young girl above them. No one knew how Mara's heart and soul ached. She just wanted this pain to be over.

"I wish I'd never met Yelsaventa and her brother!" Mara cried to the night sky. "I wish I'd never even gone to Sebaste!"

***

The next day dawned blue and bright. New. Mara awoke from a restless sleep feeling stiff and uncomfortable. She wriggled out of her blankets and climbed down from the upper story of the house, into the kitchen.

Pinchas was already awake and setting about preparing breakfast. She smiled at her granddaughter tiredly.

"How are you feeling this morning, lovey?"

Mara didn't attempt a smile back and merely shrugged.

"Do you need water, Savta? May I go to the well for you?"

Pinchas took in Mara's drawn, distressed face and nodded, thinking perhaps the fresh air would do her good.

"Don't be long though," she cautioned.

Mara took up the water jars and made her way out towards the town edge. It played on her mind that, if she had intended to run away – back to Sebaste and to Levi's arms – this was the perfect opportunity. But she did not wish to run away – not really.

If she had been a less mature girl, perhaps she would have truly considered it. But Mara understood enough about the world to realize she would be running back to nothing. Levi could not and would not have her now. Running back to Sebaste would only lead to her public disgrace.

The morning breeze was cool on her face as she made her way down the dusty, narrow streets, out towards Ya'acov's Well. Mara licked her lips, dry and parched after her night's sleep. The thought of the cool well water made her instantly feel a little better.

The sandy dirt of the path crunched beneath her feet as she left the town's eastern boundaries and neared the well. The taste of the icy, fresh water from so far below her feet refreshed her more than she could have imagined.

She could almost feel it flowing through every part of her body and washing away her tumbled mix of emotions. There was something about the taste of the water from Ya'acóv's Well that did that to her.

For a long while she just sat in silence at the rocky well's edge, watching the world around her stir gently to life. The sky, beautiful in pinks and vibrant blues, began to lift her spirits. Bird song filled the air.

In the distance she could hear the baa-ing of sheep. The sound grew closer and closer, as a shepherd lead his flock in to be watered before commencing their day at pasture.

Mara looked around and saw Shemu'el's honest, kind and weather-beaten face. It creased into a friendly smile when he noticed her slight form beside the rocky wall of the well.

"Mara? Mara bat Mal'akhiy? What are you doing here?!" He called out incredulously. "What has Sychar done to deserve to be graced by your loveliness?" He added teasingly.

Mara had been determined to keep a bold face, but something about Shemu'el's kind-hearted and pleased welcome broke down her defense and tears came. She couldn't help it.

Angrily she brushed them away, but not before Shemu'el had observed her unexpected flow of emotion. He made his way to her side, concerned and a little awkward.

"What's wrong? Did I say something I shouldn't have?" He put out a hand and placed it gently, tentatively, on her arm, seeking to console her, but unsure of how she might react.

When Shemu'el had seen her in the distance, her beautiful frame silhouetted in the morning sunlight, he'd been so happy. Mara was always a delight to have around, with her vivacious personality, ready laugh and sparkling love of life.

And today, when he'd glimpsed her, he'd seen her in a whole new way. Her beauty, as a girl blooming into womanhood, was truly apparent to him for the first time.

Her long, dark hair fell all around her shoulders, curtaining her from the world, her delicate cheekbones defining the corners of her sweet face. Her eyes, always blazing golden, were on fire today. The wistfulness in them was new and only served to make her more attractive, more enchanting.

She was lovely, there was no denying it. Shemu'el had realised this with a jolt as he approached. Other beautiful girls he had seen before faded instantly into the background of his memory, and he saw only her and knew he would forever see only her.

Her sudden tears had shocked him, leaving him unsure of how to proceed. Mara wasn't usually like this. Had he offended her with his good-natured teasing? Or perhaps had she sensed the pounding heart - as if it had never beaten before - under his words.

"Please Mara, what's the matter?" He asked gently, putting his arm further around her as she had not pulled away. *She is Dawid's little sister, Shemu'el,* he reminded himself. *Treat her like she was your own. As you always have.* Hah. Not that he'd ever be able to see her as a sister again.

Mara looked up at him through thick, tear-laden, dark slashes, her lower lip trembling despite herself.

"Oh Shemu'el, I've been such a fool!" She said bitterly. She scanned his confused, but earnest, good face and felt her tears flood back. He seemed to her, in that moment, to exemplify everything good and honest and true, every virtue she had thrown away.

"Whatever you have done, it can't be that bad," he replied, voice cracking a little. Mara laughed, the bitterness ever more present in her voice.

"Oh, yes it is!" She covered her face with her hands, feeling filthy beside him. What she felt in that moment could not be expressed by mere words, or anything so simple as common emotions. In the eyes of the world, she was tainted.

She would never be anyone. And all because she'd been foolish enough to fall in love with a man who didn't want her – heart and soul – for who she truly was. Had anyone ever? *Would anyone ever?* She ached.

Shemu'el looked on, feeling rather helpless. If she'd been one of his own sisters, he would have gathered her into his arms and just held her through her emotional turn. But he could hardly do that with Mara. If she would just explain what the matter was, perhaps he'd be able to help.

Somehow, he doubted it. In his experience, girls seemed to make even the most simple issues complex. Surely whatever Mara was upset about was just a case of this – an overreaction.

"Isn't it something you can move past, at least?" He asked in what he hoped was a comforting tone.

The cynical laugh she gave dispelled all hope of that.

"You don't understand Shem. Dawid caught me in the arms of a man." She stopped talking, giving a moment for her words to sink in. "One of my friend's older brothers sought to take advantage of me. And, silly child that I was, I thought he loved me."

A harsh laugh bubbled to the surface again, her lovely face twisting. Gone was her youthful sparkle. "I thought he wanted to marry me. But no, all he wanted was a pretty plaything."

Shemu'el just stood in silence, listening, his face unreadable. Chancing a look up at him, Mara, despite herself, felt vulnerable. What would he think of her now?

Now that she had begun talking, she couldn't seem to stop. Words poured out of her, as she told Shem the sad story of her last few months.

"Abba warned me. So did Dawid, but I didn't listen. I was so caught up in him. My friends urged me on. And now, with one little kiss, he has ruined me. No one will want a girl like me now," she finished, looking away so he wouldn't see the hot tears that fizzed up once more.

I would. Shemu'el looked down at her trying to master his raging emotions. How was it that she could tell him such things and all he could feel for her was pity and love? He should despise her for such immoral behavior, no matter how innocently born. But he could not.

"Mara, you've been listening to lies," he began huskily.

She looked up at him, distain hanging from her curled lip, but a deep longing in her golden eyes. Though it was pointless, she couldn't stop herself from hoping that his words would hold the freedom she'd been longing to hear, ever since this whole mess began. He continued shakily.

"You listened to a lie that all love is true love. And that you are a fool. You were just innocent. Your friends told you lies. And the biggest lie is that no one will want you now. Trust me Mara," he said, voice catching. "There are many who will want you. But love can't be centred on a person. If it isn't centred on Elohim, on God, it will never work out. He wants us to love Him first and to find love in Him. If things are done His way and not the world's way, it hurts less," he ended gently.

Mara snuffled to herself.

"What, you mean be a good little Samaritan daughter and marry whoever Abba picks for me, or the first man to come knocking at the door asking for me? No thank you! I want more than to marry some unimportant man. I want to be happy!" Her eyes blazed scornfully now. What Shemu'el had offered was not what she'd wanted to hear.

"Who is to say you wouldn't be?" Shemu'el returned softly. But he could see she wasn't ready to hear what he had to say, so he tried to carefully manoeuvre the conversation back to safer ground. "Either way, I am certain you are not ruined forever. You are young and Sychar is not like Sebaste. You will find the man for you." He grinned and shoved her affectionately. Mara rolled her eyes and shoved him back.

"I certainly hope you're right," she said rubbing her eyes. "Otherwise you might have to marry me," she joked, eyes beginning to glisten with their old life.

When she eventually set off back to town, step much lightened, Shemu'el watched her go. Her words "otherwise you might have to marry me", weighed heavy on him.

"If only Mara, if only," he whispered into the wind. His sheep were the only ones that heard.

*** *

As the days went by, Mara began to feel more like her old self. Pinchas and Yehudah delighted to see their youngest granddaughter starting to return to normality. There was a new, sad air of world-weariness, which lingered on though. Pinchas secretly wondered whether it would ever be gone.

Mara had crossed from childhood innocence into a new, graver understanding of the world so fast and it seemed there was no going back. Glimmers of her name's meaning appeared in her from time to time as well. It grieved her grandmother deeply, that her happy girl was no longer there. Still, she was thankful that the overwhelming depression, at least, had lifted.

Pinchas had managed to get Mara to begin engaging with people again and not just go off on those long, solitary walks through the hills. After her conversation with Shemu'el, Pinchas had managed to keep Mara from telling anyone else what had happened in Sebaste. No one else need know.

It was almost time for Yom Kippur, the Festival of Atonement, and Mara would be able to be cleansed from all her sin. It need never matter.

Chapter IX.

A.D. 2, Sychar, Samaria, Roman province of Judaea

Mara awoke on the day of the Yom Kippur festival feeling light and airy. It was the first time in many weeks she'd felt anything but sadness ruling from the seat of her emotions.

Ever since she was a very little girl, Mara had loved being in Sychar with her grandparents to celebrate their traditional festivals.

The Day of Atonement, followed by Sukkot - the Festival of Tabernacles - a few days later, had always been her favourites. Going up onto Mount Gerizim with her people at the end of Yom Kippur was always a night to remember.

Mara rushed her trip out to Ya'acov's Well that morning, not taking time to admire the flowers, or to ponder her way along the track. She drew up her water and made her way back into Sychar with a group of excited girls.

Zimra was there with her family for the festival. Mara was especially glad to see Zimra, whose kind heart flowed over into all she did. She made no mention of the scandal within Levi, much to Mara's relief. Hearing of her shame, or even hearing Levi's name spoken out loud again would have been too painful.

Zimra's pale, gentle eyes whispered to Mara that she knew all and yet there was no judgement in her gaze. Her eyes swam with aching sorrow and deep understanding.

But today would see even those looks wiped from her eyes, Mara was determined of it. The Festival of Atonement saw the Samaritan people fast for the day – from sundown that coming evening, until sundown the next – gathered, praying.

Then, they would visit Mount Gerizim's heights, worshipping at their holiest place, where their temple had once stood and finishing the festival with a great feast.

It was a long day, Yom Kippur, though the feast afterwards had always made it seem worth it to Mara as a child. This year it would be worth it in its own right – because it would see her freed from what she had done. No man could have a hold over her now.

As Mara stood beside her Savta during the long readings of the Torah, the book of the Law of Moshe, despite her stomach's near-constant rumbling with hunger, she felt satisfaction flowing through her body. She was no longer going to be held back by her past.

As she watched, the High Priest, a tall, stately man named Yonatan, chanted his way through passage after passage of their scriptures, seeming never to tire. This Day of Atonement was all about enduring physical hardship to gain its reward.

Mara figured that High Priest Yonatan's heavy ceremonial priestly robes must be an extra hardship for him to endure. Her own clothing felt loose and baggy without her usual leather belt and her feet chilly with no sandals – no leather was permitted on this holy day.

A little way from her, Mara could hear a small child whimpering in his mother's arms. It wasn't easy for any of them to endure a full day's penitence, but it was for certain hardest upon the elderly and the children.

As Yonatan switched with another priest, allowing him to continue the chanting, Mara's thoughts strayed from their proper place. She began to consider whether or not the time spent really achieved anything. Did Yahweh really hear their prayers? Did He really forgive all their offenses simply because they fasted and prayed? That is, if He was even there at all.

Still, regardless of their true state of forgiveness, there was another benefit of the Day of Atonement. It meant no one could again accuse her of immorality – she would be cleansed. And everyone would see her repentance.

Mara looked over to the men's side of the gathering and saw her Saba standing solemnly, enduring the ritual. Shemu'el was standing a few rows away. His rugged, sun-bronzed face didn't bear any trace of heavy, painful endurance. Instead, he looked deep in meaningful thought. Mara supposed that he really believed that this day-long fast once a year was the key to their cleansing, whilst they waited for their long-prophesied Messiah – the one to bear away their sins - to come and redeem them all.

She studied Shem a while longer. There was something overwhelmingly peaceful about his face. Mara wondered if she'd feel like that once Yom Kippur was over. Sniffing to herself, she tossed her hair and turned back to the assembly.

What did it matter? So long as she was purified in the eyes of the people and her past forgotten, it held no significance to her. She didn't need Yahweh to give her peace and satisfaction. She could find that herself.

* * *

As the sun began to set in the western heights of Samaria's mountains, the High Priest gave the signal and the fast was over. People began to shout and whoop with unveiled joy. Musicians struck up their instruments and everyone rushed to rejoin their families. Atonement had been made. Now, it was time for the feasting to begin.

A wave of relief washed over Mara and almost overcome, she turned and hugged her grandmother tightly, desiring nothing more than loving, human contact in that moment.

"I'm free," she whispered more to herself than to Pinchas. Mara could tell from the wetness of her grandmother's slightly wrinkled cheeks that she was feeling the same, elated feeling.

To Pinchas, there was no greater relief than knowing Yahweh had redeemed Mara, both in His eyes and in the eyes of all others in the community. No burden of shame inflicted on her, in her innocence, by an arrogant, rich, young Sebastean would follow her around now.

"Praise Adonai," she murmured, using the word for Lord God. She was so grateful.

"Mara! The maidens are getting ready for the feast – let's join them!" Zimra cried, running up in excitement. "The celebrations begin soon!" She grabbed Mara's hand, ready to pull her off to where the other girls were gathering. Mara felt something surge within her. She felt so light. Following her friend, she turned back to Pinchas and called:

"I'll see you there, Savta!"

Pinchas watched Mara run off at Zimra's side and shook her head slowly. In comparison to Zimra's slight, still childlike form, she observed the beauty which had blossomed up within Mara. No wonder that rich boy from Sebaste had wanted her for his own.

"Soon you will be all grown up and married to another rich man, who longs for a jewel like you," Pinchas whispered softly after her. "And then, I will truly call myself old, with all my grandchildren grown up."

Her mind turned to thinking of the first time she'd met her own husband. She'd thought Yehudah terribly handsome when she'd noticed his gaze from across the market square, despite the fact that he'd been quite a lot older than her fourteen years.

She could still remember how she had felt when he had come to her parents' home with gifts and she'd known without a doubt he was there to ask for her hand. The trembly, wobbly excitement she'd felt that day was still such a vivid memory, even all these years later.

She'd done well for herself, Pinchas supposed. Yehudah had always been a good husband and had provided for her well. Besides, he was kind and generous and he made her laugh. Many of her friends had not been so blessed by Yahweh.

They'd had a happy marriage, that was for certain, she mused. She'd given her husband four sons and three daughters. Two of their sons had served in the Roman army, as part of the Samaritan battalion, their oldest had become a wealthy money lender and all their girls had married well and were happy.

Pinchas knew parents weren't supposed to have favourites – she knew how their ancestor Ya'acov had suffered for that! - and yet, her youngest had always been extra special to her heart. Mal'akhiy had always been such a dear boy and he took such good care of his parents.

That he'd lost his wife, Ado, was terribly sad, but secretly, Pinchas was glad for it. She got to have her boy, now fully grown, back again. And with him, his own two precious, last born off-spring. Dawid was such a sweet, good boy. And Mara… There was just something about the girl no one could resist.

She was determined that Mara would make something of herself. If she needed any shoving from behind to get there, Pinchas would provide it. Of course, there'd been that little setback with that young man in Sebaste, but now, after Yom Kippur, that would no longer be a problem.

As she watched Mara dance away, Pinchas couldn't help but laugh at herself. As if that girl needed any help securing her future.

"Ready to go to the feast my dear?" Yehudah slipped an arm around his wife's waist. She smiled up at him. Despite his wrinkles and his tired, old face, she still thought he was the most handsome of men and her eyes tenderly whispered that up to him. She gently cupped her slim fingers around his cheek, before following him away.

* * *

Mara and Zimra emerged from one of the houses on the outskirts of town along with the other girls. Excitement rose within all their hearts as they made their way out into the street, hair bedecked with all kinds of beautiful wildflowers.

The festival which followed Yom Kippur was a time for great joy and was well known in their community as the time when a young man would choose in his heart, a bride. Mara herself was not too concerned with this. She was just glad to be feeling so light and free − to be able to adorn herself with the other maidens; not forced to hide away under an overwhelming veil of shame.

The flowers she had woven into her dark locks, brilliant whites, yellows and blooms of purple, made her feel beautiful in a way she'd never felt before. Other times, in Sebaste, when she'd dressed up, she had felt grown up and sophisticated − alluring even.

But here in Sychar she felt like a simple country girl, adorned only with nature. She felt vibrant and alive. The tinkling golden bracelets of Sebaste seemed so far away.

As the girls ran up the mountainside, leaping and laughing and singing, the rest of the people looked down at them, smiling at the beauty of these carefree maidens. It was one of the best things about the festivals their people held − the way everyone seemed to come alive, filled with life and colour.

It was as though all personas usually hidden beneath the mundane routines of everyday life simply melted away. Disguises were gone. It was real people out on display at the festivals.

She was radiant.

Even among such a score of fair maidens – some of Shomron's finest – she stood alone. Every curve of her long, slender neck, every blink of her long lashed eyes – oh, for time itself had stood still before him – every flicker that crossed her expressive face, every toss of her flowing mane…

He was lost in her.

She was laughter. Joy – they were one and the same. The moon itself ceased to shine, for all he could see was her. All he could hear was her voice, carried on the mountain wind and his own breath, deep and heavy.

Had his eyes ever seen before they had beheld her? Had his arms ever yearned to be filled with such a force? Time herself was dancing by him – wearing its palest white gown and flowers in her hair. And just like that, she slipped through his fingers.

She was gone – dancing on up the slopes.

And he was forever changed.

Could he ever breathe again, now that she had moved on, beyond him? She hadn't even noticed him. Didn't turn back to see him standing there.

Would all else of life lose its colour now?

Or would it, instead, be all the brighter because of that moment – seared forever into his memory?

Mara.

* * *

In the instant Amitai ben Yonatan glanced up and saw the group of girls laughing and dancing their way up the mountainside, his eyes fell on one in particular and he found he could not look away. He didn't *want* to look away.

The girl, willowy and slender, with beautiful flowers in her mane of hair was in the middle of the group. Oh, she had the most captivating golden eyes. In that instant, he knew his life would never be the same.

As she made her way up the grassy slopes of Mount Gerizim, dancing along with the other maidens, he weighed her beauty and knew in his heart that she was the most perfect thing he'd ever seen. She was the only one for him.

Before his people had worshipped here on Mount Gerizim, before they'd left their slavery in Egypt, those thousands of years ago and even before Yahweh had created Chava − the first woman − for their first father, Adama... Amitai was convinced this girl, the one with flowers in her hair, had been created just for him.

He was the firstborn of the High Priest of Yahweh's people and he was assumed to be the next High Priest. Surely this beautiful creature before him was his perfect match. After all, his father had always brought him up to have the best of everything and surely there was no better than this girl.

She, with her thick, dark hair, her delicately boned face and glowing fiery eyes, was in his mind, the epitome of beauty. Now he'd seen her, he knew no other woman would look as lovely to him. She shone with life and vigor. Surely, she was the purest of creatures − perfect for him.

The stars glistening in the night sky up above the mountain and the moon shone down on her and as the feasting began, he could see only her.

"Hey, Amitai, what's the matter with you?!" One of his friend's called, knuckling his hair to get his attention. "It's as if only your body is present − your mind has clearly left us behind!"

He shook his head, trying to get control of his thoughts.

"I have just seen the woman I will have as my bride," he said softly, afraid to say the words loudly, in case he broke the spell he was under.

His friend laughed.

"Will have, my brother? She may not like you!" He teased.

"Hah! What girl would refuse Amitai?" Another piped up somewhat glumly. He was, after all, the High Priest's firstborn, not to mention young and handsome, strong and learned. He was everything the girls longed for, they all knew that.

"Which one is she?" The first friend, Yehoshu'a, asked, looking down at the maidens with twinkling eyes. "My, there are many comely girls here tonight!"

Amitai looked down towards where his Flower Queen stood, holding hands with a much smaller, plainer girl as they danced around in circles.

"She is there," he said pointing. "I've never seen her before." His friends all jostled and nudged him, Yehoshu'a letting out a low whistle.

"Trust you to pick the prettiest one of all. That's Mara bat Mal'akhiy – she's from Sebaste. Dawid's younger sister. Staying with her grandparents. She has blossomed into a beauty, hasn't she?"

More than a beauty, Amitai thought, grinning to himself. She is the perfect woman. Like an angel. And she will be mine. At that moment, the girl, Mara, turned and looked up at them. Up at him. As their eyes met, a feeling unlike any he'd ever felt before struck him.

So this was love. So this was what it felt like to behold your other half. Her mesmerizing eyes, in them, he could see that she felt it too. He could tell. The way all his friends hushed their chatter and fell into a solemn silence, told him that they could feel it too.

This was an almost sacred moment. The moment Amitai ben Yonatan and Mara bat Mal'akhiy's lives had been leading up to. This was their destiny, he had no doubt about it.

***

"Mara, look!" Zimra spoke softly, not daring to look up at her friend.

93

"The young men, they have all noticed you. They're looking your way!"

Shivers began to race up and down Mara's spine as she heard Zimra's words.

"At me?! Surely, they could be looking at any of us!" She said breathily. Zimra shot her a look.

"Oh really, Mara, as if anyone can notice the rest of us when you're around. Turn, and you will see for yourself," she said, winking.

Mara turned and glanced up the mountain. At least, she had meant to just glance, but as she turned and saw the young men, gazes fixed on her, her eyes latched onto the man in the middle. He was the tallest, with a well defined and masculine figure and the fine hawk-nose borne of their people's Israelite-Assyrian mixed blood and a handsomely chiseled jaw.

His dark eyes met hers and held on, not allowing her to look away. As Levi's gaze had once made her heart pound, this man's gaze made it race. She felt her cheeks grow to flame, she held the look, feeling the fire flow between them before she turned away.

"Zimra, who is that? The one in the middle?" She asked breathlessly. "I'm sure I've seen him before."

Zimra laughed.

"Oh Mara, I think you've just won for yourself Amitai ben Yonatan." It took Mara a moment to figure out, over her heart's pounding, why that name was familiar, then she realized. He was the eldest son of the High Priest and he was the man he'd seen outside the synagogue last time she was in Sychar.

"You're imagining things, Zim. He didn't even see me," she stuttered. Zimra laughed again and danced her friend around.

"You can hardly deny that look Mara. I think everyone here tonight felt that look. We all know he will be coming to your grandparents' house soon."

The rich, heady scent of wildflowers filled Mara's lungs as she breathed deeply, trying to steady herself. In the scent of the blooms, this moment would be forever emblazoned for her.

Once more, she looked back up to where the young men were. But this time, it wasn't the young priest's eyes she locked with.

It was Shemu'el.

The look on his face told her his heart was hurting. Suddenly, she understood. Shemu'el ben Aharon had truly understood when she'd wept of unrequited love. Of course he had. Shemu'el knew what it was to love one who didn't return his love. And it was all Mara's fault.

Chapter X.

A.D. 3, Sychar, Samaria, Roman province of Judaea

The days passed and all thoughts of Levi and her life in Sebaste were forgotten – her thoughts now consumed entirely with Amitai ben Yonatan. Yet he didn't come.

As Mara made her way out to Ya'acov's Well two days later, she felt a little dejected. The warm breeze danced around her, blowing sand irritatingly up against her bare ankles. *Just figures,* she huffed.

How had she fallen into the same old trap again? Hadn't the pain and hurt she'd experienced over Levi been enough for her? Had she really learnt nothing from all that?

She'd managed to forget all about Levi and everything that had occurred in Sebaste and now, here she was, falling head over heels for yet another man who would never love her back.

And why should he? She was just some ordinary nobody from Sebaste and he was the High Priest's heir.

Amitai was well known to be the most handsome, most eligible bachelor in the whole of Samaria. It was reported that he had strong opinions, knew what he wanted in life – and always got it. He was looking for the very best Shomron had to offer. As if that would be her.

Bitter scorn filled Mara, ready to burst over and flow out into the street around her as she thought. Who did she think she was? She was a fool, a child, to think anyone would ever want a girl like her.

Levi may have been every bit as rich and almost as handsome – but he had never been looking for a bride, only a toy. Amitai wanted a wife. He wanted someone beautiful and accomplished by his side. It was the life she'd always wanted. To be someone rich and powerful's wife.

In that moment their eyes had locked, in that instant, Mara had thought there was a chance. She thought he had felt what she had. She had really thought it to be the moment that might change her life forever. That she might be free of Levi's shadow and revered by their people. Valued. Looked up to.

But Amitai hadn't come. Obviously, it wasn't meant to be.

She continued to pout as she trekked out towards the well, the pottery jar balanced on her hip beginning to feel heavier and heavier.

Mara usually enjoyed walking out in the fresh air and in the solitude, but she was always so thirsty by the time she got there and so thirsty by the time she reached town again.

Her thirst had always exceeded that of other people's. She had to drink what felt like double the amount of water others did in order to stay hydrated. It scared her to go too far from any water source because her thirst was so intense.

How she wished there was some way to get water without hiking out to the well. She missed Sebaste's aqueduct.

The well itself was surrounded by a stone wall, the yellowed blocks all worn down by the centuries of wind and sand.

As Mara approached, she could see the faint outline of a person sitting beside it, but ignored them. It was common enough for people to be found at the little man-made oasis. Still lost in her own thoughts, she approached, carefully removing the large jar from her hip.

"Can it be you, the girl with dreams in her eyes?"

The voice, soft, low and very cultured, startled her. She looked up and saw the figure by the well materialize into Amitai ben Yonatan's large frame. Immediately, her heart took up its drumbeat. He was so tall; she felt small, like an insignificant child, as she stood in his shadow. His musky scent filled her lungs and she found she could not speak.

"I heard that you often come out to the well in the mornings," he said, grinning somewhat sheepishly. "A chance meeting with the most beautiful girl — what more could I wish for?" His dark eyes twinkled. He bore the look of a man used to getting his own way and sure that he always would.

It was absolutely clear to Mara that this little rendezvous was not even the slightest bit accidental. This had obviously turned out just as he had planned it. And Mara, for one, didn't mind.

He waited, as if expecting her to speak, but she found that, much to her surprise, no words came. Amitai made her nervous, but not as Levi had. She didn't feel like an ignorant fool before Amitai — just like a shy maiden. Looking up at him through her lashes, she smiled, before ducking her head and turning away.

"Wait!" The way he said it was both a command and a request. "Do you know who I am?" Mara nodded shyly.

"Everyone knows who you are. You're Amitai ben Yonatan, our High Priest's son."

She turned again, somehow intuitively knowing that to force him to chase her was the best way to hold his attention. The way his eyes followed her, dark eyes filled with idealized adoration — though Mara did not comprehend it as such — told her that he would not let her get away.

"Please, I want to talk to you!" His voice, still deep and soft, took on an imploring tone now. She half turned back to face him, meeting his dark eyes with her golden ones.

"It isn't proper, Sir, for me to be here with you like this," she hesitated, teasingly. "People might start to think things."

His face flushed under his beard and he cleared his throat.

"Please, I didn't mean anything improper!" His words came out in a stuttering flurry. "I just wanted to hear your voice, to know your thoughts before I -" He broke off speaking, then tried again. "I'm pleased you care about propriety because the one I ma-"

He looked so very uncomfortable that Mara longed to put him out of his misery, but she couldn't think of a word to say. She could hear her pulse pumping in her ears as she waited for him to finally get out what he was trying to say. She smiled gently up at him, trying to offer the encouragement he needed.

Amitai sighed deeply and ran his fingers through his dark hair.

"What I'm trying to say is… the other night, when I saw you at the festival, I knew." He paused, looking steadily into her eyes. Her stomach flipped at the words. Could it be true? Seeming to get the reassurance he needed to continue, he went on.

"That moment I saw you, I knew you must be mine." His words all came in a rush now. "All my life, girls have been angling for me to choose them, but none I have seen before have been anything like you. When I saw you and when you saw me too, I knew. I knew Yahweh had created you to be mine. The most beautiful woman among His people, so pure and lovely."

He gazed into her eyes, and she gazed back. Pure… Maybe not so much as he thought. *Should I tell him?* She wondered. But only for a moment. Her next thought was far more forceful. *No! After the Day of Atonement, I'm as pure as any other.*

"Mara bat Mal'akhiy," he was saying softly. He knew her name! "Lovely Mara. They tell me you are from Sebaste. When will your Abba be in Sychar? I want to ask him for your hand, not just your Saba."

Mara's heart lurched again and she found she could hardly speak. She had to be dreaming this. The High Priest's son asking her to be his wife?!

"Ahh, um, he'll be here for Sukkot – for the harvest festival," she managed to get out. She looked away and began to twiddle nervously with a stray lock of hair.

"You aren't just teasing me, are you?" She asked, unable to meet his eyes as she spoke. She couldn't bear it if he was. "You're not just trying to make fun of me?"

"Make fun of you?!" The shock and horror was evident in his voice. "No, Mara! I truly want to marry you. You are the only one for me. Surely you feel it too?"

Mara gave a happy little giggle and nodded.

"I've never felt anything like it."

A little whoop of boyish enthusiasm escaped his refined demeanour at her words.

Suddenly Mara's face fell again. "But Amitai -" It felt strange to say his name. "What will your family think? I'm not from a wealthy or old family, I'm just a stone mason from Sebaste's youngest daughter. And you're to be High Priest one day!"

He was grinning now, a self confident smile that gave her heart a little twinge. It was Levi's smile. She shook herself. She couldn't be thinking about Levi ben Yehu now! She forced her attention back to Amitai's words.

"If I love you and I do, then they will love you. Besides, you're right, I am to be High Priest one day and therefore I deserve the best. There is none more lovely, more beautiful than you. You must be mine!"

That settled, there was little else to say. Amitai, it was clear, was used to have the last say in things and with such a complimentary description of herself, Mara was not about to argue.

Bending to pull the ropes, Amitai drew the leather water skin up out of the deep well and, picking up Mara's large jar, began to fill it. She watched him silently, flushing as she became suddenly aware that she hadn't paid much attention to her appearance this morning and wasn't up to her usual standards. Her hair was left loose, its dark lengths flowing in waves down to her waist, she had no make-up on and she was wearing her oldest tunic.

Mara couldn't stop a little bubble of laughter from popping out her mouth. Yelsaventa would be horrified. But what had she ever known?! She'd told Mara that in order to find herself a good match, she'd have to keep up appearances.

And yet, here Mara was with Amitai ben Yonatan himself filling her water jars and announcing his intention to seek her hand. And he was a far better match than Levi ever would have been! If God existed, Mara thought, he was certainly smiling on her today.

"Can you imagine," Amitai began softly, interrupting her thoughts. "That once, our ancestor Ya'acov might have stood right here, drawing water for his truest love, Rakhel? And now, here we are and I am doing the same for you." Despite his beard and chiseled face, Amitai suddenly looked very young, very vulnerable to Mara as he offered her a shy grin.

He was a strange mixture of things, this man - boldness and self assurance and yet also timidity and a clear desire for validation. Mara was touched by his words, so tenderly were they spoken, so sincerely. It was quite apparent that in those few days since first he'd seen her, he'd fallen head over heels in love with her. Mara knew how that felt.

Amitai picked up her jar, now full of water which sparkled in the sunlight and stepped out on the path back to Sychar.

"May I walk you back to your grandparents' house, Mara bat Mal'akhiy?" He asked, back to the confident, decisive young man she'd first seen. Nodding, she set off beside him.

She was terribly thirsty by now, but didn't really feel right asking him to stop so she could quench herself. She didn't want to cause any trouble, she was far too desperate to please him.

Amitai kept up conversation with Mara all the way back to the town, his strong arms managing the water jar far easier than she ever had.

She felt light and happy, walking along beside this handsome man and knowing everyone who saw them pass by admired her.

And the more she talked with Amitai, the more she liked him. On the whole, he seemed rather serious, but he found her quick wit amusing and he had a handsome and complimentary turn of phrase.

As they neared the town, Mara began to feel a little bit self-conscious at all the eyes turned their way – from the old beggar sitting by the wall and children playing in the street, to housewives leaning out their windows. It seemed to her that even the birds up in the trees stopped their chattering, and cooing to watch.

"They're all staring," she mumbled bashfully to Amitai, but he just laughed.

"Let them! We make a fine pair, Mara and they are admiring how well we look together. You are the epitome of a beautiful Samaritan maiden and I am one of Samaria's most famous sons. And if they talk, let them! Soon, you will be mine, not only in people's eyes, but in name as well." His dark eyes met hers, filled with reassurance.

They had reached her grandparents' courtyard now and he bent low to put down the jar, muscles rippling as he stood back up. He tossed back a stray lock of hair and gave Mara a slow grin.

"I'm so glad to have met you, Mara. I must go now, but I will return – the minute I hear of your Abba's arrival in town. Be ready!" He added, tossing a wink her way. The wink had the practiced air of one who had used it often upon giggling girls, but Mara hardly cared.

His words *I will return the minute I hear of your Abba's arrival* had set her head spinning. Feeling giddy, she watched him make his way out of the courtyard and head down onto the dusty street again. This. Was. Real.

"Mara? Who was that?" Pinchas called curiously out of the downstairs window. Hardly containing squeals of delight, Mara ran on through the courtyard and into the atrium.

"Oh Savta, you wouldn't believe what has happened!"

* * *

So, this is it then. Shemu'el sighed as he filled the trough with water for his flock. He had seen her, seen Mara with him. Amitai ben Yonatan. The High Priest's son. The man who always got what he wanted. From Mara's besotted face, Shem knew that this time would be no different.

Like the Roman horse Amitai had coveted and convinced his father to buy, like the house on the hill which had belonged to another and yet now was his. It was all too easy to see what would happen here. Before anyone else could get in, Mara ben Mal'akhiy, the most beautiful woman in the region, if not the whole empire, the world, would be his.

Despite himself, Shem felt his dark eyes fill with angry, hurt tears. He brushed them away. Mara owed him nothing. Why should he ever have thought she might be interested in a scrawny shepherd like him when wealthy, cultured men were asking for her hand? He was a fool to have ever considered it.

Shemu'el's heart ached. It wasn't that Amitai was a bad person. He was a nice enough man, he supposed, it was just that he was always so focused on getting exactly what he wanted.

He had always been vocal about only marrying when he found the most beautiful girl, the purest their nation had to offer. Did he know about Mara's little situation back in Sebaste? Shemu'el doubted it. No matter her beauty, he wouldn't have even considered her if he had.

Her beauty. That was all Amitai saw her for. He didn't see the fiery temper, or the quick laugh. He didn't know how much she loved to run barefoot in the mountains, or how thirsty she always was. He didn't know the little things that made her sad, or the way her eyes danced when she was teasing someone.

He couldn't possibly know about her sweet, lilting singing voice, or the dramatic way she loved to dance in front of a fire. Amitai knew nothing about all the doubts Mara hid inside, the doubts about her

103

Creator and of her own worth. He didn't know how crafty she was, or how she would happily twist situations to get her own way.

Both the good and the bad in Mara, Amitai ben Yonatan knew nothing about. He only saw her as his perfect match in appearance.

Shemu'el thumped his hand down angrily on the trough, making his sheep bleat in agitation. He rubbed the nearest ones' heads, seeking to calm them, despite feeling all churned up inside. Love hurt.

"Why is it, Lord, that some people seem to get everything?" He cried, face turned up to the sky. "Why?" The sky was silent, but deep in his soul, he felt the reply. *All things are designed for my purposes, my Child and they are above yours. One day, you will understand.* Shemu'el bowed his head low, frowning. "I wish I could know now, Yahweh. But I will trust you."

* * *

The next day, as Mara went out to the well to get water, she could sense things were different in town. Whenever she walked past anyone, the whispering would start. Good or bad things, she wasn't sure. Some people's eyes held encouragement, others, reproach.

There was none of the usual friendly banter, today people just watched her pass, as if she was someone else entirely, not the town's beloved young beauty. Even Zimra seemed different. Eventually, Mara could no longer bear her friend's silence and confronted her about it.

"Is that a serious question, Mara?" Zimra replied, laughing a little.

"The whole town is talking about the way Amitai ben Yonatan walked you home yesterday. They think he must have proposed to you already, or else that you are very shocking to allow him to walk you home! Either that, or very blessed to have been noticed by the next High Priest!"

Her pale green eyes glowed with the excitement of it all.

Mara snorted.

"Well, which do you think me? Shocking, or blessed?" She asked, skipping ahead of her friend, expression playful. Zimra still looked serious.

"I haven't decided yet." The two girls went back to walking in silence for a while, then she piped up again. "Still, he seemed so enamored with you, I would be very surprised if he didn't come and ask for your hand very soon." She smiled at Mara encouragingly.

Mara couldn't stop the beaming smile which blossomed onto her face as she confided.

"The minute my Abba arrives in Sychar for Sukkot, he is intending to ask!"

Zimra squealed loudly, before covering her mouth in embarrassment as half the market place looked up to see what was going on. Her cheeks flamed, but the staring only lasted an instant. Once people had satisfied their curiosity and seen it was just an excitable young girl, they'd turned back to their work.

Blush back under control, Zimra replied:

"Are you serious? Mara, I'm so thrilled for you! He is the perfect match for you, I'm sure." Lowering her voice, she added. "And what about what happened in Sebaste, how does he feel about that?"

Mara felt her own face flush now.

"Zimra! Don't ever mention that again!" She pleaded. "I haven't mentioned it and I don't intend to. Levi and everything that ever occurred in Sebaste is forgotten to me! As my Savta said, I attended the Day of Atonement and therefore anything I have done in my past is to be recalled no more. He doesn't need to know about it and neither does anyone else!"

Zimra put a placatory arm around her friend.

"I'm sorry I brought it up and I promise I won't again." She said gently. "But Mara, if he's to be your husband, don't you think he has a right to know?"

"No, I don't! And I don't want to talk about it anymore." She said, pouting her pretty lips in rage and storming away.

Who did Zimra think she was to interfere? It wasn't her life, after all! Blind in her anger, Mara crashed into one of the forum's many stray cats, making it yowl loudly. She shooed it away irritably with her sandalled foot.

She could hear Zimra calling out after her apologetically, but she wasn't in the mood. Besides, something deep down inside her was asking – what if she's right? But no! How could she possibly tell Amatai?! That would jeopardize everything.

She stopped by a tall fig tree near the edge of the forum, as her anger faded, replaced by fear. Zimra made her way up to her hesitantly – afraid she'd feel the sting of Mara's anger again.

"Mara, I'm so sorry"' she said softly. "I really didn't mean to hurt you. I'm sure you've thought everything through well. I only want to see you happy and well taken care of." She reached out to take Mara's hand. Mara sighed softly and squeezed Zimra's in return.

"I know you do. I just don't want you to question me. Amitai is a good man and he will make me a woman of standing. I will be an important man's wife, Zim," she said.

"I only hope he will treat you well," Zimra replied, with a laugh.

"What do you mean by that?" Mara asked doubtfully. She could tell her friend was trying to say something beyond her words.

"Oh nothing," Zimra replied, brushing her own thoughts away. "Nothing at all."

Chapter XI.

A.D. 3, Sychar, Sebaste, Roman province of Judaea

As Mal'akhiy and Dawid made their way down through the Mount Gerizin valley early in the afternoon on the first day of Sukkot, Mal'akhiy wondered to himself how he would find his girl.

It had been several months since he'd escorted her, silent and resistant, to his parents' home. Enough time, he hoped, for her to have returned to her old self. Sychar was her favourite place on earth – surely, by now, it would have had its effect on her.

The whole situation with the Patron's brat had all died down within days and had, by some merciful miracle, been kept from becoming a full-blown scandal. Mal'akhiy shook his head ruefully. Despite himself, he understood how the situation had come about.

Mara was a beautiful girl and if he'd been Levi's age, he also would have been tempted to chase her. Of course, Mara could hardly be blamed for what had occurred. She was far too young and inexperienced to know one kind of man from another.

Levi was undoubtedly the other kind of man. Preying upon an innocent young girl?! Unheard of! Still, Mal'akhiy mused, it was mostly his own fault – as her father, he should have kept a closer eye on her, been more cautious as to whom she befriended.

Thankfully, it was all over now. There was a new topic at the forefront of Sebastaens' minds now – Herod the tetrach would be back within the city's walls after the festival week.

The outline of Sychar was visible now, as they made their way between the mountains. There was that shepherd – Dawid's friend, Shemu'el – bedecked in a long, striped tunic and a pale turban, protection from the harsh sun. Dawid rushed forward to meet him.

"Shemu'el! I'm so glad to see you!" He shouted. The two of them embraced as brothers, clapping each other on the back and grinning widely. Mal'akhiy found himself smiling too, at the boyish enthusiasm these young men had.

"Sir, Sychar is glad to see you back," Shemu'el said, bowing respectfully in Mal'akhiy's direction. This man is a true Samaritan, Mal'akhiy thought to himself, pleased by the show of deference. One could quickly become sick of the dishonourable way the youth of Sebaste treated their elders.

"Thank you, Shemu'el. How goes it with you?" He asked kindly.

Shemu'el's face clouded over, but only for a moment.

"I am awaiting the coming of our Messiah with much delight," was his reply. It was a customary greeting amongst their people, but the sincerity with which Shemu'el spoke it made Mal'akhiy smile.

"As are we all, my son! As are we all."

"Shem, how is Mara? Have you seen much of her?" Dawid asked eagerly. "Is she well?" He had been worried about his baby sister in the months they had been separated. Shemu'el's face fell again, a fact Mal'akhiy couldn't ignore.

"She is well, I believe," Shem began slowly. "I haven't seen much of her since Yom Kippur. I think she ought to be the one to tell you, but I have reason to believe there will be someone coming to see you soon.

About Mara, I mean."

"Another man?!" Dawid asked, incredulous. Mal'akhiy silenced him with a sharp look, though he himself held similar sentiments internally.

"I'm sure she will tell us all about it when she is able," was all he said.

He shouldn't be surprised, he thought as the three of them, accompanied by Shemu'el's sheep, made their way down into the city. The sandy soil crunched beneath their sandals, the percussive effect serving to punctuate Mal'akhiy's rapid thoughts.

Mara has a new suitor.

She is going to be asked for.

This is perfect. Married in Sychar, free from Sebaste.

But what has my little girl gotten into this time?

Shemu'el loves her.

I have raised her to be a wilful fool.

The sand had transitioned into a firmer, dirt road and the pale stone walls of Sychar's homes had risen up around them without his realizing, so deep in thought had he been. There was his parents' house ahead of him - the house where he, himself had grown up.

It was from this very home, he realized with a sense of deep sorrow, that he would be giving away his last born.

Shemu'el waved goodbye and walked, shoulders slumping ever so slightly away. Dawid headed on up, into the courtyard, but Mal'akhiy remained frozen outside.

There she was. Standing at the top of the flat roof. Mara ben Mal'akhiy. His own flesh and blood. His heartbreak child.

The way she looked in that instant was how he would always remember her after that. Mara wore a simple, white dress, belted around the middle with a bright blue sash, a long-ago gift from Yelsaventa.

Mara was standing on the very edge of the roof, waving down at him. Her dark hair tumbled, loose and free over her shoulders and down her back. Her sun-bronzed skin was smooth and freshly youthful. The golden eyes she'd inherited from her mother were shining with pure joy. She was the picture of beauty.

"Abba! Abba!" She was calling out to him, her voice full of laughter. She sounded happy again. Truly happy.

Well, despite himself, he wasn't ready for her to be all grown up, to be gone, but if that was what it took to be rid of her sadness, then so be it. Mal'akhiy heaved himself together and made his way into the house.

Mara veritably flew down from the roof and wrapped her arms tightly around him.

"Abba! I've missed you so much!" She cried, face glowing as she looked up at him. Mal'akhiy wrapped his big, strong arms around her slight frame. He did it without thinking about it. He acknowledged her. The way Mara's eyes shone now, he saw what it meant to her. And somehow, it warmed him inside. Mal'akhiy felt he could face whatever the future brought, as long as his darling daughter was happy and he could learn to love her again.

* * *

"Are you sure you're ready for such a step, Mara?" Mal'akhiy asked his daughter solemnly. Mara nodded vigorously.

"Oh Abba! Why ever would you think I wasn't?! After all, I am of marriageable age now."

Mal'akhiy ran his hands through his hair, a sure sign he was troubled. What she said was true – Mara had turned thirteen in the months she had been Sychar. How could it be?!

Seated on a bench in her grandparents' courtyard, surrounded by the vegetable garden Pinchas tended so studiously, Mara could just visualize her life with Amitai.

She knew he owned a large, Roman-style home near the synagogue, at the centre of town. She could imagine herself giving orders to slaves, hosting parties and making the house a home. It would be perfect.

"Mara, being married is wonderful, but it isn't always easy," Yehudah said gently. He didn't want to upset his granddaughter's delicate emotional balance, but he did want her to consider carefully before she handed her future over to a husband, especially one like the high priest's proud, oldest son.

"Oh leave her alone Yehudah!" Pinchas said, swatting at him. "Everyone gets married at some point − even the Romans. No point trying to ruin it for her before she's even begun."

"Yes, but Mara, even if he is the High Priest's son, is he a godly man?" Dawid questioned, face clouded. He had heard about Amitai's less-than-proper behaviour in waiting for Mara at the well and he wasn't too impressed. It wasn't the done thing, by any stretch of the imagination.

Dawid and Amitai had been boys together and whilst Dawid liked the easy going, fun side of his nature, he also knew about Amitai's streak of conceit and lack of any real maturity.

"Oh, be quiet, Dawid. Just because he isn't like Shemu'el doesn't mean he isn't a godly man!" Mara snapped a little cruelly, irritated by her brother's intervention.

Mal'akhiy raised his hands to stop the discussion. He felt weary. Almost from the moment he and Dawid had arrived at the house, Mara and Pinchas had been bombarding them with talk of Amitai ben Yonatan and his impending arrival to ask for Mara's hand.

The high priest's son was a good match for any girl, especially for someone like Mara, with no dowry to speak of, as the last of six children. But still, it all seemed so sudden. He felt unprepared.

"Discussing this is all null and void, as the young man has not come. But as he is the High Priest's son, we want to do this the best we possibly can. Mara, do you know the tradition?" He asked with a sigh, wiping his brow as he spoke. Mara nodded.

"Of course, Abba. I wasn't so young when Rahal got engaged!"

Mara could still see her older sister's flushed, happy face as she poured wine for their father, for her husband-to-be who sat nervously twiddling his thumbs and when it came time for her to make her choice, one for herself to symbolize her acceptance of the proposal.

She could still remember Rahal's nervousness when Yohanan had arrived and her panicked, high pitched voice worrying she would spill the wine everywhere − a bad omen. And she could hear Mal'akhiy's calm, steady voice trying to convince Rahal to relax.

It wouldn't be like that today Mara decided. Rahal had always been a quiet, shy girl, a little like Zimra. Mara was nothing like either of them. She would be self-assured and confident. Radiant. A queen.

Still, when the knock on the door finally did come, even Mara couldn't help the little tremors of anticipation running through her veins. Perhaps it would be today that her life would truly begin.

***

"I promise I will take the best care of your daughter, Sir. I adore her, and would do anything for her!"

Mal'akhiy watched the young man before him intently. How fast this first afternoon back in Sychar seemed to have gone! It was dusk now, and Amitai was sitting anxiously before his prospective father-in-law in the atrium of Yehudah and Pinchas' home, trying desperately to prove his worth.

The high priest's son was tall, strong and handsome − the kind of man girls swooned after in the streets. His dark hair was well oiled, his hooked nose enhancing his air of grandeur. He was articulate, with a confident and persuasive personality. His tunic was made of the finest linen, his sandals the best of leather. He was wealthy and had the best in life. And all these things, he clearly knew.

Such pride always comes before a fall, the older man mused, remembering the old proverb.

Amitai ben Yonatan continued his oration, almost begging Mal'akhiy to give him his youngest in marriage. It surprised Mal'akhiy how conflicted he felt about it.

Truly, the High Priest's oldest son and heir, was a far better match than he could ever have envisioned finding for Mara. Being the youngest daughter out of many meant that, despite her beauty, she wasn't a very attractive bride, having very little to offer in way of a dowry.

Indeed, here before him stood a young man who could be the answer to all his prayers. Amitai ben Yonatan was wealthy and young, wanted Mara as his first wife, no strings attached. But Mal'akhiy felt some apprehension about saying yes.

Amitai had earlier expressed great admiration for Mara's beauty.

Mal'akhiy remembered what it was like to be a young man, swept away by passion, but there was something about Amitai's manner that concerned him.

He glanced over at his pretty young daughter, cheeks flushed in anticipation, watching intently as she poured the wine for them all.

Mara was young and impulsive and it was easy for Mal'akhiy to admit that she wasn't set to be a good Samaritan wife. She was flighty and immature, self-centered. And she wasn't very constant. Would Amitai still be so enamored with her once he realized all those things?

Marriage was hard work, he thought ruefully to himself. He and Ado had been truly happy in their marriage, but she had died when Mara was so young. She'd never seen a good marriage modelled. In fact, Mara didn't know how to be a good wife at all.

Amitai had said he liked to have the best in life, to be recognized by others as superior. He said he thought Mara to be the most beautiful in all the land and felt he must have her.

Mal'akhiy wondered silently how long it would be until the charm of her beauty wore off, or how long it would be until another woman, more beautiful and more virtuous (or perhaps less), caught his eye?

But what could he do?! There would never be another such offer for Mara, that much he was certain of. Despite his relatively good job, thanks to the exorbitant Roman taxes, Mal'akhiy couldn't afford a proper dowry for the girl. It would be a great relief to see her married off and provided for in his old age.

There was no doubt Mara was besotted with the man and he, clearly, with her.

Perhaps Amitai's assertion that Yahweh Himself had made them for each other was true. Who was he, Mal'akhiy ben Yehudah, to deny such a claim?! Besides, how would he ever be able to decline the offer of the high priest's son? He'd look a complete fool!

"So you see, sir, I truly will look after your daughter. I know she is your youngest and you will be sad to see her go, but I find must have her, I cannot live without her!" Amitai finished passionately.

Mal'akhiy sat for a few moments in silence, pretending to ponder. There was only one possible answer to this, he knew. How could he possibly do anything but agree?

Their whole community would think him a fool for denying such a match. And a fool he would be.

He glanced over at his parents, seated quietly across the room as witnesses. They each gave almost imperceptible nods. A few moments later, Mal'akhiy followed that with his own, signalling his agreement. He knew Mara would be delighted. The crafty young thing had probably planned this all, he thought, shaking his head, affectionate despite himself.

Amitai broke into a grin, the first boyish, earnest expression Mal'akhiy had seen on his face so far.

He turned his eyes to Mara. It was her move next, as to whether or not this went ahead. They were all watching her intently. She'd heard all Amitai had to say, had seen her Father and grandparents give their consent. It was up to her now.

There was one empty wine cup left. If she left it empty and turned it upside down, then Amitai would know her answer to be no. He would have to get up and leave, never to return. It would be a forever no. But if she filled the cup and drank from it, then she was accepting his terms. She would be his bride.

Amitai's eyes dark, deep and pleading, bored into her. She imagined him saying "Mara, from the moment I first saw you, I haven't been able to keep you from my mind. I must have you as my wife. You and I would make the perfect pair, you would bring me great honour. I know it is sudden, but as it was for our ancestors, Yitzchaq and Ribhqah, I have seen you and my heart loves you. It could love no other now, I am sure of that. My parents approve and your Abba says he will give his blessing. So what do you say Mara? Will you marry me?"

He seemed to be holding his breath, awaiting her answer.

Slowly, hand trembling despite herself, Mara reached for the wine beaker, meeting Amitai's dark eyes with her own golden ones as she did so. As carefully as possible, she poured a small stream of wine into the cup. The taste of wine on her tongue had never before been so strong, nor its colour so vivid. It was done, she had given her answer.

Everyone breathed out a sigh of relief The moment of torturous waiting was over.

Relief washed over Amitai's features and he uttered a relieved laugh. Now, he was free to propose to her properly.

"Mara bat Mal'akhiy, most beautiful of women. In front of your father and grandparents, I ask you this most important question. Will you consent to be mine? To be my wife?"

Mara met his eyes once again, her heart light and happy. This was really happening. She, Mara, the rejected girl from Sebaste was wanted here in Sychar. And by this most desirable of men.

"Yes, Amitai ben Yonatan. I will marry you."

Amitai's face was elated. He held out to her a ketubah – the document containing the marriage conditions which he and Mal'akhiy had just agreed on and his pledge to be true to her.

She reached forward and took it, admiring the beautiful patterns on the border. Surely, he had had it decorated by a master artist. Smiling as if he would never stop, Amitai reached for her left hand and gently slipped onto it a delicate gold band, symbolizing the eternity of the promises they'd just made.

"Mara, you do me a great honour." He said softly, huskily. He almost sounded choked up. Emotion suddenly hit Mara too and her eyes misted over as she smiled back up at him.

"It is you who honour me."

Still holding her hand, Amitai proclaimed his betrothal pledge in a loud, strident voice, claiming her as his very own. "I will betroth you to me forever;

I will betroth you in righteousness and justice,

in love and compassion.

I will betroth you in faithfulness

and together, we will acknowledge Yahweh."

"Ameen," echoed Mara.

Amitai took hold of the wine beaker, ready to complete the betrothal ceremony. The next thing he had to do was pour Mara a drink. If she drank, it would show she was marrying of her own free will. Refusing to drink would indicate she was being forced and proceedings would be halted.

This final action would seal the covenant of betrothal and make them officially engaged before witnesses and in the eyes of God. Mara took the cup he offered her and drank deeply.

Amitai looked into her eyes with such an intensity it took her breath away. "You are consecrated for me according to the law of Moshe and of Israel." His voice was soft now, but every bit as passionate.

He looked up at the family members witnessing. They nodded their assent. It was done. Mara and Amitai were now betrothed.

Pinchas gave a happy sob from the corner and rushed out of the room. She returned a few moments later with Mara's favourite blue scarf. From this moment on Mara would wear her hair covered in public to let the whole world know she was a promised woman. As if, by tomorrow, there would be anyone left in Sychar who did not know!

Mal'akhiy stood, hands raised. "Mazel tov, Daughter," he proclaimed. "Mazel tov, Son-in-law."

"Thank you, Abba!" Mara said laughing happily. She felt euphoric. Had this truly all come to pass?! Yehudah followed, embracing Mara's slight form and shaking hands with the tall, handsome bridegroom.

Pinchas came forward as well, still mopping tears and kissing her granddaughter and Amitai on the cheek, wishing them her blessing as well.

Dawid entered, grinning widely, his earlier misgivings clearly put aside.

"Mazel tov, Mara," he said, hugging his sister. The happiness in her bright eyes made him glad for her. He reached out a hand Roman style and shook with Amitai, congratulating him as well.

Pinchas brought out a tray of little round cakes, sweetened with honey and the family celebrated with the newly engaged couple. Seated at Amitai's side, Mara sensed for the first time, partnership with another.

When Amitai spoke now, he spoke on her behalf as well. He had, with the ring and the signed document, taken ownership of her. And she was more than happy with that.

There was no doubt that Mara, in all her loveliness, was Amitai's perfect counterpart. His crooked smile was out in full force and every time he went to brush his mane out of his dark eyes, Mara felt she might swoon. He was so handsome. And he was truly her fiancé! Pinchas seemed to echo her thoughts.

"Such a beautiful couple," she sighed, clasping her wrinkled hands in front of her. "It will be such a lovely wedding"

"Speaking of the wedding," Amitai began. "It will have to be a traditional Israelite wedding, as people will expect it. I will send my friend Yehosh'ua to prepare Mara for the wedding, as our people have always done and then I will come and take Mara to my home. And we will have the full seven days of feasting," he concluded.

Yehudah and Mal'ikhiy exchanged glances. Such a wedding would cost a fortune and neither of them had anything near one.

Amitai caught the look and laughed, smiling.

"My Father's wishes, not mine," he said conspiratorially. Dawid scoffed at this inwardly – Amitai not wish for a large, extravagant wedding?! Impossible! - but said nothing as the bridegroom continued:

"And since it is my Father who wishes it, he has offered to pay for the entire affair. He will arrange a meeting to discuss all the details with you," he finished, directing his gaze to Mal'ikhiy.

Unaware that she'd been holding her breath, Mara let out a sigh of relief. Her family never could have managed such a thing and she knew they would be shamed if the wedding wasn't a grand affair.

She should have been expecting it, she realised. It was their people's tradition for the father-of-the-groom to pay. This wasn't Romanised Sebaste – this was Sychar, the very heart of the Samaritan world.

The evening wore on and soon - all too soon for Mara's taste - it was time for Amitai to be gone. He stopped at the courtyard's arched doorway to say his final farewell to Mara until their wedding day. The jasmine which trailed the arch filled the night with its romantic scent.

The moon was out now and it shone down on Mara, illuminating her face. Amitai shook his head slowly as he beheld her.

"Look at you," he breathed. "You're as lovely now as the first night I saw you. And now, you're my bride." She gazed up at him through upturned lashes, not wanting to say a word in case she broke the spell of that perfect moment. It had suddenly hit her that she was standing there, looking at the man who would be her husband.

Amitai's gaze turned suddenly wistful.

"Oh, Mara, I would give anything not to have to leave you now," he was saying. He was biting the inside of his lip, looking at her own.

He wants to kiss me, Mara realized with a sudden rush of desire. All she wanted now was for him to hold her and to never let go.

"I wish you didn't have to go," she replied, licking her own lips nervously, subconsciously.

He groaned softly.

"Oh Mara, you make me sick with love for you. I will make sure this engagement is a short one!" He vowed. Reaching into his satchel, he withdrew a parcel, wrapped in soft cloth.

"This is for you," he said, the little boy shyness coming over him once more. Mara took the package from him, breathing her thanks. Before she could open it, he reached out a hand gently, cupping her chin as tenderly, gently, as one might hold a sparrow.

"Goodbye, my beautiful bride. Soon, I promise soon, I will return for you."

Mara watched him walk off, instinctively moving her hand to touch the place his hand so recently occupied. Her heart hammered and she knew that he had stolen it from her. She stood motionless for a long while, just taking in all that had happened.

Finally, she looked down, remembering the package in her hands. She unwrapped the soft cloth and found a collection of gold bangles for her arms and some for her ankles. Nestled in the middle of them was a beautiful, turquoise encrusted necklace.

Chapter XII.

A.D. 3, Sychar, Samaria, Roman province of Judaea

It was strange, Mara thought, how fast her world had changed. In one evening, she had gone from being a single young woman with no prospects to suddenly being the wife of Amitai ben Yonatan, previously one of Shomron's most eligible bachelors!

In the Samaritan culture, once the engagement had been made, a man and his bride-to-be were technically considered married, despite the fact that they had not yet consummated their union.

The Romans scoffed at this idea and yet the Samaritan people persisted in it. Mara was now Amitai's wife. He could only break off their engagement through divorce.

How much had changed in such a short space of time! People in the streets treated Mara differently now. Even her own family began to treat her as they would someone of superior rank.

Mara was, after all, a betrothed woman now, no longer just a beautiful young girl. She was to be the high priest's daughter-in-law. The veil over her hair had effectively transformed her.

Mara sat on the roof of her grandparents' home a week after Amitai's proposal, thinking deeply. It was over a year now since she had been in

Sebaste.

Looking back, she could see she'd been such a child then. She had known so little of the world! And then how her world had been rocked by Levi ben Yehu's entrance into her life!

How he would wish he hadn't let her get away when he heard the news of her engagement!

In truth, Mara hardly thought of Levi these days, not now that Amitai was hers. But sometimes at night, when all was black and silent around her, he would slip into her dreams, a handsome, charming spectre of the past.

And then she would remember. Remember the way he had held her. The way he had looked at her, the things he'd whispered into her hair when he'd kissed her. How she had loved him. And how he had, she was sure, loved her too.

After that, she would remember how he hadn't come for her. Hadn't fought for her.

At first, the sly, vindictive part of Mara's personality had been tempted to ask Yelsaventa to be one of her wedding attendants, just to spite Levi. Thankfully, her kinder side won out. Besides, she didn't want Amitai finding out anything about her little escapade outside the Patron's box in Sebaste's hippodrome. The less she had to do with the Patron's family, the better.

Zimra had reported that Yelsaventa's wedding to the rich, old patrician, Ira ben Kershon, had finally taken place. Mara hadn't been invited to the wedding feast, which was hardly a surprise, despite the once inseparable closeness of the two girls.

How Yelsaventa's family must despise Mara now, for the little scandal she'd caused. Still, in their Romanised world, the way Levi had treated her was normal, even acceptable. Mara hated the injustice of that!

Shaking her head angrily, Mara tried to rid herself of all thoughts of Sebaste. That was in the past now and she was to make her life here, in her beloved Sychar. She was of celebrated status now, as Amitai's bride. Wasn't that what she'd always wanted? Biting her lip, she told herself to be content. Her dreams were coming true before her very eyes and sandalwood scented memories of Levi ben Yehu weren't going to spoil that for her.

The wedding plans had begun the very day after their betrothal was announced in the forum. Basemath, Amitai's mother, had sent a servant girl with a litter to summon Mara to their large, opulent home. It was very Romanised in style and Mara forced herself not to think how much it resembled the Patron's Sebastean town house.

She was guided through the marble entrance way into Basemath's sprawling rooms, splendid in turquoise and royal purple. Basemath reigned as queen from a gilded couch in the centre of her drawing room and from there, plans were made.

Basemath herself was a stately woman nearing the close of her thirties. She was of fair complexion and had the much-coveted honey brown locks that blessed so few of their people.

She dressed well, in richly coloured, flowing gowns befitting her station. She had an air of such dignity and grace that, even at her age, heads would turn in the street at her beauty.

Mara found herself very much in awe of her mother-in-law and assenting to her every whim with quiet compliance.

She had already chosen her friends from Sebaste – Zimra and Hadassah - as her handmaidens for the wedding and Basemath insisted that Amitai's rather plain, gawky younger sister, a little younger than Mara herself, be the third.

Basemath had been pleased to find Mara had a good understanding of the Roman style toilette and felt the need only to tweak the way her eyebrows lay, having a slave shape them into two thin, identical curves to frame her eyes.

It was a painful procedure and at first Mara secretly resented it, but when she saw herself in the polished bronze mirror, she could see that it was an improvement. She looked much more like her Sebastean self once more and less like the simple country maiden she'd recently been presenting.

Yonatan, the High Priest himself, was at home very little. The few times Mara did see him, she found herself feeling very out of her depth. He was every bit as regal as his wife, though a lot more softly spoken.

He asked her, once, about her understanding of their people's beliefs and Mara was able to answer him satisfactorily, it seemed, on every topic. Obviously what her mother had taught her as a very little child had stuck somewhere in the far recesses of her brain.

Her own father and brother had returned to Sebaste at the end of the festival of Sukkot, which had passed almost without Mara noticing.

It had been decided that, for practical reasons, Mara would not return to her father's house before the marriage, but would remain in the care of her grandparents.

Although Mara adored both her Saba and her Savta, she somehow wished she could return to Sebaste one more time. She missed Achsah and she missed Dawid more than she cared to admit. The closeness they had once shared had disappeared the very night her engagement had been announced. Dawid had suddenly begun treating Mara as if she were another person entirely. In a way, she supposed, she was.

* * *

Before Mara knew it, they had arrived at the final week of the engagement period. At some point this week, Amitai was coming back for her, coming to take her to her new home as his bride. She didn't quite know when. But she and her attendants would be ready whenever he came, his best friend, Yehosh'ua, had made sure of that.

As the one Amitai had appointed to prepare his bride, Yehosh'ua had been very diligent. He made sure every morning of the wedding week that Mara was dressed in her finest, all ready. Her family had returned from Sebaste to be with them and had brought Zimra and Hadassah with them.

The two girls from Sebaste and Lirit all came to stay with Mara in that final week. The four of them spent many hours giggling and gossiping together and Mara was pleased to find that for all her plain looks, Lirit was an engaging and lively girl.

The day before, Basemath had sent several slaves down to Mara's grandparents' home and had collected all her belongings to take up to the new house she would soon be sharing with Amitai. Mara longed to go to it herself and pack them in, but she wasn't permitted. She'd have the opportunity soon enough, Basemath assured her.

On the second day of the week, Mara awoke feeling stiff and in need of fresh air – and some alone time. Ever since her engagement and especially now, in these final days, Mara had been surrounded by people, with hardly a moment to herself.

Before she could decide against it, or be caught by someone else in the house and stopped, Mara slipped into a tunic and a pale, lilac palla, grabbed her veil and tiptoed out of the house.

Without even considering where she would go, her feet began taking her to Ya'acov's Well and she found herself agreeing with them that this was exactly where she wanted to be.

Despite the early hour, the air was warm and a little sticky as it clung to her skin. There was no breeze and the palms stood tall and silent. It felt odd to be so alone. So nice. Mara was determined to enjoy this.

She walked slowly, enjoying the crisp crunch of the sandy earth beneath her sandals and the sounds of birds foraging for their morning meal. It was strange thinking that this would no longer be her daily walk after today. Once she and Amitai were officially married, she probably wouldn't even have to go to the well herself – she'd most likely have maids to do that. Then again, maybe she'd convince Amitai to let her go anyway. There was something she just loved about walking out in nature and getting to taste cool, fresh water, straight from the bowels of the earth.

Mara bent low to look over the well's edge and watched the water sparkle as the rising rays of the sun bounced off it. She sat for a long time, just staring down into the water, thinking.

She was beyond excited for her wedding day; to be handsome Amitai's wife. And yet there was so much she was unsure about.

She drew her palla tighter about herself, pulled her knees up to her chin as she sat. Like a child. For the last time. Mara knew that from tomorrow, she would be expected to conduct herself as an adult woman in all things. That fact both thrilled and horrified her. So, she was making the most of today and her moments alone with no one to say "Mara, behave".

* * *

Shemu'el had been avoiding Mara. After seeing her at the *Yom Kippur* feast, looking so beautiful, he'd longed to ask for her hand. But then he'd seen her walking with Amitai ben Yonatan and knew he'd never stand a chance.

Mara had become engaged the very day her Abba returned to Sychar and Shemu'el had stayed far out of her way after that. It was just too painful. And now, here she was, sitting in her old place by the well.

He watched her from a distance. She looked so young, fragile and unsure as she sat there – nothing like the mature young lady she'd been presenting to people recently. She looked like the Mara he'd grown to love. The Mara he longed to cherish. The Mara he would never be able to.

A strand of her dark hair had fallen out from under her veil and graced her brow. Her golden eyes glistened, reflecting the early morning gleam from the pool of water below her. She was altogether lovely. Any fool could see that.

More than anything else, he longed to go to her, to tell her of his love, to sweep her away. But he knew he couldn't. It wouldn't be right. She belonged to another.

As of tomorrow, she would be another man's wife, in more than just name. As he watched her, he prayed for her, asking God to bless her with the happiness she so desired and that Amitai might be the husband she dreamed he was.

Shem couldn't help but doubt if the second part of his prayer would come true. Amitai gave him the impression of cruelty. An unnaturally high desire for perfection caused that.

Shemu'el knew it was partly his own jealousy speaking but he couldn't help feeling that though Amitai was smitten with Mara now, it wouldn't last.

"Lord, you know I would love her even when she grew old and grey," he whispered. Shemu'el knew Mara would not be his, but that didn't mean his heart had stopped loving her.

One of his sheep started baa-ing and Mara turned around with a start, to see him watching her.

"Oh, Shem!" She rested a hand on her heart, regaining her composure. "You frightened me." She pulled her knees out from under her dress, jumping to her feet. She tried to laugh it off nervously, unsure how to read his expression. Shemu'el laughed half-heartedly.

"Sorry."

Mara picked up her water jars.

"Need some watering?" She asked him, with a smile. She desperately felt the need of a friend today and Shemu'el was decidedly the best option. He seemed to be the only one around here still treating her normally. Or at least sort of normally.

He looked startled.

"Er, um, yes please," he mumbled, coming forwards. Inside he groaned. *Oh Mara, my beloved Mara. Why did you have to choose today? Choose this moment to be kind to me? Now, when you are leaving, when you will be another man's wife? You are determined to make me love you more, now that I can never have you.*

Mara poured some water into the trough for his sheep, then held out the jar for him to drink from, completely unaware of his inner torment. She couldn't sense much other than her own at the moment.

"Shem, I'm so nervous! Am I making the right choice? To marry Amitai?" She asked, biting her lip.

The question startled him. Whatever could he say? He couldn't tell the truth, could he? He couldn't just blurt out his feelings, his desire to love her, heart and soul, not just her beauty and wit. No, she would only laugh at him and tell Amitai. He shook himself mentally.

"Well, Mara, what do you believe the Lord God wants for you?"

"Happiness!" Mara said decidedly. "He wants me to be happy."

"And will this bring you happiness?" Shemu'el asked softly. Everything in him longed to cry out loudly, begging her not to do it, not to marry the high priest's son, to think far beyond, far deeper than mere, unstable "happiness". He fought the urge to take her into his arms.

Still completely unaware of his inner battle, Mara snorted gently.

"Well, I certainly hope so!"

Suddenly she beamed at Shemu'el. "Thank you so much Shem, you're the best. You've been a good friend to me, all these years, even when I haven't been so good to you. You're the only one who knows my whole story and you don't hate me, even so. I'm so glad we're friends."

Impulsively, she leaned over and hugged him as she would Dawid. Then, she picked up her water jars and with a last, captivating smile, she was gone. Shemu'el, bemused, felt his heart go with her.

* * *

The day of Mara's wedding to Amitai dawned bright and sunshiny. Mara awoke as the first rays of sun hit the house. The night before, she'd been restless. She'd ended up, much to her Savta's consternation, sleeping up on the roof, wrapped in her favourite old blanket.

Now, she awoke to the sun's bright warmth and the sound of girls singing. It was her attendants, awakening the bride. Mara sat up, wriggling out of the blankets, excitement and trepidation rushing through her veins. This was it. She just knew today was the day Amitai would come for her.

She rushed down and joined her friends. They danced around the courtyard, laughing and singing. As Mara looked up, she saw Dawid watching them from the balcony, a strange look on his face. Why was he looking at Zimra that way? She only dwelt on that for a moment before whirling back into her dance with the maidens.

"Mara, you look so happy today!" Zimra exclaimed and Mara laughed.

"I am! Oh, I just feel that today he will come for me!" She said, grabbing Zimra's hands and spinning her around. The girls all squealed in delight. Hadassah grasped one of Mara's hands from Zimra.

"Mara, let's go out to the fields and pick flowers! We will make you a garland to wear in your hair."

Lirit nodded her head wildly in approval.

"Yes! My brother first fell in love with you when you were dancing with flowers in your hair. It will be a good sign for your marriage if you do it again today."

The notion delighted Mara. She quickly washed in the ceremonial washing cistern in the courtyard, dressing herself in a fine linen robe, a gift from Amitai. Grabbing some bread for their morning meal, she and her friends headed out to the fields.

The spring wildflowers were beautiful. Vibrant hues – yellows, reds, and purples – were scattered all around them. They fell, laughing, into the long, green grass, then sat, weaving garlands for each other.

The smell of the wild flowers made Mara giddy with happiness. Their scent brought her back to that very first time she'd seen her bridegroom face-to-face.

Lirit, with her long, lithe fingers was the best weaver. She made Mara's garland from the most delicate white and purple blooms, weaving in bright splashes of yellow. Once she had finished, she gently placed it on Mara's head, over her fine sheer, white veil. The girls all gushed over how beautiful it was. Mara felt truly happy.

"Amitai will be blown away by you tonight. You've looked beautiful before, but tonight, you will look like the queen he has dreamed of," Lirit said softly. Overcome by the girl's sweet sincerity, Mara threw her arms around her soon-to-be sister and hugged her.

"Gaining you as my sister will be one of the best things about my marriage, Lirit," she said, making the younger girl blush with pleasure.

Widening her gaze to encapsulate Zimra and Hadassah as well, Mara continued:

"I'm so thankful for you all! Hadassah, Zim, I'm going to miss you so much! Promise you'll come and visit?" She suddenly felt a little quavery again, as she had the morning before when she spoke to Shemu'el.

"Every festival I can, I will come," Zimra promised. Hadassah laughed.

"Maybe we'll all meet our future husbands at your wedding feast Mara! Then soon, we'll be living in Sychar, right here with you." They all laughed and Mara noticed a small blush creep up Zimra's cheeks, but she didn't ask about it. She was too full of joy and trepidation to think of anything else.

It was nearly nightfall when a shofar blast rang through the air. Sitting at the table with Pinchas, in the heart of the home, Mara felt her heart's pace quicken. The blast of the ram's horn trumpet, that was the warning – Amitai was almost here.

Mara jumped to her feet, straightening her hair and pinching her cheeks for a blush, although there was hardly any need, such was her excitement. Her jewels were already on and she was attired in her finest robe. Her hands and feet were patterned with henna and she was perfumed. Yehosh'ua had seen that she was well prepared.

Rushing to her side, Zimra, Hadassah and Lirit were all squealing with excitement. It would be any time now.

Pinchas hurriedly dispatched the girls to fetch Mara's veil. They all scurried off, searching. Once they'd gone, Pinchas sheepishly pulled it out from behind her back.

"It's the tradition for the bride to be taken in secret," she said, shrugging and smiling. Mara was surprised to hear the sound of husky tears in her Savta's voice. Suddenly, Mara realised that this was real. This was happening.

Pinchas opened her arms wide and Mara, for one last moment a little girl, rushed into them. Pinchas kissed her cheek gently.

"May Yahweh bless you richly, our Little Flower," she whispered, before making a hurried exit. Mara turned and called out to stop her.

But suddenly the door was opening and Amitai walked in, taking big, confident strides, a wide grin etching his handsome face.

As he saw Mara standing there in her wedding finery, he stopped a moment, taking in the sight of the vision before him. Dark curls dripped from under the veil, delicate blossoms topping her head. His heart stopped.

Mara looked back at him. He was here. He, in his own garland and white robe, looked like the paintings of Apollo on the walls of the bathhouse in Sebaste. More handsome even.

Suddenly aware that he was supposed to be whisking her away before anyone noticed, Amitai reached out his hand to her. Mara knew she would never forget that moment - the way it felt to hold a man's hand, and belong - as long as she lived.

As they ran out of the courtyard and on, into the dark streets, past Yehosh'ua, who began whooping wildly, shofar in hand, Mara could hear Zimra, Lirit and Hadassah shrieking that she was gone. Soon, they would be mobilizing a procession to wind its way through Sychar, to begin feasting, culminating in the wedding banquet in seven days time.

But for now, Amitai was lifting her into his arms, up against his muscled body and carrying her towards his home. That same intensity that Mara had seen in his eyes that day at the well had returned now, both thrilling and exciting her.

"You're finally here," he breathed into her hair, as he carried her through the courtyard and up, in the house. "Since that first instant our eyes met, I've waited for this moment." Mara felt a bubble of happy laughter well up inside her, unable to be stopped.

"So have I," she murmured.

Hesitantly, he reached out and gently put back her veil. She looked shyly out from under it. Did he still think she was enchanting? Did he still adore her? She saw in his expression that he did.

"Oh, surely my wife is the most beautiful of all women!" He said, awed. She smiled up at him. "And my husband most handsome of men." The next thing she knew, his lips were on hers. Feelings Mara couldn't even explain took her over. She was happy beyond anything she'd known.

She just knew this happiness would last forever. The flower crown she'd been wearing toppled from her head and went tumbling to the floor, disintegrating into a thousand pieces as it did.

Chapter XIII.

A.D. 3, Sychar, Samaria, Roman province of Judaea

The day after their wedding feast, Mara awoke feeling awful. The party had been so wonderful and she'd been so joyful, but now, her head was pounding and she felt nauseated.

Mara looked over at Amitai lying asleep, handsome as ever, next to her. She didn't want to wake him, so she wriggled out of the blankets and made her way down into the small garden in their courtyard.

The fresh air ministered to her headache and she felt her health restored. She could smell the faint scent of saffron on the breeze and spotted their brilliant, yellow, extremely valuable blooms growing by the bench.

Mara could hardly believe a whole week had passed since their wedding night, when, at the blast of the shofar, she had been swept away from her grandparents' home. And now, here she was, the wife of the high priest's eldest son.

None of it had seemed real until she was sitting at Amitai's side at the wedding banquet and the little girls of the town had brought her bouquets, curtsying as if she were truly important.

As the children looked up at her in delighted awe when she offered them a smile, she realized that now she really was somebody.

Her new mother-in-law, Basemath, was coming to visit them today, to begin educating Mara on what was expected of her as the future high-priest's wife. Mara was looking forward to this, hoping she might bring Lirit with her.

She also was desperate to learn how to please her new husband. Amitai had treated her as a precious princess from the moment they'd become man and wife, seeing to her every whim and need. Last night had taken it's toll on both of them and Mara was certain he would sleep late.

The sun flickered softly through the olive branches above her. Mara could see why Amitai had desired this home as his own. The house, tall and cool, was beautifully built, but it was the garden that made it most enchanting. The courtyard was large, the outer world hidden by tall hedges.

There were several beautiful olive trees providing shade and the fragrant blooms in the flower beds. The birds were singing, the bees humming and the sounds of the city below seemed so very far away.

The cool marble bench beckoned to Mara and before she knew it, she had curled up on it and her eyes were closed, sound asleep.

"Mara?"

She opened her eyes to see Amitai's dark, tousled head bending over her. With sleepy eyes, he bent down to kiss her soft lips. "Why are you out here, my darling? Come back to bed," he cajoled her, pulling her into his arms.

Mara shook her head.

"I wasn't feeling all that well, so I came to get air. But we can't go back to bed, your Imah is coming soon!"

Amitai pretended to pout, then laughed and poked Mara's nose affectionately.

"You've got me all organized already. What a perfect little wife you are. I can't wait until mother has you all dressed up and looking as my bride should. Then I'll take you around town and show you off."

Mara wasn't sure whether to feel flattered or irritated by this comment. What did he mean? Didn't she already look as she should? Surely, that was why he'd chosen her, wasn't it?

She decided not to let it worry her and just laughed along with him. They walked back into the house hand-in-hand.

Basemath arrived in the middle of the morning, looking resplendent in a patterned, green robe and bedecked with many gleaming jewels. Her coppery hair was elaborately coiled atop her head, topped with a fine veil of gossamer fabric. She smiled as Mara, dressed in a simple, white, linen tunic came to meet her.

"Mara, my child, I'm so glad to see you!" Basemath said, kissing her.

Mara greeted her mother-in-law and welcomed both her and her handmaiden into the home. She was a little disappointed to see Lirit was not present.

Amitai visited with his wife and mother for a while, before heading out to the temple, leaving the ladies to their own devices.

The two of them sat sipping cool water outside under the olive trees for a while, before Basemath got into the business of her visit.

"Mara, as of today, you will have maid and a cook. Amitai is used to having staff and I want him to be happy. Besides, it is not seemly for a priest's wife to be doing manual labour. You will also have a visit from my seamstress soon, as we must have some new clothes made for you. Your old things are not suitable."

Mara felt rather taken aback by this. What was wrong with her old things? Still, she wasn't about to complain! Basemath continued:

"You will spend your time either at home, or out visiting other ladies. Sometimes we go shopping in the market, but very rarely. It is not seemly for you to go out walking alone, so be sure either Amitai or one of your ladies goes with you."

Mara nodded, trying to take this all in.

"Amitai is often away, or will come home late. You must always look your best for him when he returns. Especially if he is entertaining guests. One of your most important duties is to be a good hostess. Always keep your home fresh and light. And always obey his every wish."

The list of instructions went on and on. Mara soon felt like she had forgotten important items. She wasn't sure it was going to be as easy as she'd originally thought, being Amitai's wife.

Basemath was kind, but strict, insisting Mara personify the perfect Samaritan wife for her son.

Her seamstress visited Mara the very next day and made up numerous new tunics, stolas and pallas for her, in vibrant, rich colours. Basemath had her personal jeweller come to the house and numerous new jewels were purchased.

Personally, Mara didn't really like any of the styles Basemath favoured, much preferring the delicate style of Dawid's work, but she was determined to please her new family and said nothing.

Mara's handmaiden, picked by Basemath, soon settled into the home as well. Orna was a slim girl, several years Mara's senior, with a thin face and lips that never seemed far from pursed disapproval.

Orna didn't talk much and treated Mara with distain. Still, she did her job well, ensuring Mara's hair was always well styled and her make up flawless. She dressed Mara like a queen each day and was sure to accompany her mistress wherever she went.

Mara wasn't sure how she felt about having Orna around and she struggled to like her new companion, but there wasn't much she could do about it.

As Basemath had predicted, Amitai wasn't home much, but whenever he was, Mara always rushed to greet him, to make him happy. She ensured she looked her best for her husband's return and he was always delighted to see her.

"My precious one," he would call her and hold her close, telling her she was the most beautiful of women.

A few weeks after their marriage, Amitai decided to take Mara to the synagogue, where he and all the other priests met daily. He ordered her to dress in her very best, as he wanted to show off his bride. Mara was happy to oblige.

Orna silently slipped Mara into a pure white gown, hemmed with golden thread. With the wide gold headband and a large blue stola the colour of the sky, also trimmed in gold, that covered both her hair and her entire body, Mara felt all grown up.

When she came down from their chamber, she was thrilled to see Amitai's expression of awe and pride.

"You look stunning, Mara," he said huskily and stepped forward to kiss her passionately.

"I've a good mind to just keep you here, all to myself and never let anyone else see you, looking as you do," he whispered into her tumbling hair.

But they did go out and Mara was glad. It felt strange to walk through the streets of Sychar with her husband. Amitai walked with such an air of confidence that Mara felt carried along by it. People stared as they passed by. Mara wondered what they thought of her, as she made her way along at her husband's side. Did she please them? Perhaps they were jealous of her marriage to their town's most eligible bachelor. Or did they think she made a fitting counterpart to him?

Feeling a little overwhelmed, Mara turned her attention from people's gazes and focused instead on keeping her skirts from trailing down in the dusty street.

Amitai led her into the synagogue at the centre of the town. Whilst it could never compare to the splendour that had been the Samaritan temple, once towering above on the heights of Mount Gerizim, it was still an impressive building.

The tall columns that supported the vaulted roof seemed to dwarf them as they entered.

All the priests turned to look as Amitai entered, striding forward proudly with his angelic wife at his side. Intimidation seeped through Mara, but she was determined not to let it show.

Yonatan greeted his son and new daughter-in-law. Obviously, Mara had already been introduced to the other men present, since no introduction was offered.

She wished she could remember who was who, but for the most part, the night of their wedding feast was a blur of dancing and music, of well wishes and wine. She would just have to determine their names through conversation.

Near the back of the group stood a younger man, perhaps Amitai's age. He was true "looker", with gleaming, pale eyes and olivey skin. He looked Mara up and down, nodding approvingly at her. Mara felt herself flush, but couldn't resist a small smile in return. It was hard not to feel flattered by such blatant admiration.

Amitai instructed Mara to sit on the far side of the synagogue whilst he and the other priests worked.

For several hours, she watched as the priests sat and talked, debating the issues of their faith and answering the questions the people came to ask. They read from the scrolls containing the holy scriptures, prayed and chanted to Yahweh.

After a while, Mara got very bored and thirsty, but there wasn't much she could do about that – she knew she must not leave until Amitai directed her to.

Other people came and went from the synagogue – mostly men, but also a few women. All of them stared at Mara, drinking in the sight of the new addition to the high priest's family. Mara felt a little uncomfortable. She also noticed that that handsome young priest couldn't take his eyes off her. Whenever the other priests weren't looking at him, he was gazing at her.

Later that evening, when they were back home, Mara mentioned it to Amitai. He just laughed. "That's Dan for you. He always did have an eye for a beautiful woman. Besides, let him look. Let him envy me. I have the most beautiful wife in the whole of Samaria, what is that worth to me if no one is jealous?" He moved in to kiss her, dark eyes hungry.

Mara pursed her lips and turned away. She loved that Amitai thought her beautiful, but she was hoping he was getting to admire her for more than her beauty by now. Obviously not. Still, how could she complain? He treated her like a queen.

The months rolled by and Mara grew used to life as a prominent man's wife in Sychar. She made friends with several of the other priests' wives and enjoyed entertaining Amitai and his friends in their beautiful home. She even got used to ordering Orna about and being in charge of a household. It felt wonderful.

Mara had almost forgotten what it felt like to be the youngest daughter of a poorer man. It seemed like a life-time ago that she was complaining to Shemu'el about how hard her life was.

She wondered how life was treating her old friend now, whether he'd moved on and married. He was well out of her social strata by now.

Zimra had come to visit her once and she saw Lirit frequently, but that was the only contact she'd had with her old life.

Her family stayed out of her way for the most part, perhaps feeling out of place in her new society. And perhaps, Mara realised, they were.

Halfway through their first year of marriage, Mara noticed she missed her monthly cycle. At once, her thoughts turned to a child, but she didn't say anything of it. But when the morning sickness came, she knew she had to tell Amitai.

He was delighted at the news. From the very first, he started speaking of "my son" and told Mara to take the best care of herself. He boasted to all their friends, to the whole town, that his and Mara's little boy would be the most beautiful in the whole world.

This was to be the High Priest's first grandson, making it a special child on numerous levels. Amitai sent a messenger to inform Mal'akhiy and the messenger returned with his congratulations and the congratulations of all their friends in Sebaste.

At first, with heavy hitting morning sickness, Mara was forced to become bedridden. Basemath sent Lirit to take care of her most days, as Mara became too weak to keep anything down, even water.

Her back ached. Her ankles had swollen. She felt like crying and laughing all at once. She moaned to Lirit on many occasions that she was like an over-ripe melon.

It seemed like months until Mara was feeling more like herself again. Her belly was expanding day by day and she delighted to feel the baby growing within her.

For the first time in her life, Mara began to pray. She prayed for the small life growing within her, that it might be a boy to please her husband and that he might grow big and strong. Her pace of life and ideals changed along with her body.

Now, her focus wasn't just on being seen as the most beautiful woman, with the best husband and life – she wanted to be the best mother, for her child's sake. She began to notice new and different things too.

Mara had never before seen the looks of adoration little boys gave their fathers, or the way daughters looked up at their mothers adoringly.

Now, when she saw people in the street, she really saw them. She saw emotions on their faces – the exhausted woman hurrying by suddenly became a mother doing all she could to find money to feed her babies, the little boy crying on the corner, the orphan with no one to love him.

Mara had never thought much on other people's stories, but now she did – proud and thankful that her own was very different. She and

Amitai would have no financial worries and their child would never be deserted.

Two months from her due date, Mara was surprised and delighted when her brother Dawid arrived at their front door. "Dawid! Welcome! I'm so happy to see you." She cried, embracing her brother warmly around her now slightly swollen belly.

He looked somewhat uncomfortable, coming into the grand house, but he followed her meekly.

She had Orna bring them both some water as she happily demanded to hear all the news from home in Sebaste.

Dawid's laughter rang false in both their ears. "Ah, well, I've actually come to tell you something rather important." He looked down at his hands and shuffled a bit. "Well, I'm not really sure how to tell you this. But I'm, I'm er, getting married."

Mara looked at him, shocked. "Really?" Dawid nodded, still looking uncomfortable. "Mazel tov, Achi!" She congratulated him, hugging him again. "Who is the lucky woman?"

Dawid gave another false laugh and ran his fingers through his hair. "Uh, your friend Zimra."

"Zimra?!" Mara was incredulous. "Really? Surely not! She's so young!"

She simply couldn't visualize her slight, childlike friend being married – let alone to a handsome young man such as her brother Dawid. How Zimra had even caught his eye was beyond her comprehension.

"She's no younger than you, Mara," Dawid replied, somewhat reproachfully. "Besides, she is a wonderful woman and will make me a good wife. She's responsible, hard working and loving. And she has grown up to be quite beautiful." He grinned shyly as he finished, infatuation clear in his expression.

Mara blinked. "If you say so. She is very sweet." Pulling herself together, she smiled at her brother, squeezing his hand warmly. "Well, as long as you are happy Dawid. I couldn't wish for more for you."

Dawid looked relieved. "Will you come to our wedding feast, Mara?"

Mara nodded. "As if you could keep me away. I'll just have to convince my husband I'm well enough to travel. He's being so strict about my resting and not doing anything strenuous. When will the wedding feast be?"

"In three weeks," Dawid said sheepishly. "I've been meaning to come and tell you for a while now, but in truth, I've been putting it off."

Mara swallowed. She was a little hurt that she was only hearing all this now. "Well, I understand. It's no short journey. I'm sure I can work it out to be there. With two of my very favourite people in the whole world marrying, I have to be!"

Dawid put an arm around his little sister, like he used to. "We've missed you at home, Mara. Abba misses you more that he'd like to admit."

Mara sighed and leaned her head up against Dawid's strong arm. "I miss you all too. I'm very happy here in Sychar, but I do miss our home. Sometimes I get the feeling life is moving so fast it is leaving me behind, and you'll all forget about me."

Dawid laughed, shoving her gently. "Forget about you, Mara?! Impossible! How could we ever not miss your laugh, your love of life and your dreams? Zimra misses you a lot. And so do I."

Mara shoved him back, less gently and stuck her tongue out at him. "Why is it, then, that you never come to see me?"

Dawid's face fell. "It's a long journey. We would if we could, but not all of us are as wealthy as your husband!"

* * *

It took Mara quite a bit of pleading, pouting and cajoling to convince Amitai that they should attend Dawid and Zimra's wedding feast, but at last she won out.

After their argument, he had kissed her deeply, tenderly and whispered into her hair: "How could I ever say no to you, my perfect one?"

The wedding was a small, but lovely event. Amitai hired a some camels to transport them to and from Sychar and though it wasn't the most comfortable mode of travel, Mara supposed it was far better than walking, especially in her current state.

They arrived in time to see Dawid arriving, a garland of flowers atop his curly head and his new bride at his side. He looked truly happy, Mara thought. Next to him, dressed in a plain robe, ornamented by a green palla and with simple but beautiful jewellery (clearly Dawid's own handiwork), stood Zimra.

A strand of fine, brown hair graced the curve of her face and her eyes danced, the very colour of her scarf in the fading sunlight. She looked just lovely as she beamed a smile.

Mara had never seen her friend this way before. Her beauty was far more to do with the radiant happiness on her face than anything else and somehow, that made Mara ache.

She felt almost as if she were intruding upon a sacred moment, this happy and near-perfect moment not meant for the likes of her. Looking at Zimra as she stared into her husband's eyes, Mara knew she'd never been as joyful as her friend was now. Surrounding her were all their family and friends, delighting in this special time.

Tears welled in Mara's eyes. For some reason she felt completely alone. She was alone. No one cared for her that way. Not even her longed-for husband. Amitai loved her certainly, but more as a treasure than as a companion. But she would not let this spoil Dawid and Zimra's day.

* * *

She was there. Mara.

From the other side of the gathering, Shemu'el had seen her. And he would never be able to unsee her as she was, golden eyes solemn, face pale beneath her wine-red cloak. How could anything mortal be so beautiful, he wondered? She wasn't showing terribly much, but there was certainly a new roundness about her that had never been there before.

She captivated him, as she always had. He couldn't take his eyes off her. A part of him hoped this moment would last forever, this fleeting fragment of time would hang, ever suspended in eternity. In his mind, at least, he knew it would.

He knew she was another man's wife and he shouldn't even look at her. He battled his mind, trying to remove her from it. But all he could see was Mara. Giving a slight groan he turned and walked away. He could not stay if she was here.

* * *

The day after their return from Sebaste, Mara began to feel new motions within her. The child was stirring, ready to meet the world. Trepidation and anticipation filled Mara. The birth pangs had yet to commence, but she knew it wouldn't be long now.

The next evening, after a long and grueling battle, guided by the town's old midwife and Orna, with Pinchas and Basemath both by her side, Mara brought into the world, her child. A tiny daughter.

Amitai was devastated. This was not his long-desired son. Irrational in his disappointment, he refused to see the child and would not even come to Mara's side. Mara felt broken – how could her sweet husband be so callous?

From the beginning, the baby was beautiful, her big, blue eyes wide and framed by thick, dark lashes. She had dark hair all over her head from the very day she was born. Her soft baby skin, her cooing cries... Mara adored everything about her.

Mara had never been happier than when she gazed down at the little child in her arms. She had never felt love like this, never known it to be possible. She just wanted to make the entire world right for her little girl. Amitai's anger and distress didn't disappear for the entire night and so Mara held her and adored her alone. She named the little girl Rani, "my joy".

For the first week of Rani's life, Amitai neglected both mother and daughter, refusing to see them and leaving them in Orna's care. Mara felt exceedingly hurt by this and couldn't understand where his cruelty was coming from.

Basemath sought to reassure her, saying Amitai would be alright again, once he'd received the son he longed for. But Mara wasn't willing to wait that long. She longed to chide him for his lack of feeling and for his selfishness, but didn't dare. Besides, she was too tired.

Everyone else who met Rani adored her. She was as sweet-tempered as she was pretty and had a cooing cry that could melt the insides of the most sombre person. Amitai may have disdained her from the very first day, but even he, eventually, could not resist the child's charm.

Mara had gone to fetch some water for herself one evening and left Rani cooing contentedly in her cradle. When she returned, Amitai was holding her, staring at her in awe.

"You are beautiful, my baby daughter," she heard him whispering. "You are the most beautiful daughter a man has ever had."

Mara came into the room and Amitai jumped, as if caught in some sin. He gingerly held Rani out to her. "Er, she was crying," he said hastily.

Mara took her daughter with no comment and just rocked her gently. "She is perfectly wonderful, our daughter, isn't she?" She said, not looking at her husband.

Amitai sighed. "Yes, she is. I guess you did something right, after all," he said. He gave her a half-smile – the first time in a long time– then gently rested his hand on Mara's shoulder. Mara leaned back into it.

Maybe everything would be alright after all.

* * *

The first few months of Rani's life were precious ones in Mara's life – the times she'd always look back on as the happy times. Rani was a perfect baby, cheerful and well behaved. Amitai adored "his girls", having seemingly forgiven Rani for her early misdemeanor of being born female and doted upon both wife and daughter.

Mara still felt lonely, isolated from the community of Sychar - aside from a few of the priests' wives and occasional visits from Lirit, or her Savta. But she didn't mind lonely, not with her darling baby and her loving husband. She lacked nothing.

Rani was nearing a year and a half old when that blissful time drew to an end. She had learnt to walk and was starting to babble away in baby chatter, with some real words thrown in for good measure.

Amitai took great pride in his daughter and the fact that she was recognized by all as the prettiest baby ever seen. She bore his dark, soulful eyes and Mara's fair complexion and thick, luxurious hair. They dressed her well and taught her to behave as a little lady.

Everyone in Sychar talked about Amitai ben Yonatan and his family and honoured them. Rani might not be the son he'd hoped for, but she was a jewel none the less.

Chapter XIV.

A.D. 5, Sychar, Samaria, Roman province of Judaea

It was nearing Rani's second birthday when the messenger came to town, seeking out Yonatan and his family. At the coming of the new moon, Herod Archelaus was, for the first time in a long while, returning to his Sebaste palace and would be throwing a grand party to celebrate his return.

All the most important people of the province would be honour-bound to attend and that included Amitai and Mara.

They were both thrilled by the invitation, although something in the pit of Mara's stomach clenched. She wasn't sure she was ready to return to Sebaste.

It was nearing three years since that day during the Ludi at the hippodrome, but she wasn't sure three years was enough to dull the ache of her heart. Sebaste hurt.

Mara and Amitai decided it would be best to take Rani with them and leave her with Dawid and Zimra during the party, rather than in Sychar, with Basemath. Loading up the child and all the fine things they would need in Sebaste took Mara nearly a week.

The two donkeys Amitai owned were hardly enough and Mara

wished they might hire a camel to carry everything. Part of her longed for the days of simple possessions and freedom, when she used to make the journey by foot, carrying all her things herself. This was far too complicated.

They set off for Sebaste halfway through the week. Amitai had relented and hired a third donkey, which Mara and Rani rode and he walked at their side. Rani, usually a placid baby, hated the donkey and cried for almost an hour, until Amitai finally took her impatiently and alighted her on his shoulder. She was happy after that.

This was the first trip between Sychar and Sebaste where Mara found herself fretting about the sun. The heat haze rose from the horizon, a shimmering reminder that her home climate was less than hospitable. Only tufty shrubs poking their heads above the rocky ground and loner trees survived out here.

Mara had always worried about water on such trips, but now, with her precious little girl to care for, it was far more concerning to her. Once Rani had calmed down, Mara kept her well wrapped up, under her own cloak, protected from the harsh, desert rays.

Parts of Samaria had beautiful, fertile soil and experienced heavy rainfalls. Sebaste was one of those regions. The city flourished, with palm trees and animal life abundant. It was an oasis of plenty. Emerging from the dusty plains into its shade was a pleasure.

The sun was making its final dip below the horizon as they approached Sebaste. The town looked huge and mighty, with its towering wall and the Temple of Augustus, resplendent on the hillside.

Mara hadn't remembered it being so large. After so long in Sychar's sprawling comparative poverty, Sebaste's grandeur was doubled for her.

Dawid and Zimra welcomed them with open arms. Their home was modestly furnished, but well built and their happiness seemed to fill every inch of left over space.

Amitai acted a little too pompous for Mara's liking, but her brother and sister-in-law were ever-gracious.

They both adored Rani and Mara could tell that her little one would be in good hands whilst they were at the banquet. Zimra's own slim waist had begun to expand and Mara could see it wouldn't be long until Rani had a little cousin of her own vintage.

*　*　*

Mara had forgotten what it was like to prepare for a grand event in Sebaste. Memories of the full days of preparation she and Yelsaventa had once shared in the Patron's mosaic-filled bath-house flooded her mind.

There had always been so much to do and arrange. Mara found it was much the same now, if not more. This banquet was, after all, being hosted by Herod Archelaus himself and his scandalous new wife, the Persian Glaphyra.

The Jews hated Herod Archelaus for his cruelty and his disregard for Mosaic law in marrying his brother's widow, but here, in Samaria, they were happy to have him as ruler – even if he was only a puppet ruler. His mother, Malthace, had even been a Samaritan!

Mara had only ever seen Herod once, many years ago. He was a fairly young man then and was large and strong-looking. He wasn't a handsome man, but he was very impressive and fearsome. As she relaxed back in the warmth of the baths, she wondered how the years would have treated the tetrarch.

Mara was also very eager to catch a glimpse of Glaphyra. She was reportedly very beautiful, like a goddess, with charm and a vivacious spirit to match. It was said that she'd caused much trouble in the court of Jerusalem, claiming that her lineage was far superior to the other women present.

Not only that, but after her first husband's death, Glaphyra had remarried King Juba II of Mauretania in Northern Africa, only to meet her once-brother-in-law Herod Archelaus again and fall desperately in love. They had both divorced their spouses in order to be together. Glaphyra had left a king to marry a mere ethnarch, so strong was their passion.

Despite herself, Mara couldn't help but find it all rather intriguing and desperately romantic. Amitai disapproved strongly of it all, but of course, it would not do to lose favour with the ethnarch, so he kept his opinion to himself.

Mara let her hair float out around her like a veil as she soaked in the water. How long it had been since she'd enjoyed a proper Roman bath like this!

Amitai had headed off to the men's side of the baths a few hours before, leaving her to her own devices in the women's section. Rani was safely at home with her aunt. This freedom from all responsibility left Mara feeling light and airy.

Once she felt sufficiently soaked, a Nubian slave oiled her skin and applied the hair-removal lotion. When Mara emerged from the baths a few hours later to return to Dawid and Zimra's apartment home, she felt a new woman.

The whole afternoon was spent bedecking herself in her finest clothing. Dark, tiger's eye stone earrings hung from her ears, her eyes glistening from behind their kohl lining.

The deep maroon stola, a prized gift from Amitai, hung softly to every curve of her now curvaceous body - another gift motherhood had bestowed upon her was a more well endowed figure.

Mara wore her hair loose, flowing in a thick curtain down her back. Her brow was ornamented by a single pendant – another beautifully polished tiger's eye, hung on a soft fabric band. She covered herself with a long, filmy scarf of pale, sunset red. It flowed nearly to the ground,

149

hiding most of her hair from sight.

Amitai was ready and eager to leave by the time Mara was finishing her make-up and applying her heady, musky, perfumed oil. The look on his face when she emerged from the bedroom told her everything she could wish to know about how she looked. He hadn't look at her with such desire, or such pride, in a long time.

Pressing his lips softly to the side of her temples, he whispered, passion wild in his voice. "If we weren't in Sebaste and about to attend an event, I wouldn't be able to resist you."

Mara laughed softly. "Well, my love, we better leave before you get tempted!"

Amitai grunted, holding his wife close. "I'm not sure I want to let you out where other men can see you." He gave her his half grin. "Though on second thoughts, maybe I do. Everyone will see that my wife is the most enchanting woman of all."

As Mara kissed Rani goodbye on their way out, she had a strange sense of changing seasons. Somehow she knew that things would be different after this night. Whether it would be a good kind of change or not, she couldn't tell. It left her feeling a little edgy.

The palace where Herod the Great had once resided, now occupied by the son who bore his name, was resplendent in candlelight as Amitai and Mara made their way through the main entrance way, along with the other guests.

The towering ceilings, with their ornate Grecian carvings, the majestically frescoed walls and marbled floors made Mara catch her breath in delight. The pillars were hung with magnificent, sheer, fabric hangings and scented flowers flowed in cascades from the roof. An ornate fountain held court in the centre of the room.

This is what Mara had always dreamed of – being amongst society's elite and attending parties such as this. The new moon, round and luminous, hung above as they were ushered through into the palace's peristylium – the inner gardens where they would be congregating.

Everywhere the eye could see were glittering, beautiful women and dashingly attired men – Samaria's elite. Mara tucked a lock of loose hair nervously behind her ear. She hoped that she and Amitai weren't underdressed.

However, the thought was only fleeting. The way the men were looking, well, leering, at her, she wasn't sure she'd ever felt so desirable. She knew, on her handsome husband's arm, they cut a fine figure.

Herod Archelaus was seated with his latest wife on ornate throne-like chairs, ready to greet their guests. Mara was amazed by how much Herod had aged in the years since she'd seen him. His brow was lined with dark, brooding temperament and his eyes were cruel.

By his side, Glaphyra sat, tall, and regal. She was fairly old, but still very lovely. There was something enchanting about her, with her classic Greek looks and her alert grey eyes.

She raised her gaze to Mara's face and stretched out a fair, delicate hand to cup her cheek.

"Simply lovely, my dear," she complimented in husky, cultured tones. Mara blushed, terribly pleased to be noticed by the great lady who had won the hearts of such powerful men.

As Mara and Amitai walked away after their introduction, Mara overheard a plain, but ornately dressed Samaritan women with a sour expression complaining to another.

"She may be of royal lineage, may have been raised in Cappadocia and have lived in Jerusalem, but any woman who will marry her deceased husband's brother is no better than a common prostitute!"

The woman's friend hurriedly hushed her, looking urgently this way and that, checking that no one had heard the treasonous remark.

"I hear she had an awful dream about her poor, dead, first husband," another woman whispered conspiratorially. "She dreamt that he was terribly angry with her for her faithlessness and that he was coming to reclaim her."

"How horrendous!" The first woman piped up. "No wonder she looks so distant!"

Mara looked back at the once-Queen of Mauretania. There was something faraway and desperately sad in her eyes.

The banquet master, almost frighteningly illuminated by the blazing torches, was announcing the pre-dinner entertainment and people were gathering to watch the dance girls, dressed in glistening, bejewelled dresses with tiny bells.

Amused and endeared, Mara watched Amitai turn his flushed face away, shocked. She'd forgotten that this Romanised side of Sebaste's culture was not something he was accustomed to.

The hypnotic rhythm of the music lulled the guests into a sort of peaceful trance. Very little chatter went on as they reclined to eat all sorts of strange, Roman delicacies such as stuffed dormice.

Reclining at her husband's side, Mara felt so safe and happy. She noticed lots of people in the room staring at them — jealous-looking women and lustful men.

One woman in particular reminded Mara much of Yelsaventa, as she had been years before. Her heart rate quickened as she began to panic. She wasn't ready to face Yelsaventa! Thankfully, a second glance revealed that it wasn't her.

The banquet hall — the size of five tricliniums in any regular home — was far too large to see right across, so Mara contented herself with looking at the guests near their end. The fashions, it seemed, had changed a lot in her absence from the city.

Eventually, after Herod's speech and speeches from other important citizens, the banquet master summoned more entertainment. The acrobats were wonderful, as was the magician — a dark skinned man named Shim'on, with flashing eyes and a strong brow.

As Mara watched him perform, he reminded her of someone else.

Though he bore no physical resemblance to the man, he had the same look of desperate passion that Severa, the charioteer who had tossed Mara his victor's wreath, had once had.

Mara felt her heart constrict at the memory. Why had she had to be reminded of that tonight? Not wanting to watch any more, she tugged Amitai's arm.

"Come with me into the gardens, my love. It's too hot and loud in here. I'm sure we'll be able to find people to converse with outside."

Drawing her knuckles to his lips, he kissed them, his eyes meeting hers.

"For you, my perfect one, anything."

Chapter XV.

A.D. 5, Sychar, Samaria, Roman province of Judaea

It was much cooler out in the gardens and Mara felt better almost at once. She drank in the cool breeze, scented with blooms from the palace gardens and felt her senses clear.

Taking Amitai's arm, she led him further down the torchlit path, to the fountain at the bottom of the tiered garden. A collection of people were standing there and they joined them.

Amitai soon struck up a conversation with a broad-shouldered soldier. Mara wasn't at all interested in their conversation, so she drifted off into oblivion, staring into the fountain's depths, which shimmered prettily under the flickering torches.

Mara shivered slightly, pulling her stola tighter around her shoulders. It was a little too chilly out here. Or was it something else making her skin crawl? She felt distinctly strange.

Mara glanced across at her husband. Having only just coaxed Amitai out here, she wondered if she'd be able to convince him to return inside again so soon. She looked across to where he and the soldier, resplendent in his red centurion's cloak, stood talking. Not likely.

"Mara? Mara ben Mal'akhi! What are you doing here?"

It wasn't the abrupt and unexpected nature of the exclamation that made Mara start in shock. The voice that uttered it both chilled her to the bone and made her heart race at an alarming rate.

She knew that voice. It was a voice she'd never forget. Even before she turned, she knew it was Levi ben Yehu.

And there he was, looking as roguishly handsome as ever. His Roman-style tunic and citizen's toga were the same as ever and his face, though three years older, was unchanged.

In that instant, every line, every curve of his chiseled jaw... everything, flooded back to her. The feeling of his lips on hers, his arms surrounding her, was forever emblazoned on her heart. One look at his face, and his incredulous expression told her it was written on his as well.

Mara knew she was staring, but she just couldn't shake her gaze away.

She'd fought so hard to forget, to remember only Amitai and yet, there he stood and her heart remembered. It remembered everything.

The clever inflection of his speech, the way his eyes flashed, the way, so like Amitai, he would toss his hair from his eyes. She remembered his scent and the way he made her feel. And those eyes told her that he remembered every little thing about her, too.

"Levi...." Mara stammered, finally finding she could talk again. Everyone around her faded into nothing and she saw only him. "I..." She couldn't think straight. She felt her cheeks redden, as they always had in his presence.

"I never thought I'd see you back in Sebaste. Can it be that your father has allowed your return?" She could hear the sardonic tone in his voice, but his eyes, burning with passion, told her he loved her still.

She was helpless to answer. All she could do was stand, gazing at the man she'd always wanted, but had never been able to have.

"Mara? Who is this?"

She'd forgotten all about her husband, standing close to her side.

155

Amitai's voice was almost angry, protective. For all his talk of showing her off, there was no disguising the jealousy in his voice.

Feeling guilty and flustered and breathless and confused, Mara turned back to face him.

"Amitai, this is my friend Yelsaventa's older brother, Levi ben Yehu," she managed to stutter out. "Levi, may I present my husband, Amitai ben Yonatan."

The expression that crossed Levi's swarthy face was indescribable. Pain. Anger. Jealousy. Bitterness. And then, a lazy grin and a cruel understanding swept through his features, coming to rest in his glittering eyes.

"So, they managed to find you a husband, did they? And the High Priest's son, no less. Well, well, well, you have done well for yourself, Mara. I can't say I'm surprised, you always were that kind of girl though, weren't you?"

The pounding in Mara's heart was no longer the result of Levi's mere presence, now it was based on horror. The past was announcing itself to Amitai in the worst way possible and there was no way she was going to get out of this unscathed.

The look in Levi's eye told her that he knew it. He knew exactly what he was doing. She should never have come here.

"Whatever do you mean?!" Amitai was asking, his voice indignant. His usually composed, cultured face was shocked and he flung an arm possessively about Mara's shoulders. He looked from his wife to Levi and back again, unsure how to proceed.

Levi began to laugh, a deep, self-satisfied chuckle.

"Oh? You don't know? I do apologize then – I seem to have made a mistake." His sly grin remained and Mara loathed the way he clearly seemed to find her predicament amusing. In that instant, she almost hated him.

But how could she, when every part of her was crying out to be his?

Levi's eyes caught Mara's once more, sending her a silent, cryptic message.

"Well," he said, turning to acknowledge Amitai, then back to Mara. "I'd love to stay and chat, but my wife is waiting for me," he said, pointing to a tall, slender woman of fair complexion and golden, Roman hair.

Be jealous. His eyes taunted Mara. *This is what you've missed out on. I would have given everything for you. But you didn't give your everything for me.* If only he knew.

Then Levi was gone and the steady, secure and prosperous world Mara had fought so hard to construct seemed to walk off with him.

Amitai didn't waste a moment on courtesy, but grabbed her wrist tightly and pulled her from the gathering, marching out without so much as a farewell to anyone. The curt bow to Herod Archelaus and his wife was all he stopped for. Mara could feel him trembling with rage. She'd never seen him like this. Her wrist hurt.

"Amitai," she cried, as he pulled her, stumbling down the marble steps. "Please stop this! I can explain!" She was begging, pleading now, but he ignored her words entirely.

He dragged her on, out of the fashionable district, not stopping until they were in an alley down by the forum, deserted at this time of night. He flung her painfully up against a wall. She could feel a statue digging into her back.

"Go on then. Explain." He ordered. Betrayal dripped from his every feature. She ached. She wanted to go into his arms, to comfort him. But she could see he would never accept it from her now.

"Amitai, I..." The words died on her lips and she broke. The tears flowed, but he just watched her, stone faced.

"So it's true is it, what he implied?" He looked down and cursed. "I should have known. Why did I ever marry you? I should have known. The beautiful ones are always poison. I was warned, my father told me you were a selfish little vixen. Was he ever right?!"

"Amitai, don't accuse me of those things without at least hearing what happened." Mara was angry now, not just ashamed.

"None of it was my fault. I was a child, a naive child. My friend's older brother expressed interest in me and she encouraged it. I thought he wanted to marry me. I had no idea how cruel men could be." She let the words drip from her tongue. "I thought Levi loved me. When he kissed me I -"

"No!" Amitai groaned, his rage suddenly abating, swapped for desperate grief. He sank to the ground. "No! No! Mara, tell me it isn't true!" He was heartbroken, she could hear it.

"It is true. But it wasn't my fault. My father brought me to Sychar the next day, to sit it out until it had all boiled over. And after the Day of Atonement, I thought I was free from it all." Tears dripped in murky black kohl rivers down her face.

She knelt beside her husband, trying to take his hands in her own. "Please understand Amitai, I never meant for any of it to happen. It wasn't my fault."

He pulled away from her.

"Not your fault?! As if a woman like you doesn't know what she's doing to a man." Scorn hung off his words and the look he cast her burned her almost physically. How had he moved from adoring to despising so fast?

Something Yelsaventa had once said played through her mind. "Love and hate are the two closest linked emotions in this life..." Now, Mara knew for herself that this was true.

"Perfect, pure woman. A rare bloom. All those things I said of you. Why didn't you stop me Mara? What didn't you tell me?" Amitai's voice cracked and suddenly he looked terribly vulnerable.

Everything within her cried out for him. She wished he had never had to meet her. A sob bubbled up from deep within.

"Because I loved you, Amitai. And I wanted you to love me too. You were everything I ever wanted." She clung to his arm, but he wrenched himself free.

"Of course I was. And you used everything within your power to get me, seducing me as you seduced that Levi ben Yehu. I see it all now. You're nothing, Mara. Worthless. A man is a fool to want a woman like you."

He was on his feet now, but she stayed crumpled to the ground. She couldn't move as his harsh words cut her to the core.

"As of this instant, you are no longer my wife. Your child is no longer my child. And you are never welcome under my roof again. I hope I never see you again. You are a seducer, Mara, but I am no longer under your power."

Amitai began to stride away. Mara scrambled up, screaming out his name, begging him to listen, to stop. He turned back and for a moment, she had hope.

But all he did was pull the scarf which had covered her, the very symbol of his protection over her, from her head. And just like that, he was gone.

* * *

Mara had tried everything. After Amitai had left her, crumpled and sobbing in the alley behind the forum, she'd felt alone in a way she'd never experienced before. She'd just sat and cried, rocking back and forth, until she had no more tears to cry.

How could he have done this to her? How could Amitai have deserted her so suddenly and without hearing the truth?

How could Levi have done this to her? Was this his revenge because she hadn't run away to be with him? Or was this simply the world's revenge against her? In that moment, she wished she had never been born.

The dawn was breaking over the city walls when she finally peeled herself off the street and began to make her way back to their lodgings.

People stared at her and no wonder. Her clothes, which had been splendid the night before, were now creased and stained, her make up washed down her face until she was left with a blotchy mess. She was pale and her hair tangled, falling loose around her face.

Anyone who had seen her at the palace would never now recognize her as the woman Glaphyra herself had complimented.

The walk to Dawid and Zimra's apartment seemed to take an eternity. Mara was beyond caring now what people would think of her – even what Dawid and Zimra would think – she just wanted to see Amitai, to plead with him once more.

Zimra opened the door, with a sleepy Rani on her hip. Upon seeing Mara, her mouth formed a silent O.

"Is Amitai here?!" Mara asked desperately. Dawid emerged at the sound of her voice, slipping an arm around Zimra as he did so. Mara nearly cried at the sight of it.

"No. We haven't seen him. He sent a slave for his things about an hour ago. What's going on?" Dawid's voice was concerned, but only mildly. He looked confused more that anything else. Somehow, with her own world falling down about her, it made her feel angry.

"I have no idea! I have to find him!" She spat, then turned and ran, before they could stop her, or ask anything else. Behind her, she could her Rani begin to cry, calling out plaintively for her Imah.

Mara finally spotted Amitai leaving the city by the south gate. She cried out his name, rushing after him down the cobbled street.

He didn't stop, didn't look back, didn't do anything. He'd heard her, that was for certain.

"Amitai, please!" She cried once more, running in his wake.

This time he turned, and she saw the sorrow, saw the pain etched into his features. But there was a hardness about his face that told her the decision was made and there was no changing it.

"It's over, Mara."

* * *

Mara cried herself to sleep that night. Zimra kindly looked after Rani and she and Dawid left Mara to herself.

The next morning, Mara awoke still feeling miserable, but knowing she couldn't just sit there, taking up her brother's home. Despite their many assurances that she was no imposition and was welcome to stay as long as she liked, she packed up her things and took herself home.

Mal'akhiy welcomed her with open arms. Achsah, ever the nursemaid, plucked Rani straight from Mara's tired arm and left father and daughter alone to talk. Mal'akhiy was outraged at what had happened, but hardly surprised.

"I saw it in him from the first. If he doesn't have what he perceives as the best, then he is not happy. I'm so sorry Mara, I'm so sorry he couldn't see past what happened with Levi and see the truth. I should have warned you. I saw the tendencies and did nothing to help you. I should have made you tell him before the engagement."

"He wouldn't have married me if I had," Mara sighed, raking her fingers through her tangled mess of hair. "And perhaps that would have been better. But ah well, what's done is done. I just never expected my life to be over by sixteen." A bubble of sardonic laughter popped out as a hiccupy sob.

Mal'akhiy wrapped his arms around her and drew her close. Mara leaned gratefully into his embrace.

There's nothing like a father's arms, she thought. Something Rani will never have now. She shook the thought away. Now Amitai had shown his true colours, she'd never want her precious girl around him anyway.

"Your life isn't over, Little Flower," Mal'akhiy was saying. "You are still young and lovely. And there are good men out there who will understand that you've been unfairly cast off." Mara couldn't help but hope he was right. It was too painful to think of any other outcome.

Chapter XVI.

A.D. 6, Sebaste, Samaria, Roman province of Judaea

That first morning on which Mara awoke back in her father's home, she expected to hear that her husband's desertion was the talk of the city. But there was greater news afoot – Herod Archelaus' wife, Glaphyra, had died.

Achsah was quick to pass on the street's gossip – that Glaphyra's deceased first-husband had come and taken her to himself once more, as her dream had said. Mara had scoffed at the notion, but she couldn't help but wonder, deep down, if it was true.

Mal'akhiy dispelled the notion as well. His interpretation was that it was Yahweh's punishment to Herod for disobeying His ways.

Mara was sad to hear of the once-Queen's passing. It was strange to think that only two nights ago, Mara was in the resplendent palace, being paid compliments by the lovely Persian princess. And now she was gone forever.

In some horrible way, Mara couldn't help but also feel a little glad for it. It meant that she herself, was forgotten for a while. And for once in her life, that was exactly what she wanted.

At first, it felt terribly strange to Mara, being back in her Father's home. She had never noticed how simple and plain things were before, but now she'd lived a life of luxury, she certainly did. There were no marbled staircases here, no beautifully carved benches under swooping olive branches. No sunlit reading rooms, no small, private baths. This home was wooden. Rigid. Dark.

And it felt odd to be living once more in her father's care, but this time with a child of her own.

Rani, poor girl, was irritable and weepy those first few days. What had occurred was far over the two year old's head and she was disturbed by all the new and different things that suddenly shaped her life. And the new people.

She lay, her curly dark head in Mara's lap, liquid brown eyes red and teary. Mara just rocked her, holding her baby as tightly as she herself wished to be held.

Achsah was delighted to have a young one in the home once more and did everything in her power to make the little girl happy again. Even Abihud, Mal'akhiy's elderly slave, couldn't hide the fact that he enjoyed having Rani around.

As time when by and Rani recovered her equilibrium, the child brought life and vitality to the home as only a child can. It didn't take long for her to stop asking for her Abba and to form a new rhythm of life. It was a quieter existence than they had known in Sychar, but Mara didn't mind. It was happier.

Amitai wasted no time in having the divorce finalized, under charges of adultery. Mara was incensed, but at least it was all over now. As the old year flicked over into the new, she was contented to just mother her daughter and look after her Abba's house.

But all that changed one day in the forum.

Usually Achsah went to the market to do the shopping, but she had fallen over one of Rani's toy and hurt her ankle. Mara felt bad, as she should have ensured Rani's toys were put away and insisted on seeing to everything until Achsah had healed.

Though it was now several months since her arrival at her father's house, it was the first time she'd since ventured out in public. She breathed in deeply as she set foot out onto the dusty, busy street, trying to drum up her courage.

The world all seemed incredibly bright and alive. After her months cocooned inside the haven of Mal'akhiy's walls, it was almost overwhelming. Mara just stood for a while, letting the city wash over her senses.

It felt good to be out of the confines of the house for a while. The sun was warm on her dark hair and Mara began to feel light and happy as she walked. It wasn't so bad, after all, to be out, to be seen. Not everyone knew her story, not everyone knew of her humiliation. It wouldn't all last forever. She didn't have to be tied to her past any longer.

Mara began to walk faster along the *decomanus maximus*. The streets were crowded with people going about their business, just like her. For once, Mara enjoyed blending in.

It was so long since she'd been to a market. She'd never really gone when she was married to Amitai. It felt wonderful, being able to trawl from stall to stall, looking at the exotic wares and enjoying the smells of the foods and spices.

Her arms and bags were soon filled with a wide array of the things they needed and she was almost ready to return home.

As Mara was preparing to leave, she noticed a thickset man standing by some camels, his eyes never leaving her face. She looked away the first time she saw him, but when she looked again, his eyes were still on her face.

Flushing, Mara looked down. Why was he watching her? He was much older than she was, at least part of the way through his twenties and very statuesque. Amitai was a tall man and strong, but compared to this man, he would have looked a young boy.

This man had a well whiskered face and sun-beaten skin, but there was something knowing about his thickly lashed, dark eyes. They looked almost out of place on his otherwise rugged face. There was something familiar about his appearance too, but Mara couldn't quite place it.

She was unable to keep herself from looking back once more. This time, she offered him a tiny smile. He grinned in return. Her heart gave a tiny flutter. Maybe all hope was not lost. Maybe this was a sign to her that the universe wouldn't be against her forever.

When she returned to the market a few days later, she looked out for her giant with the lovely eyes, but he wasn't there. It surprised her how disappointed she felt and she told herself off in rueful frustration. *You're hopeless Mara. Always falling in love with men who have no heart for you.*

She felt resigned as she walked away from the market, having completed her shopping. Between them, Levi and Amitai had ruined her life. It was useless to imagine otherwise.

Mara took Rani over to visit Zimra later that afternoon, bemoaning her plight to her. Zimra, deep into the last months of her pregnancy, was sympathetic.

"I'm sorry all this has happened to you, Mara. You know I am. But I don't believe that Yahweh is finished with you yet."

Mara snorted disdainfully, bouncing Rani up and down on her knee. She didn't say anything, knowing Zimra would disapprove of her thoughts.

Yahweh never even began with me. I don't believe he ever cared about me at all. Or our people. Why else would he leave us to the mercy of the Jews and the Romans alike?

Zimra reached across, grasping Mara's hand. "I know what you're thinking, Mara. I do. But some change is coming for you, I feel it!"

Suddenly, she grimaced. "For both of us perhaps."

Zimra proved to be exactly right. It was late into the night when, after a hard labour, she gave birth to a baby boy. They named him Eli, after Zimra's father. He was a lovely baby, although small. As soon as his eyes lost their newborn blue, it was beyond apparent that he bore his Aunt Mara's looks. His eyes became fire golden and engaging.

Rani was delighted with this new addition to her world and would often coo on about "Baby 'li" as she referred to him.

Mara loved seeing her own baby becoming a little girl.

Rani's hair was long enough to tie up now and her little voice forming a sound of its own. She would often follow Mara about on her pudgy little legs, chattering away. There was no question that times were changing, for all of them.

Mara watched Dawid and Zimra bond over their shared new experience of parenthood. The love between them and Eli was so tangible, one could almost taste it.

It made Mara sad, thinking that she'd missed out on that experience with her firstborn. She and Amitai had never shared such a relationship and Amitai had never been like that with Rani. It broke Mara's heart that her little girl's father had never so much as asked after her. Amitai had cast off both Mara and Rani as surely as one casts off a ruined garment.

Achsah's ankle had made a fine recovery and she was back up on her feet again. All the same, Mara wasn't ready to give up her newfound independence, getting out into the town each day or so.

It was somewhat embarrassing at first, being among the older of the unveiled – clearly unmarried – women, but that soon wore off and Mara found new confidence in elaborately styled hair and having her face lifted to the sun.

Chapter XVII.

A.D. 6, Sebaste, Samaria, Roman province of Judaea

It was some weeks after Eli's birth when Mara first saw her "giant with the knowing eyes", as she'd come to think of him, again. She was passing into the forum when she saw a caravan making it's way into the town.

There were numerous camels, laden with exotic fabrics, boxes, baskets and led by sun-bronzed camel men. At their head rode the man Mara had seen. His eyes met hers as he passed by. Still so bold, so vibrant and full of life, so expectant.

Mara felt carried along by his expression and found herself moving, along with the rest of the crowds, to where the caravan stopped at the centre of town.

The wares being unpacked all around her were magnificent, but Mara couldn't do anything except watched the muscled merchant unloading. She felt herself grow giddy, watching him sweep things down from his beast's back. This was a man that could make a girl feel like a woman.

The camels moaned and groaned their melancholy cry. The sound of bartering began and people began moving again. Mara just stood.

The man turned and seeing her watching him, grinned widely. Out of all the crowds, he saw only her. Mara knew she should blush and run away. What was she thinking, looking at a man that way? She was a divorcee and a mother, after all. But she didn't. She blushed and stayed.

Once the unloading was complete and the rest of the crowd had melted away entirely, only Mara remained. Wiping the sweat off his glistening brow under his turban, the merchant made his way across to her. So, he was the sort of man who would speak to a strange, unmarried woman in a market square? Mara was liking him more by the moment.

He towered over her, a head and shoulders higher than the top of her head, although Mara herself wasn't a short woman.

"I hope you won't run away, now that I've come to talk to you," he began, his voice coming from deep within his chest. "But somehow, you don't strike me as the sort of maiden who would." He wasn't smiling, but Mara could hear the amusement in his voice.

"I'm not your average woman," she rejoined, allowing her eyes to glisten with life. This time he really did smile.

"Oh, I've noticed that much. No other woman has so captivated me that I've remembered her face for months on end." Mara felt her heart begin it's race as he continued. "Years even."

Mara was confused. What did he mean years?

The man laughed at her expression.

"My name is Micah ben Yosef. I'm a merchant. But you might remember me as a young cavalry officer from the Ala I Sebastenorum. I first saw you at the Patron's banquet many years ago. You were beautiful then. But now..."

He let out a long, slow whistle, making Mara blush to the roots of her hair.

She remembered him now. He'd been the officer to supposedly ask after her, the one Yelsaventa had been so enamored with. She had first met him on the very night she first fell in love with Levi...

Mara ignored the twinge of her heart as Micah continued speaking.

"I left the army two years ago. It wasn't the life for me and so I paid my way out early. I became a merchant. I'm making far more than I ever did in the service. And now... Well, you see, I'm looking for a not so average bride and I think you might be just the perfect fit."

Mara found herself laughing now.

"I'm sure you must be. Any average girl would be frightened off by such an advance."

Micah offered her a sly wink. "Which is exactly why I use it. I have no use for a nervous, flighty young girl. I'm looking for a bold, passionate woman who isn't afraid of life. And when I saw you for the first time in the market, I knew you were that kind of woman. It's clear you've grown up remarkable, Mara bat Mal'akhiy."

Mara looked away. "I may be all of those things, but I'm not an ideal bride." She looked away here, frustrated that she was on the verge of tearing up.

Micah laughed, a rich, deep sound. "I've yet to meet one woman who is. Or one man who is the ideal husband. I travel enough to know that there is no such thing."

Mara shook her head. "No, you don't understand. I...I am a divorced woman. My husband accused me of adultery and left me and my little girl for lost. You see what I mean?"

To her surprise, he didn't turn away, but looked interested. "Did you?!"

"Did I what?"

"Did you commit adultery?"

She felt her cheeks reddening, but refused to look away. She had nothing to be ashamed of.

"No, I didn't. But now, I almost wish I had, just to spite him!" She lifted her chin defiantly, only making Micah ben Yosef grin more widely. He didn't say anything, but Mara could tell her answer pleased him.

A moment passed in silence, as they appraised each other. It wasn't an awkward silence, just a silence.

Micah broke it a while later.

"How old is your girl?"

"Nearly three. She's a treasure!"

"If she's anything like her Imah, then I can't say I'm surprised." His face was solemn as he continued. "I've always wanted a daughter."

He couldn't be serious. Was he really saying what she thought he was? She looked down at her dusty sandals, unsure of how to reply. He seemed to sense her confusion and continued. "How about it? If I asked you to marry me and let me be a Father to your baby, would you say yes?"

Heart pounding, Mara dared to raise her eyes to his handsome, earnest face. This wasn't a joke, this was real. Could she say yes? Would she dare?

"I know this is sudden," Micah was saying. "But once I saw you, I knew there was no going back. I liked you as a girl, but I know I could love you as a woman. I've been waiting for a woman like you all my life. One who isn't afraid to live. Who would travel with me sometimes, would be my companion. Your eyes hold a fire I can't resist. Mara bat Mal'khiy say you'll be mine!"

Mara was barely aware that she was nodding her head. This was real. A wealthy merchant wanted to marry a divorcee with a baby – and that was her! If only Yelsaventa could see her now!

* * *

It seemed Micah ben Yosef was a man of action. He wasn't interested in waiting months to have Mara as his bride – he wanted to marry her that very day. In the army, it seemed, he had learnt how short life was and wasn't willing to waste a moment of his.

Somehow, there was no trepidation in Mara's heart, only excitement, as he rushed her off to the court.

Standing in front of the presiding community elders with her tall, good looking new husband, she felt a sense of elation she hadn't felt since her first wedding night.

But this was different. Perhaps it felt even better. She had a sense of redemption in this new marriage, even at only minutes old. She was a status-less disgrace no longer!

The feeling of Micah's hand around her hand, the way he looked down at her now... Mara felt dizzy and happy and wonderful. There was no better feeling, Mara concluded, than that of new love. If only she could feel at every moment as she did right now!

She looked up at Micah. He was broad-shouldered, a manly man in every aspect. His face bore the scars of a soldier and yet they only added to his appeal. He may have left the military, but there was no pretending Micah was not a warrior inside. Mara was besotted.

The reaction she received upon her arrival back at her father's home was not on a par with her own elation. Shock was a far better word to describe it. Dawid and Zimra were visiting and Eli was propped up in a basket cooing away with Rani.

When Mara entered, with Micah by her side, all the chatter stopped and eyes turned their way in shock. Rani began to scamper Mara's way, calls of "Imah!" dying on her little lips.

"Abba... Dawid, Zimra... I'd like you to all meet my new husband, Micah ben Yosef..." The words sounded strange, surreal, even to her own ears. The shocked expressions gazing back at her and the hasty congratulations being made, were just as false.

Rani sidled up to Mara's side, tugging at her Imah's skirts, seeking reassurance in all the confusion. Mara swung the pudgy little girl up into her arms.

"Rani, meet your new Abba."

***

And so Mara created another new life. Being married to Micah was nothing like it had been being married to Amitai. Where Amitai was steady and monotonous, Micah was lively and continually changing.

His stint in the army, it seemed, had failed to instill any sense of order, or discipline in him. The merchant lifestyle he had chosen granted him the freedom to explore, to change, to make almost any choice he liked.

Micah's home in Sebaste was a small, but elaborately furnished apartment, filled with art and beauty from all around the empire, it seemed. Persian rugs lined the floors, intricately woven hangings from Greece on the walls, beautifully crafted Greek and Roman pottery was displayed everywhere.

When Mara first entered the apartment, she felt like a viewer at a fine art collection, but Micah ensured she was soon made to feel at welcome in his life and in his home.

Rani loved her new surroundings and all the pretty trinkets, but often, she would cry at night, asking for her Saba Mal'akhiy, or for Achsah. That, in Mara's opinion, was the only downside to her new arrangement.

For the first few weeks of their marriage, Micah was happy to remain in Sebaste, selling the wares he had most recently brought up from Jerusalem. It didn't take long, however, for his restless spirit to return to him and then, he was ready to move.

Mara found this thrilling. Arrangements were made for the journey – Rani was left with Dawid and Zimra and the caravans were prepared. They were to head to Corinth.

It would be a long journey, first across land and then across the *Mare Internum* sea. It would be many months until their return to Judaea and still more to Samaria.

Before they were to leave their homeland, Micah was determined to take his remaining wares down to the region's political centre – Sychar.

Trepidation and anticipation merged within Mara at this idea. Was she willing to risk facing Amitai, face humiliation? With Micah at her side, she felt perhaps she was.

Riding a camel felt powerful. As they made their way through the desert hills of Samaria, Mara felt like a goddess in her colourful, billowing robes and glittering jewels.

Micah, riding up ahead of her on a magnificent, golden beast, dressed in flowing robes and his turban, composed a mighty sight. He moved as one with his camel's rocky gait, completely at ease. He was a desert king and she, his queen. She'd never entered Sychar in such style.

* * *

She was here.

There was no one else it could be but Mara. No one else had a brow that noble, nor a gaze so fierce and wild, so golden. Even under her flowing veils, Shemu'el could see it was her.

A year had passed since Amitai ben Yonatan had return to Sychar alone, leaving his wife and daughter in Sebaste, disgraced. He had claimed adultery.

Shem wasn't sure he believed that. He knew Mara enough to know that she had truly loved Amitai, in her way. But all the same, Amitai had returned alone and angry. His marriage vows had been swiftly destroyed.

Shemu'el had longed to go to Mara, to rush to her side and make her his own… But he knew he mustn't. Knew she wouldn't want him.

The year had passed by and he had done nothing.

And now, here she was, riding in a caravan, the reds and golds of her robes catching the sunlight and casting light all around. She didn't see him up on the hill, amongst his sheep. He wasn't really surprised. Why would she? Her eyes were fixed ahead, on the man leading the caravan.

Mara was veiled again, it suddenly struck him. She must have remarried. Could this giant be her new husband? The pride in her gleaming eyes told him it must be. He couldn't help but wonder how it had come about.

No doubt the man had ridden in on his camel and swept her off her feet, he thought bitterly. A powerful looking man, with such wealth would have had no trouble winning a woman like Mara.

Oh Mara, Mara… I hope he is everything you need. I hope he loves you as you deserve to be loved. Shemu'el's heart clenched with pain, as it always did for her. *Oh Yahweh, please. Unchain her from my heart. I know she can't be mine.*

* * *

Corinth was beyond Mara's wildest dreams. The mix of languages, people, sights and sounds made her feel both small and insignificant and as though she was really somebody. With the exception of rulers and soldiers, Mara had never known any one of their people who had journeyed further than Jerusalem.

Micah enjoyed her excitement, taking her to all his favourite haunts and showing her off to his business associates, who seemed to greatly appreciate his elegant, exotic looking, young wife.

Micah spoilt her, buying her all sorts of beautiful and valuable items. The new clothes were what Mara liked the most. The daring cut and bold colours made her feet enchanting and entrancing. The way the fabrics hugged her curves and accentuated her shape was more bold than anything she'd ever worn before, but she was exhilarated by the riskiness of it all.

Micah made the most of having Mara by his side as a beautiful bargaining tool. As he explained to her, people in his business were easily swayed by a lovely woman in their presence.

At first, Mara wasn't sure how she felt about being called on to parade before his business associates, but it didn't take long for it to become normal to her.

In fact, she started to enjoy the way she could change the atmosphere in a room with one single appearance. She had always known how to catch a man's eye – it had come very naturally to her – but now, she began to practice it as a craft.

A mere swaying walk and a flirtatious glance; a playful laugh and a certain way of sitting. Micah encouraged her, saying it made him feel good to know other men desired his wife as much as he did. Besides, she always seemed to help smooth the lining of his pocket and that was almost as good.

Mara loved to hear Micah's clients' proclaiming her beauty, saying how there was no doubt Judaean women were the most beautiful in the world. She was proud of her good looks.

When they returned to Sebaste several months later, with a loaded caravan, Mara realized she was an almost entirely different person. The curve of her smile was less girly and more that of a sophisticated, worldly-wise woman. The smile she now wore was the smile of Yelsaventa's she'd long desired to emulate.

Mara herself wasn't the only thing different in Sebaste now. Herod Archelaus, the tetrarch, had been banished from Judaea by the Roman Emperor Augustus. His immorality had become so unpopular with the Jews that they'd begged for his removal. And now he was gone – exiled to Gaul.

When Mara and Micah arrived at Dawid and Zimra's tiny apartment to collect Rani, Mara felt somewhat self-conscious for the first time. What would they think of her, in her revealing dress and with her dark, heavy make up?

The contrast between herself and Zimra had never been more apparent. Zimra was pregnant again, eyes shining with true joy. She looked tired, but satisfied. Youthful even.

Eli and Rani were playing happily when they arrived and Rani was happy enough to greet her Imah. Both she and Eli were little children now and no longer babies.

But when it time for them to leave, Rani screamed and cried, clinging to Zimra's skirts. It was then that Mara knew she had been replaced. She had given up the role of mother in her own daughter's life. Zimra was her daughter's real Imah now.

After a long, tearful night, Mara took Rani back to her brother's apartment. There was no denying it was the little girl's home now. Rani had cried until she'd made herself sick and Mara knew it was the right thing to do to take her "home", no matter how it pained her.

After relinquishing Rani to Zimra's arms, Mara turned, ignoring her sister-in-law's tears and walked away without looking back.

Chapter XVIII·

A.D. 7, Sebaste, Samaria, Roman province of Judaea

Micah took Mara away with him to Jerusalem to take her mind off Rani.

Mara hated Jerusalem, hated being amongst the Jews who so despised them. She began to regret that she had ever accepted Micah's proposal – as much as she enjoyed his wild company. She'd been happier, as she was, in her Abba's home. Was being married to a wealthy, handsome and thrilling man worth this misery?

From Jerusalem, they headed up to Tarsus in Cicilia. There, Micah took Mara to more parties and frequently used her as his bargaining tool. Mara became used to him summoning her to meet his clients, though she was fast growing to hate it. She felt used and trapped. The strong wine that kept her from feeling anything became her dearest friend.

She missed the cold, clear waters of Ya'acov's Well more than she'd ever thought possible. She missed childhood. Missed innocence. Missed the days that had gone before. All she had hoped for in her future had come to naught.

It wasn't long before they next returned to Samaria that Mara first noticed a stirring in her womb. She said nothing until she was absolutely sure. Micah, to her dismay, was not pleased.

"What use are you to me pregnant?" He bemoaned. "You can't travel with me and neither can a baby! Besides, my clients won't be a swayed by a fat melon of a woman!" Mara felt her cheeks flush angrily, but Micah seemed not to notice.

Kissing her ear, he whispered that he'd miss her too much and begged her to visit a certain woman he knew of who dealt with these matters.

Furious, Mara declined and so the child continued growing within her. It was spring when it came. A boy. Micah wasn't there and so Mara bore the burden alone. She called him Yathom, feeling that somehow Orphan was an appropriate name for the child.

From the first, the baby was sickly and would spend nights coughing until he was blue in the face. Mara was broken with concern. No one could do anything. Even the strongest of herbal potions, the offerings in the temple of Augustus, the magic spells cast by Shim'on, the Wizard of Sebaste had no affect.

Mara wished beyond all wishes that she could go back and never marry Micah, never give up her beautiful baby girl for this poor, sick child. He should never have been born.

Micah finally met his son two months after his birth. Indifference. There seemed to be no paternal instincts in him.

Mara began to resent her husband. Even Amitai had shown love for his little Rani after a while.

It was all becoming clear to her now. Micah had needed a woman for his business and he had seen one who was both fair of face and vulnerable.

The snake of a man had seen her desire to be loved all those years ago when they'd first met. Then he'd seen her failed past and the unfulfilled longing for love and had capitalized on it. She had been used. And now that she was no longer useful... He had never cared for her.

Yathom grew sicker after Micah left on his next journey. Mara began to pray like she had never prayed before. She prayed to Roman gods, to the gods of the land. She even prayed to Yahweh. But she could see the child slipping away before her very eyes. He was too weak even to cry. Within two weeks, he was gone.

Mara did not weep. She didn't move. She didn't do anything. There was too much pain for that – an agony that gripped her in the gut. She couldn't bring herself to do anything at all.

Zimra found her sitting there with Yathom, cold, tiny and still, cradled in her arms.

Zimra wept for the child. Mara did not. She could not. She'd never known pain could be this deep. She had no words left in her, now that Yathom was gone. Finally, as Zimra dressed her in her black robes for the funeral, Mara began to wail. It was an unearthly sound, even she could hear that. She frightened Rani and Eli. Their people traditionally lamented this way, but Mara sounded as if she would break open, so deeply was she mourning.

All of Mara's family came for the funeral, her brothers and sisters and their families. And at the back, trying to stay out of sight, she spotted Shemu'el. Their eyes met for a second. Mara saw he felt her grief. He clearly saw her vacant, anguished expression and he felt that too.

People came and told Mara how sorry they were and offered their support. She didn't know what to say to them. What could they know of her pain? Her loss? All her happiness was gone. Why had God done this to her? She couldn't understand it. She was a wreck.

After Yathom was buried, Mara felt she had nothing to live for. Pain ruled her days and weeping, her nights. When Micah finally arrived back in Samaria from his latest trip, he gave a half-hearted attempt to cheer her up, but she could not be comforted.

Mara longed to have her baby back, to hold him for just one more day, one more moment. She lamented for the childhood he'd never get to have, the life he'd never get to experience. But there was nothing she could do, Yathom was gone.

It was some weeks until Mara began to feel human again. She'd sunken into such a deep, dark place that once she came out if it, she hardly recognized herself.

When she looked in the mirror, she saw just a shell of what had once been. She had not reached eighteen years old, yet the blossom had faded from her now-sunken cheeks, her eyes dimmed from their once bright sparkle. The fire was gone. As she looked, Mara wondered if she'd ever get it back.

For the first time in weeks, she got up, washed properly, clothed herself well again and went out. She felt weak and a little unsteady, but it felt good to be alive again.

But she soon realized it would not be easy. When Micah returned home that evening, to find her up and about, his reaction was not what she'd expected.

"Oh, so you've finally pulled yourself together," he muttered and slumped down in his ornate Persian armchair. He looked haggard and tired, his face pinched under his shadow of a beard. Mara tried not to be hurt, but knew she deserved it.

"Forgive me Micah," she whispered. He looked surprised, scornful. "What, no more excuses?"

Mara looked down, ashamed.

"I truly am sorry. I don't know what came over me these last few weeks. But I've determined to get through it now."

Micah put his head in his hands. "About time." He looked back up at her. "I've had to bear everything alone since the child died, Mara. Do you realize that? You've had not one thought for me and I've lost as much as you have. In fact, I've lost more. I lost my beautiful wife. And now all you've left me with is a haggard, helpless girl."

Tears sprung to Mara's eyes, but she could not deny a word of what he said. It was all true. As he walked away from her, she felt the tears and the depression wash over her again. It was all just as he said.

* * *

It came as no surprise when Micah returned from his next business trip with a new woman – voluptuous and bubbly - on his arm. The simple words "get out of my home" didn't surprise her either. What else could she have expected? Micah had never wanted her, only what she could give him. And now, she had nothing left to offer.

As Mara numbly packed her things, she found herself laughing sardonically at the way things had gone. She was such a fool. The man she'd thought would see her life changed for the better had been the one to push it to the breaking point.

As she walked away from Micah's house, she would have given anything to return to her happy existence at her Abba's house. But she couldn't bring herself to. She had to get out of Sebaste.

Mara made her way down town and into an area she had never before entered. She managed to find herself a room in a small, fairly respectable establishment. Rats and bugs were her companions for the night, sleepless though it was. As the first rays of dawn crossed the horizon, she set off from the city. Sychar was calling to her.

She found a cart heading south and managed to convince its elderly driver to give her a ride, at least part of the way. She curled herself into a ball in the back, amongst the hay and bundles and tried to make herself comfortable.

As they neared the town, Mara suddenly wanted to be alone. Pulling her bundle from the cart and waving goodbye to the driver, she began on foot.

Somehow, the walk was healing to Mara. The desert hills spoke to her lamenting heart and suddenly, the tears came.

She started to run, not caring where she went. Finally, she crumpled down on a ridge, under a tree. Her legs simply gave way and she began sobbing as if her heart would break. She didn't know why life was this cruel, why God had issued her with such a life. She couldn't see at all how this was the life she herself had created.

In the distance stood a shepherd, watching. He saw Mara running, saw her collapse to the earth in anguish. Everything in him longed to go to her, to hold her tight, to wipe her tears and to make it all alright again. But he knew he couldn't.

Shemu'el just watched.

"Oh Mara, Mara," he whispered to the wind. "Why couldn't you see true happiness is never found through riches or a life founded on pride?"

He had grieved with her for the little boy taken too early, but what he saw today spoke of yet more hurt. What had Micah done to her? He felt anger sweeping through him. Clearly, the merchant had never seen anything more than a pretty face in Mara, he'd only ever wanted her to complete his fancy life. But now that she was a faded flower, now that she'd failed him, he would cast her off.

Shem wished he could have taken Mara from him, stolen her away rather than let her be subjected to such rejection. But it couldn't be. All he could do was watch her weep in the distance. And pray.

* * *

As Mara arrived at her grandparents' home, Pinchas greeted her granddaughter with open arms. She had aged in the year and a half Mara had been away. Pinchas brought Mara out into her kitchen, giving her a warm Roman posca to drink.

Suddenly, all the kindness proved too much for Mara and she began to cry again, weeping for all that had been in those last few years. As she had always done, she poured her heart out to her Savta.

"I'm so sorry, Mara," Pinchas whispered tearfully. "I can't help feeling partly responsible. I'm the one who encouraged you to marry Amitai and to keep your past from him."

Mara shook her head wearily. "It's not your doing Savta."

Pinchas clasped her wrinkled hands nervously. "You should know, Mara, that Amitai has remarried... Your friend Hadassah..."

Mara snorted bitterly. "She's welcome to him. I want nothing to do with such a man. Less to do with a man like Micah. No, if I marry again, I want to marry a compliant man. I'm still young, but I'm not foolish anymore. I know what I want now."

Pinchas pulled Mara close. "My precious girl, what's become of you?" Mara stiffened in her embrace.

* * *

"What do you mean she's gone?!" Dawid's face was blotchy with fury and pain. Mal'akhiy reached for his son's arm. Shouting wouldn't help anything here, that much was clear. Micah's stony face, many inches above both of theirs was impassive and likely to remain so.

"I told you, she's been gone for days." A sneer formed across his features. "Some family you are, to not even know that!"

"Please, young man," Mal'akhiy begged, raising his hands in what he hoped was a placatory gesture. "We don't meet to interrogate you. We just want to find my daughter. She hasn't been herself since -" He broke off speaking. Since what? Since the baby died? Since she lost Rani? Since she married either of her husbands? Since she first met Levi ben Yehu? What did he mean?

Micah gave a hollow laugh. "Don't you think I know that?" He shrugged his large, muscled shoulders. "But what does it matter to me? She's no longer my problem and I have no idea where she's gone. Probably to her beloved Sychar."

He closed the door in their faces, effectively dismissing them. Mal'akhiy was too upset to feel the full burn of the insult. His heart ached for his daughter.

"Oh Ado," he murmured, wishing his wife was still with them. "I've let her down so badly." His poor, sweet little girl. Not even into her second decade yet and already so ruined.

"Abba, do you think she has gone to Sychar?" Dawid was asking. Mal'akhiy nodded vaguely. "Perhaps. It sounds like the sort of thing she might do. She always has loved to go to that well when something has gone wrong."

Sychar? Should he go there and bring her home? Why hadn't she come to him first? Oh Mara. He could see her now, as she had been at only four years old. She had been such a pretty child and those eyes – wide and bright – had always been captivating.

Mal'akhiy remembered the first time he'd taken her to the synagogue. She had been awed by the towering pillars and the ornate carvings, her little lips open in a round O of wonder. He could still hear her little voice asking: "Abba, does only Yahweh have buildings like this? Or do people sometimes get to live in places this pretty?"

He had laughed and replied: "Oh Mara, if only you had seen the temple before it was destroyed by the Jews. It was much more beautiful." Her little face had grown incredulous, as if unable to comprehend anything more wonderful than this place.

"Maybe, one day, I'll get to have a house that beautiful," she had whispered.

"As beautiful as a temple? No, my daughter. But maybe you will have a lovely home one day. A happy home is a lovely one."

The obstinate look he knew so well had entered her eyes then as she ran her chubby little fingers over the pillars. "I don't just want lovely. I want the most beautiful. And Yahweh knows that! So he'll give it to me."

He hadn't bothered trying to correct her. Arguing with a four-year-old had always seemed so pointless.

But maybe he should have. Maybe he should have taken her by the shoulders and broken her childish illusions then and there, told her she was entitled to nothing, not even breath. Life was hard enough as a Samaritan these days. She should be grateful for whatever she was given and not always be trying to get more.

But he hadn't. Mara was almost eighteen years old, twice divorced and still living in her childish fantasies. *I should have been firm with her. Should have forced her to marry someone good and steady, like that shepherd friend of Dawid's,* he lamented. But he hadn't. And now it was too late.

Chapter XIX.

A.D. 8, Sychar, Samaria, Roman province of Judaea

The Day of Atonement was the first time Mara saw the rest of her family again after her flight from Sebaste. She was scared to face them, scared to even show her face at the gatherings of people. If Amitai, or anyone from his family had seen her, she knew she would be more ashamed than she could bear.

And so Mara had donned a mourning veil. No one would ask who the woman in the veil was, or question her weeping. As she gathered amongst their people, she watched in silence, watched their lives.

She saw Dawid arrive with Zimra and their little family. She saw Eli and the new baby. And she saw Rani, a little girl of four and a half now, skipping along happily, hand in hand with Dawid, looking up at Zimra, eyes full of adoration.

The feeling that hit Mara at the sight couldn't be put into words. She felt she was being ripped apart.

How was her baby, her beautiful baby, that tall child, with the long, dark curls? Rani couldn't be so grown up. Couldn't be so pretty. So happy. Turning, Mara began to run – anywhere – just to get away from all she'd left behind. Blinded by tears, she ran.

Stopping out near Ya'acov's Well, Mara finally managed to gulp her tears to an end. She hardened her heart, forbidding it from feeling. She was done. No more the human fountain. She was so tired of weeping!

Mara picked up a small rock and tossed as hard as she could away from herself, crying out in her frustration. "Arggg! I'm so sick of this life!" She yelled towards the hills. The wind whipped the words back into her face, the trees echoed it to her in the waving of their branches.

"Aren't we all?" A voice asked. Mara whirled around, trying to spot the speaker. It was a strangely dressed man, sitting on the well's edge. His hair was dark and he wore luminous Arabian robes of bright golds and blues. But his eyes – they were the palest Mara had ever seen on a Samaritan. They almost looked like Roman or Germanic eyes, they were so blue.

She stared at him and he stared right back. His eyes were intoxicating, Mara found. She was unable to look away.

"Who are you?" She heard herself ask, her voice quavery. The man smiled a mysterious smile. "They call me Naftali, O Woman of Bitterness."

Woman of Bitterness? Did he know her name?

"What are you doing here, at our well?" She heard herself asking.

He looked quizzically at her. "Our well? What makes it yours?" He asked. "Wouldn't the Romans say it is theirs, since Judaea is their province?"

Mara wasn't quite sure how to answer. "Er, my ancestors built it. And it's on our family land."

Naftali frowned at her. "But how does that make it yours? What is to say heritage assigns it to one? Or conquest? Or anything like that? Why are we so interested in ownership anyway?" Mara thought about his words, wondering what he was getting at. She looked at him in silence as he continued. "What if we were just content to enjoy something then move on and let others enjoy it. Why is owning and belonging so important to us?"

The more Mara thought about his words, the more she saw merit in them. Naftali, whoever he was, didn't think like anyone she'd ever known, that much was clear.

"What is it that makes you sick of life?" He asked, coming back to her original statement, skipping over her question entirely.

"My first love betrayed me. My first husband accused me of committing adultery then divorced me. My second husband forced me to be his own personal business tool and made me desert my first daughter. My baby boy died and his father threw me out, after using me," Mara said hollowly.

It was more than she'd intended to say, but somehow, she just couldn't stop it. There was something about this mysterious Naftali that made her want to share her truest thoughts and her feelings.

He blinked at her, pale eyes expressing thoughts Mara couldn't read. He was an enigma, there was no doubt about that. What came out of his mouth next was not at all what she expected.

"I suppose people have told you need to be content, that the Lord gives and the Lord takes away."

She nodded and he continued:

"I think there's more to life than contentment and birthing and dying. I think life is here for us to make the most of, to enjoy. I think if we're not happy then we have a right to seek happiness, whatever that looks like. There are too many rules, too many ways of living life 'acceptably'. Why can't we feel free to just be ourselves, even if that doesn't look the way everyone else thinks it should?"

As he finished speaking, Mara found herself nodding wildly in complete agreement. "Yes, exactly! Freedom! That's what I want."

Naftali grinned. He looked like one of Sebaste's stray cats, satisfied to have found the full milk pail. "And why not take it? Why not?"

She laughed cynically. "How? Have you done it?"

Naftali stoop up, his full, flowing robes dancing out around him. As he lifted his arms and turned, the gold threads caught the sunlight. "Of course I have. I've wandered for years now and travelled to many different lands. I do what makes me happy."

"Where are you from? Originally, I mean."

"Oh, my mother is a Samaritan, like you. My father was a Roman." So that explained the pale eyes. He continued speaking. "Naturally, my father deserted my mother before I was born. I grew up as an outcast halfling, in the hill country, north of here."

"What are you doing here in Sychar then?" She asked. He shrugged.

"I want to be here. I got tired of being in other parts of Judaea where people look down on me because I'm part Samaritan. Besides, there's something about this place that seems to call me home. My family are all here for the festival. I wanted to see them, but when I did, I realized I'm not who I was when they were my family."

Mara considered his words. *Not who I was when they were my family.* The words rang so true to her now.

Suddenly realizing how thirsty she was, Mara moved past him to the well and drew up water from its depths. He stood by her, watching her intently. She felt his every glance. She was enchanted. "Will I see you again?" She asked, as she prepared to go.

For the first time since she'd seen him, he gave a genuine smile, revealing a row of crooked, but very white teeth.

"Will the wind continue to blow?" Reaching into the folds of his clothing, he pulled out a flower and presented it to her. As Mara walked away, she realized she'd never even told him her name.

* * *

From that time on, Mara was different. She didn't feel tied to her past anymore and that brought a strange sense of satisfaction. No one had a hold over her anymore and she could do as she liked.

Her mind kept going back to the strange man she'd met by Ya'acov's Well. He was not at all as handsome as Micah, or as Amitai, but there was something captivating about Naftali.

He was so different from anyone she'd ever encountered – so intriguing. She desperately wanted to hear more of his thoughts, to understand more of his way of thinking.

Naftali had engaged her mind on a new level, spoken thoughts she'd never verbalized, or even formalized in her head. All that evening, his words kept playing through her head. Why shouldn't she seek happiness her own way? Why shouldn't she feel free to really be herself?

She was able to find the resolve to meet with her family again and even to stay strong when Rani came and greeted her as "Aunt Mara". It is better this way, she reminded herself.

Seeing her Abba – suddenly so frail, and tired looking - and sitting amongst her loved ones at her grandparents home was lovely, but it all felt a little hollow to Mara. "Normality" wasn't a reality to her anymore and it felt too foreign.

The next day, when Mara went out to the well, Naftali was there again. His gaze met hers as she came over the ridge. Normally, Mara would smile and greet a person when she saw them, but not with Naftali. Somehow, it would have felt wrong. He wasn't the sort of person you tried to strike up conversation with. He had to be the one to initiate anything, Mara was sure of it.

As she approached, he stayed stationary, watching her with luminous eyes. He didn't look at her with the obvious desire with which so many others beheld her. It wasn't like that at all. He looked almost as though he was judging her. Weighing up her worth in his scales, to confirm whether or not she was worthy of his insights, his conversation.

Mara continued walking, the heavy jars slipping a little in her hands, as they became clammy. Naftali's pale gaze made her heart race, though not in the way Levi's, or Micah's or Amitai's once had. Naftali's gaze did nothing to make her feel desired.

Instead, his gaze made her desire him – his knowledge, his thoughts, his words. His approval. Mara walked on towards him and continued right past him. Her eyes met his, but she said nothing.

Naftali nodded, a small smile playing on his thin lips. Mara got the impression she had somehow passed some form of test. She bent to draw water from the well. It sparkled down below them, reflecting the morning sunlight in bright flashes. She pulled the bucket of water back to the surface and began tipping it into her jars. Naftali just sat watching her. Suddenly, he spoke.

"You never told me your name."

"You never asked it," she returned softly, keeping her eyes on the task.

He chuckled softly, and Mara felt as though she'd somehow passed another test. But he was clearly still waiting for the answer to his question. "It's Mara bat Mal'akhiy."

"Mara? So, I was right, O Woman of Bitterness. You've become what you were called."

Naftali somehow turned her to face him without even touching her. She just couldn't seem to help it. "There's a way to fix that. To change things for you."

"There is?" Mara asked curiously. She was excited to see what he would come up with.

"Think of yourself by another name – another name which I will call you also. We will find you a name with words that represent who you are, not who you have become." He said.

Mara nodded slowly. She liked this.

"Yaffa. We will call you Yaffa. Beautiful queen. That is far more appropriate for you. And it is a name you can live up to." He said decidedly.

Mara laughed.

"I like it. Yaffa. That feels nice." *He thinks I'm beautiful?* Her insides clenched.

His pale eyes appraised her yet again.

"Make sure you live up to it. A queen lives for no one but herself. She pleases herself and rules her kingdom her own way. Live that way, Yaffa, just as I am my own king."

"So don't you respect Roman rule?" She asked, cynically.

Naftali smirked at her, as if she was stupid to have asked such a question.

"Oh, you will learn, Little One. All things serve a purpose. Respecting Roman rule serves mine. At least for now. But they say the Jewish Messiah has come. Maybe that will change things and serving the Romans will no longer suit me. We have to be flexible."

Mara nodded as she tried to make sense of his words. She, too, had heard the rumours that the Messiah had been born, when she was a child. But nothing had come of it yet. Perhaps it never would.

This new idea of shaping all things in life to suit one's own purpose pushed every boundary Mara had ever known. She'd grown up in the knowledge that you did what was expected of you and no more. You never challenged authority. You never did anything outside of ordinary.

But she loved Naftali's suggestion that one could rule one's own destiny. Shape one's own future.

"You mean, we use circumstances to our advantage?" She said slowly, feeling that she was beginning to catch on.

"Exactly," he agreed, nodding. "Why should another be in control of who we are, or who we are permitted to be? We can let them think they have control of us, but inside they never do."

These thoughts were nothing short of revolutionary and somehow, Mara loved them. They made her feel brave, free and fearless. She longed to hear more, but she wasn't quite ready to put these thoughts into action. She needed more time.

"I should head back," she said slowly.

This time, she'd clearly failed the test. He looked at her with disappointment. She felt crushed. She wanted his approval so desperately.

"Alright, Yaffa. Remember, you can be a queen. But you have to take it, your life, in your own hands." He said softly. His eyes blazed a message into her own, but she could not decipher it.

"I won't forget," she said, hefting the water jars onto her hip and heading back along the dusty road. She would never forget.

Chapter XX.

A.D. 8, Sychar, Samaria, Roman province of Judaea

Over the next few weeks, Mara saw much of Naftali. He was out by the well nearly every morning. Each day, she'd stay longer, listening to him talk. Some days, they would walk out into the hill country as he talked.

Before she knew it, she was changed. She spoke differently now – more and more, it was Naftali's turn of phrase coming out of her mouth. Mara acted differently too. Gone was the depression and the anger. In its place, was a new manipulative streak, disguised in honeyed words and sweet smiles.

Yehudah and Pinchas liked this new change in their granddaughter, unaware of her deception and not noticing that she was constantly disappearing off. She treated them with much affection, was happier, and that was all that mattered to them.

Another saw through her ruse. From his distance, Shemu'el noticed the growing difference in Mara's character and disliked it immediately. She was becoming craftier. She treated people just nicely enough to get by with, whilst stripping her relationships of anything that didn't directly benefit her. Mara had never been like this and Shem wondered sadly where it was coming from.

One day, he was out with his flock when he saw two figures walking in the distance. One, was tall and bedecked in flowing robes, the other, slim and willowy.

As he approached, he saw that it was Mara and a strange man. His heart lurched. How could Mara do this? But as the man came clearer into view, he saw exactly how.

He'd encountered men like Naftali before. They thought themselves "enlightened thinkers", filled with Greek philosophy and their own self-importance. They drew people to them and convinced them to their way of thinking.

From the way Mara looked up at him, entranced, he could see that this was exactly the case. Shemu'el knew he had to do something. Before she got hurt. He only hoped she might actually listen to him.

He stepped out towards them.

"Mara? What are you doing?"

Mara stopped walking, a strange expression on her face. The tall, robed man regarded him cooly with eerily pale eyes. Shemu'el felt distinctly uncomfortable, but he knew he was doing the right thing.

Mara looked across at the pale eyed man, as if gauging how she was supposed to react. Shem did not like this at all. "I'm walking, Shem, what are you doing?" She responded blithely. The man smirked.

Shemu'el ignored him and looked at Mara.

"Are you thinking about this Mara? What would your family think? You would destroy them."

Mara laughed out loud.

"What? By walking? Very likely," she teased cruelly, eyes glistening golden at him. Shemu'el shook his head. "That's not what I mean, and you know it."

Mara tossed her hair at him. "Why don't you just go home, Shemu'el and focus on your own life. Surely you've something better to do than follow me around constantly."

He ignored the sting of her words and nodded.

"I will go, but bear in mind what I said, Mara. Think of your family. They love you. Think of all the others who this would hurt."

Her eyes became cold. "I don't know what you're talking about. You're rude to accuse me of things with no proof."

Shemu'el didn't bother to continue the conversation and walked away. *As if any more proof is needed than what I just witnessed,* he thought sadly. *Oh Lord. Mara is so lost. Please find her before she loses You entirely.*

As Shemu'el's figure and his flock disappeared over the horizon, Naftali turned to Mara. "You did well, Yaffa. Why should he, or anyone dictate what you can and cannot do? If you want to walk with a man, why shouldn't you?"

Mara glowed under his praise. "I agree entirely," she said. "Shemu'el is always trying to boss me around."

Naftali laughed. "Of course he is, he's lovesick for you."

Mara turned her head away, a little embarrassed.

"I can't help it. I've never felt that way about him."

"And why should you? You can't force feelings. You don't have to love someone just because they love you." Naftali sat down under a tree and Mara sat down beside him.

"Tell, me," he asked. "Did you love your first husband?"

"Amitai?!" Mara spat a laugh. "No. I wanted him for his money, for the status he would give me and the way he'd enable me to live a new life, here in Sychar. He was handsome enough and he was kind to me once. But I never loved him. I don't think he loved me either. He just wanted a pretty wife."

"And did you love Micah?"

Mara sighed. "I don't know. He turned my head for certain, with his handsome face and his charming nature. But now, I hate him."

Naftali looked long and hard at her.

"Yaffa, you are a queen. You deserve more than the boredom of your current life. You deserve passion and desire. Why aren't you seeking that?"

Mara shrugged.

"I wouldn't know where to begin."

She didn't say that the only person she could imagine desiring right now would be him. Though he wasn't so typically handsome, his intellect had captured her heart. Naftali smiled slowly at her.

"Ah, but I do." With that, he got up and walked away, leaving her sitting under the tree alone and bemused.

It was some days until Mara saw Naftali again. She was busy with chores and helping Zimra, who was due to have Baby Number Three in a few weeks. She was glad, despite herself, that Dawid and Zimra had moved home to Sychar.

Every time Mara went to the well seeking Naftali, he was not there. Soon, she stopped looking. Maybe he was gone. It seemed like the sort of thing he would do, just disappear one day without saying goodbye. But later that afternoon she was surprised by a knock on the door. She opened it to reveal Naftali standing there, eyes glistening with life.

"Yaffa, I want you to come with me. There are some people I want you to meet."

Still somewhat surprised that he knew where she lived even though she'd never told him, Mara put down what she was doing and silently followed him.

He led her through Sychar to the far side of the town, where she very rarely went. On the very outskirts of the town was a small, run down dwelling. It was built in the traditional Samaritan style – a square sandstone dwelling with a flat roof.

Inside were a collection of men and women, sitting around talking, some dancing, some eating, some playing hypnotic sounding music on drums. They all looked up as Naftali entered the room, suddenly falling silent. The air was aromatic with strong wine and burning incense.

"Friends, this is Yaffa, the girl I spoke of," Naftali said, holding out his hands sideways as if presenting Mara for inspection. Everyone sort of nodded and smiled in her direction, then went back to what they were doing. A whole cluster of girls made their way of Naftali's side, vying for his attention, but he wasn't interested.

In Mara's mind, she heard Shemu'el's voice – or was it really Shem's? - calling to her. *Mara, leave here now. This is not a good place. These are not good people. Leave before you fall under their spell. This is not the freedom you are searching for.* She looked around, a little upset. She should go. She hesitated.

But then she looked back at Naftali. His pale eyes were boring into her, urging her to stay. She suddenly knew that she would. She wouldn't disappoint him. She couldn't.

Tossing her hair over her shoulder as a defiant act to the voice of caution in her head, she set off across the room and found herself a seat. She had stepped over an invisible line now. She'd moved into new territory, a kind of life she'd never dared to encounter before. She was both terrified and elated. Behind her, she could feel Naftali smiling.

The next day, he left Sychar. And somehow, a piece of her heart went with him.

Time passed and things changed. Mara, despite herself, longed for a husband; to have someone to hold her tight and love her. She hated feeling alone.

And that's when it happened. She saw him, from across the crowded forum. And he saw her.

There was no mistaking the dark, passionate eyes that locked onto her own, nor the feeling that rushed through her. It was Levi. Heart hammering, she didn't know what to do. A part of her hated him for what he had done to her... But another part... Oh, how could she hate him? Levi. Levi. Levi.

She felt frozen, completely unable to move. How could she turn away when he was right there? Did anyone else exist other than the two of them? She wasn't sure.

Suddenly, there he was, right in front of her. Oh his face, did it never change? Something in the way he was looking at her now made Mara want to fly to his arms. As she had always wanted to. All thoughts of Naftali dropped from her mind, like scales from her heart.

"Mara? Mara bat Mal'akhiy?" He was asking, voice husky. "Can it really be you?" The look in his eyes was both vulnerable and pained.

"Hello Levi," she replied softly. "It's been a long time." Her breath was coming fast, but she hid it under a false bravado. She wasn't going to fall into his trap, not this time. "What are you doing here, in Sychar?" She asked.

"I... I came with my wife to visit her family..." He replied, shaking his head as the memory that he had a wife seemed to hit him. "How is your husband?" He asked, swallowing nervously. There was none of the old confidence in Levi that Mara remembered. He was completely entranced by how she looked. Her hair, so dark and thick, was bound back under a scarf, her eyes lined in dark kohl and her body was covered in a shapely palla. She knew she looked beautiful.

"My husband?" She laughed. "I'm no longer a married woman." She looked at him through her eyelashes. She could feel the power she was wielding over him, feel his desire for her.

She began to turn away.

"Mara, wait! Don't go."

She looked back at him solemnly. "Why? What do you have for me?"

He opened his mouth to speak, but she stopped him, finger raised. "I loved you once, Levi. I would have given everything for you. And in a way, I did. But not again."

"Mara, please. I'm sorry! You know you're the only one I ever wanted." He was pleading now, and Mara had to fight not to laugh. The mighty Levi ben Yehu reduced to begging – and for her.

"Well, if that is true, then you know where to find me. You know what it costs." And with that, she turned and walked away, hips swaying under her dress. She felt powerful.

* * *

"What were you thinking Mara?" Dawid's normally placid face was lined with explosive anger. "A married man? And Levi ben Yehu no less? Don't you remember all the pain he has caused you? Caused us all?"

"It's not my fault!" Mara spat back. How dare her brother lecture her! "I can't help who turns up at the door looking for me! I can't help it if he thinks me enchanting!"

"Yes, but you can help whether or not you let him into the house!" Dawid's voice cracked with emotion. "You don't think of anyone but yourself, do you Mara? What of Abba? You know he vowed never to let you be with that Sebastean. He's old Mara, do you really expect him to fight for you now?"

Mara flushed with anger. Dawid was so self-righteous, thinking he could control her life. She was his sister, not his wife or his daughter. Rani wasn't even really his!

"Dawid. Leave me be. I will make my own choice," she said through gritted teeth. She could almost hear Naftali's voice in her mind telling her that she was Yaffa, queen of her own life and it was her right to choose her own future.

Dawid's head drooped. She had broken his resistance.

"Mara, our father is dying. At least wait until he is gone before you make this foul choice. At least keep him from seeing the shame you are bringing to us all."

Mara turned her eyes away, as tears picked at them. She knew the choice she wanted to make, but she didn't want to break her poor Abba's heart. She would wait.

Mal'akhiy passed away at the end of his long illness as winter reached its height. The family mourned deeply for their kind and gentle patriarch. Only a few weeks after Mal'akhiy's death, Yehudah had a fall and within days, he too was gone. The family reeled.

It was at that point that Mara realised she was beyond caring. Life was all just a miserable joke anyway. Why shouldn't she make the very best of it that she could? Why shouldn't she be happy? Levi was all she'd ever dreamed of. Why shouldn't he be hers? There was nothing to stop her, now that Mal'akhiy was dead. Fortune may have kept them apart for these six years, but he was her first love.

Mara stood at her grandfather's funeral, thinking deeply. She was to return to her father's Sebaste town house, to organise the estate, ready for sale. When she was there, she would seek Levi out once. If he wanted her, she would be his.

Selling Achsah, her once beloved nursemaid, was one of the hardest things Mara had ever done. She kept up a bold appearance, but watching the old woman head away with her new owners – a friendly family who lived near the theatre across town – she began to cry.

This is ridiculous, Mara. She told herself firmly. *She's just a slave.*

But Achsah had never been just a slave. And now she represented another piece of Mara's crumbling life.

Mara dressed in her best stola, hair pinned up Roman-style, lips stained berry red and headed down to the forum. She made sure that Levi saw her. His chiseled face clouded with longing as he saw her leaning on one of the tall, marble pillars.

The last time he had seen her, Mal'akhiy had shouted at him, banishing him from the house. But this time, she was alone and unencumbered. He knew what he had to do.

Just seeing her seemed to change everything.

A few days later, as Mara walked through the forum once more, she heard a voice at her shoulder. "Mara." It was Levi. She turned to face him.

"I've done it. I divorced her. Come home with me. Marry me. Please." He was breathless as he spoke. "The past can stay in the past, but I must have you as my bride. No matter what. There can be no one else for me but you."

The words were carried with such urgency, such earnestness that Mara couldn't resist.

"Nor anyone else for me," she whispered in return. What had she got to lose?

Chapter XXI.

A.D. 9, Sebaste, Samaria, Roman province of Judaea

Levi and Mara were married in the courthouse in Sebaste's basilica that very evening. They spent their wedding week in a guest house on the edge of town. Mara wasn't sure she'd ever felt such happiness as she did now, in her lover's arms.

She could see now that it was Levi. It had always been Levi. As the old feelings she'd always had for him rose to the surface once more, she realized that she'd never loved anyone like she loved him.

He drove her wild. He was everything she'd ever dreamed he would be. When he held her, when he kissed her...

What she'd experienced – even the good things – with Amitai and Micah paled in comparison. Levi. Levi. Levi.

When they returned to his Sebaste town house, Mara was nervous despite herself. She feared what his family would think of her – whether they would accept her at all.

She could still see their faces as she was torn from Levi's arms by Dawid in the hippodrome all those years ago. It seemed almost as if it was from another lifetime entirely.

Yelsaventa, her old friend, her teenaged face was burnt in fire onto

Mara's memory. Guilt. Horror. Disgust. Shame. Sadness. Pride. All of those emotions, they'd been there in her lovely features.

What would it be, to see her once again? Mara nearly hated Yelsaventa for all she represented in her memory. Her lost innocence; lost childhood. Lost everything. And yet, as she always had, she longed for her acceptance.

As for the Patron and Chavvah, his wife? What would they make of Mara? Surely, they'd see her as a wicked woman, the kind who lured and tore from their wives' sides. As she sat, feet hanging down in the cool fountain in the garden of Levi's home, she realized in a sort of numb horror, and fascination that this was exactly what she was. What had she become?

Self-questioning overtook Mara as she began to wonder where she had gone wrong? Where had she gone from a desire to have the best to this strange life of finding people, of losing them, of losing everything.

Soon she had plunged into the bottomless vortex of self. Why her? Why did her life have to look this way? Be this way? Why couldn't it have worked out that she and Levi had married when they'd first fallen in love? Or better yet, that she'd never even met him.

What would Mara's life had been if there had been no Levi in it? Would she have happily married another and be living with them still, surrounded by their children? Would she have married well? Would her family have been pleased with her?

Now, all she'd managed was two failed marriages, two lost children and a third marriage that she could already feel, somehow, was doomed. And she'd lost the support of all who had ever loved her.

Dawid and Zimra had made their stance very clear – they loved her, but could not support her lifestyle, nor have her around their children. Even her grandmother was ashamed of her now. Without Mal'akhiy's or Yehudah's presence... Mara had no one left.

How was it that her life had gone so wrong? Other people around her seemed to have gotten on with life just fine. Did the gods hate her? Perhaps, like so many in the stories of the Roman deities, the gods had been jealous of her beauty and had doomed her to hopelessness because of it.

And what of her own people's God – Yahweh? Did He hate her as well? Mara had heard the words "I am a jealous God" - perhaps He had been jealous to the extent of stealing her happiness from her. He had started early, then, she mused. He had made her a Samaritan and not a Jew. He'd made her the youngest daughter and not the eldest. He'd taken her mother. How could a God such as Him, love her?

"Oh Mara, Mara, Mara," she whispered to herself "you shouldn't be thinking these things!"

The fountain's water chilled her toes to numbness as she sat there. Rather like her heart, she mused. Somewhere in between her delirious happiness at finally marrying Levi and in moving to his home in Sebaste, she'd lost all feeling. Her heart felt heavy, like stone, within her.

A new realization had dawned. No matter who controlled her destiny – be it the God of her ancestors, or the strange gods of other people, or be it no one at all – it was Mara herself who had gotten herself to where she was now. She had no one to blame but herself.

Mara had finally gotten all she'd ever wanted in life – and now that she had it, she somehow didn't want it anymore. It had cost her too much. But, once again, it was too late to change.

* * *

It didn't take long for their marriage to fall apart. Levi adored Mara, but her feelings for him had cooled to a dull toleration. The worst of it all was that although Levi longed to take her out into society and to show her off, Mara wasn't interested.

Sebaste was Romanized enough for a divorced woman to be acceptable, but Mara could still feel the distain the other women had for her. She resented the way shame seemed to shroud her – surely, they didn't consider themselves better than her, did they? Hah. Mara knew the truth of Sebaste's culture – it was rotten to the core and those who posed as the best society had to offer, they were the very worst.

She realised many of Sebaste's society had known and loved Levi ben Yehu's first wife, Julia and blamed Mara for her suffering. Mara hated the injustice of it all.

All the same, Levi dragged her along to party after party, banquet after banquet. The constant cycle of beautifying and parading and having to outdo, exhausted Mara. She was tired of pretending to be someone she wasn't. But every time they went out, on when the mask of "model wife" and Mara would pose as Levi's happy, adoring bride. Pretend her world wasn't a mess. That she didn't dream of her dead son every night, or lament her lost daughter at every moment. That she didn't miss Sychar and the memories of her old life. That she didn't long for what could have been. That the darkness wasn't threatening to overwhelm.

And as for Levi himself, the man who had once occupied so many of her thoughts and dreams, she soon found out he wasn't as exciting or thrilling now that he was hers. He no longer intrigued her. After all these years of fantasising about Levi's character, Mara finally realised he was rather ordinary underneath the mask of bravado.

Almost despite herself, Mara began to feel herself longing for new romance, deeply desiring to be wooed and won once more. She was tired of rich men like Amitai and Levi, who had life handed to them, seemingly with no problems.

She wanted someone exciting, someone thrilling. Someone who would take from her the emptiness of herself – or at least serve to cover the ever-expanding the void.

At first, it was the handsome servant from the kitchen. Mara loved to brazenly catch his eye as he stared at her and make him blush. And slowly, she seduced him. That was thrilling. The young man, perhaps a few years her junior, after he got over his terror at being caught, proved to be filled with desire for her. He made Mara feel beautiful again.

But soon, Levi began to suspect something and had the lad sent away, though he never mentioned a thing to Mara.

Before she knew it, there was another man taking her fancy, then another, then another. Sometimes things never got beyond a low-level flirtation, other times things went much further.

And yet, Levi never complained. He never even said a word.

* * *

Mara could hardly believe that five years had passed since she and Levi had married. Five miserable years. It was no use pretending otherwise. This marriage had been a huge mistake.

She was so tired of living this way.

The ever grasping for more affection, more acknowledgement, yet never feeling full. She was so sick of it all.

Levi had long since given up on seeking her heart. He seemed to be resigned to the way she was living. And somehow, that hurt Mara more. Hurt her that he hadn't tried. That he hadn't pursued her beyond her borders.

* * *

He had lost her. Before they'd even half begun, she was no longer his. That much was clear to him now. Angrily, Levi pumped the weights in the large gymnasium at the temple baths. Veins in his upper arms bulged as he strained, not with physical exertion, but with pain.

A sense of loss settled over Levi as he trained.

Mara bat Mal'akhiy was the only one he'd ever wanted. He could still see her as he had the first time, entering the garden for the banquet at his parent's home. Beside Yelsaventa she'd looked so small and yet there was something about her even then that had taken his breath away.

Those golden eyes had ignited a fierce passion within him from that very first moment, despite the innocence with which she had gazed at him.

The innocence was all gone now and Levi ached for that too. It was mostly his own fault.

He could recall every little conversation they'd had back then. He had memorized her mannerisms. The way she tossed her dark hair when she was angry. The way her eyes sparkled with life and passion. The flirtatious laughs; the shy smiles. In those days, those smiles had been for him alone.

A heaviness rested over Levi and he put the weights down. Life itself felt heavy. He suddenly felt incredibly sad. He made his way into the next room, snapping his fingers to summon a slave to massage his tired muscles.

Why had he been so stupid? He should have married Mara then and there, when they were both still young, despite what anyone would have thought of him. Though he'd had the pick of Shomron's women, he had always known he'd never be happy with anyone but his Mara.

But no. He'd played the role of fortune's fool. It had been his choice and he'd blown it.

A shudder ran through him as he recalled the first time he'd taken her into his arms and kissed her. That fateful moment. He'd never felt anything like he had then. It was her. It had always been her. It would always be her. It had felt so perfect. As if it had been "meant to be".

And then she'd been torn from him. He could still see her anguished face. Why? Why hadn't he fought for her? Married her? For so long he'd blamed her for not running away to be with him. But how stupid of him.

How could she have?

He'd have never been able to marry her if she had – the shame would have been too great. It was his fault. He should have fought for her.

On the day of his wedding to Julia, Levi had imagined her to be Mara. In place of the blonde hair and blue eyes, he'd seen dark and golden. What a fool.

He winced, as the slave rubbed at a tender spot in one of his shoulders. The calming oil being rubbed into his skin seemed to be having no effect on it, nor on his emotions.

What kind of idiot was he to think that ruining her marriage to Amitai ben Yonatan would make her love him again? Why hadn't he left well enough alone? She'd seemed happy with that arrogant, one-upping Sycharian. But no, he'd been determined to make her suffer as he had.

It was his fault that she'd become as she was now. Never trusting, never contented, never settled. He knew she was seeing other men. Everyone did. But what could he do about it?

He rose from the massage table, paid the slave and made his way through the pools to wash and robe. As he made his way through the crowded streets, a realization struck him.

You've ruined Mara. You've lost her forever. And you can never win her back. You fool.

The thoughts stuck in his gut like a knife and he had to stop, leaning up against the city wall as he sucked air into his lungs.

He loved Mara like he'd never loved another. But maybe now it was time to let go. To walk away. Maybe she'd come with him. Or maybe now she'd inflict on him what he had inflicted on her. Agony.

It was a chance he had to take. He couldn't go on like this. He'd either have to have her as his own, or leave and start a new life.

***

210

"This town is dying."

Mara wasn't really listening when Levi first spoke those words. She hardly even looked up from her sewing.

"Mara, I'm serious!" He continued. She could hear irritation lacing his voice – most likely feeling that she wasn't taking him seriously. Did she ever, these days?

"Since Herod's banishment, Sebaste is losing what little life it has left. The whole of Samaria is. Nowadays Shomron is just seen as the back country of Judaea and it's not worth anything to live here. We've got to get out whilst we still can."

"And go where?" Mara scoffed cynically. "We're Samaritans, Levi. No one wants us!"

He shook his head. "In Rome, they don't care where you're from, so long as you have money. And I've got enough money not only to be prosperous, but to be upper class. My father bought me citizenship, Mara. We could go anywhere in the empire! But I'm thinking Ephesus."

"You can't be serious!" Mara exclaimed, almost laughing, lip curling in disgust. "Leave our homeland? No thank you!"

"You don't have to come."

The words chilled Mara to the bone and she felt her heart constrict into nothingness. Again. "What, you mean, divorce me? Leave me here?" She spoke with no emotion now. What else could she expect? What else should she expect?

"Oh, come, Mara." Now it was his turn to look scornful. "As if a divorce and my being gone would end this farce of a marriage. No, we both know that was over a long time ago."

Levi's eyes filled unexpectedly with tears and he turned away angrily. "I don't know why I ever trusted you, why I ever wanted you. I don't believe you ever truly wanted me. You just wanted the life I could give you. And once you had it, you stopped pretending. Oh, I was such a fool, to give up Julia for this. For a woman like you."

Mara just took the words, having nothing to say in return. What he said was right, to a degree. Their marriage had been over pretty much before it began. But she had wanted him, once. Wanted him more than she ever could have expressed. Those days were long gone now.

Mara wasn't sure she even knew how to love a person anymore. She knew how to pursue love, that was for sure. She knew how to bask in the beautiful feelings of a new flame, how to set men's hearts on fire.

But real love? Love like that which belonged to Dawid and Zimra? No. She'd never known that. She supposed she never would.

Sighing heavily, brokenly, she got to her feet and moved to one of the windows, looking out across Sebaste.

Levi was right. The city was dying. It was time to leave, or die with it. But behind that, she knew it was also time for them to both move on, or to become ghosts themselves, in this farce of marriage.

"I'm sorry it went like this Levi," she whispered softly. "I'm sorry we never really stood a chance. I know we both dreamed of being together… But I think by the time we got there, it was too late." Her voice trembled despite herself. She'd long since promised herself it was safer never to let another know what she was truly thinking. "Maybe we were never meant to be Levi. All these years we tried. But maybe we should have just left well enough alone."

She didn't look over at him, but she knew he would be brushing his curly hair out of his eyes, as he always did when he was upset and wanted to hide it. As he always had.

"So, this is it then," he said, voice cracking. "Time to let go."

Pain racked Mara's body. Physical pain. She just nodded silently.

When they said goodbye a week later as Levi prepared to head off to the coast, ready to sail the Mediterranean, Mara felt the familiar numbness come over her. She was now a three-time divorcee. Her father was dead. Only her grandmother was left of those who accepted her. She had nowhere to go but to the family home in Sychar. She was twenty-four and all alone in the world.

Levi was taking all their slaves, all the furniture and treasures – everything. He'd left her enough money to get by. Mara almost wished he hadn't. She almost wished for nothing, wished that it could all be over. Almost.

She stood on the marble steps of the Sebastean townhouse she and Levi had shared, watching him load the wagons with their things. He'd be heading down through Galilee to get out of Judaea. So this was it.

He made his way up those steps for the final time with such a sadness in his dark eyes. And resignation.

"Goodbye Mara," he said huskily. "I wish things had been different for us." Tears sprung up in Mara's eyes. "Me too," she whispered back.

For one final time, Levi kissed her. He crushed her lips to his with such agonizing passion and regret. Regret for what they could have had, but never did. It was a kiss filled with salty tears and broken dreams. Their eyes met one last time and then he pulled away and was gone. He never looked back.

Chapter XXII.

A.D. 14, Sychar, Samaria, Roman province of Judaea

The journey Mara made across the hills to Sychar after Levi left was the worst she'd ever known. Dark thoughts tormented her and at every peak she felt drawn to throw herself off, to end it all. But she couldn't quite bring herself to do it. She was too scared of the pain.

It came as no surprise to her that the first person she ran into on her way into Sychar was Shemu'el. He was always there, in her every time of need. In her every desperate moment.

Mara was kneeling under a gnarled old olive tree, shaking uncontrollably, when he found her. She was gripped by a deep-seated terror she didn't understand. She felt nauseous and out of control.

Her breathing was coming fast, in panting gasps. Panic. Her vision was blurring and sensations fleeing from her limbs. She felt as if she was dying.

Shemu'el lowered himself to the ground next to her, just comforting her with his present.

"Mara. Breathe. Slow down," he urged her soothingly. Her muscles were seizing up now, over-oxygenation fueling her fear. Shemu'el breathed along with her, helping the overwhelming sense of panic to slow.

"God. Help Mara. She needs you right now. Help her to breathe. Help her to trust you. To know that you are taking care of her."

Finally, Mara was back in control, feeling steady again. Her limbs returned to normal and her mind was on track again.

"What has God ever done for me, that I should be grateful?" She asked bitterly. Shemu'el looked across at her in amazement. Was she really asking such a question?

She was. In that instant, pale after her panic attack and with her knees drawn up to her chest, she looked like a petulant child, dressed in her Imah's clothing.

Slowly, Shemu'el replied.

"You know, it's funny that we ask questions like that. It's almost as if one of my sheep were to ask me "what do you do for me anyway?""

Mara raised a cynical eyebrow at his analogy and opened her mouth to respond, but Shem raised a hand to halt her.

"Hear me out, Mara, would you?" He implored. A moment later, she nodded her assent. Shemu'el continued.

"If one of my sheep were to ask me such a question, I would be hurt. I do everything for them – I feed and water them, I keep them safe and warm... As for what God does for us... everything we have at all, we have from Him."

Chancing a glance to his left, he could see Mara was listening intently.

"The very air in your lungs, Mara, is only there because Yahweh chooses that it should be. And we don't really think of that as a blessing, but without it, without God speaking life into us day after day, we would cease to exist!"

Mara teared up and turned away. The talk of breath was too painful after her recent experience.

"My life is miserable. It would have been better if I'd never been born." Her words were thick with pent-up emotion.

It was on the tip of Shemu'el's tongue to tell her how wrong she was, but something urged him not to. Instead, he reached his arms around her, as a brother would his sister and just held her as she cried.

A while later, as her sobs subsided, he began to speak again.

"When I was a little boy, only five or six years old, I remember my Imah calling to me from the house. I had been outside, playing with my friends. I went to her and she said 'Tomorrow, there will be a wedding feast in our home. It will be the best party you've ever been to, my son. If you are a good boy, I will permit you to stay for all of it.'

"I grew very excited at the prospect, until my Imah continued speaking. 'But in order for you to come to the feast, I need you to help me clean out the house and the stables today, so we will be ready for tomorrow.'

I was horrified and stamped my feet and refused. Do something awful like that, when I could play with my friends and do as I like instead?! Absolutely not! I told my Imah I would rather not attend the feast, if I had to help with the cleaning.

I can still remember my mother's face at my words. She looked so sad and disappointed in me. 'Very well', she said. 'It will be as you wish'.

She did all the cleaning herself and when it came time for the feast, she shut me upstairs and wouldn't let me come down.

I cried and wailed, but it didn't change anything. My Imah let me have what I had chosen. But watching that beautiful feast and everyone enjoying it from afar, I found I no longer wanted what I thought I had."

Mara looked up at Shemu'el, confused.

"What are you trying to tell me?"

He cast her one of those deep looks she could never quite interpret.

"God has promised us the wedding feast, Mara. Right now is the time for preparing – for cleaning and waiting. The Messiah will come and one day we will be with God. We'll never even remember what it was like before the feast began. I promise it will be worth all the pain we face here. But for those who don't do what is asked of them and prepare for eternity as Yahweh has commanded... they'll be left outside. As I was. And no one wants that. I don't want to diminish your current suffering Mara. I'm not denying it. All I am saying is that if you make the right choice, one day, all the pain will be worth it..."

Shemu'el's words stuck with her as she walked away later that afternoon. Those words, paired with the water she drank from Ya'acov's Well, tasted of healing to her. It seemed to wash away the darkness and give her a little hope for the future. Perhaps she might be alright after all.

It didn't take long for Mara to come across a banker, Keren ben Yonah, a relatively wealthy widower of mature years, with a reputation of generosity. Mara had made it her business to seduce him and gain herself a place to live and someone to look after her.

Her plan had worked. She was nearing twenty-six now and whilst she was still beautiful, she was nothing compared to the younger girls. An older man had been her best bet.

Mara had known Keren all her life – he had always been the chief banker in Sychar, like his father before him. As a young man, he'd been rather handsome and strong, kind and well-liked among the people. He'd married young, a sweet, but frail girl. They'd struggled to have children, but had been happy together.

Nearing middle age, she'd finally become pregnant, but had died in child-birth. Keren had been broken-hearted, but had slowly come back to his normal self.

Mara couldn't help but feel a little smug that she'd managed to keep people from disliking her through all these marriages and the numerous changes of life she'd been through.

No one had blamed her for the failure of her first marriage. Micah's divorce had happened so quietly and out of the way, no one really questioned that either. When Levi left, everyone said he was a rascal and poor, sweet Mara had deserved far better.

But now, she realized things might change. She had only been married to Keren a few months when she began to feel bored. Mara liked the man – he was kind and cared for her well – but he certainly wasn't her equal in many ways.

She had vowed to herself when she'd married him that she'd leave her past in the past and start behaving more honourably. Mara had fully intended to be a good wife to Keren, focusing on making his home nice and on caring for him. She wanted to repay him for the kindness he'd shown to her.

However, Keren often travelled and if he didn't take his wife with him, Mara found herself longing to return to her old haunts, to get into her old trouble. She wanted to have fun and enjoy herself. She wanted to feel the wind through her hair, to enjoy the freedom of youthfulness once more. She wanted to join the traders by their fires under the stars and sing and drink and be merry...

As Mara lay in bed one sunny morning, tears rolling down her cheeks, she cursed herself. Who was this woman she'd become?

Keren was a good man. He treated her well. And he deserved far better. How could she think of searching after young lovers when he had taken her in so kindly, looked after her so well?

True, she did not desire him, nor truly love him, but what did that matter? She should treat him better – with respect at least, that was certain!

He was leaving again today, on another of his trips and she was so scared that she would ruin everything, slip back into old habits. She couldn't do that. She couldn't. But she would, she knew she would.

She heard shuffling through in the main part of the house – Keren getting ready to leave. Footsteps headed towards their bedroom and she hastily dried her eyes. He still spotted the tears on her long, dark lashes.

"What's the matter, Mara?" He asked gently. Under his thick salt-and-pepper beard, his face was lined with years, but they were kind lines, forming smiles by his eyes and his mouth. Mara shook her head, swallowing her tears once and for all. No more crying, she resolved.

"Nothing to worry about. I'm just emotional."

Keren looked deep into her eyes, gauging her truthfulness. Finally he nodded, satisfied that she was alright.

"I'm sorry I have to leave you, if you're in such a state," he said. Mara looked away. He was such a good man. How could she even consider hurting him so?

"I wish I could come with you," she said softly. That would fix everything, wouldn't it?

He smiled down at her, such a gentle, trusting smile that it twisted the knife of her guilty conscience all the more.

"I wish you could also, my dear. But this will be a rough journey and I don't wish you to endure it." He patted her hand in a fatherly manner, as he often did. Mara sighed softly and moved closer to him, just longing to be held, even for a little while. Keren was one of the few people who truly, deeply cared for her. He cherished his little wife in a way she had never been cherished.

How strange, being married to a man who gave you the relationship you'd never truly had with your father, Mara mused after he'd left a few minutes later. Though he was her husband, Mara couldn't help but view him as a father figure in her life.

He was, without a doubt, the best husband she'd ever had. Amitai had been a selfish boy, she saw now, Micah, he was cruel and self-seeking. Levi, a lovelorn man who knew nothing of caring for his woman emotionally. He was no true husband.

Keren knew she didn't desire him, knew she didn't truly love him and yet, he loved her so well. He gave her everything she needed and more, and even didn't seem to mind her reputation of failed marriages. He was a righteous man for certain. Why could she never bring herself to love him, stay with a man like him?

Why was it that there was always something inside her searching for more? To be desired, prized and honoured? To be looked at as the most beautiful, to be lauded above other women. There was something about the thrill of a new relationship that Mara found she sought. Over and over again.

Now, it was almost an addiction. She was never at peace with the same man for long. Never satisfied with one lifestyle for more than a few years, no matter how good it was.

Mara moved out of the bedroom and resorted to her usual cure-anger tactic – a walk out to the well. This was her parents' fault, for never loving her as a child. It was Levi's fault, for forcing her to become someone she was not, for being unfaithful. It all began then. It was God's fault for taking Rani away and her baby boy. For taking her father. For never giving her a truly happy existence.

At the well, she drew up water and gulped it down as if she would never stop. Being angry always made her thirsty. When she finally finished, she gasped for air, then stood, panting, as she contemplated her life. Deep down, she knew that she could blame circumstances and people all she wanted but that her way of life was her own fault. She was the culprit. She wanted to rip herself open and tear out all the rotten bits.

Somewhere, deep inside, was the real Mara. She had been a nice girl once. She'd cared for others. She had truly loved, once upon a time. *I must still be in here, somewhere,* she thought miserably. Bitterness. Naftali was right, she thought, remembering the man she'd met here so many years before. I have become my own name.

Mara longed to be free of this torment. She wished she was a simple country girl, married to her love, as Zimra was. It was strange now, to think back on the two girls growing up together.

Zimra had never changed. She'd always loved Dawid and had longed to be a wife and mother, faithful always. Mara had never stayed the same for long. She was tossed this way and that, constantly.

If only I had listened to Zimra, to Dawid, to my Abba, to Shemu'el she thought. They had all warned her before she'd married Amitai that marriage was not the key to happiness.

Were they ever right?! She sighed deeply. The key to happiness was something beyond that. And so far out of Mara's grasp. Out of her comprehension even.

She thought back over the things Naftali had told her, that she could be the queen of her own life, could be in charge of her own happiness.

Well, that hadn't worked out so well so far – all she had to show for this so-called freedom was three divorces and an insatiable thirst she could not quench. Chasing her own whims had not won her any happiness at all. But what else could she do but keep chasing it?

Mara lowered herself to sit on the well's edge, feeling weighed down by the burden of life. She wondered if she would ever feel light and free again.

A memory washed through her mind of a trip to the port city near the Egyptian border on Sinai with Micah, in their first year of marriage. There, they had seen a boat carrying Greek entertainers who had been travelling the world with a band of curious people and animals they had collected from all over.

One of their curiosities had been a small, yellow monkey in a cage. Mara remembered watching it, entranced, as it tried over and over again to escape its prison, even though that was the only thing keeping it safe from the lion in the next cage, pacing and salivating as it considered devouring the wee morsel.

Mara had asked the trainer why the monkey was so determined to escape though freedom would carry it into danger.

The tall, dark African had laughed and answered that the monkey had once lived in the wild and longed for that once more – though getting out of the cage would not return it home and would only bring it pain.

Was it stupid? She had asked. Couldn't it see the lion waiting to eat it? He had replied no, it wasn't stupid, just stubborn. It was determined to have something that would not be good for it.

Mara felt like that monkey. She longed for romance, to find love. She wanted to feel important and of more worth than others. She was determined to have something that would not be good for her. Why couldn't she just be content?!

Chapter XXIII.

A.D. 18, Sychar, Samaria, Roman province of Judaea

Keren returned from his business trip in but a few days. Mara was glad to see him home, for it meant a cap would be kept on her emotions and upon her behavior. She would not do anything silly whilst he was there.

As soon as she heard word of his return, she rushed out into the street to meet him, excitedly running into his arms. His warm smile and tender eyes were a balm to her aching heart. He bear-hugged her and picked her up as if she were as light as a feather.

"Oh, Mara! What a welcome!" He said, laughing heartily. Mara found herself laughing along with him. "I'm glad you're home, Keren!" She said, her face buried in his shoulder.

The eager welcome had, of course, been partly as she said, but there was more to it than that. It was a reminder to her that she had not dishonored him this time. She'd made it thus far.

People passing by in the streets watched the reunion fondly. Keren was a much loved member of Sychar's society and his wife was like the city's daughter. It pleased people to see them both apparently so happy.

Once they were back in their home and the servants had finished unpacking Keren's spoils, the two of them sat down to dinner. It was a comfortably silent meal, both of them lost in their own, contented thoughts.

Keren eventually broke the silence as he held out a package to her. The look of boyish excitement on his face endeared him to Mara so much.

"I saw this in one of the bazaars we visited and I couldn't help but get it for you," he said. "I hope you like it," he added, hunching his shoulders around anticipating her reaction.

Thrilled, Mara pulled away the plain cloth that wrapped the gift and brought out a beautiful necklace, silver, set with stones in all kinds of blues. She gasped slowly, completely taken aback by the loveliness of the gift.

"Keren, it is beautiful," she said quietly, tears pricking the backs of her eyes. He smiled broadly.

"It's lapis lazuli. I hoped you would like it," he said shyly. Mara leant across and kissed his cheek.

"I do! Thank you."

He helped her do the clasp of it around her neck and nodded approvingly as he admired it on her slim, olive-toned neck. "It looks as though it were crafted just for you, Mara," he said.

She smiled. It felt nice to be given gifts and to feel beautiful. The necklace was heavy and cool against her skin.

Keren sighed. His face clouded a little before he spoke again. "I'm sorry to do this to you, Mara, but I'm afraid I'm leaving again soon. I have to travel all the way to Corinth this time. I'll be away for a few months and I cannot take you with me." He admitted slowly.

Mara felt herself go cold. No! She wasn't sure she could hold out for a few months. This couldn't be happening.

"Are you sure I can't come?" She asked, biting her lip. Keren shook his head with another sigh.

"I wish I could Mara, but the folk I'll be travelling with are rough and will not take kindly to a woman journeying with us. Besides, you would be mistreated and I couldn't bear that. I want you to be well looked after and safe, not at risk. I know you'd enjoy seeing the sights and experiencing the journey, but you're too beautiful. The men would punish you for it, or take advantage of you," he said ruefully. "What kind of husband would I be to subject you to that?"

She knew he was right – it would not be safe for her to go. Still, perhaps it would be better for her to be with him and in danger, than to stay here and risk falling into old patterns once more. But she couldn't very well tell Keren that.

* * *

The weeks passed swiftly and all too soon for Mara, Keren was leaving again. She walked out to the edge of town to wave farewell to him and the caravan of servants. The sun was still rising as they wound their way out of town and on, into the distance.

Mara sat on the ridge watching them for a while, a hot desert breeze ruffling her hair. The early morning sun cast their shadows far across the sand around them, bobbing up and down as the camels moved. The further away they travelled, the more convoluted and misshapen the shadows became.

Mara felt terribly alone as she watched the shadows grow longer and longer, then merge with the horizon. Alone with her thoughts. Alone with herself. It wasn't a place she wanted to be in.

She sat out on her hilly vantage point long after the band of travellers had disappeared into the distance. The dry yellowed grass began to heat beneath her as the day wore on.

She watched the sun turn the sky from grey to brilliant, bright blue, as bright as the necklace Keren had given her. It would be a beautiful day, she was certain of it.

Summer was at its height and it was hot, even so early in the morning. She could see the heat-haze flickering over the sandy earth below her feet as she headed back into town alone.

Their big house seemed so empty to Mara. She ran her fingers wistfully over the stone walls as she wandered her way through the courtyard and past the small water pool in the inner garden.

The little atrium, the large inner sanctum – it felt so much more vast and empty today. The kitchen in the back courtyard, the servants' quarters, currently unoccupied, with Keren on his trip, their own rooms up on the second story. Emptiness surrounded her.

Mara went and sat on the roof, watching people hustle and bustle below, as they began their day. She couldn't quite bring herself to do the same.

She wished that she had a maid servant here, to keep her company, to keep her from her past. Keren had often offered to hire one for her, but she'd always declined, saying she was more than capable of running the home on her own. If only she'd accepted.

Sniffing determinedly to herself, Mara got to her feet. *Well, I didn't accept and I need to move on with life*, she thought. She climbed down from the roof and made her way into the heart of the home. Looking around her, she tried to gauge what needed doing. Everything was pretty well in order and she wasn't sure where to start. She just knew she needed to do something. Or she would go mad.

Days rolled on after Keren had left. Mara managed well to fill them all with productivity and visiting her friends. It wasn't the days she minded, it was the nights. Being alone with yourself, she discovered, was difficult. When there were others around, you never had to focus on your own thoughts, or face what you'd become.

Mara thought a lot of Keren, tried to visualize him and his routes. Corinth, in Greece, was a long, long journey from Palestine – she remembered it all too well from her trip with Micah.

It would not be a safe journey at all. Keren, and his companions would be in danger from robbers, wild animals, pirates on the sea, and....

She stopped herself considering any other potential outcomes. Mara was not passionate for her current husband, but she truly did love him, in a way. If something were to happen to him... No.

Days spun by one after another, rolling together and forming an endless web of sameness. Each day played out identically, as she'd long since given up practicing the Sabbath rest.

Mara would get up early, fetch water from the well, return home, clean, cook, wash and tend to the animals. It wasn't too bad a life, as long as she kept busy, kept her thoughts at bay. In the afternoons, she would get out, visit friends, or walk, or visit the market. She'd visit Dawid, Zimra and the children.

Before Mara knew it, the first two months of Keren's travels were over. He must have reached Corinth by now, she thought and was surely working hard, trading and expanding his financial empire. She hoped it wouldn't be much longer until his return, or at least until news of his whereabouts came.

One afternoon, Mara finished all of her chores early and headed out for a walk in the hills. She enjoyed the slightly cool breeze blowing down off the mountains as she went, for it had been a hot day. As she approached the road to Sebaste, she watched a gathering of Jews pass by in the distance, doing their utmost to keep away from any of the Samaritans.

She snorted. It always made her laugh the way the Jews turned up their noses at her people, avoiding them completely if possible.

It seemed strange to Mara that Jews and Samaritans had once been brothers. But much had changed since those times and the split of kingdoms. Now the Jews, with their thick accents and strict rules, thought themselves better than the Samaritans.

They thought they knew better what God wanted, that He wanted their worship in Jerusalem and that to worship on Mount Gerizim made the Samaritans inferior. They'd steer well clear of the Samaritans, if at all possible.

Mara enjoyed the irony that all good Jews had to pass through her people's land. The Samaritan hill country was in the heart of Palestine, in the very middle of Judaea and was the only way to get from the coast and beyond, into Jerusalem. And Jews had to go to Jerusalem if they were to give proper worship.

She lifted her head high as she made her way past the Jews on the road. They wouldn't make her feel ashamed!

The Jews averted their eyes and swerved so as to avoid touching her, or even her shadow. Once they were past, one of the youngest men at the back, turned and called in his foreign accent "Samaritan pig!". Mara returned his remark with a rude gesture and kept walking.

Up ahead stood another man. Even from this distance, Mara could see that he was laughing at her. Feeling infuriated, she pulled the gesture at him also and went to walk straight past him.

The man just stood in the road, still laughing.

"Oh Yaffa, you haven't changed a bit," he said once she was beyond him. If it hadn't been for his name for her, Mara wouldn't have known it was Naftali.

Slowly, Mara turned around. Yes, it was him. He looked very different from the last time she'd seen him. Gone were the flowing robes. His hair was short, Roman-style and his clothes nowhere near as flamboyant. In fact, what he was wearing was all round very Roman – a short, plain tunic and sandals. His face was clean shaven.

But there was absolutely no doubt it was the same Naftali. His pale eyes bored into her, as they had always done. Some things, clearly, never changed.

This couldn't be happening now.

He grinned at her shocked expression and paced towards her, still chuckling at her expense. "Have you missed me Yaffa?" He asked as he arrived at her side, arms held out in a welcoming gesture.

Mara felt tense, disturbed and unsure. For so long, she'd longed for Naftali to return, to be her teacher and advisor once more. But now that it had really happened, she wasn't sure she wanted it any more. Her life had begun to change, she had remained faithful to her husband and she wanted to continue to be. For Keren's sake.

"Have you missed me?" Naftali asked again. Mara snapped out of her trance. Naftali. The man whose words had plagued her dreams more than anyone else. How much she'd thought of him! She blinked up at him, long-lashes fluttering.

"Does the wind continue to blow?" She replied huskily. She wondered if he would recognize the words he had spoken to her by Ya'acov's Well, those ten years before. His intense expression told her he did. That she had spoken well, that she had pleased him.

There was something else in the way he looked at her that had never been there before. Before, she had been so young, so naive – she had been a child in his eyes. And now, she was twenty-nine, a woman by anyone's standards. Something about the way he looked at her now told her that he had noticed and it was effecting him.

"Yaffa, I hear you have married again. To an old banker." He said, eyes fixed upon her face. Slowly, she nodded, waiting for his disapproval. "And, are you happy with this?" He asked. Mara snorted in an unladylike manner.

"Well, I'm far happier than I ever was with my previous husbands. Keren treats me well, gives me everything I could wish for," she defended herself, subconsciously fingering the stone studded necklace encircling her slender neck.

Naftali looked at it. "I take it this is a present from your doting husband." Mara nodded. "And do jewels make you happy Yaffa?"

"He's kind to me," Mara defended again, pouting a little.

Naftali backed off.

"Don't argue with me, not now that I've just arrived back. You're the queen of your own life, remember?" Something in his eyes told Mara that she was queen of more than just that now. Something in what he was saying spoke of jealousy. He was jealous that she was happy, jealous that it wasn't him creating her happiness, creating her.

Slowly, she turned and started walking back to Sychar. She glanced back over her shoulder and beckon to him with her eyes. To her delight, he followed. Mara felt powerful. The one who had been her teacher was under her spell.

"So, Naftali, what have you been doing with yourself since you left us those years ago?" She asked. He shrugged. "Oh, this and that," he replied airily.

Mara laughed. "Oh come on, you'll have to give me a better answer than that – you've been gone a long time! You must have done something!"

Naftali shrugged again. "I haven't really. I've traveled around a lot, met some interesting people and stayed out of trouble. I went back home to the hills for a while, spent some time in Italia, some in Greece and so on," he said.

"In Italia?!" Mara exclaimed. "No wonder you're looking so Roman these days!" Naftali looked a little uncomfortable at her observation – the first time she had ever seen such an emotion flick over him.

"I hadn't really thought about it," he replied.

They continued on into the town, winding their way through the twisting back alleys that characterized the outskirts of Sychar. It felt a little uncomfortable being with Naftali again after all this time, but also sort of natural. It was just like it used to be and yet, not at all.

"Where are you staying?" Mara heard herself asking.

Naftali shook his head, looking rueful. "I had thought to stay with all my friends, but I hear that house is owned by someone else now. I'll figure something else out though," he said.

It felt strange to walk through town with another man, one who wasn't her husband. And yet, no one seemed to noticed. Part of Mara wished someone would; someone would call out to her, call her away or even call Naftali to them.

She knew she should beg her leave and never allow herself to see this man who so enchanted her again. But she also knew she wasn't strong enough to turn away herself. She needed someone, anyone, to be her voice of reason. *Please help me.* She didn't realize it was a silent prayer.

Chapter XXIV.

A.D. 19, Sychar, Samaria, Roman Province of Judaea

Morning dawned pure and fresh. Mara lay quiet in bed, listening to the birds cheeping in the date palm outside her window and musing to herself. Listlessly, she rolled onto her side, stretching out her tired muscles. Today was a new day and it would bring new things. She sighed softly to herself.

Last evening, Zimra had met her on the road, inviting her to dinner. She had agreed and Naftali had slipped away, into the streets, saying he wouldn't be back for a while. It was strange how it had happened, almost exactly what she'd hoped for.

For now, Mara was managing to keep her resolve to be an honorable woman. However, she wasn't sure she could keep it up. Already she could feel the pull upon her heart to seek Naftali out. To walk with him. To hear his thoughts. To be his.

She'd been through this all before. She wanted it out of her head. Mara wanted desperately to remain here for Keren, to repay his kindness to her.

She rolled out of her bed, wriggling her toes to wake them up. She made her way out into the courtyard and splashed icy, morning water onto her face. Immediately, she felt alert, ready to face the day.

Mara spent the morning trying to distract herself, by washing all her clothes and cleaning the house from top to bottom. She loved to see the dirt wash away with the water, to see the shine the floors took on as they lost their coat of dirt.

She sang as she worked, songs of her childhood – anything to keep her mind from Naftali. She thought back to her frustrated explosion to Zimra last night, as the two of them had walked back to her home. "Why do our hearts always want what is not good for us?" Zimra had been confused by this, unable to fathom Mara's meaning.

After a while she had replied finally that she thought perhaps one desired what one shouldn't have because they were fallen descendants of Adama and Chava. She suggested Mara could perhaps head over to the synagogue and make an offering to atone for her unfaithful heart.

Mara's immediate response had been "absolutely not!" She had not been back there since the Day of Atonement five years ago and she wasn't going to return now. But perhaps it was her only hope.

As she cleaned, she mulled it over and over in her mind. She wasn't sure she wanted to return to the synagogue. So many bad memories had their root there, it seemed.

But what if she could do it? If atoning for her sin would make her more faithful, ensure she was a better person, then it was her only hope. There was no doubt in her heart. She went back to her scrubbing.

Before Mara knew it, it was getting dark and she realised she'd been working all day. A feeling of pride swelled within her at the fruits of her labour so apparent in front of her eyes.

As for the synagogue? Tomorrow. Tomorrow she would go.

Early the next morning, her hands trembling, she dressed in a plain, white linen robe, then covered her hair with a rich, red and gold wrap – a gift from Keren.

She applied make-up to her face, especially her eyes, trying to ensure they appeared darker than usual. They would be the only part of her left out on view and she wanted to ensure they would not be recognized – she was well aware they were her most distinctive feature.

Satisfied that she looked different, Mara pulled numerous gold bangles onto her slender arms, so they chinked together musically as she walked. She felt mysterious and beautiful.

Amitai would not know the mature and hidden woman before him and neither would any of his fellow priests, she was sure of that. She would go, stay just long enough to make her sacrifice, then return home. Mara was determined to stay in the synagogue not a moment longer than necessary.

As she made her way into town, she found herself shaking a little. She'd walked out this way before, but it had been years since she'd come as far as the synagogue.

Mara had to laugh at herself. She hadn't realized that there were still so many unresolved hurts in her heart over what Amitai had done to her and over her lost baby.

The entire walk was painful. Images of the past kept flicking before her eyes. First, she remembered how happy she'd been on her first night of marriage. She remembered how Amitai used to hold her, the sweet things he'd whispered into her hair.

She remembered how he would look each morning after he woke, all bleary-eyed and groggy. She remembered the way Basemath had treated her – kindly, yet also demanding her absolute obedience, her perfection.

She recalled the way Amitai had treated her in Sebaste. How it felt to be abandoned.

Mara remembered the moment Rani entered the world – excruciating pain, followed by sheer bliss. Her perfect little baby. No child had ever been as beautiful as sweet Rani and none ever could be. No pain could compare to losing Rani. And then, of having her baby boy die…

She had not been able to conceive again. She and Levi had tried desperately for children, each secretly hoping it would mend the great rift torn between them and mould their hearts together once more and yet, none had come. It was almost as if Mara's body refused to conceive, subconsciously knowing the pain was too great.

"Oh Rani, my baby," Mara whispered to herself, tears slipping down her cheeks under her scarf. Every time she saw her daughter, now a beautiful young girl, she felt crushed. It would have been easier for Mara if she had died, as Yathom had. The pain would be less then.

Her heart ached deeply, but she kept her feet moving forward, on towards the synagogue. If this sacrifice would help things, then she would do it, no matter how hard it might be for her.

The familiar sights and sounds of the forum met Mara with rush as she arrived. It was all as it had ever been. It felt strange being back here. She recognized every house on the way to the synagogue, every roadside shrine to local gods, every stone on the street.

She recognized people too, as if out of a bad dream. Could it really be nearly fifteen years since last Mara was here, at the synagogue?

As she pushed her way through the streets filled with crowds of people and animals, noise and confusion, part of her began to wonder what it would be like to see Amitai again. Would he still be so handsome? She doubted it – he had been eighteen when they'd married, twenty two when he'd sent her away. He must be pushing his mid-thirties now.

She chuckled bitterly to herself at the thought. Where had all this time gone? So long now since he was the most desired bachelor in all of Shomron. She wondered if he was happy with his new wife – her once-friend, Hadassah.

As Mara walked, she began to feel rather brave. Part of her began to want Amitai to see her. She wanted to prove to him what he'd missed out on when he farewelled Mara bat Mal'akhiy. He'd missed out on having the most beautiful, most vivacious and charming wife in the land. She, however, had missed out on nothing. Marrying Amitai had, most assuredly, been a mistake.

As she approached the hill where she had once lived, Mara slowed. Slipping under the overhanging roof across the road, she paused and looked back. The house was the same. Still white and tall, still with the pillared courtyard and creepers growing up the walls.

Memories of mornings spent sitting on the roof looking out over the town flooded her mind. She'd spent four years there and yet not even once had it felt like home. A slow smile crept across Mara's face, beneath the scarf. It had never been home.

And somehow, that thought made her feel free.

She turned on her heel. She had left nothing of her heart here.

Mara walked fast, determinedly. She couldn't believe how different she felt after making that realization. She wished she'd come back to this street long ago, to set her mind free.

When she reached the synagogue, she sneaked in with a pack of other women. Some of them she recognized, but none of them realised who she was, she was certain of it.

The Samaritan synagogue was still as dark and cool as ever. The ridged pillars loomed overhead, making the people seem small and insignificant.

In the back, the priests were gathered, as they always had been. Yonatan – once Mara's father-in-law – was still high priest and he stood in the centre of the building, next to the altar. He looked older, but just as intimidating and regal as ever in his long, loose-fitting robes. Mara stood at the other end of the building and watched for a while as the priests administered people's offerings and chanted.

There he was. Amitai. He was at the far end of the gathering of priests. He looked just the same, Mara realized with a small chuckle. Time had been kind to the golden boy of her people.

Now, as she gazed at him, there was no skipping in her heart, just resignation. Beauty is never what it seems. Oh how obvious to her now was the pride in his brow.

Taking up her grain offering in her hand, Mara headed towards him. Some vindictive part of her lesser self wanted it to be Amitai who oversaw her offering. The same part of her wanted him to recognize her, to see what he had lost.

She walked slowly, deliberately towards him, offering held out in a bag.

A bored expression on his face, Amitai took the offering from her and emptied its contents onto the altar before him.

"What are you atoning for?" He asked, his voice as disinterested as his face. Mara spoke in what she imagined to be a beguiling, mysterious tone.

"My past. I'm atoning for what has been done to me and for my heart."

At the sound of her voice, a strange look passed across Amitai's face and his eyes flickered, as if he were trying to place it, but he said nothing.

He began to make the offering, looking hard at her all the while, trying to figure out how he knew her, but she kept her eyes lowered.

Inside Mara was laughing hard, having forgotten the true reason for her offering entirely. Once he had finished, she would tell him who she was.

A tall, thickset man bumped her from behind, causing her to stumble and drop her scarf. She spun around to frown at him and he muttered an apology. The man looked up and his eyes met hers. Shock filled her as clearly as it did the man.

"Mara?!" He gasped, cynical laughter written in every line of his face under his thick beard. It was Micah. Time froze. Not Micah. She hadn't wanted to see him. Not Micah, the cruel man who had hurt her so badly. Her heart pounded. Why was he even here?

"Mara?!" Amitai echoed. She spun back to face him and saw disbelief. No, this wasn't how she'd planned it. She'd wanted him to be awed and regretful, but as she looked at him now, she didn't see either of those emotions in his handsome face, only disgust.

Suddenly, she had to leave, to run. She couldn't stand here with her first two husbands – the "betrayed" and the betrayer – both staring at her.

Pulling her scarf back across her face, Mara ran. She fled. Out of the synagogue, away, never to return. She should have never gone back. The past was not a place to visit.

***

Mara sat crumpled down by the well sobbing her eyes out. Shemu'el watched her cry and felt his own heart twist at her pain. What had happened to her now? Her life seemed never to let up on her.

Shem shook his head sadly – this had been coming to her from her very youth. There was no doubt that she'd brought all of this, whatever it was, upon herself.

Sob after sob filled her. He couldn't just leave her to cry like this, no matter what she'd done.

"Mara?" He said gently. She lifted her head and looked up at him. Black smudges of eye make-up ran in tiny rivers all down her cheeks and her face was pale. She looked pathetic, completely undone. "Oh Shem," she whispered, lower lip trembling.

He couldn't help himself, he held out his arms to her. Mara buried herself into them, clinging on as if she'd never let go. She cried and cried, head buried in his chest.

He just held her in silence, hoping no one would come to the well and think anything improper of him. Mind you – Mara had done many improper things over the years and no one seemed to blame her, he thought.

But no matter what Mara had done, he couldn't help but love her, beyond her faults. He longed to fix everything for her, to make her mistakes alright, to clear away her pain. If only he could.

Eventually her sobs slowed and she sat up, hiccuping and wiping her weepy eyes with her scarf. She glanced across at him, clearly a little embarrassed.

"I'm sorry Shemu'el, I don't know what came over me," she said formally after a little while.

He smiled gently at her, squeezing her hand. "It's alright Mara, this happens to the best of us sometimes. Life is heavy."

Mara snorted a little laugh. "You can say that again!" She shook her head slowly. "Oh Shem, I've been such a fool. I've thrown my life away in my pride and I don't know how to fix it. I'm trying desperately to change, to be faithful to Keren, to be an honorable woman, to be the true Mara that's somewhere deep in side of me, but I just can't seem to do it. I feel so lost. I've messed up so much, I just don't know how to change."

She looked up at him with her streaky make-up covered face, still red from crying and her gaze pleaded with him.

"What should I do? How do I fix everything? How do I turn my life around?"

She looked so very vulnerable, so like the child he'd once known in that moment. She didn't look like a woman of over a quarter of a century, married to her fourth husband.

Her dark hair framed her slim face, only intensifying the youthful illusion. He swallowed hard. She was not a girl anymore, she was a woman, a very desirable woman and she needed him. He would have to be careful.

He extracted his arms from around her and got to his feet. He reached out a hand to Mara, pulling her up as well.

"You should get home and rest Mara," he said thickly. "You'll feel better after a sleep, I'm sure."

She nodded, using her scarf to wipe the last few kohl rivers from her face. "I'm sure you're right. There isn't much I can really do, is there?"

Shemu'el shook his head.

"You can't change your past, that's for sure. All you can do is hand it over to God and keep moving forward. You can't just be better because you decide to, either, you have to trust God with that as well. We cannot change ourselves for the better Mara,"

They walked in silence for a while, then Mara nodded slowly. "Yes, I suppose you're right. I'm not sure I'm able to give it all over just yet though." Shemu'el sighed. "Well, you need to know it is the only way Mara. It's the only way any of us can have hope."

Mara nodded again.

"I went to the synagogue today, to offer a sacrifice, to make it all right again. But I bumped into Amitai and... and Micah," she admitted heavily. "And I just lost control." She shrugged. "It just seems to be the way of my life, every time I try to fix things, I only make them worse."

Shemu'el sighed deeply. Oh Mara. He thought. Her heart was trying desperately, but she was so lost. He longed to help her change, but knew it would be no use. Only God could do miracles.

They arrived at her home on the backstreets of Sychar and he waved to her as she went on into the courtyard. He watched her all the way up the steps. Finally, she turned back to him and gave a watery smile.

"Thanks for listening, Shem, you are wonderful."

He returned her smile. "God chooses where we'll be at any given time. He just placed me in the right place for when you needed someone."

Mara offered one more heart-stopping smile to him. Then, she was gone.

As Shemu'el made his way home, he ached all over. Why? Why? Why did he have to feel this way about her? Why did he have to love a woman like Mara?

"Yahweh, help me!" He groaned to the sky. He couldn't just go home, feeling this way. He guided his sheep into their pen, then set out to the home of the one person who might understand what he was going through. To her brother, Dawid.

His friend welcomed him with open arms. Zimra was settling the children for the night, so Dawid suggested the two of them head out for a walk. They walked long into the night, as Shemu'el poured out his heart to Dawid.

"I love her." He began simply. "She is married and can't be mine, I know that. But still I love her." And then it all came pouring out, expressed as he'd never dared express to anyone but God.

"I love her above all else and all I long for is for her to love me in return. But that is the thing with love – you cannot force it. If I try, any fragments of love that have been forged will shatter and it will all be over." He sighed deeply.

"I love Mara more than I love myself. Though she is no longer a virtuous woman, that is how I see her in my heart, how I long to see her again. I remember her beauty. I remember her true heart. Now, it is hidden away and I long more than anything else, to coax it out, to see the real Mara once more. But I cannot. I love her more than that. And her love cannot be forced."

Dawid shook his head slowly, feeling his friend's anguish of heart.

"I understand, my brother. Mara is still Mara deep within, though she has lost the essence of who she was. But my sister isn't the right one for you, Shem. You should let it go now."

Shemu'el shook his head.

"Don't you think I've tried Dawid? I've prayed and prayed that Yahweh would take this from me. But He has not."

Dawid shoved his friend in a brotherly way.

"I guess it's as you say, love cannot be forced." Then his eyes became serious once more. "But I will be praying for you. For freedom."

Chapter XXV.

A.D. 19, Sychar, Samaria, Roman province of Judaea

It was nearing three months since Keren had left on his journey and a few weeks had passed since Mara's trip to the synagogue. She was feeling more in control of herself, more normal.

She was worried though, as she'd heard nothing at all from Keren. It was unlike him to be gone this long without sending word.

Mara was preparing her dinner one evening, when she heard a knock on the door, she went out to open it, only to find a pair of pale eyes looking intensely back at her. Naftali.

He came in before she could say anything, making his way into the kitchen and sat down. Mara followed him through, a little taken aback, but used to his erratic, unconventional manner of behaving.

She returned to her cooking as if nothing had happened, as if he hadn't just appeared back in her life after a month of absence. This was how their relationship worked. He just sat in silence.

"I can't focus. I'm not happy Mara," he suddenly blurted out, using her given name for the first time since he'd first called her, "Yaffa".

She looked up sharply, surprised and unsure how to proceed.

"I am heading back to Italia in the morning, but I couldn't leave without seeing you again."

Italia? He was really leaving. Mara could feel the blood pulsing steadily in her temples. Naftali always came and went, why was he coming to see her this time? "How long will you be gone for?" She asked shakily.

Naftali shrugged. "Perhaps forever. I think I will be happier there than here, in Palestine."

Mara continued to stir her stew.

"If that's what you want, then I'm glad for you Naftali," she said. "I hope you'll be happy." This felt strange. Why was he coming to farewell her this time? She decided to just ask him outright.

"But after all the times you've come and gone, why this time? Why this time do you say goodbye, seek me out? I don't understand. What's different this time?"

Mara didn't need to turn around to feel him rise to his feet, to sense him make his way across the room towards her. Part of her knew what was coming, even before it occurred.

For the first time ever, Naftali touched her, his hand light on her shoulder, as he turned her to face him. She was trapped between him arms, looking straight up into his mesmerizing eyes. They pierced her, tore her open to her very core.

"Yaffa, my queen." His words caressed her as he lifted his other hand and gently, almost tenderly, brushed her cheek with his long, cool fingers. "How could I leave you without saying goodbye?"

Mara knew she should turn away, tell him to go now, anything, but she found herself powerless in his embrace.

Every good part of her told her this could not happen, but every other part of her insisted that it was and it must! She could not bring herself to move, she was rooted to the spot.

"It's always been you, Yaffa, surely you know that," Naftali continued, fingers now lacing their way into her thick curls, pulling them out from under her headscarf. "From the first moment I saw you. Yes, I've been

243

with other women, but none have pulled my heart as you do. You're...
You're what keeps me coming back here," he breathed. Mara said
nothing. The fiery passion that lit his eyes was transferring its power to
her. She was shaking all over at the war going on inside her.

"You're like my other half, Yaffa, the other wanderer, dreamer and
visionary. I've never met another woman like you. No other so strong in
herself, so determined to achieve her own ends. And when I saw you last
time I was here, out on the road to Sychar, I saw how you'd grown and
changed," he continued, cajoling her.

"You are so beautiful, perfect, like a goddess."

Desire rose within her, completely against her will. This one man
she'd never been able to resist. She'd thought him under her spell, but in
truth, she would always be under his. When his lips descended towards
hers, she didn't turn away. She didn't pull back as he drew her close to
him, holding her tight as he kissed her, over and over.

Mara's head began to spin and the confused voices within her told
her both to get out and to give in. Eventually, she pulled away, panting.

"Naftali, I cannot do this," she said, turning away.

Confused, he turned her back to him. "Why not Yaffa? Don't you
know I love you? Don't you know you're the only woman I've ever loved?
Am I not enough for you?"

A frustrated tear made its way down her cheek. She felt the weight of
the world on her shoulders. She knew she must send him away, but she
wasn't sure she was strong enough.

"You are more than enough. More than my dreams Naftali. Surely,
you must know I wanted to be yours from that first day I met you. Yet
I thought you did not want me. I thought I could never win you. But I
cannot. I'm married. You know that. I cannot dishonor my husband this
way."

Ever so gently, Naftali captured Mara's tear on his finger and pressed
it to his heart. His eyes held such a look Mara knew she couldn't bear

it much longer. "Yaffa, do I not make you happy? Don't you deserve happiness? I will be gone by morning. Can I not leave with the knowledge that we had one, perfect night together, you and I? Your husband need never know."

Temptation wore a face in that moment. A thin, bony face with pale, mesmerizing eyes.

Before Mara knew it, she was back in his arms, his lips swapping secrets with her own. Her head began to spin again as he caressed her and drew her closer still. She no longer had the ability to resist what was going on.

Later that night, they lay side by side on the bed that Keren and Mara shared, gazing into each other's eyes.

Naftali had made Mara forget that the world and its troubles even existed. He ran his fingers through her long hair, eyes filled with adventure never leaving her face.

"Yaffa, you are my one unforgettable thought," he whispered to her. She dipped her head shyly.

She could hardly believe that after all the years of longing for him to come to her, for him to claim her as his own, he had. And no one need ever know. This night and their secret love might remain just that, a secret, forever.

When she awoke the next morning, the bed beside her was cold and empty. Naftali was gone, leaving her alone once more, with just her memories.

She pulled herself up, out of bed and wrapped a blanket around herself, before making her way up onto the roof that overlooked Sychar.

She looked out over the city as it woke. The light was still low, but her neighbours were all up and moving. The old man next door was washing in his courtyard, his wife beating out old rugs from their balcony.

Mara watched as he called up to her, a term of sweet endearment. The old woman gazed down at her husband with such a look of love and fondness that Mara's heart began to ache. Wasn't that how love was supposed to look?

True love shouldn't up and leave.

Down in the street below, she saw the shepherds herding their flocks out for a day on the hills.

There was Shemu'el at the back of the pack and Dawid walking alongside him. They waved up to her as they passed by and she returned their wave. Such good men. Like her husband. And she was a filthy woman.

But why should she feel so guilty merely for loving? Shouldn't it make her happy, as Naftali had said? Why should it be wrong to love a man? To delight in his embrace, in his raw, undisguised desire?

She pulled her blanket tighter around herself, despite the heat. She longed for some comfort. Mara thought she'd sought comfort in Naftali's arms last night, but she found today, the experience left her hollow. She had not changed. She was the same unfaithful woman she'd ever been.

Poor Keren. He didn't deserve this. She closed her eyes against the pain. It would be better for him never to have met her. What kind of woman would treat a man like him in such a way, with such contempt, after all he'd done for her?

Why was it she thirsted for attention so much? Why did she have to always be seeking more? Could she never be content just with what she had been given?

She cursed herself bitterly as she descended back into the house and began to prepare for the day. She dressed in a plain tunic, with her hair wound back, no nonsense. She was in no mood for fussing over her own looks today.

Once Mara was set for the day, she gathered her jars and headed out to the well, hoping that the walk would make her feel better. It did. The warm air was cooled by a gentle breeze and it lifted her spirits.

She made her way through the dusty streets, blending in with the other housewives out on their errands.

As Mara walked, it struck her that she wasn't so very different from any of the other women around her. Perhaps, her sister-in-law, Zimra was more virtuous, but most of these other women were much like her. Maybe they didn't all move through men like a reaper through a wheat field, but certainly they had their own faults. And none of them had endured her life. She was not a bad person truly, she just suffered because of her past. That was what had made her the way she was today – she could not be blamed. Indeed, no one would blame her.

The further Mara walked, the more certain she became that she was not a bad woman. She began to reason that it was not true adultery – not if it was only once and Keren never found out. Naftali was gone. It would never happen again. She would probably never see him again.

But she would always have the memory of their night together. Truly, it was the most beautiful one she'd ever known. Naftali was a veritable enchanter, the way he strung words together, making her melt like a candle and mould into whatever form he seemed to desire.

Mara laughed softly to herself. If anyone else had tried to shape her life she would have turned them away, told them not to bother, that she'd figure her own life out.

But Naftali was irresistible to her. And secretly, a part of her was glad that this was the case. She had enjoyed the way he made her feel – desired, longed for, interesting. Unforgettable. It was that feeling she had spent her entire life searching for, she realized.

First, she had sought it in her parents, then in those around her. As she had grown older, she had began to seek it in men – first in Levi, then Amitai. When that failed, in Micah, then Levi once more, then a whole raft of others. Naftali had been her ultimate goal ever since she'd met him. But now that she'd been his, he was gone. Was this truly all there was to such a powerful connection between two people?

She hauled the water up to the surface of the well and drank. She was so very thirsty today. How is it that someone can mean so much to you and yet the feelings never, ever lasts? Mara wondered internally.

She watched the water drip off the edge of her cup and fall back into the well, far below.   Love and desire is never enough. You can never get enough. Just when you think you've had your fill, you realize it has all run out and you must seek it all over again.

Her walk back to town with the heavy water jars was a slow one that day. She felt lethargic in the heat.

Mara was suddenly so tired. She was weary of life and the monotony of it. She could just never be truly happy for more than a few moments at a time. It all seemed sort of pointless. A never ending cycle of chasing love, being loved and happiness. Completely pointless and unattainable.

Chapter XXVI.

A.D. 19, Sychar, Samaria, Roman province of Judaea

A knock on her door midmorning a few weeks later changed everything. Mara put down the dish she was in the middle of washing and opened the door, hands still dripping, to find a solemn-faced young man she didn't recognize standing before her.

"Are you Mara, wife of Keren ben Yasriel?" He asked gruffly. She nodded.

"Yes, I am. What can I do for you?" The youth cleared his throat awkwardly and stood shuffling his feet a few minutes, clearly unsure how to proceed. He was a gangling young thing, with greasy hair and an awkward manner. Clearly, she overwhelmed him.

Mara waited patiently. Eventually the young man raised his eyes to her face and slowly exhaled. Something in his gaze made Mara's stomach lurch. Something was wrong.

"Madame, I am sorry to be the one to bear such ill tidings to you, but your husband's ship has been wrecked off the coast on his homeward journey from Corinth. There were no survivors."

And with that short statement, Mara's world began to come crashing down around her. She gasped and lurched backwards, nearly toppling over.

Suddenly, the world began to flicker in and out of focus. The young man began to fade before her eyes. She could vaguely hear him saying:

"Madame? Madame?" but it was getting softer and softer.

She would not faint. She could not faint. She forced herself to breathe and gradually the world stopped spinning.

The earnest young man looked concerned. "Are you alright?" He questioned, eyebrows knitting together under his tangled mop of greasy hair. Mara took another deep breath and nodded.

"Yes. I'm just shocked. My husband is dead then and all our servants? All his possessions gone?"

The boy said nothing, but she knew this was the truth of it. There was a silence that seemed to go on forever and ever.

Eventually, the young man began to speak again.

"Ma'am, you don't need to fear for where you will live, nor what you'll live on, for Keren has left you everything in his will. It was his lawyer that sent me to you, you see."

Even in death, her kind husband had taken care of her. She did not deserve such a man.

Mara nodded her understanding to the young messenger and he hurried away, leaving her to stumble into the house alone. She went up into the bedroom she and Keren would never share again and found her way under the covers on the bed. She did not cry. She had no tears.

Poor Keren, what a way to go! She thought, sadness gripping her heart. And once again, she was alone in the world, husbandless. At least Keren would never know about her unfaithfulness.

Mara lay there, completely still and wrecked with pain. Late in the afternoon, Mara heard a clattering out in the courtyard and Zimra's voice calling out for her.

"Mara? Oh Mara!? Where are you?" Footsteps inside the door told Mara that she had entered the house. Heaving herself up from the bed,

Mara walked unsteadily out into the doorway, hagged and pale.

Zimra paused for a moment, an expression of heartache and deepest sympathy etched on her features. She rushed to Mara, arms open.

"I'm so sorry Mara. I came the minute I heard. I am so, so sorry," she repeated, hugging Mara tightly, rocking back and forth as she held her.

In Zimra's kind arms, Mara felt something give way within her and a tumult of sobs rising in her throat. Before she could check them, they exploded out of her – she cried as if her heart had broken in two.

Zimra sank to the ground and held Mara as she wept, crying along with her. The tears flowed on and on. Mara didn't know she had so many tears still inside her.

She wept for Keren, wept that he was gone and she'd never get to see him again, or let him know how much she truly appreciated him. She wept for herself, that she'd lost such a kind and gentle advocate, a true friend.

She wept for all the loss she'd ever experienced. She wept for Rani. For Yathom. For her father. For the years she'd lost with them. She wept for Micah and the way he'd broken her heart. She wept for the way Amitai and Levi had treated her. She wept that life was not what she'd expected. Not what she wanted. And then she just wept.

When she could cry no more, Zimra helped her into bed and urged her to sleep. And sleep, Mara did. She slept the sleep of the dead until just before dawn. Then dreams came.

The dreams were mostly of Keren, with Amitai also there and Micah and Levi and Naftali, Shemu'el, Dawid, her father - all the men she'd ever known it seemed. They haunted her so she awoke more tired and in pain than rested.

Sweet Zimra had made her a meal and left it on the kitchen table. There was a beaker of water there too. She knew Mara so well. The meal tasted good after yesterday's lack of hunger. Mara still hurt inside and yet, today she felt as if life might go on. Yesterday she had felt as if it never could.

"Keren is never coming home." She spoke it aloud, needing to hear it.

"I am alone again and he will never be here again." There, it was said. This was real. She was a widow now. She'd been a divorcee three times over, but never a widow. Somehow, it felt much the same.

In some strange way, she felt betrayed by Keren. He'd promised he would return to her and he had not. He'd broken his promise to her, just as every man before him had. Maybe it was her destiny to be promised things she would never get.

* * *

A few weeks later, Mara realized something that chilled her blood. She'd missed her monthly cycle. This couldn't be. Her heart started hammering, as she counted back the days since she'd last had a flow of blood. Forty days at least. It was too much.

Perhaps it was the grief that was doing this to her, she thought desperately. Maybe that had simply caused her to miss out on having a flow at all this month. She would be back to normal next month, surely.

A few days on, as Mara was walking in the market, buying some spices she needed for her kitchen, she passed a food house. Usually, she loved the smell of cooking, but today it made her stomach turn.

She hurried away from the market, trying not to look too conspicuous. She made it around the corner into a back alley, just in time to violently lose the contents of her stomach over the filthy ground.

Shakily, she wiped off her mouth and made her way upright again. This was not at all like her. Mara normally had a sturdy constitution.

A thought came into her head, causing her stomach to clench again and she bent over, retching. This could not be the sickness that came with a pregnancy, could it?!

Walking as fast as she could, Mara headed home, slamming the door behind her. She leant heavily against it, breathing deeply as she tried to keep from panicking. She remembered how she had felt when she had been pregnant with Rani and Yathom. No. This couldn't be. It was only one night. Surely she wasn't pregnant after just one night!

Four and a half months had passed since she'd last been with Keren. If she truly was pregnant, no one would possibly believe that it was his child once she began showing.

Everyone would finally know what kind of woman Mara bat Mal'akhiy really was. She would be hated forever. Keren had been a well-liked man. If she was suspected of committing adultery, she might even be stoned.

The very thought had her retching again, running for the latrine at the back of the home. She crouched beside it, feeling sweaty and miserable. What had she done? *You fool, Mara!* She cursed herself. What had she been thinking? No! This was a disaster and all of her own making too. How could she have been so stupid?

As the pattern of smells making her sick became more regular over the next few days, Mara realized that she was, without a doubt, pregnant. Her life would be over. There was no hope left for her.

All her life she'd gotten away with living just how she pleased and avoiding all repercussions, but this time, there was no way out! She knew that she would be punished for this. The people of Sychar would see her suffer for the wrong she had done. And she deserved no less.

Resignation to her fate filled her as she left the house, heading out to the fields. She just needed to get out and clear her head. There was a baby growing within her and it would have a terrible life – shunned along with its mother. If they were allowed to live at all...

"Naftali!" Mara cried to the wind. "Why did I believe you? Why did I ever think that it could have worked, that we could have gotten away with it?"

She stumbled out to a ridge and lowered herself shakily down under a tree. She shivered violently, although it was a warm day. She felt desolate. Hopeless.

Lowering her head, she looked down, cradling her stomach in her hands.

"I'm so sorry, little baby," she whispered. "I'm so sorry. You should never have been and it's not your fault. It's all my fault your life will be terrible and you'll have no father. No one will ever respect you, you will be scorned. I'm so sorry. I wish I could fix it all. But I can't."

Tears flowed silently, freely down her cheeks as she spoke. There were no great, violent sobs this time, just resignation, pain and self-hate. Mara felt lower than a worm. She felt like the biggest harlot this world had ever seen. In a way, she may as well have been.

"Mara?" A soft voice behind her called. "Mara? Is everything alright?" Sniffing, Mara dried her eyes and turned to see Shemu'el. Dear, sweet Shem. Always right there when she needed someone.

"Can I do anything to help you?" He asked, his face filled with concern for her. Mara sucked in a breath.

"No Shem. I'm not alright. I'm far from it. I may as well tell you, for everyone will know soon, then my life will be over."

His face lined as he tried to comprehend her words. Mara sighed deeply, trying to work up the courage to confess what she had done.

"I'm pregnant Shemu'el."

"Pregnant?! But how?"

She could see him mentally counting the months since Keren had left.

"I've been despicable Shem. The worst of the worst. I committed adultery. I lay with a man who is not my husband and now I am paying the price."

Shemu'el looked at her with a deep understanding as he took in her declaration.

254

"Oh Mara. They will kill you when they find out," he said, pain filling his face.

She nodded bravely, though she couldn't quite prevent her lower lip from wobbling slightly. She knew as well as he did the customs written in the laws of their people. Death by stoning was what rightfully awaited her.

"I know they will. And it's no more than I deserve. I am a terrible person, Shemu'el and I can't bear to go on with this life anyway. Naftali came in to the house and I didn't know how to ask him to leave. And then, one thing led to another. But it was only once. Why is it that once has to be one time too many?" Mara asked, bitterly.

Shemu'el reached out to her and she buried herself in his arms. The tears came again then and she cried and cried. Shem just sat up on that ridge and held her. All the while, he was thinking.

When she finally stopped crying, he spoke.

"Mara, I don't want you to take this the wrong way. But there is a way in which I might help you. Please don't think I'm suggesting this for any reason other than your own well being..." he trailed off, too embarrassed to even finish. Mara looked up expectantly at him with red eyes and spiky, wet eyelashes.

"Well, I was thinking, if, er, if, um, you marry me today, then no one need know." Now that he'd said it, he couldn't stop speaking, garbling out the rest of his statements.

"No one will think anything strange of our marrying – I'm still unmarried and you aren't too old. People here know I've cared for you for many years, I'm certain people will just think I finally convinced you to be mine. And as for your baby, I promise, Mara, I could love it as my own."

Mara felt her heart soar as she listened to him. He was so kind, so generous. And this might just save her. Shemu'el was offering her a lifeline. She would be plucked from death, free. She began to cry softly again and he looked panicked.

"Please don't cry Mara, I'm sorry, truly I am. I was only trying to help. I wanted to keep you from danger, that's all. Please believe me!" He said, clutching at her hands. Mara shook her head, tears still flowing.

"No Shem, you don't understand. I'm crying because I'm so thankful. You have no idea..." She trailed off as she began sobbing again.

"Oh Shemu'el. You are my hero. You have saved me." She choked out. Relief washed through her, filling her with peace for the first time in days. In fact, she felt weightless. She hugged Shemu'el tight. Rather surprised, he took a moment to return the gesture.

*　*　*

Part of Shemu'el couldn't help but wonder what he had just done. He had just agreed to marry Mara, the girl he'd always loved, not because she would be a wonderful, virtuous wife, but because she needed him. He'd agreed to hide the fact that she was expecting a baby before they married, to bring the child up as if it was his own.

It was Naftali's baby, that strange, wandering man that Mara had always been obsessed with. That didn't surprise him in the slightest.

Poor, foolish Mara. Why had she always been so easily swayed by people? He found himself angry beyond words with Naftali, taking advantage of Mara's weakness in this way. And even more than that, for in leaving her to bear the burden and the consequences alone.

He had been waiting for many years to find a woman he wanted to marry, but always, Mara's face had come into his mind. He'd never been able to see another woman the way he saw Mara.

Perhaps, he reasoned, as he looked down at Mara's slight form in his arms, this was the reason why he'd never found anyone else. Perhaps God had never allowed him to find another woman so that now, in this moment, he might be here to rescue her.

*　*　*

That evening, in the sight of two of Sychar's elders, Shemu'el and Mara were married. It was a short, simple ceremony. It hardly felt as if the two of them had truly been joined in the eyes of God, but that was the case. They were now one.

Earlier that afternoon, as they'd walked their way back into Sychar, they began to make practical decisions. They would live in Shemu'el's home and rent out the property left to Mara by Keren.

Shemu'el lived in a small, traditional stone house, built into a row of other houses, near the edge of the city. The two of them spent the afternoon moving Mara's few possessions over to the home, then visiting their families – Mara's grandmother and brothers and sisters and Shemu'el's parents.

All the relatives were incredibly surprised, but delighted all the same. Dawid and Zimra in particular were thrilled to hear the news.

"So, Mara, you've finally realized what a special man Shemu'el is, huh?" Dawid said, clapping Mara on the back affectionately. "It's only taken you over a decade and four marriages to notice!"

"Dawid!" Zimra exclaimed, embarrassed at her husband's bluntness. Mara just laughed, knowing her brother well enough to know he meant no offence.

"You're right, Dawid. I am a slow learner, but I know for absolute certain that Shemu'el is a man beyond reproach. I am blessed indeed," she said, smiling up at Shemu'el. He smiled back at her, his dark eyes full of unspoken words. Only the two of them knew the depth of what he had done for her.

Zimra blinked her eyes fast, keeping tears of joy at bay. She clasped her husband tenderly around the waist. "Oh Mara, that is so sweet! I'm so happy for you. I hope this marriage is a blessing to you both and that you will be as happy as Dawid and I are together," she said, reaching up to kiss Dawid's cheek.

Mara sincerely hoped they would be.

And now, here they were, truly husband and wife. It felt a little awkward as they headed back to Shemu'el's house after their marriage was confirmed by the elders. Shemu'el had always been a close friend to Mara and she'd never thought of him in a romantic way. She knew he had always viewed her in that light, so she wasn't quite sure what to expect.

Mara wasn't sure she could fake romantic feelings for him, if that was what he would want. She was exceedingly grateful to him, but even that could not make her conjure up something that was not a reality.

Shemu'el unlocked the door and led Mara on into her new home. She had seen it earlier today as they moved her things, but it felt strange to be here now, knowing this was her dwelling place. She looked around, nervously. The roof was low and the walls close, but it somehow felt cosy and more homely than anywhere Mara had ever lived.

Shem shrugged his shoulders, obviously feeling a little embarrassed. "I know it isn't much, especially after what you're used to, but I hope you'll be happy here. I'll do everything I can to make you feel at home."

Mara smiled and reached out to squeeze his hand gently. "Shemu'el, I love it. And I am so grateful to you, anywhere would make me happy. You have saved my life, there are no two ways about it."

Feeling relieved to the extreme, Mara began to explore the little home properly, enjoying its little cut stone window and carved arch doorway. She entered the narrow kitchen, delighting in the strangely shaped nooks and crannies.

Much to her pleasure, the kitchen was well stocked with herbs and spices. At the back of the home was a small bedroom. It looked cozy, with its simple pallet. This was a nice home.

It felt strange, lying down to sleep at Shemu'el's side. Mara felt a little bad that he had given up his life to marry her – this was her fifth marriage, making her hardly the blushing, virgin bride – and yet he had never married. This was his wedding night and he had not tried to touch her even once.

As they lay in the silence, Shemu'el in the far corner of the bed, Mara across on the other, she looked up and noticed something she had not seen before. On the roof was an ornately painted tree, each branch intricately woven with leaves, each one delicately and precisely formed. The paint used was almost golden, from what Mara could make out. It was a truly lovely image.

"Shem, who painted that tree?" Mara asked, awed at its beauty.

"I did," he replied huskily. She rolled over to look at him in the dark. She could hardly make out his expression, but his discomfort was clear.

She reached out for his hand, trying to put him at ease. "It is beautiful. I don't know that I've ever seen a more beautiful painting. You have a gift," she breathed. "What does it mean?"

"I painted it when I was younger," he began shakily. "I painted it to remind me of the trees in the garden of Eden at the beginning of time. God gave Adama and Chava instruction, told them what was permitted, what wasn't, yet they followed their own wills, not His guidance. Look where it got them, where it got all of us. I painted it to remind me that God has shown us the way, which tree to choose, I just need to be strong enough to choose it," Shemu'el said, voice still full of emotion.

It was clear to Mara he had just laid open a piece of his soul to her. She knew she would never forget the wisdom he had just offered to her.

"And do you choose the right tree?" She asked softly. He shuffled around for a bit, trying to form words to answer her.

"Mara, I painted that tree the day you married Amitai," he said, surprising her entirely. "I painted that because for as long as I can remember, I loved you. I wanted to have you for my wife. But you were searching for other things, things I could not and would not offer. Besides, you didn't want a man like me as your husband. I painted that tree to remind me that God knows what He is doing when life doesn't go our way, doesn't go to plan."

He sighed in the darkness. "It is a long time now, since I first painted that tree. Eighteen long years in which I have tried to forget you every day of every year. Eighteen years in which I have not been able to. Each time I struggled with discontentment, with longing for you to be mine, I painted another leaf, another branch, another aspect to the tree. With each stroke of my paint brush, I reminded myself that God knows better than me. He is in control of my life and He has planned out each step along the way. He knows better than I which way I am to go."

Mara listened in silence, her heart clenching for this incredible man, so devoted and honourable. She felt tears slipping down her cheeks again, but she did not check them. Shemu'el continued.

"You see Mara, God has taken care of you in your time of need through this. If I had been able to forget you, to marry someone else, I would not be here to help you, now that you needed someone. You would be in deep trouble. But God has used this to save you. I believe He will have saved you from your sin for a reason. He's planned it all out from the beginning."

He turned to face her, reaching out a hand, and brushing her hair from her cheek.

"Don't think this is easy for me, Mara, lying next to the woman I've longed for since she was a girl and doing nothing, not touching her, just respecting her. I'll admit that this is a struggle. But I love you more than for your captivating beauty. I love you more deeply than that. Mara, I am able to love you this way because God has shown me. He has given me insight to see how the tree represents our own free will. We, all of us, have the choice to choose the right tree. I have tried to, with God's help, each and every day. You can too, Mara. We all have the choice."

Mara sighed shakily in the dark. "Yes, I understand Shem. If only I was as good a person as you," she said, rolling over. She'd seen a new side of him this day and it unnerved her a little. How could anyone be so honourable and good? Surely, it couldn't possibly be real. It just didn't make sense to her that it could be. But she knew Shemu'el and she was sure that it was.

Could he truly have loved her all these years? She didn't know it was possible to really love someone that much. Granted, Zimra seemed to love Dawid with that kind of devotion and Dawid loved Zimra equally well, but they were the only ones she knew. Other couples fought, or divorced. Other people did not remain content. She, of all people, knew that.

Her heart could not comprehend that anyone could love a woman like her. She was unfaithful, unkind, selfish, brazen and at times…

"Why me Shemu'el? Why me, of all the women you could love?" She asked, unable to help herself and desperate to understand. "I'm not a good person. I'm not constant, I focus on myself − forget others exist − I can be awful really, I don't…"

"Ah yes, but you are more than that," Shemu'el cut her off. "I love you beyond the imperfections I see, Mara, for I saw who you were as a child. I've seen glimpses of who you truly are, hiding somewhere within. That is the woman I love, the hiding one. If only she would come out for all to see, no one could help but love her."

His words touched Mara deeply. How anyone could care that deeply about another was beyond her. As she finally dropped off to sleep later that night, it was with a peaceful understanding that she was loved, even in her imperfection.

After Mara had fallen asleep, Shemu'el lay awake for hours. He simply couldn't sleep, not with Mara just across the room, under his very roof. He had not really considered how difficult this would be.

She looked so beautiful lying there, contented and sweet, sleeping soundly. Her features looked perfect to him. Long eyelashes lying against pale, soft skin. Slender nose, delicate rosy lips. Those lips called out to him, making him ache inside, but he resisted. She was too precious to dishonour by forcing. He wanted her to come to him, to want him.

Silently, he prayed as he watched her sleeping. He prayed that God would transform her life, help her to see things in a new light, to see that there was far more to life than happiness. He also prayed for himself, that God would make him patient.

Her little feet poked from under the blankets at the end of the bed. So small, almost childlike. He'd never studied her feet before, but as he stared at them tonight, he saw that they were just like the rest of her – beautiful, delicate and very much in need of looking after, protecting from the hard path.

Chapter XXV.

A.D 20, Sychar, Samaria, Roman province of Judaea

The first few weeks of her marriage to Shemu'el were fairly uneventful. Mara tried hard to adjust to life as a poor shepherd's wife. She was determined to be a good wife to him, to make up for the sacrifices he had made for her – cooking, cleaning and generally making life easier for him.

Her morning sickness continued a few weeks more, but it was not as bad as it had been when she carried Rani, or Yathom.

It took Mara some time to start showing the baby within her and she was thankful for that. If she wanted people to believe that it was Shemu'el's baby, she needed it to take as much time as possible to show.

The baby carried low within her, well hidden by the folds of her clothing. She could feel the little one growing and along with it, her love for the child also grew.

Shemu'el announced to their families that Mara was pregnant with a convincing grin and with much holding Mara tight. People were delighted for them, wishing them all the best and teasing them for "being busy". No one guessed that it was all a hoax, a sham. Shemu'el played his part to perfection and there were no words to express Mara's gratitude.

For the most part, the two of them lived together in a companionable manner. Friends, as they had ever been. Mara felt sorry for Shemu'el, knowing how hard it must be for him that she was his wife and yet only in name. But Mara was not ready for anything more than that. She was too scared of hurting him, more than anything else.

As the days went on, Mara was delighted to feel the baby moving within her. Excitedly, she called Shemu'el to her, wanting him to share this special moment with her. She grabbed his hand and lowered it on her belly. She watched his face as he felt, for the first time, the child moving within her. The look of awe on his face touched her deeply.

"That's our baby Mara," he whispered. "That's our little one." Tears sprung to Mara's eyes as he spoke. Our baby. He was accepting her child as his very own. There was no mention of Naftali, no accusing, just acceptance. "Isn't it incredible to think that a child is forming right there inside of you?"

Mara giggled softly.

"It's the strangest feeling. Another life, right here inside of me. And so tiny!"

Shemu'el left his hand on her belly, feeling the baby, which was full of movement.

"How long until we get to meet it?" He asked, his voice still filled with awe and love.

"Not for another four or so months," Mara replied, calculating in her head. "Hopefully a little longer, especially if we want people to..." she trailed off, not wishing to speak the reminder that the child was not Shemu'el's.

Shem got up from the ground where he had been kneeling and moved to sit beside her. "Mara, you need to understand something. We don't need to convince people that it is my baby. Because in my mind, it is. When I agreed to marry you, I knew you were expecting. I married you knowing and in doing that, I've claimed your child as my own as well. When this baby is born, no matter what it looks like, no matter its blood, it will be my son or daughter as much as it is yours. You don't need to worry about that."

Mara, filled with wonderful emotions and joy, suddenly longed to hold Shemu'el close. She leaned into his body, silently thanking him once again. She'd said it all before and he knew her thoughts, but he didn't know how very much this meant to her. That her baby would not be born fatherless meant the world to her.

She looked up at him and started to lean her face towards his, her lips leaving a sweet kiss on his. She could feel him melting beneath her lips, but he stopped her, lifting a hand up.

"Mara, wait," he said, eyes bright, and tortured with passion. "You don't have to do this. I don't want you to feel you have to do this in order to thank me. I want you to kiss me, to touch me because you want to, because you love me, not because you think it's what I want."

Mara leant in and kissed him gently again.

"Sweet Shemu'el," was all she said. She hoped that would be enough answer for him. It was.

* * *

The months of Mara's pregnancy sped by. She was thankful that she didn't begin truly showing until the very last month before the baby was born. And even more to her delight, she went overdue.

The pangs of labour didn't come upon her until nearly two weeks after the due date she had predicted for herself. This made her only a month and a half early in other people's eyes, which was normal enough.

A number of the local women had planned to attend the birth and assist with it, but the baby came fast, in the middle of the night.

Shemu'el, filled with the anxiety of a first-time father, had wanted to go and get someone to help, but Mara was too scared to let him leave her side. So it was he who caught their baby boy as he burst into the world.

The child was healthy and strong from the very first, bawling loudly at his rude removal from his comfy home. Both Mara and Shemu'el cried as they held their little boy together.

Mara named him Raphael – God has healed – for this child had mended her hurt over losing Rani, and Yathom.

Raphael was born with the big blue eyes all babies have and pale brown hair. His skin was fairer than Shemu'el's, but similar to Mara's. She could only hope no one would look closely and see differently.

The time she and Shemu'el shared with their new baby in the early hours of the morning, with the flickering light of the candles dancing off the walls, were precious ones. Raphael fell off to sleep almost immediately Shem had swaddled him and laid him in Mara's waiting arms.

Mara and Shemu'el watched him sleep in pure delight, before drifting off themselves.

When dawn came, Shemu'el made his way into town, proclaiming loudly to anyone who might listen that he was now the proud father of a son!

* * *

As Rani had once been, so many years before, Raphael was an easy baby. He behaved well and was cheerful most of the time. Mara was a much happier new mother this time, with so many women around her to help her care for him. She was double the age of most women birthing children now, but somehow, that didn't seem to matter.

Shemu'el loved the child and would often take him from Mara when he returned home in the evenings, playing with him, or just cradling him whilst he slept.

To Mara's dismay, Raphael retained his blue eyes long after he was supposed to, but no one seemed to think anything of it. They would just comment how beautiful his eyes were and wonder if it was passed down from a further back generation, as his Aunt Zimra's grey green eyes were.

As Raphael grew, so did Mara's love for him. He was her redemption in so many ways. Having Raphael kept Mara from becoming distracted by life, or from getting complacent. She loved the cheerful little boy and treasured each moment with him.

As a toddler, he would often curl up in her lap in the late afternoon and fall asleep. She cherished this sweet time, for once Shemu'el arrived home, it was as if she ceased to exist. Raphael loved his "Abba" more than anyone else and would follow him around, imitating him, all day if he could.

Shemu'el loved the way Raphael loved him, treating him as if he were his own flesh and blood, just as he had promised Mara he would. Everyone loved Raphi. He was irresistible.

Before Mara knew it, Raphael was three years old. It was a bittersweet thing for her, to recognise that her little boy had grown so big and that it was so long now since Naftali had left.

Rani had been gone before she reached three years of age, Yathom dying far earlier and it felt strange to Mara that she should have a child of that age again, nearly sixteen years later. She was pushing thirty years old now, terribly old to have had her "first" baby.

Mara wondered if Raphi would grow up asking questions about her past, about why she was so much older than his friends' mothers. She hoped not, that his childhood innocence would last forever.

For now, it was enough that he loved Shemu'el as his father, and adored his mother, regardless of her age and past. Love was what bound their little family together.

Chapter XXVI.

A.D. 24, Sychar, Samaria, Roman province of Judaea

But it did not last. It seemed to Mara that nothing good ever did. Raphi was approaching five years old now. It never failed to amaze Mara how fast time slipped by. She had been married to Shemu'el for five and a half years. How long now since she'd been a desperate widow, pregnant to a man who was not her husband, so long since Shemu'el had rescued her from her fate of death.

It had been a good five years, Mara mused, as she washed their clothes in a large bucket, the morning sun kissing her cheeks. She had never come to truly love Shem the way he loved her, but she did care for him, much as she had for Keren. It wasn't true happiness she had in this marriage, rather safety and a home for Raphi.

She hoped Shemu'el was happy though. After all, he'd given up everything for her. It felt strange to be so in debt to someone, yet for them to have no expectation that she repay them.

Mara didn't really like it. She always felt that she owed Shemu'el, no matter how many times he reassured her that she was an entirely free woman.

Raphi was a Daddy's boy through and through. He simply adored

Shemu'el and wanted to follow at his heels everywhere he went.

Mara began to feel a little jealous of the relationship her little boy had with his surrogate Abba. She felt left out and sad that Raphael always wanted his father to do everything for him.

In order to distract herself from her jealousy, Mara began to occupy herself with other things – such as ensuring her home, left to her by Keren, was well looked after and had suitable tenants.

Her first tenants moved out and she was determined to get the house all spick and span before new ones came. She spent many days cleaning, mending, tidying and polishing. The house had never looked better. She was proud of herself for all her hard work.

It didn't take her long to find a new tenant. A Jewish man, run away from his people, came to Sychar from Jerusalem in the south, looking for a home. He was also hoping for a housekeeper to care for it, as he had fled without his wife and was calling himself unmarried. Someone from town sent him over to Mara's house, to enquire with her.

The knock on the door surprised Mara. She was wearing her apron and her hair was tumbling from her headscarf when he arrived, soot from the fire on her face. She looked up with a start, trying hurriedly to rectify her appearance. The man stood in shadow in the doorway, face obscured.

"Excuse me, I'm looking for a woman name Mara bat Mal'akhiy. I was told she owns this home?" The man asked. His voice had a lilting tone to it.

Mara swept her headscarf off her dark curls and retied it. "That's me," she said, offering what she hoped was a friendly smile. "How can I help you, sir?" He stepped a little further into the doorway. "Well, I'm looking for accommodation. Are you able to assist me with that?" He asked. He was not as tall as Shemu'el, but he was still substantially taller than Mara. He was as tanned as a field worker, but his hands were smooth and unhardened by the work of the land. He must be wealthy,

Mara realised.

Mara lifted her arms and gestured at the house around her. "Well, this home is for renting and I would be happy to show you around, to see if it is to your liking."

The man nodded his approval. "Yes, I would appreciate that."

Mara smiled and hurriedly put away what she was doing by the fire. "Please follow me sir and I give will you a guided tour."

She showed him all the rooms, indicating any special features, but mostly keeping silent in order to let him think. Once she'd taken him everywhere, she returned to the kitchen and sat down.

"Is it satisfactory?"

The man — he had said his name was Eber ben Natan — took the seat next to her.

"Yes, I like the house. The only thing is, I was looking for a home with a house keeper," he said solemnly.

Mara nodded, wondering if it was merely her imagination, or if the man in her doorway was flirting with her. "That could be arranged. I only have one child and he is out with my husband all day, so I have the time to keep house for you. I can also cook meals for you and do your shopping if that is the kind of thing you would be needing."

Eber nodded back, his face thoughtful. "Yes, that sounds like it would be acceptable. What would the payment be?"

Mara named an amount for the rent and added a figure for her services. Eber considered it for a few moments, then nodded a second time. "Yes, I will take it! When am I able to move in?" He asked. "Any time from tomorrow, I suppose," Mara replied, smiling. She was glad to have a project upon which to focus.

Perhaps, she dared hope, this would give her a sense of purpose once more! The prospect thrilled her. Mara had always been the sort of person who needed more in life than simply keeping a home and looking after her family.

By the next day, Eber had moved his possessions into the building and Mara had taken up her new position as housewife at home and housekeeper in Eber's home. Mara enjoyed the hustle and bustle it brought, the excitement of having another person in her life to care for. She was planning to be the best housekeeper Eber had ever had.

At first, it was a bit of an adjustment cooking and cleaning for two homes each day, but she soon formed a routine, caring for her own home in the morning, sending Raphi out in the fields with his father, then heading over to Eber's home to work.

Quite often, it meant she was late home to get Shemu'el and Raphael's dinner, but they were kind enough not to complain.

And so Mara once more fell into the trap so many other women had fallen into before her. It was almost without realising it that she found her fickle heart turning towards another man yet again.

Mara had always longed for admiration and affection from those around her and couldn't resist encouraging it. At first, she thought nothing of Eber other than caring for his home, but then she began to notice little things in the way he treated her, that made her think he was beginning to have feelings for her.

He was always exceedingly complimentary of all she did, of her cooking, her cleaning, or how nice she kept his clothing. He started talking to her more and more, asking her about herself, asking her thoughts, seeking out her opinions and stopping what he was doing to deliberately engage in conversation with her. Mara knew she was being pursued.

It wasn't that Shemu'el didn't appreciate her hard work around their home, or try to talk to her. It was just that she was so used to him. He had always been there and, she reasoned, always would. He was more focussed on Raphael than on her, anyway. Eber pursued her in a new and exhilarating way. He excited her emotions simply by walking into a room and smiling at her. Seeing him somewhere she had not expected to see him always made her heart skip beats, or sent her stomach into flips.

Mara hadn't meant for this to happen. She had had no intention of leaving Shemu'el, no intention of ever looking at another man again, not after what had occured with Naftali. But somehow, it happened.

Eber was funny, he was sweet and gentle. And he was a "higher-class" man than Shemu'el. He bought her sweet little gifts and listened intently to her always.

It didn't matter to Mara that he didn't worship the God of their ancestors. It didn't matter to her when she found out that he was a Jewish man who had denied the faith and fled to Samaria in order to save his own skin.

It didn't matter that he had chosen to worship a Roman deity. He favoured the chief of Roman gods – Jupiter – over his own people's God. Instead of worshipping Yahweh, as Shemu'el did, many Samaritans worshipped idols, so this didn't seem like too much of an issue to Mara.

In fact, she rather liked the idea of a powerful thunder-and-lightening god. If the mighty Romans could worship him and conquer with such success, then maybe she would find her life went better if she also chose to follow him.

Besides, Mara reasoned, why should she obey a God who had never seen fit to bless her in any way? None of her marriages had worked out – *you'd think one out of five might have!* She thought indignantly. So why should she continue to live with a man she did not truly love, nor felt affection for? Why should she not pursue her own happiness once more? She was sick of living her lives for the approval of others!

Soon, Mara was spending long evenings at the kitchen table in Eber's home discussing all manner of things and sharing times together. There was no doubt in Mara's mind that she had fallen hard for this man. When, one evening, he kissed her tenderly, she knew he felt the same.

"What about your wife?" She heard herself asking, as she gently pulled away.

Fingers curled into her hair and voice soft, he pulled her back to him, whispering,

"She no longer exists for me. She was always nagging me, telling me what to do. I could never feel free when she was around. But you, Mara, you make me feel young once more. You delight my senses in every way. I feel like I could fly when I'm with you," he said.

He kissed her again, stronger this time.

"You never try to make me into a man I am not, nor force me to worship what I do not believe in. With you, I can be Eber, as I truly am. And you can be the true Mara, not held back by a solemn husband, or a child who does not love you." He held her tightly, kissing her to make her head spin.

In her mind, Mara heard a voice saying "Run! Go now!". She had heard it so many times before. But she did not listen. She ignored the memory of Naftali's similar words, the way he'd gone and left her, never to return, left her with a baby and plenty of hurt.

All she could think about now was Eber and how it felt to be in his arms. How it felt to be in love.

As she walked home in the cool evening air, Mara cursed herself. How could she be doing this again? She knew it was wrong! She knew what had happened to her the last time she'd tried this. Adultery would get her to no good place, she knew that.

And yet, *why* was it so wrong? How could something that felt so good, so sweet, be so immoral? It felt good to be in Eber's arms, for him to treat her kindly, to lavish on her the romance her heart so longed for.

For weeks, she refused him, but when, for the tenth time, he invited her to come and live with him, she felt her resolve wavering.

"Why shouldn't you, Mara? We are happy together. Your husband will most likely be happier with your son all to himself anyway," he cajoled her, using words she'd once spoken to him. His sweet tasting, corrupting kiss on her lips and his hand about her waist convinced her.

She could hold out against temptation no longer.

***

Shemu'el wasn't surprised. He had been waiting for the moment when Mara would tell him she was leaving. He begged her, for Raphael's sake not to. She spat that the boy would be happier with him anyway.

"But Mara, he needs his mother. He needs his family! He needs us both – we are his parents," he pleaded. He couldn't keep the hurt from showing in his face. After all he'd done for her, it hurt that she would do this to him, but it hurt far worse that she could simply desert her son.

"Oh Shemu'el. Though he isn't your blood, he is far more your son than he is mine. He loves you more than he loves me. He would rather stay with you and have me out of the way," she replied coldly.

"How can you even say that Mara?!" Shemu'el asked, shocked. "He loves us equally! Do not do this to him. I'm begging you." Mara unwound her headscarf and tossed her hair. "I am doing this Shemu'el, I've already made my choice. You cannot convince me otherwise. Besides, I know you'll parent Raphi better on your own than with me there to hinder you."

An image of the tree painted on his roof suddenly came into Shemu'el's mind. This was another of those defining moments in his life. This was a moment when there were two trees to choose from – which one would he choose? He wavered a moment.

It was clear that Mara had once again chosen a different path from him. But what was his best move? His head ached. His heart hurt. *Why, Mara? Why?* He cried internally.

"What will you tell our boy?" He eventually asked.

Mara waved her hand, dismissing this as a concern.

"Tell him whatever he needs to hear – that Imah needs to take care of Eber's house all the time, or that his great-grandmother is sick and I am assisting with tending her. I will still come and see him occasionally, of course."

"This is cruel, Mara. He won't be a child forever! And one day he'll have a right to know why his mother doesn't live with his father," Shemu'el said, head hanging.

"And one day, when he is no longer a boy, I can tell him why," Mara replied, all decided in her mind. "As for everyone else, I don't care what they say. You can tell them the truth. That I have moved to live with Eber, for that is what I need for my happiness."

But what about mine? Or your son's? Or anyone who isn't you? Shemu'el thought sadly to himself as Mara turned tail, collecting up her things to leave.

He swallowed deeply and moved to help her, despite the dull throb in his chest. He remembered the last time he'd help her collect up her belongings. Then, he had been helping her move to his own home, to save her from ridicule and harm. Now, she was bringing it upon herself and there was nothing he could do to stop it.

"I don't need your help Shemu'el," Mara snapped as she pulled her belongings together into a basket. Suddenly she felt teary again. Why did he have to be so good, so kind? Did he think his kindness now would stop her from leaving? Then he was a fool.

Once she had all her things together, she took a deep breath, then walked out of the house without looking back. Mara walked brazenly through the streets of Sychar and straight on into Eber's home.

She had done it. The choice had been made. Now, everyone would know what kind of woman Mara bat Mal'akhiy truly was.

* * *

It was always seemed odd to Mara that life could change so much and yet go on, days turning over as ever they had. Life was strange. Their people had never been like their Jewish neighbours, living governed by rules and regulations. The Samaritans were proud of their freedom, proud that they were not tied back by the bonds of tradition. Mara had never felt judged by her people. Not when Amitai sent her home, nor when she left Micah. Not when Levi deserted her, or when she married just weeks after Keren was reported dead.

But when she left her fifth husband, the town's beloved shepherd, Shemu'el and her little boy with him, she felt the icy wash of shame. People looked down on their town's pretty prize for the first time.

Leaving a good man like Shemu'el and a sweet, kind son such as Raphi behind for a Jewish runaway? It was not something people liked to hear about, even if it was Mara, the woman no one could dislike.

But, after a few days, people shrugged and got used to it. After all, what right did they all have to tell someone they were wrong? Each person had to do what would make them happiest.

Dawid and Zimra were devastated to hear the news. They went straight to Shemu'el and wept with him, once Raphi was safe in bed and asleep. They grieved for the lost family and for the poor little boy, left without a mother.

Zimra went to Eber's house one morning after he had headed out to work in the town. She tentatively knocked on the door. Mara let her in with a big, beaming smile on her face.

"Zimra, I'm so pleased to see you, my friend! How are you?" She welcomed, ushering her into the kitchen.

Zimra could feel her knees shaking a little, so nervous was she about what she knew she had to say. She hated standing up to anyone, let alone Mara, who had always been the leader in their friendship. Taking a deep breath, she opened her mouth and began.

"Mara, what you're doing is wrong. Have a care for Shemu'el. For your son. It is wrong for you to live with a man who is not your husband, to just desert your family on a whim. You must return to them. They will forgive you and you can learn to love them again. Get rid of that renegade Jew from your home. He has corrupted you! No matter how much you think you care for him, you cannot. Worshipping a Roman god, turning from the only life you've ever known? You just can't do this, Mara!" She found she was panting as she left off speaking.

Mara's eyes had become twin cold slits. She too was shaking, not from fear, but from terrible anger. "Have you said your piece?" She asked icily.

Zimra opened her mouth, then shut it again. She'd never seen such a look of distaste on Mara's usually lovely face. It disfigured her entirely. She looked almost venomous, Zimra thought, horrified. She nodded, slowly.

"Yes. I'm sorry to speak so bluntly, Mara, but someone has to be honest with you. You know I love you, it would be wrong of me to say nothing -"

"Get out."

Mara spoke the words flatly. She'd heard them spoken like that before. When Micah told her to leave. And the expression that flashed across Zimra's face as she spoke them was the same she'd worn on the day she'd been banished from Sebaste – betrayal.

Zimra turned to leave. Tears blossomed in the corners of her green eyes, but they didn't quite spill over.

"Mara, just remember that truth tellers are important. Even if I'm the only one who is brave enough to tell you, this is still the truth. And no matter what you've done, you will always be my heart's sister."

She turned and ran out of the house, leaving Mara feeling shocked and in pain.

Who does Zimra think she is, thinking she can just come barging into my own home, and tell me I am living my life wrong? How dare she? Mara raged internally. She picked up the clay cup she'd been washing and hurled it at the wall. It split into a million jagged little shards. Like my life, Mara thought miserably.

She was furious with Zimra and yet, in the core of her being, she knew without a doubt that she was right. About everything.

Mara was being selfish. She was thinking of no one except herself and her own feelings, but she didn't care. She didn't want to care.

Slowly, Mara sank to the ground. The pain within her was too much to bear. How could she have messed up her life so badly? Why was it she could never feel good enough? Pretty enough? Valuable enough? Loved? Cherished? Wanted? Anything? Even when she was clearly all of those things. Internally, she could never reach the standard of perfection she so desired.

Sitting amongst the shards of clay cup, Mara began to think of her splintered life. She could never stay joined to anyone for long. Either because they left her, rejected her, or because she was so afraid of being left, that she herself went before it could happen.

Her family. Amitai. Her sweet baby, Rani. Micah. Her baby, Yathom. Levi. Keren. Naftali. Shemu'el. Her own little boy, Raphael. She could see it now, it was a pattern.

She began to gather the broken cup into her hands, piece by piece. It had all begun as a child, when she knew her parents did not want her, couldn't truly afford another child. She knew it was her fault her Imah had died. That was when the desire to fly, to move on before pain took hold began. From then, it was a pattern. A cycle. Mara was afraid she could never escape from it. She felt trapped. Alone.

As the pieces of clay cup became too many for her hands to hold, she transferred them into her apron. How was it she had been so blind?

Thirty-five years and she had never noticed that she had such a fear of real love. How could she never have noticed that she was forever following it, wherever she could find it, then fleeing before it could end?

And why was it Mara had never found the true love she desired? She ached for something real. Something lasting. Yet, the long-lasting love Shemu'el had given her did not seem to be enough.

She could not understand it. Shem had always love her and yet, she had run from him as surely as she had run from everyone else.

Mara just could not rid herself of the feeling that he was better than her, that she wasn't good enough and never would be. She grasped a shard of the cup too tightly, cutting her finger open. She yelped, both in pain and in extreme frustration. Blood dripped down onto her skirts and she began to cry.

"Will I never be good enough?!" She shouted. The words echoed around the high walls of the house. Good enough. Good enough. Good enough. It felt almost as if even the house itself was mocking her. She felt desperate. She called out to the God of her ancestors.

"Yahweh, if you're out there, please. Help me. I am so lost. I'm drowning in this life and I can see no way out. Please." The last word came out as a bleat, a cry so drenched with pain, it had lost all sense of dignity. Mara had come to many low points in her life, but never before had she felt so undone. So lost. So completely deserted. And yet, she knew it was she who had done the deserting.

"What's the use of even praying?"

She saw Eber's idol of Jupiter on the shelf in the corner and filled with anger, rushed at, throwing it on the ground so that its face cracked off.

"What is the use of having gods if they bring us nothing good in this life?! I married a priest and nothing good came of that! I married an ordinary man. A strong man. A rich man. A godly man. And none of that came to anything. What is the use?" She screamed.

She kicked the Jupiter statue hard, so that it rolled out of sight under the table. "What is the use?"

Emotion over, she finally sat, panting on the doorstep. She had no hope left. She was certain she had ruined her life for good and there would be no redeeming it.

Chapter XXVII.

A.D. 25, Sychar, Samaria, Roman province of Judaea

Mara soon recovered from her fit of hopelessness. She'd always had the sort of nature that just bounced back after a while. Zimra's visit had affected her more than she cared to admit, but all the same, life went on, as it always did.

Often in the evenings, she and Eber would head out to the tavern down the way and mingle with the other townsfolk. Mara enjoyed getting back into visiting the tavern.

She'd missed the raucous company she'd once kept, the honour she was given as the most beautiful lady present and the male sense of humor which always had her laughing. Mara liked the fact that men got on with her so well. She liked that she could just slip back into her role as honorary man. They didn't care what she had done. They liked her. She could tease and joke and laugh and bat her eyelashes all she liked. Eber didn't mind if she behaved that way, as long as it was always him she came home with at the end of the night. And she always did.

As much as Mara enjoyed flirting and being flirted with, she found that no other man was really attractive to her now. Though she wasn't quite sure how, her renegade Jewish lover had woven a complicated enchantment over her.

It was much like the spell Naftali had once cast. She could think of no one else, dreamt of him all day, longed for his touch at night.

Mara wondered to herself why it was she was so susceptible to this type of man. Why was it that the men she desired were the kind that consumed her, heart and soul? Once upon a time, that had been Levi's role. Though she knew so very little about him, she had become obsessed with the idea of belonging to him. The pull to belong to a strong, confident man consumed her. She hated it. Why could she not just be content to be her own person, a woman free of any attachment?! But life as a single woman did not bear thinking about!

The nights around the flickering fire, surrounded by the traders, foreign camel drivers and the most unscrupulous of Samaria's people, enchanted Mara. Like the hypnotic beats of the cow hide drums they played and the high pitched wailing of their music, Mara found herself lulled into a sensuous rhythm of life. With Eber's strong arms about her shoulders and her old friend, powerful wine, in her hands, she felt invincible.

The nights by the blazing bonfires, or in the taverns went late. The laughter and song filled every moment. "You Samaritans are nothing like us Jews!" Eber shouted in Mara's ear over the noise, one night. She laughed as she turned back to face him, eyes blazing gold.

"You are right, Eber. We are far better. Shomron is nothing like the Jewish land either. Our land is richer. Our people more beautiful. Our lifestyle more desirable. Our food better. Our cities have better architecture. Everything about Shomron is better! Samaria!" Her voice had risen to fill the room and as she finished, she was met with a chorus of "Here here!" and clinking cups. Mara was elated. This was an exhilarating life, for sure.

Before she knew it, Eber had collected a group of fellow idol worshippers from all around Sychar. They weren't people Mara had ever spent time with before, but they were friendly and inclusive. Many of them were divorced, or unmarried people living together. Being around them made Mara feel better about her own living arrangements.

There was another side to these meetings that Mara couldn't abide. A man named Shim'on was a sorcerer in one of the towns further north in Shomron. Many years ago, Mara had sought the man out, looking for a cure for Yathom. The magic he was said to be able to do had made Mara's insides quake then and it still did now. Deep down, Mara knew there was something terribly wrong with it all and she hated the obsession Eber and his friends had with it.

Eber brought along his statue of Jupiter (whose head he had reattached after Mara's vicious attack on him) and taught them more about the Roman gods. It interested the idol worshippers that Jupiter was so similar to Baal, the traditional god of their land, and that Venus represented Ashterah so well. These were the same old gods with new names.

Mara hated attending their worship ceremonies. They would burn incense and chant and present offerings before their idols. Sometimes they would also engage in obscene acts together as acts of worship and practice a dark form of magic. They called it worship, but it made Mara's skin crawl and shiver.

Sometimes she would have to run from the meetings down in the wooded glade, hurrying away before she vomited. Mara had lost touch with the very idea that there was a God whom her people had worshipped for centuries who prohibited the worship of other gods. She'd lost touch with the knowledge that these things were forbidden for a reason.

After a particularly intense worship session, Mara fled. She just needed to get away. As she sat out by Ya'acov's Well, shaking like a leaf in the wind, she knew, deep down, that she'd never been more lost. She had doused herself in cold water, trying to wash away the feeling of creeping evil running through her hair. But it didn't work.

As she raised her eyes to the horizon, she saw Shemu'el approaching in the distance, Raphi running at his side. How was it that Shemu'el always turned up when she was in her worst moments, Mara wondered?

She hadn't seen him since the day she'd left and it felt heinous to see him again now. Mara was so filthy, so very sinful and he was so very good, so godly. She hated the way that made her feel – insignificant. Wrong. As always, her reaction to such a feeling was to put on a mask of pride.

"Imah!" Raphi cried, rushing up to her. She laughed and caught the small boy up in her arms.

"Raphi! How are you?" She asked, kissing his nose.

Raphael giggled, wrinkling. "I am great! Abba and I are working hard! We miss you though, Imah." Tears sprung into her eyes and she buried her eyes in his soft curls.

"I miss you too, Raphi," she said huskily.

Shemu'el approached now. His face was guarded and he looked thin and pinched but he managed a small smile for his son's sake.

"Mara. How are you faring?" He asked. The monotone of his voice was broken only by a slight crack halfway through. He tried hard to hide his feelings with Raphael around.

"I'm well, Shemu'el. Raphi tells me you have been busy." Her voice was as strong and proud as ever, but she was pale and her face was gaunt.

He looked down at her hands and saw the faint outlines of henna patterns drawn on her olivey skin. He knew what that meant.

"Mara, don't go there!" He said urgently. "Don't get caught up in that! It isn't ever too late to turn back, but if you continue down that path, there will be no way back."

Mara fought the haughty instincts rising inside herself. She knew Shemu'el was telling the truth. She was getting herself into more than she had bargained for.

"I know Shem. I'm here because I ran away and left it behind. I know

283

I've done many things, but I can't do that."

He nodded slowly, relief on his face. He pulled Raphael to his side and the boy snuggled in close.

"It's never too late Mara. I mean that. There's always space in our hearts, right Raphi?" He said, smiling down at his son.

"Right Abba!" Raphael replied, grinning widely. He had no idea what his parents were talking about, but he trusted Shemu'el implicitly.

Mara watched his grin and saw Naftali looking back at her. Her stomach lurched and she turned away. She didn't want to confront her past now. She had moved on.

* * *

"Mara, Shemu'el is seriously ill and I think you should know." Dawid's solemn words and anguished face crushed Mara. Dawid had pulled her aside in the street on her way home, saying he needed to tell her something urgent.

Mara couldn't believe it. Not Shemu'el. Not good, solid, sturdy Shemu'el. He couldn't be sick.

Mara had taken it for granted that Shemu'el would always be there. He was the one she always turned to. Even now, she had continued to think of him as her best friend.

"H-how sick?" She stammered, her proud mask slipping despite herself. "I saw him out walking, just this afternoon!"

Dawid shrugged. "Sick. He wasn't able to get out of bed for days. He's very weak, although I think he is recovering. But he'll never be strong as he was. He is keeping up appearances for Raphi. That's probably why they were out walking. He's had to sell his flock to pay for medicine though. His lungs..."

Dawid trailed off, running a hand through his dark hair, a shaky sigh escaping his lips.

"Why didn't he tell me?" Mara asked softly. "I would have helped nurse him."

Dawid turned a scornful gaze her way.

"You, Mara? The one who deserted him? Why would he turn to you?!"

Mara felt a physical knife blow at his words. What her brother said was true. Why would anyone turn to her? No one wanted her. Even Eber was growing tired of her...Dawid's words broke through her thoughts. "I think you need to consider the possibility that he won't be around forever and you need to consider what will happen with Raphael. Zimra and I can't take in another..."

"Dawid, stop!" Mara turned away. She couldn't bring herself to listen.

Shemu'el couldn't be in danger of dying. It was unfair.

Tears brimmed in her fire golden eyes. Shemu'el didn't deserve this. If anyone should be in danger, it was her.

"Please, just leave me." Mara choked out the words.

She couldn't bear the weight of guilt that was bearing down on her shoulders in that instant. Guilty. Guilty. Condemned. Worthless. Unwanted. Failure. The words beat her down.

As soon as Dawid was gone, sobs racked her body. She hurried on her way home.

"Why Shemu'el? Why not me, God?" She cried to the heavens as she walked. "He deserves better than this."

"I just don't understand. It isn't fair. Why?!"

But she heard no answer.

Chapter XXVIII·

A.D. 26, Sychar, Samaria, Roman province of Judaea

Jewish travellers very rarely made their way as far into Samaria as Sychar. The next day, Mara made an extra trip out to Ya'acov's Well and was surprised to see a Jewish man sitting on its rocky edge.

The past few days, filled with stress, had made Mara extremely thirsty. She didn't usually go to the well in the middle of the day, but she had run short on water and she and Eber were having guests that night.

After the happenings of the day before – in the grove, then meeting Shemu'el and her son by the well, then finally hearing how sick Shemu'el was despite his pretence of health – Mara had hardly slept.

She had tossed and turned, head pounding, until finally, she had given up on the idea of sleep at all and slipped out from her place at Eber's side.

Sitting out in the cool night air under the stars, she had wept until her eyes hurt and her whole body ached. She hated her life. Hated that she was always crying. Hated everything she had become. Hated her own pretence of happiness. She was miserable. She couldn't even remember ever feeling happy. Not truly.

The stars above her had flickered. As they did every night. They, at least, were constant. Unlike everything else in her life.

"How have I gone so wrong?" Mara had whispered up at the night sky. She thought wistfully of all the childhood nights she'd spent sleeping on her Saba and Savta's flat roof. All her idealized childhood dreams. Gone. Crushed. Nothing.

Sleep had stayed far away after that and she was feeling incredibly irritable by the time the sun rose. She just wanted to be free of this sad existence she led. Thirty-five years and all to naught.

And now, here was this man. Slumped sideways across the well's edge, he looked even tireder than Mara herself felt.

He was unmistakably a Jew, with his dark beard and his prayer shawl poking out from under his robe. It was decidedly strange for a Jewish man to be sitting alone by a Samaritan well, but Mara didn't care. She'd found enough strange people here over the years, as it was.

She approached somewhat warily, feeling suspicious. Hopefully he wasn't one of those Jews who would spit on Samaritans – she wasn't in the mood for dealing with that. As she drew close, the man sat up, lifting his eyes to her face.

There was something about his eyes. Mara had never seen eyes like these before. It wasn't to do with the colour, it just seemed that this Jew's eyes were more penetrating, held more something than other eyes.

Mara had always been drawn to eyes. Perhaps it was because her own were so unusual, but the first thing she ever took in about a person was their eyes. One of the few things she could remember about her Imah was her saying "eyes are the window to the soul". You could tell a lot about a person just from looking into their eyes. Zimra's green eyes, for instance, held a world of kind compassion. Amitai's dark eyes had always blazed with a deep rooted pride and entitlement. Rani's bright little girl eyes had always been so full of life, as Raphael's blue eyes were now. Shemu'el's eyes had always held a love Mara couldn't quite comprehend. Her own eyes... an unquenchable thirst, a longing for... something.

The man before her now, his eyes were different. It wasn't the thick, dark Jewish lashes, either, that made them so intriguing. It was something far more profound than that. Mara couldn't quite put her finger on it.

"Will you give me a drink?" The man asked, in a typical coastal Jewish accent. He must be from Galilee, Mara thought. She half-laughed at his request. "You are a Jew and I am a Samaritan woman. How can you ask me for a drink?!" She snorted scornfully at the end of her sentence. What kind of self-respecting Jewish man would ask a Samaritan for a drink, let alone a woman?!

He gave a half-smile, ignoring her scorn. "If you knew the gift of God and who it is that asks you for a drink, you would have asked him and he would have given you living water."

The words mystified Mara. This man spoke cryptically. Not cryptically like Naftali – attention seeking and mocking. This man's words were kind. She'd only spoken a few words to him and despite his unusual turn of phrase, the kindness that underpinned what he said made even someone as good as Shemu'el sound like the worst person in the world.

And yet, Mara could not help the sarcastic response that sprung to her lips – her usual reaction to feeling out-of-her-depth, or unsure of herself. "Sir, you have nothing to draw with and the well is deep. Where can you get this water? Are you greater than our father, Ya'acov, who gave us this well and drank from it himself, as did his sons and livestock?" She was incredulous as she finished. Who did this Jew think he was, saying water elsewhere was better than that found in the depths of Ya'acov's Well?!

Why, Ya'acov wrestled with God and gave the twelve tribes their birth! To claim to be greater than Ya'acov, one of the Patriarchs, was almost unthinkable.

The man spoke slowly, deliberately.

"Everyone who drinks this water will be thirsty again," he said. "But whoever drinks from the water I give them will never thirst."

With that, he smiled — such a beautiful smile, it lit up his plain face in a transforming way. "Indeed, the water I give will become in them a spring of water welling up to eternal life."

A deep longing, unlike any Mara had ever known suddenly overcame her. She wasn't sure she'd ever wanted anything so desperately in all her life.

"Sir, give me this water, so that I won't get thirsty and keep having to come here to draw water."

Suddenly, he looked at her with such a piercing gaze, she felt as if he saw right through her.

"Go, call your husband and come back," he said. He knew.

Mara bowed her head, trying to hide the shame suddenly washing through her. She tried to answer nonchalantly.

"I have no husband."

The man looked deeply into her eyes again. What he said next rocked Mara to the very core.

"You are right when you say you have no husband. The fact is, you have had five husbands and the man you now have is not your husband. What you have just said is quite true."

Mara felt her eyes widen in shock. She stumbled a little, almost dropping her bucket and jars as she tried to regain her composure. "Sir," she said, trying to breathe steadily. "I can see you are a prophet. Our ancestors worshipped on this mountain," she pointed up to Mount Gerizin, "but you Jews claim the place we must worship is in Jerusalem."

She wasn't ready to deal with this. She tried to distract him with this age old debate between their two people groups — anything to keep him from making any more observations about her own life! She suddenly felt filthy. He knew.

"Woman," the man said, his eyes filled with kindness and deep compassion. But there was also something shrewd and unrelenting in his gaze. He wasn't letting her ploy distract from what he had just said.

"Believe me, a time is coming when you will worship the Father neither on this mountain, nor in Jerusalem. You Samaritans worship what you do not know; we worship what we do know, for salvation comes from the Jews. Yet a time is coming and has now come when true worshippers will worship the Father in the Spirit and in truth, for they are the kind of worshippers the Father seeks. God is spirit and His worshippers must worship Him in the Spirit and in truth."

As Mara listened, his words took hold of her, making her heart pound with excitement. This was no ordinary man, she was sure of it. She wasn't sure what she should do next, or how, even, to truly understand what this man was saying.

"I know that the Messiah is coming," she said slowly. "When He comes, He will explain everything to us."

The man got to his feet and stood before her. There was something about this moment that Mara knew she would never, could never, forget. It was as if time itself froze as he spoke.

"I, the one speaking to you – I am He."

Mara felt overwhelmed. How could this be real? Only a few days ago, she'd been crying on the kitchen floor, begging God, if He existed, to save her from herself and the night before, crying out to the universe for answers.

And now, here before her, apparently, stood the Messiah.

Mara stumbled again, suddenly dizzy. She felt her jaw go slack. But as she looked at him, she knew. She knew it was true. This Jew standing before her, He was the long-awaited Messiah. Their salvation. This changed everything.

Mara stood, her energy sapped by shock.

A bunch of Jewish men were heading towards them, looking questioningly at Mara, probably wondering why the Messiah Himself would bother talking to a sinful Samaritan woman like her. She could see the surprise on their faces, but none of them called out, asking her who she was, or what she was doing.

She lowered her water jar to the ground and began shakily to run. She slipped through the crowd of His followers and didn't stop, all the way from the well back to town.

Over her shoulder, she heard the Messiah's followers saying to him, "Rabbi, eat something," and His quiet reply, "I have food that you know nothing about." The words made Mara smile. Perhaps He meant food like He had meant the water – spiritual food.

Mara knew where she must go first. She ran to Shemu'el's little house. Flinging open the wooden door, she rushed in, but he wasn't there. Running into town, she was surprised to see him standing in the market, near the meal house, Raphi at his side. Shemu'el's face was drawn and pale, but his eyes grew brighter as he saw her.

Mara rushed up and breathlessly exclaimed: "Come and see a man who told me everything I ever did! Could this be the Messiah?!"

People all around turned curiously to look at Mara. No one had ever seen her, usually so composed and world-wearied, in such a state of excitement. For a moment no one seemed to know what to do. What could she mean?

Mara saw the faces she'd known all her life looking back at her. Her true husband, Shemu'el. Her son, Raphael. Zimra. Dawid. Her birth-daughter, Rani. Her uncle. Eber. Cousins. Friends. Acquaintances. They were all staring at her, none of them moving. They were all completely unsure what to do.

Mara made her statement again, more urgently this time. "Come and see a man who told me everything I ever did! Could this be the Messiah?!" She looked around, searching for even one face that seemed inclined to believe her.

Mara held out her hands, begging someone, anyone, to follow her. She met Shemu'el's gaze. His eyes were solemn as he analyzed her.

A truly happy laugh bubbled up inside her as she saw his eyes light up. Reaching out for Raphael's little hand, Shemu'el stepped forward, following Mara out, back towards Ya'acov's Well.

Mara felt her face begin to beam, as person after person followed along. She lead them back, talking excitedly and sharing what the Man had said to her. Raphi reached for her hand and held on tightly. Mara wanted to weep happy tears. This was real. The Messiah had come to them, to Sychar – a small town in the hated province of Samaria. Yet, He was really here. This changed everything.

Chapter XXIX.

A.D. 26, Sychar, Samaria, Roman province of Judaea

The Man was still there talking to His followers as the towns-folk approached Ya'acov's Well. Gradually, drove after drove of Samaria's people came out of Sychar to meet this Messiah. Some hung back, nervous to get too close to a Jew. Others had no such scruples, pushing and shoving in close, desperate to catch a glimpse of this Man that Mara bat Mal'akhiy had spoken of. Could what she had said be true?

Mara herself pushed right to the front, Raphael at her side, his small, soft hand clasped tightly in her own. Raphi stared up at Him in awe.

The Man smiled down at him and ruffled the boy's hair affectionately. Raphael laughed in delight. Then Mara was laughing, all around her people were laughing. They just couldn't help it. They were all so happy.

They believed. As she believed, they believed. This Man, Yeshua, His followers called Him, was truly the Messiah. Yeshua. His name meant Salvation.

The town elders, Avraham, Ilan and Yoel came forward, begging Yeshua and His followers to stay in Sychar. Everyone was delighted when they agreed that they would.

How strange – never before had practicing Jews been welcomed to Sychar! And yet, everyone was elated. There was something about this Man that superseded even the generations old race war.

Things change fast, Mara thought to herself later that evening as she sat on the step outside a house in the forum, listening to Yeshua teaching her people.

A great feast had been prepared in His honour – a prize calf was slaughtered and carefully prepared by Yom, the great, fat butcher. He slaved over the spit all evening, sweat running down his vast arms in rivulets.

Everyone had brought along the best food from their homes – breads, meats, nuts and the finest of wine to be had.

Out had come the drums, the lyres and the Arabian flutes and the rhythmic music had began. It was subdued and soft now, as the Rabbi talked, but soon, as the night grew old, it would become a mixture of bold rhythms and stamping feet, wailing voices and swirling scarves.

In the few short hours since Mara had first encountered Yeshua at the well, everything had changed for her. She would once have been at the very heart of the celebrations, dancing and seeking attention. And now, here she was, hanging back, content just to listen in the background.

She wore her coarse, woollen cloak about her shoulders and fiddled with it as she sat listening. Yeshua spoke of a new way of life. He spoke about not worshipping on a mountain at all, but in Spirit and in truth. Mara wondered what he could mean by that.

This Man was speaking of change, big change – living a life that truly pleased God, based solely on their love for Him. Yeshua told them that there was one way to God, one way to be saved from one's past – to trust and believe in Him, the Messiah.

Hugging her knees close to her chest, Mara wondered if this could be possible. Could it really be that simple? Just trusting in this Man would wash her clean of every foul and evil deed she had ever committed? She bit her lip. Surely, she had sinned too much in her life for this to be true.

But then again, she reasoned, He knew all her sin – He'd shown that clearly. Could she truly trust Him to free her from the web of wrong-doing she'd long-since woven into her life, tying her down and closing her in?

Mara watched Him as he sat by the fire, talking, little Raphi sat right up close, all the other children of Sychar around his feet.

People were listening to Him talk without interrupting at all. There was no lapse of attention, that was for sure. Mara had never seen anyone captivate her people in such a way before.

As the town settled down to eat, Mara found herself too deep in thought to join them. Living water. She wanted this water. Spiritual water. Water that would quench her thirst for happiness. For fulfillment. For love. For purpose. For belonging. For all her fears and concerns. She wanted it so desperately she could almost taste it on her tongue.

"Please give me this living water," she whispered, looking straight at Yeshua, begging him with her whole being. She knew her voice could not be heard over the din of other voices and over Yeshua's own words, but she saw that He had heard all the same.

His eyes met hers, filled with compassion.

It started in her middle, a tingly feeling dancing its way through her body. It filled her fingertips, ran down to her toes and put light – true light – in her eyes and bubbled out of her as laughter.

Living water. Mara laughed again, jumping to her feet. She felt free. For the first time in her life, she did not feel weighed down by the weight of the world, by the weight of her own life.

This was the most beautiful feeling she'd ever know. Far more powerful than being admired or respected, far more than the deepest human love she'd ever known. Suddenly she knew it was as her ancestors had written.

"O God, You are my God, Earnestly I seek You; My soul thirsts for

You, My body longs for You, in a dry and weary land, where there is no water. I have seen You in the Sanctuary and beheld Your power and Your glory. Because Your love is better than life. My lips will glorify You, I will praise You as long as I live, And in Your name will I lift Up my hands."

Mara knew without a single doubt that she would never be the same. She had been changed from the inside out and she could not continue to live life as she had.

She would follow this Yeshua wherever He would have her go, for she knew in all certainty that she had seen the very Messiah of God.

With a joyful cry, unlike one she'd ever heard leave her own lips, she began to dance. She whirled and twirled and moved with a new delight in her heart. Soon others began to dance with her. There was nothing sensual in their dance, Mara had never danced like this before – this was altogether different. Innocent. Clean. Beauty in its truest form. The music rose to meet the dancing feet of the people. Soon, it felt as if the whole of Sychar was dancing and swirling together in true joy. They had seen the long awaited salvation of mankind. There was no greater joy than what they were experiencing right now.

Yeshua spent the next day with the people of Sychar again, teaching them and showing them the right way to live. He was still teaching in the centre of town as night began to fall.

Mara sat back under a tall date palm, just watching and learning from a distance. It was wonderfully liberating not to feel the overwhelming pressure to impress anyone. All she desired now was to follow Yeshua.

Halfway through the evening, Shemu'el came over to her. He was still pale and gaunt, but his eyes were so happy. He didn't say a word, just sat down quietly at her side. He reached out gently for her hand and Mara slipped her own hand into his.

He understood. He knew what she was going through, the transformation that had taken place within her. He knew how hard this must be for her. "It changes everything, Shem," she whispered quietly, after a while. "It changes my whole life. I've wasted every minute thus far, but now that no longer matters. He has changed my whole world."

Shemu'el nodded. "I know what you mean. I no longer believe just because of what you've said; now I've heard it for myself and I know that this man really is the promised Saviour of the world!"

Tears filled Mara's eyes. Yes. It was true. Yeshua was walking there with them and He was the Saviour. The only one who could ever rid people of their sin. Into her mind flashed glimpses of some of the sins she'd committed and she was overwhelmed. Yeshua was setting her free from all she'd ever done.

"I can hardly believe this is real, Shem!" She said shakily. He put an arm around her tenderly. As he had always done. "I feel like a new woman. I feel like one of the birds, caged for sacrifice, but set free before it is killed. I feel like I am walking up on the clouds, like nothing could ever be better."

He grinned down at her, tired, but delighted.

"You are free Mara. Your sin cannot hold you back anymore. Who you had become has no hold on you. You are the real you now, Mara. In fact, Bitterness is a bad name for you! Why, we should call you Galiliah – God has redeemed – instead!"

Mara thought back to the last time someone had suggested she change her name. Naftali had called her Yaffa – Queen, urging her to become ruler of her own destiny.

Huh. Some success that had been. Looking back, she could see now that her life became far worse once she started living a completely self-centered life. Mara had thought that when Naftali had left, the whole concept of Yaffa had fled from her life, but retrospectively, she could now see that Yaffa and the desire to be queen of her own life had ruled up until the very day she had met Yeshua.

But "Yaffa" was dead to her now. She had walked out of Mara's life the moment Yeshua first spoke to her.

Suddenly Mara was hit with a wave of remorse and her eyes filled with tears.

"Oh Shemu'el, I'm so sorry! I'm sorry for everything I put you through. I can't believe what a terrible person I have become," Mara said almost inaudible in her distress, wriggling her toes in the sand beneath her feet. It felt soft and was still warm, even now that the light had faded from the sky.

Shemu'el squeezed her hand. "You have been forgiven Mara. I do not hold you accountable for what you have done. It is in the past now."

Suddenly Mara knew what she had to do. She knew what Yeshua would want her to do in order to move on with her life. She jumped to her feet. "Not quite, Shem. Yeshua said repenting means turning from our sins and there are still some things I must do in order for it to truly be behind me!"

Pulling her cloak tight against her, Mara slipped from the gathering. It saddened her to miss some of Yeshua's words, but she knew she had to do this, before anything else happened.

She found Eber and his friends gathered in the home of a woman called Lali, as far across town from Yeshua as they could get. From the very first, they had turned from Him, unwilling to be in His presence.

There were none of the usual smiles as Mara entered the home through the cut stone door way. The people, who used to be her people, were seated on the floor of the second storey of the house. They stayed silent and unwelcoming as Mara climbed up to be with them. She could see their magic symbols etched into the floor, smell the strong, spicy incense they had been burning. It repulsed her, but she managed to keep her face from showing it. Eber got to his feet, looking surly.

"What do you want Mara? Is your precious Messiah not enough for you?"

His lip curled down and he spat at her feet. "If you've come to apologize for your crazy behavior, you'll find it might take more than just words."

Mara could feel her old nature longing to strike back with a sarcastic comment and a decisive departure, but she knew she must not. The others all gathered around Eber, watching the stand-off and knew she must answer well. Silently she prayed that Yahweh would guide her tongue, then began to speak.

"No Eber, I'm not here to apologize for the last few days. I'm here to apologize for the last year. I should never have done as I did and left my husband and son to be with you. I should not have deserted them. I should not have deserted the faith I knew my whole life, the faith I knew was the truth. But now Yeshua is here and He is changing everything. He is the Saviour of the world! Everything I've ever done wrong has passed away. He has set me free now, of all the pain I've been carrying for so long." She breathed deeply, the incense in the air burning in her lungs.

"And so I'm here to tell you that I'm leaving you Eber. It isn't right for me to live with you when I am already married. Please forgive me for the wrong I have done you. You may have my house until you can find somewhere else, but as of right now, I no longer live there." As Mara finished, no one around her spoke. No one knew quite what to say. Lali was looking at Mara with wide, kohl-outlined eyes, Eber's jaw had dropped and his lip curled almost back on itself.

"Where will you go Mara?! Surely, your husband won't have you back after what you did to him!" Eber said, incredulous.

Mara shrugged her shoulders. "That is true, he may not and I wouldn't blame him. But God always provided for our forefathers and Yeshua says we have but to ask Him and He will provide for us too. So from now on, I'm not trusting in my looks, or my charm, or any man. I'm trusting in the God of my ancestors."

She moved towards the ladder, feeling she'd outstayed her welcome. One, final thought crossed her mind before she clambered down. "Come and hear Him speak. He is changing lives right across Sychar. Maybe He will have something to offer you, too? Come and see."

They watched open-mouthed as Mara descended the ladder and made her way back out through the front door of Lali's home, never to return again.

Chapter XXX.

A.D. 26, Sychar, Samaria, Roman province of Judaea

As Mara returned to the square where Yeshua was teaching, surrounded by his disciples and his brand new followers from Sychar, person after person came to greet her. Each one stopped and told her that they had been inspired and were prepared to rely on Yeshua after hearing from Him with their own ears. At first, they'd believed based on what Mara had shared with them, but now, they truly believed because of their own experiences.

Hearing that warmed Mara's heart more than she'd ever thought possible.

She wanted everyone to find the new freedom and happiness she now had. All her life, she had been longing for something – if only she had known this was it.

Mara made her way back into the circle of people sitting around Yeshua, listening to his words. She squeezed in next to Zimra, who was surrounded by little miniatures of herself and Dawid. Eli sat beside her, a young man now of nineteen. He was every bit his father's image.

Zimra smiled warmly and stretched an arm out around Mara, pulling her sister-in-law close. Mara leaned into Zimra as she had so often as a child. "Isn't it wonderful, Mara?!" Zimra whispered delightedly. "Isn't He incredible! He's everything I dreamed the Messiah would be and more!"

Mara laughed softly. "I always imagined He would come on a war horse and declare us free of the Romans, making the nation of Israel whole and great again. But I'm glad I was wrong, because I cannot imagine anything better than this!"

The two women listened intently as Yeshua spoke, taking in every word. They were hearing the answers to questions they'd always wondered about and learning more about how they were to live their lives. Watching Yeshua, Mara thought back to the old stories that had filtered out to Sychar long ago, of a baby being born to a virgin, before Herod the Great murdered every little boy in his region. It was hard to imagine that the man before them was that very baby.

"I heard from one of His followers that He turned water into wine at a wedding feast over in Cana!" Eli said excitedly, leaning across to his mother and aunt. "I heard that He cleared the temple of Jerusalem, because all the people inside were hypocrites!"

"And I heard He knows each of us so well, He knows everything we've ever done!" Zimra whispered back, eyes twinkling at Mara. Mara smiled softly to herself.

How incredible to think that anyone should even want to know about her! As she sat thinking, a poem penned by an ancestor, which she'd learnt as a child, came floating back to her.

"Lord, when You look at me you know all about me.

You know when I sit down.

And you know when I get up.

You understand what I'm thinking about.

Even when You are far away.

You see when I go.

And You see when I stay.

You remember everything that I do."

There was no doubt in Mara's mind now that Yeshua was the prophesied son of God. How could she have been so blind for so long – thinking God did not really exist, or that He no longer cared for the people of this earth?!

"Zimra, I want you to know how sorry I am. For everything," Mara whispered across to her friend. The emotion filling her made her voice tremble involuntarily but she was able to hold her friend's gaze strong and true. "Please forgive me. Yeshua has made me a new woman and I will no longer live as I have done in the past. I have left Eber for good now and I intend to fix as much of my wrong-doing as I possibly can."

Tears filled Zimra's eyes, green as the sea, as she nodded. "Of course I forgive you my friend. However could I not?" She reached out her arms and hugged Mara tightly. "I'm so glad to have you back!" Mara let out a watery hiccup. "Don't speak too soon! You may regret having said that!" They both laughed and Mara could feel a change between them. Their friendship was renewed and it was better than it had ever been before.

A little while later, Mara made her way over to where Raphael was sitting, in the branches of a sycamore tree. He looked down at her solemnly with his big, pale eyes and then grinned.

"Hi Imah!" He held out his bony little arms to her and swung down. She caught him as he landed and hugged him tightly. Her boy. Her own flesh and blood. How could she have turned away from him?! What kind of woman had she been? Raphael hugged her back for a little while, but then he began to squirm, wriggling out of her grasp. "I want to go and hear Yeshua, Imah!" He said. Mara stroked his soft hair. "My precious boy," she murmured. "Raphi, I want you to know that I love you very, very much. I haven't been a very good Imah to you, but I want you to know that. And I have changed. I want to be a good Imah to you now, if you can forgive me."

Raphael's eyes lit up and glowed, their own pale blue replica of Mara's. "Does that mean you'll come home and live with me and Abba again?!" He asked excitedly.

Mara bit her lip. She so desperately wanted to say yes, to say everything would return to just as it had been, but she could not do that. Not without speaking to Shemu'el. Not without making amends for her other mistakes.

"I hope so, sweet boy, I hope so," was all she said.

He raced off towards Yeshua, as fast as his legs could take him. Six years had gone so fast.

Mara could hardly believe she'd wasted an entire year of Raphael's life with Eber, when she could have been loving her beautiful son. She must have been crazy.

* * *

That night, they all sat listening to Yeshua teach, as the embers glowed bright in the dark, night sky. Mara was sitting as close to his feet as she could get. She was so happy.

Raphael had curled up next to her and with them sat Shemu'el, Dawid and Zimra and their family. And there was Rani.

Her precious first born. Mara gazed at the girl. Rani was long legged and willowy – tall, like her birth father, Amitai. She had his eyes too, Mara noted. Twenty-one years had passed since her birth. Could it really be true?

She was beautiful. Stunningly beautiful. Dark hair swirled down to her waist, thick and shiny. Her high cheeked-bones emphasised the lovely lines of her face. Long eyelashes and shapely brows... Mara couldn't stop herself staring as she took in the woman her baby had become. Rani was gorgeous.

Zimra had told Mara that Rani had been proposed to several times, but hadn't yet found the right man. Mara had almost wept when she'd heard those words. If only she herself had been that wise. But none of that mattered now. Dawid and Zimra had brought up her baby girl well. And for that, she was eternally grateful.

* * *

The night was growing late. The stars were winking up in the night sky. Most of Sychar had headed back to their homes, ready to sleep after two long days of feasting and listening to Yeshua teach.

But Mara couldn't bring herself to leave – not that she had anywhere to go now that she had left Eber.

As the fires started dying down, the last few people were starting to wrap up for the night. Mara sat, knees hunched up to her chin, warming by the dying coals. She was alone. Right now, she had nothing. No home. No core family. No money. Nothing.

And yet, somehow, it didn't matter at all. Mara had everything she wanted. All she wanted was what Yeshua had to offer. All she wanted was to go with him. Wherever he went. Mara sat quietly, listening to Yeshua and His disciples discuss where they would be heading next – down into the Galilee.

Near the back of the group sat the youngest of Yeshua's disciples. He couldn't have been much more than fourteen. His curly head was nodding with sleep. Mara's motherly instincts kicked in and she fought the urge to guide the boy off to bed.

The boy glanced up and saw Mara's gaze on him. He smiled sleepily over at her.

"You should get some rest," Mara said softly. He raised his thick, dark eyebrows in surprise, not used to being addressed by strange women. Mara had forgotten how bold she was in the eyes of many. She'd have to work on that.

All the same, the boy gave a gentle smile. "I find it hard to sleep when Yeshua is awake." The grin turned rueful on his boyish face. "I don't like to miss any of His teaching."

Mara laughed softly.

"I can understand that. How long have you been travelling with him?"

The boy shrugged. "Several months, I think. But it feels like forever. I can't remember a time when I didn't journey with Him now. He has changed my life." His thick Galilean accent made the words musical.

"He's changed mine too." Mara spoke the words quietly, but there was so much meaning behind them. The boy looked at her and she saw a deep understanding in his gaze.

He may have only been about fourteen years old, but he understood at a level far beyond that. Of course he did – he was growing up steeped in the Messiah's teachings, surrounded by His wisdom at every step. Mara thought back to when she herself had been fourteen – married to Amitai and with Rani on the way. Oh, how different their two paths. And yet, somehow, they'd led them to the same place.

"I want to follow Yeshua, as you do." Mara heard herself saying. She knew there were several other women among His followers and she desperately wanted to join them.

The boy beheld her for a long while with his doe-brown eyes. Something in his gaze told Mara he didn't think she should and somehow that hurt.

"Has it ever occurred to you that it might be Yahweh's will that you don't? Or at least not right now?" He began hesitantly. "Perhaps He might want you to stay amongst your people, and tell them what He has done for you?"

As much as Mara didn't want to accept it, something about the boy's words resonated with her. Yes, she should stay in Samaria, and tell others the truth. She raised her eyes to where Yeshua Himself and the other disciples were seated. For a brief moment, Mara's eyes locked with His. Warmth and reassurance flowed through her. In that moment, she knew that there was nothing she could do but tell of what He had done for her!

* * *

Yeshua and his followers set of early in the morning. All of Sychar came out to fondly wave them off. The town would never be the same again, that much was for certain. It felt strange to stand out on the road, watching Him leave the same way He had come. Almost as strange as knowing that they had seen the Messiah and had Him stay amongst them.

At first, no one wanted to go about their regular work, they all just wanted to sit under the big olive tree in the centre of the forum and talk about what Yeshua had taught them, what He had shared. It delighted Mara to see so many people so happy, so very alive.

She had spent a cold night, sleeping under the stars, hidden from the world in a small cave out near Ya'acov's Well. She didn't want to admit to anyone that, having left Eber, she had nowhere else to go. For the first time ever, she was completely homeless.

Mara was hungry too. She had stretched her cold, stiff bones out and washed with water from the well before making her way back into town. She didn't really know what she was going to do next, now that Yeshua was gone.

She had desperately wanted to follow Him wherever He went, but after her talk with the youngest disciple, she couldn't shake the feeling that it wasn't Yahweh's will for her. She had a strong pull to go to other of the Samaritan towns and villages, to tell them what had happened to her and tell them where they also could find new life.

Mara wasn't sure how she was going to manage it, but she had a new hope. She trusted that God would provide for her, as He does even for the sparrows. Yeshua had given her a faith she'd never had before.

Halfway through the morning, people started dispersing from town and going on with their work. Mara was left virtually alone in the square, with just a few feral dogs for company. She sat in silence for a while. What would her first move would be? Could she just take off and leave? What about her family here?! What about Raphael? She bit her lip and played distractedly with the straps on her worn sandals. She had no clue where to begin.

"Mara."

It was Shemu'el's voice. He said her name like a statement.

"You left Eber." Another statement. Mara nodded slowly, raising her eyes to where he stood, arms folded, expression stern. He was so much thinner now – she could see his illness clearly now that she was looking beyond herself. "You have your things with you." He said. She nodded again.

"Where did you sleep last night?" He asked, eyebrows raised into a firm, uncompromising wall. "In a cave by the well..." Mara said slowly. She trailed off, as Shemu'el's eyebrows shot to new heights. She was expecting him to reprimand her for her foolishness, but instead, he just reached out his hand. "Raphael told me what you said to him last night. He wants you to come home." Hesitantly, Mara took his hand, allowing him to help her to her feet. "I couldn't do that without asking you, Shem. You gave up so much for me and I just threw it back in your face. I wasn't sure you'd want me to return."

She realized what she'd just said and blushed a deep red. "I mean, that is, return to live in your house. If you were alright with it, I understand I could sleep out in the stable area, I wouldn't mind! It would be more comfortable than the cave and a lot warmer and I-"

"Mara," Shemu'el cut in. He stepped forward, his rough shepherd's hand cupping her delicate chin. "Sweet Mara, I want you to come home. I have forgiven you. We don't have to live as husband and wife, but I want Raphi to have his family back. I want to try again."

Mara felt her eyelids become slick with tears at his generous, tender-hearted words. Shemu'el had always been kind, but this was a gesture far beyond mere kindness. Yeshua had changed them all, that much was for certain.

Settling her things back into the old room she and Shemu'el had shared for the first five years of Mara's fifth marriage seemed a little surreal. This time as she settled herself in, she did not have an unborn baby deep within her womb, but a rambunctious six year old running about excitedly. He was overjoyed to have his mother home.

The tree up on the roof had grown, Mara noted. Dear, sweet Shemu'el. He had always loved her. Always been faithful to her, no matter how far she strayed from the real her.

For the first time, she began to see the parallels between her relationship with her husband and the nation of Israel and their God. Promised love and providence, they had remained true for a while, but then they had strayed far away from the God of their ancestors. And yet He loved them, yet He made a way for them. And Mara had seen that Way. His name was Yeshua.

Happy tears filled her eyes again for what felt like the hundredth time in the last few days. She was just so happy she could not contain it.

That night as she, Shemu'el and their boy Raphael sat down to eat the evening meal, her heart was more at peace than she could ever remember it feeling.

Shemu'el prayed a blessing over their food, thanking God for His great love for them in sending them Yeshua and asking Him to guide them as they lived for Him now. He held Mara's hand tightly all throughout and when he looked up, Mara saw there the love he still held for her, deep inside. For the first time, this love didn't make Mara uncomfortable, it overwhelmed her.

She was wanted. She was desired. She was loved. By Shemu'el. By

Raphael. But more than that, but the eternal One, the God of Israel.

* * *

It seemed surreal to Mara once again as she settled her little boy into bed in their home, to think that only a few weeks ago she had been living with another man, having left her precious baby and her husband who loved her so very deeply, all alone.

And now, she was back with them, the poorest she'd ever been in her entire life and happier than she had ever been. She couldn't help but laugh. If only her twelve year old self could have seen her now!

Mara and Shemu'el were learning to have a new kind of relationship, one where they learnt to love each other entirely self-sacrificially, as Yeshua had taught. Shemu'el was ahead in this, Mara felt, but she was determined to learn, to be a good wife, as she should have all along.

As she sat by Raphael's bedside, softly singing him to sleep, she thought of all the pain she might have saved if she had simply been content when she was young to marry a poor shepherd who loved her very much. If she had married Shemu'el and not Amitai, when she was thirteen, the two of them would have had over twenty years of marriage in which to learn to love each other. They would have had many beautiful and happy children. She would never have lost Rani. Never have hurt so many men, or been hurt by them.

She said as much to Shemu'el as the two of them settled into bed later that evening. Shem ran his fingers tenderly through her long hair. "Oh Mara, we can't think like that, think of the 'might have beens'. God has planned out all our steps for our entire lives, before we even start. He's mapped out paths for each of us and they are His perfect will. Besides, do you really think that we could have had a successful marriage before we knew Yeshua?"

Mara sighed softly. "You're right. I just wish there wasn't such a past behind me."

Shemu'el kissed her gently.

"It isn't there anymore, it has been forgiven."

Mara rolled over onto her back and looked up at the tree on the wall. The branches extended far out across the plaster, leaves jutting out in every direction.

"I've missed looking up at that tree every night before I sleep," she confessed. Shemu'el chuckled.

"It's been there looking back at me every night for the last twenty three years. Every paint mark, every brush-stroke on it holds a memory for me. But it's time to move forward with life, to leave the past behind. Somehow, the past doesn't feel so very important anymore. I'm ready to face the future now."

* * *

For a few, blissful weeks, Mara, Shemu'el and Raphael lived as a real family. It was wonderful. Blissful. Peaceful. Everything seemed so right in Mara's world.

But somehow, it didn't last. Shemu'el's illness returned in full force as the winter began. Mara sold the home left to her by Keren, now vacated by Eber, in order to pay for medical care for Shem, but it was no use.

There was no denying it. Shemu'el was dying.

Day by day, he grew weaker, his face thinner and his voice softer. But even as he lay pale and sickly between the sheets, his eyes grew brighter, ever more hopeful.

"I'm going home, Mara," he said to her one evening. "I'm going to be with Yahweh!"

Mara turned away, trying to hide her tears, but he caught her face in his frail hand and turned her back to look at him. "Don't mourn for me, Mara. I'm going to the best place. And one day, I have faith I will see you and my son, there, my love."

"I don't want you to go," Mara whispered softly, voice breaking with emotion. His face clouded with compassion. "Sweet Mara. Trust the God who sent Yeshua to you at the well. He guided your life to that point and He will continue to guide it, as He has guided mine. And His will, now, is that I go home, and you stay on here."

Mara bit her lip.

"I know. I'll just miss you." She buried her face in his chest, and he held her, stroking her hair until she fell asleep.

Raphael was heart-broken when he realised his Abba was dying. Shemu'el held Mara's son, who he'd made his own, as tightly as he could, rocking him and whispering Yahweh's truth into his little ears. "You're the best gift Yahweh has ever given me, Raphael," he said, eyes meeting Mara's as he spoke. "Now, look after your Imah for me." Raphael nodded bravely, as Mara came and rested her hand on his little shoulder, blinking back tears. Yahweh had been so good to her.

Shemu'el passed away the next day, under the tree he had so lovingly painted over so many years. Mara was at his side as he slipped from this world into the next. He died as he had lived – peacefully and with Yahweh's praises on his lips.

Mara sat at his side until morning. She couldn't bring herself to believe that he was really gone. Not her sweet Shemu'el – her advisor, her confidante, her best friend. Her ever-constant one. And yet, she was glad for him. Shemu'el was out of pain and where he had always longed to be.

How much she had changed, Mara realised. Before Yeshua had come, she would have taken Shemu'el's death as a personal attack of the universe, or from Yahweh Himself. Now, she knew that it was nothing of the kind – Mara was not the centre of the universe – it didn't revolve around her own life. What happened in life was all part of Yahweh's divine and beautiful plan – to glorify His name.

Looking back, Mara could see how all her own terrible choices had led up to that time at Ya'acov's Well. She had faith that Shemu'el's death would lead on to something wonderful too, even if she didn't see how until eternity!

The community of Sychar mourned Shemu'el's loss, but none more than Mara and Raphael. Their lives would never be the same without him. And yet, they had hope. They would see him again one day.

Chapter XXXI.

A.D. 27, Sychar, Samaria, Roman province of Samaria

Several months after Shemu'el's passing, just into the new year, Mara made the decision that she would now go out into the world to hear Yeshua once more, taking Raphael with her. The idea of walking away from the only true home either of them had ever known carried a strange, almost foreboding feeling. But they had a hope for their future, greater than any concerns.

Early, before the day had fairly broken, Mara made one last trip out to Ya'acov's Well. She filled water skins for the day and drank her last, cool, refreshing, early morning drink at the place where her life had changed. As she drank, Yeshua's words echoed through her mind.

"Everyone who drinks this water will be thirsty again, but whoever drinks the water I give them will never thirst. Indeed, the water I give will become in them a spring of water, welling up to eternal life."

How strange His words had sounded when first she had heard them. But now, she understood. Now it made sense. The water He gave was to quench the universal thirst for something. To give life true sense and meaning. To transform. Mara drank that last drink from Ya'acov's Well with a contented smile on her face and joy in her heart. Finally, she would live a life that meant something.

Leaving the well, she made her last walk back through Sychar. She gazed fondly upon all the old buildings. Their crumbling yellowy stone had never looked more beautiful, nor the rocky dirt walls felt as smooth under her caressing fingers. She loved this town. And she dearly loved the people in it.

And now Sychar knew the truth. It was only right that Mara should go out and tell more people the true wonder of what God was doing, right under their very noses! Their house was empty now and Mara handed over its guardianship to the Dawid until they should return.

Kissing goodbye to all their family and loved ones was hard. Since Yeshua had been with them, they'd all grown much closer. His presence had somehow sorted those who believed from those who didn't. Those who believed became as true family to one another. They had gathered together night after night, talking about what Yeshua had taught them and discussing what this would mean for their everyday lives.

Mara had been in the thick of these gatherings, where people were excitedly sharing the transforming power of Yeshua's words in their own lives. She finally belonged, finally knew how to truly live and yet, they were going to leave it all behind?! It felt crazy.

Saying goodbye to Zimra and Dawid had been especially hard. Mara and Zimra had wept in each other's arms for quite a time, their tears dripping down onto each other's backs. They had journeyed their entire lives together up to this point and parting now felt so wrong.

"I'll never forget you, Mara, no matter what happens," Zimra promised tearily after she finally released her friend. "I'll never forget the girl playing out in the fields with me, nor the young bride I helped prepare that first time. I'll never forget how you looked running through the hills, flowers in your hair, when we were children, nor the glow on your face when you first told us all you'd met Yeshua. I'll never forget anything about you."

"Oh Zimra," Mara held her hands tightly, biting her lip to keep from going into tears once more. "You have been so good to me. You are a faithful friend. I will miss you beyond all imagining. But one day, we will see each other again." She smiled and drew Zimra in for one last hug. "If not here, then in eternity! Though I don't think Sychar can be rid of me that easily."

"Learn all you can from the Messiah and come back and tell us all about it one day!"

Dawid said, giving her a bone crunching hug. "Take care of yourself, little sister." As they were picking up their bundles to leave, a figure came running up, a bundle upon his lean shoulders as well. It was Eli, Dawid and Zimra's oldest.

"Abba, Imah, I want to go with Dodah Mara and Raphi. I want to seek the Messiah also. I've thought about it and prayed about it all night. I want to go."

Rani stepped forward, a resolute look on her face.

"So do I, Abba."

Dawid looked shocked, but Zimra carried a resigned air about her. She moved into her husband's arms and hugged him close.

"I prayed about it too, Dawid. I believe it is the Lord's will for our Eli to join the travelers, to seek Yeshua once more. He is a man now and what better decision could we hope for, from our son than for him to want to follow the Messiah? And Rani, she would be in the best of hands," she said shakily.

Dawid shook his head in amazement. "I see this has all been thought out." He sighed and ran his fingers through his hair. After a few minutes, he looked up, decided.

Resting his hands upon Eli's shoulders, he addressed him. "My son, I want nothing more for you than for you to love God and to serve Him. If following Yeshua is what you believe He is calling you to do, then how could I stand in your way? Promise me you will continue in the ways we have taught you. Make sure you are always honest, always good and always hardworking. If Mara permits you to travel with them, make sure you serve her well."

Eli nodded his head solemnly, suddenly looking much older than his nineteen years.

"Yes Abba. I will bring honour to you. If I am permitted to join my relatives in their journey, that is."

Mara gave a happy laugh as she nodded her consent. "Of course we want him to join us, Dawid. Although we will be sorry to take him from your family!" Eli whooped joyfully, hugging his mother tightly and spinning his little sisters around. He hugged Rani as well, dancing her around the courtyard, too. Suddenly Mara was reminded of the cheerful little boy she'd once helped care for, after her failed first marriage. She could see his sallow little cheeks and soft baby skin, see the big round eyes that took after her own and the cheeky grin.

Eli was a man now, a beard showing along his jawline, his shoulders strong, though slender. Yet, she knew his parents must be seeing him as she was, as their precious baby, about to spread his wings and leave their nest.

Rani stepped forward to Dawid, awaiting his permission for her to go also. Mara's heart nearly stopped in her chest. "My daughter." Dawid rested his hands on her shoulders. "My beautiful daughter. What more could a father wish for than a child who would seek God above all else? You, too, have my permission."

Tears fell afresh on all the adults' cheeks. This already tender moment had become more bittersweet still. They knew. All three of them knew what Dawid had just done. He'd given Mara her daughter back. Zimra and Mara embraced wordlessly once more. A moment of painful loss and gracious regaining. Distance would never lessen the bonds of friendship and love that had forged in fire over the years. "Tell her, Mara. Tell Rani the truth about her past. You can tell her," Zimra whispered as they separated. Overcome, Mara began to sob.

Raphi tugged at his mother's arm. "Stop crying Imah! This is an adventure, not a funeral!" His childish impatience lightened the mood, and they all laughed.

And so they began their journey – Eli with Raphael on his shoulders, Mara with Rani at her side and a song in each of their hearts. It was a song of hope and a song of remembrance. This was a new season for each of them and they were all determined to begin it well.

As they reached the valley carved out between Mount Gerizim in the south and Mount Ebal in the north, Mara paused to look back. Sychar, behind them, knew the truth. Soon, more towns would hear it from her own lips. It was now that the adventure began!

Chapter XXXI.

A.D. 27, Sebaste, Samaria, Roman province of Judaea

Their first stop in the journey was Sebaste. The town had none of the splendour Mara had once remembered. Levi had been right in his prediction those years before – Sebaste had been dying.

All the same, Raphael was in complete awe of the town's large wall and the temple up on the hill.

Mara led her charges up the central Roman road into town, seeking out the forum. She wasn't quite sure how she would begin, or what she would say, but she prayed that Yahweh would give her the words. As the four of them traipsed into the forum, Mara heard a voice call out her name.

"Mara, Mara bat Mal'akhiy? It can't be you!"

Mara turned, trying desperately to place the older-looking woman, attired in a Roman stola, with expensive jewellery around her slender neck, an African slave woman at her side.

"Don't you know me? It's me, Yelsaventa!"

"Yelsaventa?!" Mara could hardly believe how her once-friend had aged.

"What are you doing back here in Sebaste?" Yelsaventa asked. "I didn't think you'd ever return, after that nasty divorce with my brother!"

Mara looked closely at her once-best friend and realised that, despite the aging, much had remained the same in her. Her haughty lips were as pronounced as ever, her eyes heavily made-up under her swooping brows. Yelsaventa was, as ever, a proud Romanesque goddess.

Gathering her thoughts around her, Mara shook her head.

"Neither did I, Yelsaventa. But, something happened and, well, here I am!" She hoped to spark Yelsaventa's cat-like curiosity. It worked.

"Something certainly must have, to have convinced the great Mara bat Mal'akhiy to return, dressed in country clothing and surrounded by a pack of children!" Yelsaventa laughed patronisingly and Mara resisted the urge to make a sharp retort. She could feel Eli bristling with enough indignation for all of them.

"You're right. You see, something incredible happened to me. A Man from Galilee came to our town with His followers. But He was no ordinary Man!"

Mara gulped nervously and licked her dry lips. This was the moment. There was a crowd of people gathering around to listen. Praying that God would guide her tongue, she felt her usual, confident spirit return, replacing the fear in the pit of her stomach.

"I was going out to the well, when I saw a Jewish man sitting there. He spoke to me – a Samaritan woman! - and asked for a drink. But then, instead He told me about the water of life. He told me things I'd never heard. He changed everything..."

Yelsaventa stood listening intently to Mara's words as she continued speaking. Mara saw a range of expressions flit over her former-friend's face.

Mara proceeded to tell her the whole story, how Yeshua had known all about her even before He had truly met her. How He had stayed amongst her people for two days, teaching them and changing their world by changing their hearts.

Eli and Rani stood close beside her, affirming the truth of her every word with their tall, solid presence. Once again, Mara was desperately glad that her lanky nephew and her beautiful daughter had joined them. Even Raphael's small, but comforting presence encouraged her on.

When she finished, Yelsaventa raised a cynical eyebrow.

"How can I know you're telling the truth?! How can I know you're not just making up every word of it? You've never really been known for your truthfulness, have you?" She finished pointedly. Mara felt her heart began to thump. "I can't do anything to prove that I am truthful," she admitted. "You know as well as anyone that I have messed up my own life entirely over the last twenty years. I have been selfish, self-centred, manipulative and unkind. I was so deep in sin I couldn't even see a horizon anymore. But Yeshua has shown me a new way, He has changed me and that's all I know. I wanted to share that with you. With everyone. I want you to know Yeshua as the Messiah, as I do."

Mara turned her eyes to Yelsaventa's slave woman also. She remembered her name now – Ere. "There's freedom for everyone in Yeshua's teaching. Even slaves. All we have to do is turn from our sinful pasts, and follow in Yahweh's way. Yeshua is the salvation we've waited for, for so long!"

Yelsaventa's face turned sour. "Oh come off it, Mara. No one is going to believe any of that, not coming from you!" She spat.

Rani's dark eyes blazed.

"It's true. If you don't believe it from my aunt, believe it from us!"

Yelsaventa gave a harsh laugh.

"Your aunt?! Oh, I see. Just another one of your little deceptions, Mara. You might as well give up telling your little story. No one will believe it coming from you. You're just a poor man's daughter from Sychar who got above herself. I think it's time you left Sebaste already. You're disturbing us all."

With a snap of her fingers, she turned on her heel, Ere following in her wake.

Mara's heart broke as she realised Yelsaventa had no intention of hearing her message, or of changing her ways. But something about Ere's eyes told her that the moment had not been totally lost.

"Excuse me?" A soft voice piped up from within the shadow of the wall. A thin young man with a patchy beard and nervously rounded shoulders stepped forward from the group of dispersing onlookers. "Is what you say true? About the Messiah, I mean?" He asked. His voice cracked at the end of his sentence and he flushed.

Eli turned to him.

"Yes, every word of what my aunt said is true. But why take our word for it? You may not believe me, or my family, or anyone from Sychar who met Him, but don't let your mistrust of us blind you. Yeshua is the Messiah! Go to Galilee and hear Him speak, listen to him..."

The young man nodded.

"Oh, I will! I'm not missing this, not for all the world!" As he finished, he smiled. He wasn't a handsome boy, but his smile was beautiful and completely transformed his ordinary face.

Mara found herself smiling along with him. This young man clearly loved Yahweh.

"We're travelling to Galilee tomorrow. Why don't you journey down with us?" The words popped out of her mouth before she had thought them through. *God, please don't let me have spoken in haste and endangered us!* She prayed.

But as she watched the young man's grey-green eyes light up in delight, she knew that she had done the right thing.

"There is nothing I would like more."

He introduced himself as Shimrit ben Colev, a cobbler by trade and Mara introduced her charges in return. She couldn't help but notice the way his gaze alighted on Rani, turning him pink to the tip of his ears. Stifling a laugh, she hoped Rani wouldn't be upset by the young man's attentions.

Shimrit took them to his boarding house – a Roman-style apartment building, much like the home Eli had been born in those many years before. He shrugged shyly.

"It isn't much, but it's all I have. You're welcome to stay here for the night."

They were all touched by Shimrit's generosity. He gave up his bed for the ladies and Raphael and chose instead to sleep on the floor alongside Eli.

The next morning, Mara awoke early. Her limbs ached after their long walk the day before and she was covered in itchy, red bites – Shimrit's bed was infested with a friendly family of bed bugs.

Rani, it seemed, had missed out on the pleasure of itchy bites and was looking as lovely as ever in the morning light.

Once Shimrit had paid for his lodgings and gathered his belongings, they prepared for another long walk, their new companion at their side.

As they set out from Sebaste, they walked onwards in the knowledge that it was now that their journey truly began. For the first time, Shimrit, Rani, Eli and Raphael would be leaving their native Shomron.

Mara remembered the excitement flowing through her veins the first time she had ventured beyond her native horizons – on a camel, at Micah's side. She felt some of the same excitement now, knowing she would soon see Yeshua again, but there was also anxiety in her mind as they made their way down, through the hills of Samaria, out and on Galilee..

From what they'd heard, over the last few weeks and months, Yeshua had gathered a crowd of followers from all corners of the Roman empire. Hopefully they'd be less out of place in Galilee now than in former times, but still, the idea of being a small group of Samaritans in a Jewish world was unsettling. There was no one the Jews hated as much as the Samaritans and they would surely be targets of derision. Mara bit her lip.

With the exception of Raphael, who had inherited Naftali's paler tones, they all had the darker, sun-kissed skin of their desert mountain people and their Samaritan accents would be impossible to disguise.

Mara steadied her breathing as they began their descent from the mountains. Surely she just needed to trust. Yeshua would keep them from harm. And it was clear they were being provided for already. Shimrit, although shy, was proving to be a most useful addition to their party. He was resourceful and adept at finding everything they needed as they travelled.

He was also lovely with Raphael, which endeared him greatly to Mara.

Having both him and Eli to protect herself and Rani was reassuring. There was no doubt in Mara's mind that Rani, at least, would be in good hands. Despite having known her only a day, Shimrit was clearly besotted with her.

The morning on which they left Sebaste, heading out to the smaller hill country towns, was dull and grey, the skies brooding and heavy. Mara knew it wouldn't be long until clouds released their burden of torrential rain, soaking the traveller. But no matter, the warm, desert wind dancing skittishly around, would soon dry them off again.

Eli walked out ahead, determination filling every stride and Raphi, who was a big fan of his older cousin followed, taking at least two steps to each of Eli's one. Shimrit followed not far behind them, leaving Mara and Rani walking companionably.

It always amazed Mara what an incredible young woman her daughter had become. Rani was bright, intelligent and although fairly quiet, funny. Silently, Mara thanked Yahweh for placing Rani in the best place for her childhood. Dawid and Zimra had brought her up wonderfully. And to have this opportunity to get to know her first-born now... Mara felt beyond blessed.

Making their way through the rocky hill country of Samaria, it didn't take them long to reach another village. And another. And another. They made their way through three small villages, telling people all about Yeshua. Some people were very open and receptive, others barely gave them the time of day.

The travellers spent the night in the hut of an old shepherd, not far outside the final village they reached. He was a man of few words, but he welcomed the five of them to share his home for the night. They gladly agreed.

Mara cooked them all dinner, using one of her own pots over the shepherd's well-wooded hearth. As she cooked, Rani at her side to help, Mara listened to Raphi and Eli play out on the field's edge and Shimrit talk to the shepherd.

The more she got to know the young Sebastean, the more Mara liked and admired him. He was nearing twenty-three, he reported and was an orphan. But he had worked hard to get through life. He seemed compassionate and generous. Mara felt overwhelmingly contented. How Shemu'el would have loved this journey, she thought. She missed him more than she could have even imagined possible.

They ate well that night and slept even better – it had been a long twenty-four hours and all of them were exhausted for some reason or another – Mara emotionally more than anything else.

The dawn had not yet broken as they set off the next morning. The air was cool as they began their climb through the foothills and on towards the coast and Galilee. Mara felt wide awake and full of thoughts.

The men were singing as they walked up ahead, Raphael's legs dangling from where he sat on Eli's strong, sinewy shoulders. Mara tried not to lag behind, smiling to herself as she noticed Shimrit and Rani had fallen into step.

Yellowed, grass covered hills rolled on and on, as far as she could see, the occasional tree standing above it all, majestically staking out a kingdom of its own, where birds congregated and wild animals took their rest. Thankfully, they had not encountered any particularly dangerous animals so far, unless one counted deer.

What is it I was searching for all my life that I have found now? She wondered as they walked. Obviously Yeshua, the Messiah, and what He taught us, but what was it that so desperately changed everything for me?

Mara's thoughts fluttered around her in a confused manner as she pondered exactly what had changed in her life with Yeshua's arrival. One word kept coming back to her. Hope. That was it.

Before Yeshua had come to her people and had met her at the Well built by an ancestor to them both, she had had no hope for her future, no sense of purpose, no idea what she could look forward to in this life. In fact, she had been utterly hopeless.

But everything was different now. Yeshua was the very Messiah of God, the one long promised who would change history forever. And she was here, alive at this very time!

If Mara had been her father's age, she would not have lived to see the Messiah come. All who had come before her had missed out on knowing the greatest One of all time. If she had been born later, at least there would be the memory of Him, the knowledge that He had been on this earth. And, Mara was sure, He would not be leaving this earth in the same state He had found it in. He would surely be making drastic changes. His disciples had spoken of Him as being King of the Jews – perhaps that meant He would free them from Roman oppression – what relief that would bring! But as Mara thought back over all He had shared with the people of Sychar, all He had said, she couldn't help but wonder if He had come to do something entirely different.

Making their way through a narrow, rocky ravine, Mara turned her thoughts back to the task at hand. The boys helped her over the tricky bits of the climb, whilst Raphi, full of energy, scampered on ahead. Unlike Mara, Rani was also an able climber and didn't seem to be bothered in the slightest by the restrictions of her long tunic.

Once they'd made their way through the pass and were coming back to the main road to Galilee, Mar went back to her previous thoughts.

"Everyone who drinks this water will be thirsty again, but whoever drinks the water I give them will never thirst. Indeed, the water I give will become in them a spring of water, welling up to eternal life." Yeshua's words played through her mind once more.

He had spoken of Yahweh as His own father and Mara believed it to be true. She had heard what the young disciple had said, how the spirit of God had descended upon Him as a dove and voice from heaven had been heard saying:

"This is my Son, with Whom I am well pleased. Listen to Him."

Mara knew she, for one, would always listen to him! The "water" He gave had quenched every longing she had ever known.

"For we, like sheep, have gone astray, each one of us has turned to his own way; and the Lord laid on Him the iniquity of us all." The words of the old prophecy, spoken first by God, then verbalized by Yesha'yahu, floated through her mind. We, like sheep, have gone astray, she thought. I couldn't have gone much further astray, and yet God has brought me back into the sheep fold! She smiled at the thought.

Yeshua had spoken of Himself as the Good Shepherd – how true was that?! He had brought her and so many of her brothers and sisters from Sychar back to the true ways, the almost-forgotten ways of their forefathers. It was a new fulfillment of an old plan; words breathed out centuries before were now coming into being and transforming lives all around them.

Chapter XXXIII.

A.D. 27, Nazareth, Galilee, Roman province of Judaea

They stopped for a meal near the main road to Galilee. Compared to the quiet roads they had travelled earlier further back into Samaria, this road was packed.

People were coming from all directions – some from Judea in the south, others from Peraea or Decapolis to the East and more from Samaria itself, all heading down to Galilee to see Yeshua.

The five travellers from Sychar found themselves in the midst of mass of travellers. Most of the Jews ignored them, which was no true surprise, but people from foreign lands mingled with them, talking and asking what they had heard of this King of the Jews.

Mara told many people what had happened to her by Ya'acov's Well those weeks ago.

She noticed a cluster of nearby Jews who couldn't keep themselves from listening. Once she'd finished her story, a poorly dressed, but pretty young Jewess, called out in spite of herself.

"You mean Yeshua asked you for a drink? From the well of our ancestors?"

"Ya'acov was our ancestor too!" Eli shot back, automatically. Mara gave him a softly rebuking look, then answered the Jewess.

"Yes, it is true, He did. It surprised me as much as it must surprise you, but it is the truth." Her eyes were shining brightly with joy and excitement as she went on. "Just wait until you hear Him speak. It is like nothing you've ever heard!"

"What does he look like?" Another of the Jews, a young man, perhaps the girl's brother, piped up now. "Does he look like a king?"

Mara gave a gentle laugh.

"Well, not what you'd think one might look like. He's fairly ordinary looking, not particularly handsome, large, or strong. He does have a sense of authority when He speaks, but He doesn't look like a ruler. His eyes are different though. It is like His eyes contained a beautiful secret, that couldn't help but spill over. I could just feel it."

"How can He be the Messiah if He doesn't look like a King?" The Jewish youth asked cynically. An old man, near the back of the group spoke up now. "Remember when God chose our ancestor Dawid to be King, He said this: 'Do not consider his appearance or his height, for I have rejected Saul. The LORD does not look at things man looks at, man looks at the outward appearance, but the LORD looks at the heart.'"

The travellers let the old man's words sink in in silence, as they considered their profoundness. Dawid had been the King of Kings for Israel and He had not been chosen based on appearances. How much more the Messiah – the true King of Kings?

* * *

Eli couldn't believe the change in his aunt. For as long as he had been able to remember, his Dodah Mara had been a selfish, self-absorbed woman. She had been the centre of attention. Always.

She had always been a beautiful woman, even Eli could see that. She wasn't anything like the simple "lovely" that was his mother, Zimra.

No, Aunt Mara had always been the sort of woman to make men stop and gawk in the street. Even now, more than halfway through her third decade, she was striking to look at.

But after meeting Yeshua, Mara was different. She'd always been so flighty. Now, it seemed, she had become steady. She'd always been likeable – friendly and funny, fiery. But now, Eli decided, she could even be considered trustworthy.

So much about his aunt Mara's life had always been a secret from him, his parents had ensured that. He knew she had been married five times and that she suffered ill-fortune, not all self-imposed. But he did know that when he was about thirteen, she'd left his uncle Shemu'el for that Jew, Eber ben Natan – that was definitely her fault.

Walking through the hills was something Eli was accustomed to, but even he found himself a little puffed as they went on into the heart of Galilee. He was leading the pack, with his cousin Raphael at his side.

Behind him walked Shimrit, with Rani not too far behind.

Eli smiled to himself. He liked Shimrit a lot, despite his slightly awkward nature. The two of them had talked late into the night and Shimrit reminded Eli very much of his own father – contemplative and quiet. A real thinker. A deep carer.

There was no denying that Shimrit had noticed Eli's pretty older sister and Eli smiled again at the thought. He may have only known Shimrit a few days, but already he knew the older boy was a wonderful match for sweet, gentle Rani.

Rani. As he looked back at his sister, he considered her past. He couldn't ever remember a time when Rani wasn't at his side. The two of them had always been inseparable. Rani was a year and a half his senior, a fact which confused him. His parents had been married only just over a year when he was born and there was no question that they would have borne Rani in immorality – they were too righteous for that.

And then there was Rani's appearance. She had dark eyes like Dawid, but other than that, she looked very little like either of their parents. Whilst Zimra was slight and plain, and Dawid dark and strong-featured, everything about Rani was delicately striking.

As Eli glanced back once more, he saw both Rani and Dodah Mara in the same moment. They were, with the exception of the eyes, perfect mirrors of each other.

The woman from Sebaste's words filtered back through his mind.

"Your aunt?! Oh, I see. Just another one of your little deceptive webs, Mara."

So it was true. As he had long suspected. Rani was Mara's daughter. And yet, neither his parents, nor Mara had ever breathed a word. He glanced back at Rani once more, wondering if she knew.

* * *

As they descended from the hill country of Samaria onto the low, flat plains of Galilee, they joined an even larger crowd. Mara had travelled a lot more than any of her people, thanks to Micah and Keren, but she had never been to Galilee before. She wasn't prepared for how beautiful it would be.

The lush greens of the farm-land below them and the brilliant, vibrant blue of the Sea of Tiberius – Lake Galilee – sparkling far away on the horizon at the edge of the land was breathtaking. Raphi, Rani, Shimrit and Eli, who had never seen the ocean before were all completely awestruck.

They stopped in their tracks, just gazing down at this beautiful corner of Judaea, so unlike their own. Samaria's heights were barren, with brown as the dominant colour – brown dirt, brown shrubs and grass, brown animals, brown buildings, brown clothing – with only the occasional green tree for relief.

Here, it seemed, there were no dominant colours, instead a fantastic mixture of shades meeting the eye from horizon to horizon.

"It's so pretty, Imah!" Raphael breathed. Mara couldn't help but smile. Her son was all boy and was usually far to busy to notice anything like scenery!

"Yes, Raphi, it is beautiful." She replied softly.

The crowds continued to grow as they made their way further through the region. That first night, after more than five, long hours of walking, they made it to Nazareth – the town of Yeshua's childhood.

The next morning, they set out early, despite their aching legs. They came first to Cana, the place where, the young disciple had reported, Yeshua turned water into wine! Four long hours later, they finally made it to the lakeshore, at a place called Tiberius.

The crowd there was immense. Mara held tightly to Raphael's hand. She wanted him close in amongst all these people. But there was something else, too; before long, she knew he would be all grown up and she didn't want to miss out on more of his life than she already had, thanks to her own terrible choices.

The crowds had gathered on the shore and Mara strained to see what was causing interest. Fishermen. There was fresh fish galore. She tried not to feel disappointed, but she had so hoped it would be Yeshua, teaching the people and that she would get to hear Him.

They made their way down anyway, feeling some fish would not go amiss after their long and tiring journey. Mara bartered her way to three fresh fish, all shiny and silvery, just waiting to be cooked and eaten.

"Hey, have you seen Yeshua here?" Eli asked the fisherman after Mara had finished making her deal. The Jew wiped his hands on his grimy tunic, trying to decide whether to ignore this Samaritan's question or not. Eventually, he answered. "The Nazarene? I've heard he's up north of here, at Bethsaida. It's not all that far, maybe half a day's walk." He looked over at Raphi, now tired, moaning and leaning up against Rani, then amended his statement. "A day's walk."

Eli nodded his thanks.

"Looks like we'll be staying here for the night then." He lifted his cousin onto his shoulders once more and began to lead the group off to find a place on the rocky shore.

They all sat down, tired from their journey. Mara and Rani set about making a little fire and slowly cooking the fish over it. Fresh fish had never tasted better. Raphael, never having tasted anything like it, pulled faces and wanted to spit it out. Rani reprimanded him.

"Just because it's different doesn't mean it's bad Raphi, you know that. God made fish good for eating. Besides, your Imah put effort into it. You'll eat it even if you don't want to."

Raphael hung his head and sulked a little, but then Eli, recently Raphael's biggest hero, proclaimed that he liked the fish and Raphi tucked in, sulks forgotten.

Mara watched their little group as they ate. She noticed Eli had been casting her strange looks for some time now and wondered what he was thinking. Turning to the left, she looked to where Rani was helping Raphael with his food. Her two precious children. Yahweh had been so good to her.

After they'd all eaten, they got up, ready to go and seek somewhere to stay. They weren't really sure where to start, but before they'd got far in their considerations of it, the fisherman they'd been talking to earlier came over to them.

"You're followers of the Nazarene then?" He asked in his strong, Galilean accent.

Mara nodded. "Yes. He came through our village and taught us."

The fisherman sighed and wiping his hand on his tunic again, he stretched out his arms to them. "People will think me crazy for doing this, but having heard Him speak, I believe it is what the Nazarene would want of me. Please, come Samaritans and be my guests for the night. My family and I would be happy to have you stay with us."

Eli's eyes widened. "You'd really let Samaritans stay with you?" He asked incredulously, eyebrows almost meeting his straggly hairline.

The fisherman rolled his eyes. "I know, I know, I've lost my mind. Come with me, this way, before I realize my madness and send you away," he said somewhat sardonically. Picking up their bundles, they followed him with no more questions, bemused, yet thankful.

Chapter XXXIV.

A.D. 27, Tiberius, Galilee, Roman province of Judaea

The fisherman's house wasn't far from the shore, in a line of other houses. As they stepped in side, they all blinked, trying to adjust their eyes, after the bright afternoon sun outside.

It was a small dwelling, much like their own in Sychar, with mud brick and stone walls and slit windows to allow the air and light in. The roof was fairly low and Eli had to stoop as he went about.

The fisherman called a short, stout woman with a round, smiling face and introduced her to them. "This is my wife, Leah. And since I didn't mention it earlier, my name is Daniyyel." Leah came over and bobbed a sort of curtsy to the strangers her husband had brought into their home.

"My name is Mara bat Mal'ikhiy," Mara offered. "This is Rani, my nephew Eli and son Raphael. And this is our new friend, Shimrit. We have travelled to Galilee to see the Messiah."

Leah's face bloomed into a friendly smile. "You and half the world with you!"

Daniyyel ran his hands through his hair, grimacing. He was no doubt considering how he would be looked down on by all in his neighbourhood for inviting the Samaritans to share his home for the night.

"I couldn't just leave them out there, with nowhere to go," he said softly in his wife's ear.

She just nodded. Louder, Daniyyel continued. "I'll go back and fetch my fish now. Leah and our children will see you settled in and comfortable."

"I'll come and help you with the fish," Eli offered, trying to repay the Jew's kindness. Shimrit stepped forward too. Daniyyel considered for a moment, then nodded.

"Alright, thank you lads. I could do with a couple more pairs of strong arms and you look like yours will do." He clapped Eli on his muscular, yet slender shoulders and grinned. "He looks much as I did as a young man, doesn't he Leah? Thin, but sinewy, strong as an ox, I'll warrant."

Leah just laughed and watched her husband lead the Samaritan lad and the cobbler off. Eli and Shimrit followed Daniyyel with lanky strides, towering over the Jew's shorter, stockier frame.

Leah turned back to face Mara and Rani.

"I'm so glad you've come seeking Yeshua, my dear," she said kindly, resting a hand on Mara's shoulder. Mara was surprised to find herself almost overcome by the gesture. She was exhausted, mentally and physically and had been longing for a spot of kindness. For it to come from a Jewish woman was even more surprising.

"How could we not come to Him?" Mara said haggardly. "We meet Him as He came through Sychar and He changed our lives. All I want is to see Him again, to hear Him speak." Her voice cracked on the last word, betraying her exhaustion to her host. Leah wrapped her arm right around her and hugged her.

"You poor dear, you must be absolutely exhausted. Come sit down now. I'll send your boy out the back to play with my little ones and you ladies can rest."

Wearily, Mara lowered herself onto a seat by the kitchen table and watched as Raphael was ushered out to play with the children in the yard. She was so grateful to this woman for her sweetness, yet she didn't have the energy left to do more than utter a simple thank you. She hoped she would understand!

Later that evening, they had the chance to meet all of Daniyyel and Leah's children – quite a brood, aged from a fifteen year old boy not much shorter than Eli, down to a little girl of three and a baby. In between there were five other children.

The one that stood out most to Mara was the oldest daughter – fourteen years old and just beginning to bloom into the flower of womanhood.

The girl, named Avigayil, was willowy, with long hair of a reddish-golden colour. She was very clearly aware of her beauty and from the flirtatious glances she made in Eli's direction, well aware, also, of its advantages.

Mara watched her, a vice of regret taking hold of her heart. Her mind flashed before her eyes picture after picture of her own such behaviour when she was Avigayil's age.

She watched Avigayil cast through-the-eyelash glances at her nephew, a sweet and seemingly innocent smile on the girl's lips and thought of similar glances she had cast Levi's way, Amitai's way, Micah's way…

She wondered if there had ever been a time when her eyes had been truly innocent, with no flirtatious undertone, or sense of false modesty. Had her fiery eyes ever carried less than a subtle hint that she knew her own beauty and was just daring some boy to come and get it? If only she'd listened to those who tried to warn her away from her foolish course.

Avigayil was laughing now, a musical little laugh, eyelashes batting and auburn hair forming a sort of halo around her head. She was a beautiful girl, no doubt about that and she seemed vivacious, full of life.

Eli, Mara was thankful, seemed to have missed the girl's flirtatious advances and was much more interested in talking to her father and older brother. Mara laughed inwardly. Oh, how that would irritate the young heroine – that any man could look past her, especially one as handsome as Eli!

Eli was, of course, the very picture of how a young male of Israelite descent should look and the girl would want his attentions, even if he was a Samaritan. Mara couldn't help noticing that Shimrit, less good looking and quieter, was not a target of Avigayil's advances. Not that he would have noticed anyhow – his eyes were for Rani alone.

Mara looked over and was pleased to see Raphi playing contentedly on the floor with the other children. Leah was watching them all carefully as she nursed her baby.

Taking her opportunity, Mara moved across the room to where Avigayil was sitting and attempted to strike up a conversation with her.

"So Avigayil, tell me about yourself. Are you promised in marriage yet?" She asked with what she hoped was a friendly smile. The girl sighed melodramatically.

"Not yet. Abba and Imah are ever so picky and all I want to do is get married. Almost anyone would please me, provided he were handsome and had enough money."

She laughed playfully and Mara laughed as well, although she didn't really find it a humorous statement.

"You know, I'm somewhat an expert on what kind of man not to marry," she began, trying to engage Avigayil's curiosity. It worked. "What do you mean?"

Mara shook her head ruefully, smiling at the two brown eyes gazing up at her intently. "I married five of them," she said sheepishly. "Well, actually four, but that's a long story."

"Tell me!" Avigayil demanded. Mara smiled again. How very like herself this girl was. She couldn't help but wonder if Yahweh had brought her to this home for the express purpose of warning the girl what her future could look like if she wasn't careful.

"I was much like you as a girl, I suppose. Popular, witty and everyone told me I was pretty. All I wanted was to get married, to get away from my family at home and to begin my own life, my own way, with a handsome, rich husband to care for all my needs and to make me look good. I wanted that more than anything else in the world. When I was eleven, a rich girl in Sebaste befriended me, made me her companion. And before I knew it, I had fallen desperately in love with her brother. And I thought he loved me too. But it wasn't as I thought and eventually, my father sent me away from Sebaste to save my reputation. Back in Sychar, I was determined that I would still marry well. When I caught the eye of the Samaritan High Priest's oldest son, I was delighted! Before I knew it he had proposed and I was betrothed. People warned me not to be foolish, not to be swayed by my dreams of a good life. They assured me that there was more to life than money, that a man of good character is worth more than a handsome face and wealth. I didn't believe them though. I thought they were all just jealous. I married Amitai six months after my thirteenth birthday. He told me the day of our wedding that he had known the first time he saw me that I was the most beautiful girl and since he was determined to always have the best of everything that I must be his. Little did I know what a curse that kind of attitude would be..."

For almost an hour, Avigayil sat, enthralled, as she listened to Mara's carefully edited tale. She didn't want to give the girl too much to consider. As she came to the part where she left Shemu'el to live with the runaway Jew, Avigayil shook her head sadly, brown eyes showing sympathy, regret, understanding and distaste.

"That's so sad, lady. I can see why they call you Bitterness."

Mara nodded frankly. "Yes. All my life, I've hated my name, yet I never saw how appropriate it had become. But all that has changed now. You see, when I met Yeshua, He knew every single detail of which I have just told you and more, yet He'd before never set foot in my home

339

town, met me, or heard my story. He knew me. He knew what kind of a woman I had been. But still, He came to me. He told me of His water of life, and He shared the truth with my people. He transformed everything about me. I am a new woman. I am no longer bitter, but redeemed. Galiliah."

Avigayil smiled. "That name suits you far better!" She said. Mara nodded.

"I heard one of the Jewish men speaking of a Scripture from one of your prophets on my way through here – talking about your city of Jerusalem – but I feel as if describes me too.

The nations will see your vindication and all kings your glory; you will be called by a new name that the mouth of the LORD will bestow."

Avigayil laughed. "Yes, it does seem to describe you! And there's another thing the prophets said that makes me think of you.

Do not be afraid, you will not be put to shame.

Do not fear disgrace; you will not be humiliated.

You will forget the shame of your youth

And remember no more the reproach of your widowhood."

As Mara heard those words, emotion swept through her again. How incredible to hear those words that the God of the Angel Armies had spoken over His people so long ago.

Yeshua had spoken of how He had come to set all of His people free – both Jews and Gentiles, for all Yahweh has chosen belong to Him – maybe now those words did speak of her.

She held out her hand to Avigayil and tenderly gripped the younger girl's slender fingers. "Avigayil, the Lord has changed my life entirely. I am so thankful for that. I hope that He will use my story to change the hearts of others too. All I have been through has brought me to this point, and therefore, it is all worth it. But if I can help prevent anyone from going through what I went through, I will."

She looked deep into Avigayil's eyes.

"You are a beautiful girl, Avigayil, and you will make some man a beautiful, and wonderful wife one day, there is no doubt about that." Avigayil blushed prettily, smiling at the compliment.

"But," Mara continued, "I want to caution you. With great beauty comes great responsibility. I mistreated my beauty and hurt many people because of it. People I genuinely loved and cared about. I was not a good person. And I hurt myself as much as everyone else. I want to encourage you to always be kind, Avigayil, not to manipulate people, or shape events your own way. Trust God with your life, trust Him to provide for you, to give you everything you need. Don't try and create your own future outside of His will. It doesn't work. It isn't worth it. Avigayil, please, try and save yourself the hurt I endured and caused. Wait on love, it will come. Don't marry for looks or money. Marry for a true heart. Marry a man you can serve Yahweh with."

She squeezed Avigayil's hand tightly, delighted that she was holding her attention so well.

"I saw the way you were looking at my nephew before."

Avigayil blushed and Mara continued, trying to use her sweetest tone.

"I understand that he is a handsome lad and he is a good man. But I cannot believe you really wished to marry him, for he is a Samaritan and you are a Jew. I know you wished to seduce his heart and win his love anyway, for it makes one feel good to have such power over a man. I know this because I was once exactly like you in this. But don't make the mistake I did. Seek God, not men. All my life I searched for a love that would last, but only God is truly faithful."

Avigayil had tears in her big brown eyes as Mara finished speaking.

Mara was aware of Leah watching from across the room, a tender smile on her face, but Avigayil was commanding all of Mara's attention. "Thank you," the girl said thickly. "Thank you for being brave enough to be honest with me and for telling me what you really think. I needed to hear that, although it wasn't easy." She laughed a little, the tears still gleaming in the edge of her eyes.

Mara squeezed her hand again. She felt such an affinity with the younger girl before her and was only too thankful to have the opportunity to share so much with her.

"Thank you for listening to me, Avigayil. I appreciate that you did and I hope that you will truly take it to heart as well."

Avigayil nodded. "Oh, I will. I know it's wrong of me to seek attention the way I do, but I've never really considered the consequences. My parents have warned me, but, well, meeting you is different."

Mara laughed softly, sadly. "My father warned me too. If only I had been sensible enough to listen!"

Avigayil looked sympathetically at her. "I guess we all make mistakes, don't we?" She said. Mara laughed again. "That is for certain! I only wish every young girl could know the love of Yeshua, the love of God, the way I do now. If I had known it as a girl, I'm sure I wouldn't have fallen into the traps I did."

The two of them talked on, for many hours, until Leah shooed Avigayil off to bed. She came over to Mara and gave her a warm hug. "Thank you! I heard some of what you were saying to my daughter and I appreciate it very much. To share your own personal story so that she might learn to follow Yahweh better? Thank you!"

Mara shrugged. "I have nothing to offer other than what Yeshua has done for me." She smiled. "Avigayil is a lovely girl, inside and out. As I saw her this evening, she reminded me of myself as a child. But she is better than I in that she has a heart willing to listen to advice, to be shaped. I never had that."

Leah teared up a little at Mara's words and hugged her again, tighter this time. She didn't say any more, but it was clear to Mara that she was incredibly thankful.

Chapter XXXV.

A.D. 27, Tiberius, Galilee, Roman province of Judaea

Mara and her young companions ended up staying three days at Tiberius with Daniyyel, Leah and their family. By the time they were ready to leave, it felt as though they were saying goodbye to long-time, precious friends.

Even Daniyyel, who had been so gruff at first, embraced each of them and wished them well. Mara and Avigayil had a particularly emotional farewell. The young woman hugged the older tightly, kissing her cheek.

"I'll never forget you, Mara. Or what you taught me. Yeshua has changed my heart!" Avigayil said softly. Mara embraced her in return, then held her out at arms length.

"I'm so proud of you. You have the character I never had. You will grow into a wonderful woman, I can tell. And one day, you will make some man very happy."

Mara couldn't help but notice the way Avigayil's eyes flicked up to where Eli stood wrestling their things into bags with Shimrit. But Mara was delighted to see that the old flirtatiousness was gone, replaced by gentle admiration. Good.

They set off, journeying on all the way around Lake Galilee to where

Yeshua was said to be with His followers. The journey only took them a little over three hours, despite the roads being packed with other travellers. They had originally intended to head all the way to Bethsaida, but new reports were heard – Yeshua was in Capernaum.

Mara noted that there were a lot more Roman occupiers here in Galilee than at home in Samaria. Many of the soldiers bore a look of the Samaritan people, which was hardly surprising considering the Ala I Sebastenorum cavalry and Cohors I Sebastenorum infantry were based in Capernaum, only a few miles up the road.

The soldiers walked tall, resplendent in the red and brown uniforms of imperial Rome. The pride in their eyes and the arrogance in their step made Mara understand why the Jews hated them. These were their "supposed brothers" aiding the regime of the enemy. The hatred in the eyes of the Jewish people was burning hot, though silent.

As Mara watched, fair-skinned Roman commander on horseback swept through the people on the road, riding as though he was in a great hurry.

"Imah! Imah! I see the disciples! I see Yeshua's followers!" Raphi's excited voice rose above the resentful mutterings of the crowd. His face was flushed with excitement as he pulled at Mara's stola. She felt the excitement rising within herself as well.

Grabbing her son's hand in one hand and Rani's in the other, Mara set off as fast as she could, Shimrit and Eli following along closely.

The Messiah was sitting under a tree, a crowd surrounding him. Delightedly, they joined the throng, ready to listen to him speak. Although they struggled to see Him through the masses, even just hearing Him teach was wonderful.

Mara sat enthralled, Raphael on her lap, surrounded by the others.

They were not the only non-Jews, or even the only Samaritans in the region. Everywhere, it seemed to Mara, there were Gentiles, all seeking to hear this mysterious Prophet speak.

Mara was surprised to see that amongst them was the Roman centurion she'd seen earlier. She mentioned it to her companions. Shimrit leaned across to explain, eyes shining. It seemed all of their eyes were shining these days.

"I hear that Yeshua did a miracle for that soldier. His servant was on his deathbed and the centurion trusted that Yeshua would heal him. So He did. No wonder the centurion is back here listening again."

Mara looked across at the tall, powerful looking man. Earlier, she had noticed his authoritative presence. Now, as she looked at his clean-shaven face, Mara saw something else. Light. This man believed, as she herself did, that Yeshua was the salvation for all.

A man standing nearby, overhearing their conversation, spoke up.

"Yeshua himself said that He had not seen such faith as that centurion had, even here in Israel!"

Mara looked at the centurion once more. Yes. She could see the faith in his gaze.

Capernaum was a beautiful town. It lay on the edge fringes of Lake Tiberius, the Sea of Galilee. The brilliant azure blue of its waters reminded Mara of the necklace Keren had once gifted to her. That necklace was long gone, sold off to raise money for Shemu'el's treatment.

Day after day, the people gathered beside the waters to listen to Yeshua teach. The Jews also went to hear him speak in their majestic synagogue. Eli bemoaned the fact that they were not permitted to enter, but Rani rebuked him softly.

"We should be grateful to have heard Yeshua at all, Eli. He didn't have to come to our people..."

The time they spent each day beside the Lake, as close to the water's edge as they could get, were always happy ones. Mara was beginning to realize what Yeshua meant by never again thirsting – hearing His words made her joyful in a way she'd never experienced before.

At night, groups of Gentiles would gather together by blazing fire pits on the lake shore and discuss what they'd heard during the day and tell their stories. In amongst the mixed group were Greeks, Romans, freed men, tribespeople from the neighbouring lands and runaway slaves from far further afield.

Most nights, a group of the tall, dark Arabs would pull out their flutes and play beautiful, melancholy music long into the night, whilst people dozed, or talked. Rani would raise her beautiful soprano voice along with them. Most nights ended up with Raphael fast asleep on one of their laps, or curled up at Eli's side.

Night after night, Mara ended up telling the story of her life and what had happened to her beside Ya'acov's Well, to interested listeners.

Sometimes she ended up with crowds of listeners, reducing the women to tears.

One night, amongst the listeners, Mara spotted several Roman legionaries. She had to hold back a laugh of wonder. She had never in her wildest dreams imagined that one day, she, a simple Samaritan woman, might be telling the tale of how she met the Messiah, to Romans.

Each night, no matter how the story was received – sometimes well, sometimes badly – Mara went to sleep happy and satisfied. She was surrounded by a little family who loved her, regardless of her past. And she was sharing what Yeshua had done for her, with others.

A particularly starry night by the fire pits saw Rani and Eli sat side by side, Shimrit across from them. Mara was off talking to a group of women and Raphi was long since asleep.

Eli found himself unable to stop the question slipping out.

"Rani, have Abba and Imah ever talked to you about your history?"

Rani looked across at him, confused.

"What do you mean?"

"Have you ever wondered, well, if they're really your parents?" Eli hesitated.

"What a thing to say, Eli!" Rani turned her back on him, shocked.

Shimrit bit his lip nervously, then piped up.

"I think I know what Eli is trying to say, Rani. You know in Mara's story, she talks about how she had a daughter with her first husband and lost her when she married her second husband... Well, when she talks about Yathom, her first son, she names him and says he died. She's never named the daughter, nor mentioned her death. And you do look an awful lot like Mara..."

He trailed off, shrugging nervously under Rani's heavy gaze.

"You really think so?" She was also biting her lip. She felt as if her whole world had just been ripped out from under her. Eli and Shimrit both nodded solemnly.

Getting shakily to her feet, Rani moved away. Shimrit started, as if to try and comfort her, but she waved him away.

"I want to be alone for a while."

The stars were reflecting in the still waters of Lake Galilee when Mara found Rani, sitting alone on the rocky shore. She had her knees drawn up to her chin and her dark eyes bright with tears. "Is it true?" she asked thickly, without even turning around. Mara lowered herself slowly down beside her daughter. "Rani, I didn't know how to tell you. Or if I even should..." she broke off, unsure of how to continue.

Rani turned her dark, tearful eyes towards the woman she'd always called her aunt. "So, you really are my mother then?" Mara reached out for the girl's slender hand.

"Sweet Rani. It is true that I am the woman who bore you. But Zimra is and always will be your true Imah. Zimra and Dawid gave you what I never could have – a real home and real parents. They brought you up to be the woman you are now. I never could have done that... And your father, Amitai, cast you off because of me."

Rani shook her head in disbelief. "I can't believe none of you ever told me."

Mara sighed shakily. "We thought it to be for the best. I wanted you to have the best life you could, without the shadow of my past over you. My beautiful daughter." She spoke the words for the first time.

She was waiting now, waiting for Rani to explode in anger. To run off. To never want to see her again. Mara could see the anguish crossing Rani's face, flowing out as tears. But what the young woman said surprised her more than anything else she possibly could have done.

"Thank you. Thank you so much. You gave me away and that must have been so hard for you. But you gave me a gift. You gave me my life."

Grace flowed freely between them as, for the first time in over eighteen years, the mother and daughter embraced as such.

For a long while, they just sat and cried together. But then, there was something new. A bonding of hearts, the like of which Mara had never experienced. As she sat with her precious daughter, she raised her eyes to the starry skies, she whispered her silent thanks up to Yahweh.

* * *

"Rani! Mara! Eli! All of you! You won't believe what happened!" Shimrit's excited voice startled the little family as the deep of night rolled into the yawning purple of dawn.

"What is it?" Mara groaned, a little irritable to have been woken so early.

"Yeshua has done something radical! Like really, incredibly radical! You won't believe it!" He repeated. Something in his tone of voice made them all sit up and pay attention.

Mara pulled Raphael onto her lap, her thick, woollen cloak around them both. At her side Rani and Eli were struggling upright, rubbing sleep from their long lashes.

Shimrit planted himself down by the now, almost-dead, embers of last night's fire. When he saw they were all listening, he imparted his big news with an air of incredulity.

"Yeshua has claimed to forgive sins."

"What?!" Eli was completely alert now. "But only God Himself can do that!"

"Does that mean He is claiming deity?!" Rani asked in amazement.

Shimrit shrugged, and nodded excitedly. "I guess He must be. He's always claimed to be Yahweh's own Son, born of Mirayim, when she was virgin. But what if He wasn't just His Son, but in very nature, God!"

Mara felt her head spinning.

"You better start at the beginning, Shimrit. Where has all of this come from?"

Shimrit nodded, slowing to catch his breath. Rani stoked up the fire, as the early morning air was chilly, even so far into the year.

"So last night, after you all went to sleep, I found myself wide awake. It was almost as if Yahweh didn't want me to sleep. I found myself compelled to go for a walk and so I did." He paused a little shyly, looking through his tangled fringe to see if he held their attention.

"As I was walking, I heard the noise of a party coming from one of the houses near the synagogue. I thought I heard Yeshua's voice, so I stopped." He began to look sheepish as he continued.

"I guess I probably should have minded my own business and continued on my way, but I let my curiosity get the better of me. I climbed an olive tree overlooking the garden and saw that it was the home of one of the Pharisees – the man named Shim'on. The party was in full swing. But as I watched, well, this is where it got interesting."

He paused again, this time to sip the hot, spiced wine Rani had put into his hands, then continued, as his listeners waited in expectant silence. "A woman entered the gathering then. Not just any woman, but one of those who, ahem, works at night..." he explained delicately, flushing as he spoke. "A bad and sinful woman."

Mara's heart ached as he spoke. She knew just the kind of woman he meant.

"The woman approached where Yeshua sat and she stood behind him. She was crying. Her tears fell all over His feet, as if she were trying to wash them. And then she wiped them dry with her hair. She kissed his feet over and over and finally she poured expensive perfume all over them. Everyone just watched in stunned silence."

Shimrit wrinkled up his face. "You could see in that Pharisee's face, how disgusted he was, how he thought Yeshua should have known what kind of woman she was. But Yeshua did know, there is no doubt. That's when He spoke. He spoke softly, I had to lean in close to hear.

He told Shim'on he had something to tell him, and Shim'on listened."

"What did He say?!" Eli begged eagerly.

"He said: "Two people owed money to a certain moneylender. One owed him five hundred denarii and the other fifty. Neither of them had the money to pay him back, so he forgave the debts of both. Now which of them will love him more?" Shim'on replied, "I suppose the one who had the bigger debt forgiven.""You have judged correctly," Yeshua said. Then He turned toward the woman, and said to Simon, "Do you see this woman? I came into your house. You did not give me any water for my feet, but she wet my feet with her tears and wiped them with her hair. You did not give me a kiss, but this woman, from the time she entered, has not stopped kissing my feet. You did not put oil on my head, but she has poured perfume on my feet. Therefore, I tell you, her many sins have been forgiven—as her great love has shown. But whoever has been forgiven little loves little." Then Yeshua said to her "Your sins are forgiven".

Shimrit gave a moment for his words to sink in.

"I heard all the guests murmuring in shock "Who is this who even forgives sin?!" I was wondering the same myself. Then Yeshua said to the woman, "Your faith has saved you; go in peace." And she left. But I stayed in that tree for a long time, just thinking. And now, here I am."

None of them knew quite what to say next. What Shimrit had shared was a life-changing utterance. And yet, they all believed it.

Listening to Yeshua the next few days as he taught, they were all in shock. He was God's own Son. He could forgive sins. It was incredible.

A few nights later, Mara and Rani sat companionably beside the lake as the sun set, as they had been doing most evenings now.

"What do you think of Shimrit?" Rani asked shyly. Mara felt herself begin to grin as Rani continued. "I know he is quiet and shy, but he truly loves the Lord and -"

"I think he is a wonderful man," Mara interrupted. "I wish I had looked for young men like him when I was young. I think he would make anyone a perfect husband."

A tell-tale blush spread to Rani's cheeks.

"He asked me if I would consider marrying him – with your consent and Eli's, in place of my Abba, of course." She dipped her head, allowing her curls to fall across her face.

Mara laughed delightedly.

"Rani, I think that is wonderful!"

Rani blushed once more. "So does Eli. Do you think... Do you think it would be suitable for us to be married soon?"

Mara rested her hands on her daughter's shoulders. "Rani, marry him the moment he wants to. Don't waste a moment of your life! If it is with him that Yahweh wants you to be, then so be it!"

Rani looked happily up at her birthmother. "The moment he asks, I'll be ready."

A few nights later, on the lake shore, Shimrit took Rani as his bride. Mara didn't know she'd ever felt such happiness as she did now, watching her baby marry the one her soul loved. Rani looked radiant as she stood in her ordinary everyday tunic, her hair filled with flowers.

Shimrit, at her side, bore no trace of the awkward, shy youth he had been only months before. The Shimrit Rani married, stood erect and confident, although still quiet. And no one could have wiped the delighted grin off his face.

Along with this wonderful happening was another. Yeshua was said to be moving on the next day. They, themselves were running out of money and Mara knew that it was time for them to return to Samaria.

There were so many people she had to tell her story to. So many people whose lives would be forever changed once they knew Yeshua, knew Him to be the Messiah. She wanted to settle down, back in her home town with her seven year old little man and give him a proper home.

She wanted to give Eli the opportunity to settle down as well, to marry and be happy. To serve the Lord with a wife and family by his side. She had great confidence that her nephew would make a good life for himself and those to follow him. He had, after all, seen Yeshua and believed.

Saying goodbye to those with whom they'd spent so many nights felt hard, but they were preparing to move on as well.

"How can anyone go back to normal life after this?" One woman asked Mara as they embraced for a tearful goodbye.

"I'm not sure we can – at least not the normal we used to know." Mara replied softly. "I think that Yeshua would want us to have a new kind of normal. Where living the way He has taught us, is matter of course."

* * *

Mara stood alone on the lake shore, looking out in the direction where Yeshua's boat had gone. The other lady she'd been speaking to, the Greek, had been right. It felt strange to even consider leaving the place where Yeshua had been.

Eli and Raphi had gone off to find provisions for their journey home, leaving Mara to her solitary thinking. Eli had, it seemed, sensed her need to be alone for a while, to think through everything that had happened. Everything they'd left behind.

"Mara? It is you, isn't it?" The quiet, pained voice spoke out from behind Mara, surprising her. It was the voice she'd know anywhere. Without even turning around, she breathed out his name.

"Levi."

What was he doing here in Galilee? Hadn't he gone to Corinth? She didn't want to turn around and face him. She was too afraid that the past would rise up once more, making her its prisoner.

Levi, her first love. The one who, for so long, she'd thought might be her forever love. Mara couldn't bear to have the feelings rise up once more. Not now that she'd come so far.

"I knew it was you." His voice was saying. He sounded so sad. Breathing up a prayer to God that He would keep her from sin, Mara turned around and faced him. She felt… nothing. Nothing, but pity for the sad shell of the man she remembered so differently, standing before her now.

For a while the two of them just stood facing each other. For about the tenth time in the two days, Mara thought how times had changed. Levi was forever etched in her memory with the lazy grin he'd used to win her when she was a girl. He was painted in her memory with the look of awe he'd had for her on the day she arrived at that feast, so long ago. With the weepy, undone eyes he'd had as he left her in Sebaste. His eyes still carried traces of that betrayed man. He looked back at her and she couldn't help but wonder if he, too, was imagining her as she had been – young, naive and sparkling with life, or defiant, selfish and determined.

So much had changed and yet the memories remained so strong. They had shared so much of their lives together, it felt absurd to just see him and know nothing of his life.

Eventually, Levi cleared his throat and broke the silence, his always husky throat cracking a with deep-felt emotion. "It was you I heard speaking last night, wasn't it? The moment I heard your voice, heard the words you spoke, I knew it was you.."It wasn't a genuine question, just a flat, sad statement. If sadness and remorse had a voice, it was his in that moment. Mara could hear so much more than the meaning of his words in what he said.

"Yes, it was me," she replied, looking away. She couldn't bear the melancholy in his eyes, knowing she was the cause of it.

"I heard what you were saying. Is it true?" Levi asked, still in that depressed monotone. There was no hope in his words. It was almost as if he expected this to be another lie, as Mara had always lied to him.

"It really is true, Levi. Every word of it." She looked back at him, willing him to see the truth in her eyes. "I'm a changed woman. Yeshua saw right through me and my sinful lifestyle. He saw that I had done so much wrong in my life and showed me that I needed to change my ways, to follow Him. I wish I could show you my heart, so that you could know it was the truth."

Levi sighed and shook his head slowly.

"I thought there was something different about you. I can hear it in the way you speak. You're not being devious like you used to, you sounded more truthful. So, you have met the Messiah, the Savior of the world! What I wouldn't give to have been there, to see Him!" The longing in his voice was evident.

"You can!" Mara said. "He was here, in Galilee. And now, he is heading on to Jerusalem. Why don't you go and hear Him speak for yourself? It will change your life to hear Him, Levi. He is not like anyone else on this earth."

Levi gave a soft chuckle, a flicker of the past, as he listened to her.

"Of course not. He is the Messiah – God's chosen one, after all."

"You believe then?" Mara asked, hardly daring to breathe. Levi nodded, his dark hair falling across his eyes. He brushed it back irritably.

"I believe because I can hear that you are telling the truth. Even after all these years I can still remember how you look and sound when it is the truth coming from your mouth. I believe because of what you have told me, Mara. But I want more than that, I want to believe because I have heard it for myself. I came back to Judaea because I heard reports of a prophet... I never dreamed it might truly be the Messiah!"

At that moment, Raphael came running up, face alight with boyish joy. He threw his arms around Mara's waist and began telling her about the game he'd been playing. When he noticed Levi, intimidating in his fine, ornate clothing, he shrank behind her a little, gazing warily up at him.

Levi bent down, smiling at the boy.

"Is this your Imah?" He asked Raphael, who nodded slowly, his pale eyes solemn, a little unsure.

"This is my son, Raphael," Mara inserted. Levi half-nodded his understanding. Mara couldn't stop a small smile from passing over her lips. It was that very chin-up gesture that had once made her insides flip. Levi continued speaking to Raphi.

"She's a very special lady. You are blessed to be her son," he said. Raphael blinked in silence. "What's your Abba's name?" Levi asked.

"Shemu'el," Raphael mumbled into Mara's side. Levi's eyebrows went up and his gaze moved up to Mara's face, though he stayed crouched down by the child.

"Is that right?"

"It's a long story," Mara murmured. Levi gave another grunted chuckle.

"Oh, I have no doubt of that." Pulling himself back up to his full height, he gave Mara a nod and tousled Raphael's hair. "Well, don't let me keep you. You've given me something to think about and it was nice to meet your boy."

Mara directed Raphi off to go and find Shimrit, Rani and Eli. Levi turned to go, but Mara caught his arm.

"Levi, wait."

He looked back at her solemnly.

"There's one more thing I want to say. I'm not sure how welcome the words will be, but I need to say them anyhow." She took a deep breath, tears burning the back of her golden eyes. "I'm sorry Levi. I'm sorry for everything. For all the pain I caused you. For the hardship. For the loss. For my cruelty and selfishness. I cannot tell you how sorry I am."

Her voice cracked and she turned away as a rogue tear broke through the front and trickled its way down her cheek.

"I know you're sorry." She could hear the sad smile in Levi's voice. "I can see you are different now. You're finally happy. And you're free. I can see it. That roaming spirit is gone."

Mara turned her face back to him. He looked resigned now, the sadness still lingering behind his eyes, hardened by the years, yet melted a little in this moment.

"Please forgive me Levi. I know I ask a lot of you, but I beg you, forgive me for the wrongs I have done you. I wish I could go back and change everything, never hurt you, but I cannot. This is all I can do."

Levi put a hand gently on her shoulder. He saw her as he had once seen her, in that box at the hippodrome, so young and nervous. She had been so vulnerable then.

Now, she was also vulnerable, but in a new way. She was vulnerable because of the compassion she was seeking to show. "I will forgive you Mara. Nothing can fix the past now. But I will forgive you all the same. It is all over now. The past." He laughed softly, a trace of his old crooked grin on his face. "Doesn't it seem strange to you now, to think that once we were so young and so very in love? It feels like another lifetime entirely."

Mara gave a watery smile.

"It is, in a way. I'm an entirely new person now." She turned to face

Levi directly once more. "Thank you for your forgiveness. It means more to me than you would realize."

Levi shrugged.

"It's time to let the past be the past, no matter how painful it once was." He gave her a final nod, and turned to go once more. "Say hello to your family for me. Maybe I'll see you in Sychar one day. But for now, I want to see this Yeshua myself."

With that, Levi was gone, off through the crowded market place. Mara watched his tall frame through the mass of people surrounding them.

As he went, she felt as though he took the past with him, pulling it away from her in his wake, removing it from her. The moment of history they had spent together was gone now. She didn't have to feel it any more.

She squeezed her eyes closed, preventing any more tears from slipping their way down her cheeks. Face raised to the skies, she whispered her most heartfelt thanks to God. And with that, the moment had passed.

She made her way back to find Rani, Shimrit, Eli, and Raphael. It was time for them to part – Shimrit and Rani to follow Yeshua; Mara, Eli, and Raphi to return to Sychar. It was time.

Chapter XXXVI.

A.D. 27, Sychar, Samaria, Roman province of Judaea

Returning to Sychar felt like coming home. Mara was filled with overwhelming joy as they made their way up the valley between Mount Gerizim and Mount Ebal.

Yeshua's words, "A time is coming when you will neither worship on this mountain, or in Jerusalem" filtered through her mind. "Yet a time is coming and has now come when the true worshippers will worship the Father in the Spirit and in truth, for they are the kind of worshippers the Father seeks," he had said. How true.

Now, Mara worshipped in her heart all the time.

It had been a long journey and with their stop over in Tiberius, to visit Daniyyel, Leah and their family, it seemed like forever since their time in Capernaum now.

They were welcomed back by their family and friends with a feast which went on long into the night. Over and over, the travellers told of Yeshua's teachings and all the new sights and sounds they had seen, and heard.

Dawid and Zimra wept bittersweet tears as she told them of her conversation with Rani and of Rani's marriage. It was all so sad and yet so wonderful. So redeemed. Mara couldn't wait until Rani and her new husband made their way home to Samaria, as well.

It was strange to be back, strange to be in Shemu'el's house without his presence there. Raphael was delighted to be home. Mara, however, felt incredibly alone and a little lost. After all their adventure, after all they had been through, somehow, she was expecting something... more. Something different.

The first few days after their return, Mara really struggled. She just felt so hollow.

Shouldn't their experience with Yeshua mean more change for her, for all of them? Being back in a "normal life" phase just felt so empty.

Dawid had arranged for Raphael, who was nearly eight years old now, to work for one of the shepherds who had worked with Shemu'el in the past. During her days, Mara was all alone.

Often, she would go over to visit Zimra and the two of them talked long and deeply about Yeshua. Especially about His alleged forgiving of sins. But talking wasn't enough, Mara just knew she had to do something.

Shimrit and Rani arrived back in Sychar several weeks after Mara, Eli and Raphael had. Mara hadn't realised how much she had missed them until she saw them walking up towards her. She ran to meet them, the years falling off her bones as she went.

The embrace with which she met her daughter was heart-felt. Rani was looking so happy, Mara realised, as she held her daughter at arms length. Marriage to Shimrit was good for her.

Mara invited the young couple to make her home their own, giving up for them the room she and Shemu'el had once shared. They were happy to accept.

Shimrit set up a new cobbler's stall at the home's front and life was breathed once more into the old cottage.

And that's when Mara had her idea. She knew what she should do. By the flickering light of a candle, she had sat for many nights thinking and praying to Yahweh for guidance. She wanted to make her life count, to do something more meaningful than just eat, sleep, repeat.

Then she remembered Mariam the Magdalene – the woman Shimrit had seen anointing Yeshua's feet with her tears. Mariam had been a woman of the night and Yeshua had cast seven demons from her. And Mariam had been changed forever – she loved Yeshua now. Just as Mara did.

Suddenly, it was as if a voice within her way saying *Go to women like her, Mara. Women like you. They need freedom too.*

It was so strong, Mara couldn't even imagine trying to resist. She would go.

It was a long time since Mara had set foot in an establishment such as this. The dark tavern was filled with incense-spiced smoke and sensuous music. As it was early morning, there were few people about; last night's drunken rabble having already made their way home. It felt so wrong for Mara to be here now.

But taking a deep breath, she went in.

Near the back of the tavern was a gathering of girls. Their gaudy tunics – low cut and tight - made her wince. She remembered all too well what it felt like to dress this way. The tinkling anklets, the jingling bracelets. The heavy eye make-up and the sensuous lip stain....Her heart broke for them, many younger than her own daughter.

"Hello, my sisters!" She called out. The pack of women regarded her suspiciously as she made her way forward. Mara held out her hands.

"I've brought you some food."

Hesitating only a moment, the women converged on Mara. She had been right. Although some of them made enough money to live quite comfortably, most of their income went right back into paying for the upkeep of their appearances. They were hungering physically as well as spiritually.

After a while, one of the older girls looked across at Mara.

"Why have you done this? Why have you brought food to us? Don't you know what kind of women we are?" Mara nodded slowly.

"I know. And I remember what it feels like to feel you have to give your all to look right. To be something you no longer desire to be. To be forced to play a part. And what it feels to hunger."

She gave a rueful smile and saw she had captured their interest. One girl near the back, with lovely, dark eyes, filled with deep pain, drew Mara's attention. Perhaps this girl was the reason she had come here.

"What do you mean?" Another girl asked. Mara smiled again. And so she began her story. She told them of Ya'acov's Well and of Yeshua and of Mariam the Magdalene. She told them what Yeshua had done for her. What he could do for all of them.

All the women listened with baited breath. The youngest one with the dark eyes couldn't conceal her tears.

After that, Mara went back day after day. Not everyone amongst Yeshua's followers in the city understood, but Mara didn't feel they had to. She knew what she was doing was right.

Each day, she built a relationship with the girls as she lived life alongside them. Not all of the girls would listen, but the young one, Mara learnt her name was Kerah, always would.

Kerah was deeply touched by the message of the Messiah. Mara could see that the girl hated her life in the Night House and yet, there was something holding her back from leaving.

One afternoon, Mara took the girl out for a walk to Ya'acov's Well and asked her life story. They both cried as Kerah related the tale of her parents' untimely death and the cruel uncle who sold her to a tavern lord when she was only seven. Now, at fourteen, she could see no end to her torment, as she didn't have enough money to pay her debt to the Sebastean tavern lord who held the keys to her freedom.

Mara held her tightly, as a mother would. Kerah's story touched her deeply. *I always thought I was so badly off,* she thought. *And yet, there are people like this poor, innocent girl who suffer far more.*

And so, Mara sold Shemu'el's home to Shimrit and Rani. Taking the money in her hand and Kerah with her, she marched the three hours to Sebaste. The tavern lord was surprised and somewhat amused when the feisty older woman and the timid girl approached. The money Mara offered him was more than enough to buy Kerah's freedom.

The girl wept with joy as they walked away.

"I cannot believe I am truly free of that life!" She kept repeating as they headed through Sebaste's filthy backstreets and out towards Sychar, once more.

As they made their way between Sebaste and Sychar, just past the ruins of what had once been Shechem, Mara was surprised and delighted to see Yeshua and his followers. Kerah was overwhelmed at the sight.

As Mara listened, she could hear the youngest disciple – the boy she remembered – now two years taller, and his older brother animatedly talking to Yeshua.

"Lord," they were saying. "The people of this town refuse to accept you merely because you are heading to Jerusalem! These Samaritans have no shame. The prophets told them time and time again that Jerusalem is Yahweh's chosen place for our worship."

Even from a distance, Mara could clearly hear their words and sense their fury.

"Lord, do you want us to call fire down from heaven to destroy them?" They asked now.

Kerah's jaw fell slack as she listened. But Yeshua didn't give the two young disciples approval to call down the heavenly judgement. Instead, as they watched, He rebuked them. And they began to head out for Sychar instead.

Mara and Kerah ran all the way home, arriving just before Yeshua and His disciples. Sychar didn't turn Him away. They welcomed Him. In delight.

And nothing made Mara's heart gladder than hearing Kerah's softly spoken words.

"I believe."

* * *

After Yeshua left Samaria again, heading down to Jerusalem, Eli made the decision to go with Him and his growing body of believers. It was strange not having Eli home in Sychar, but everyone was thrilled when one sunny evening, just into the new year, they saw him approaching up the road, a young woman at his side.

At once, Mara knew who it was. She ran to greet her nephew and the young Jewess she loved so dearly.

"Avigayil, my dear! I'm so pleased to see you!" She cried, embracing her tightly. One look up at Eli told her all she needed to know. He had taken Avigayil as his bride.

"Your parents approved?" She asked the girl, who blushed and nodded. "It was hard for them, but in the time Eli spent living with our family throughout the last year, they came to love him as a son. And they were pleased I wanted to marry one who loves our Yeshua so much!"

The few years had worked wonders for Avigayil. She was as lovely as ever, but now, her beauty was also flowing from her heart.

Dawid and Zimra embraced their new daughter-in-law with open arms. It was, after all, very hard not to love Avigayil.

That night, as the family sat around feasting, Mara wondered again at Yahweh's grace to her. She was surrounded by her brother, Dawid, his sweet Zimra and their children. Rani, her own beloved child, was there with Shimrit, Eli and Avigayil, her sweet Raphael and now Kerah too, like another daughter. Mara only wished her own Abba, her grandparents and Shemu'el could have been there to see this day.

They all listened intently as Eli told them the stories of Yeshua he had heard in his time away. Their favourite was the story with the Samaritan in it.

"A teacher of the Jewish law asked Yeshua what he must do to inherit eternal life. Yeshua asked him what the Law said, and the man replied. "Love the Lord your God with all your heart, and with all your soul, and with all your strength, and with all your mind" and "Love your neighbour as yourself". Yeshua replied that this was correct. Then the man asked "Who is my neighbour?"

Eli's eyes, as golden as Mara's, shone brightly as he related Yeshua's answer.

"A man was going down from Jerusalem to Jericho, when he was attacked by robbers. They stripped him of his clothes, beat him and went away, leaving him half dead. A priest happened to be going down the same road and when he saw the man, he passed by on the other side. So too, a Levite, when he came to the place and saw him, passed by on the other side. But a Samaritan, as he travelled, came to where the man was and when he saw him, he took pity on him. He went to him and bandaged his wounds, pouring on oil and wine. Then he put the man on his own donkey, brought him to an inn and took care of him. The next day he took out two denarii and gave them to the innkeeper. 'Look after him,' he said, 'and when I return, I will reimburse you for any extra expense you may have.'

Then Yeshua asked the teacher of the Law; "Which of these three do you think was a neighbour to the man who fell into the hands of robbers?" The law man replied. "The one who had mercy on him." And Yeshua told him to go and do the same."

They all sat in wonder, as they realised what the story told them. That even they, Samaritans, hated by the Jews, could inherit eternal life if they lived as Yeshua called them to.

"The miracles He did! You should have seen them!" Eli continued. "He fed five thousand of us in one sitting. He even raised a man from the dead!"

Dawid shook his head slowly.

"It's hard to comprehend." He looked thoughtful for a moment, before he continued. "You know, it's strange. We've talked for so long about the Messiah coming and now He is finally here, I get the feeling the liberation He brings will be nothing like we imagined."

None of them could have ever guessed how right he would be.

Chapter XXXVII.

A.D. 28, Sychar, Samaria, Roman province of Judaea

It was during the Jewish Passover when it happened. Mara knew it was something momentous. And that it had something to do with Yeshua.

It was the middle of the afternoon when the sky went black as night. And then the whole land began to shake with a tremendous earthquake. It was like the earth itself was lamenting a loss.

And then, as suddenly as it had started, it was finished.

***

"He's dead! He's dead!"

A few weeks later, Mara looked up from her weaving, startled by the frantic tone of Kerah's voice.

"Who is dead?!" She heard Rani asking, as she hurried out into the front of the house to join them. Mara had expected to find Kerah in floods of tears, but the girl's eyes were bright with excitement.

"Yeshua! But He's alive!"

"What are you talking about?" Shimrit joined the conversation, voice gruff in his confusion.

"I met some disciples on the road! He's alive! He's alive!" Kerah was clearly overwhelmed by her own words.

Mara stepped forward and put her arm around Kerah.

"Sit down. I think you better start from the beginning."

Kerah stayed standing, quivering with emotion.

"This is the best news we've ever had, Mara. Yeshua gave himself as a sacrifice for us all. We're all free! He died in our place. And He didn't stay dead. He rose. He's alive! They've seen Him all across Jerusalem and in Galilee!" She was garbling now.

"I don't understand!" Raphael piped up. "Why did Yeshua die?"

"The Jews had the Romans put Him to death, they charged Him with blasphemy." Kerah started again, trying to make sense of all the thoughts whirling around her head. "A false claim. And so He died an innocent death. And only a perfect sacrifice could bring complete freedom for us. It is the blood that makes atonement for one's life." She finished, quoting the Scripture they all knew so well.

For a while, they all stood in shocked silence as they tried to take in the full magnitude of what Kerah was saying. All their lives, the Samaritans had sacrificed animals to Yahweh, seeking cleansing for their own sins through an animal's life. And thousands of years before, Yahweh had promised their forefather, Avraham, that He would send them the true lamb of sacrifice. He would send the perfect Lamb to atone for them once-and-for-all.

"That's true," Mara breathed finally. "Only the best of our animals are able to be used as atonement offerings. We are only redeemed by an unblemished, pure sacrifice."

Rani's eyes were awash with unshed tears.

"Yeshua died? For us?!"

Kerah began to smile. "Yes. Isn't it incredible?! He lived the life none of us ever could have – a life of perfection. He's the promised Passover lamb! And when He died, the great curtain in the Jews' temple – the one that closes off the holy of holies – it tore down the middle!"

Shock ran through all their bodies. Yeshua's death had opened the Holy of Holies? The curtain in the Jewish temple was designed to prevent the people, in their sin, from entering the place that would destroy them. Did that mean what it seemed to? That through Yeshua's death, anyone could come to Yahweh?

"I am the way and the truth and the life. No one comes to the Father except through Me." Shimrit softly whispered the words they had once heard Yeshua speak. Suddenly, it all made sense.

"And you say He is alive again, Kerah?" Rani asked, hardly daring to believe. Kerah nodded her head violently.

"Yes! Yes! Yes! Three days after he died, Yeshua rose again. And now He has returned to Heaven to be with Yahweh, the Father. And we have been set free from our sins!"

Epilogue:

A.D. 35, Sychar, Samaria, Roman province of Judaea

"Imah!" Mara looked up as her tall son ran towards her. She could hardly believe Raphael was now fifteen years old! Where had the time gone? Her little boy was now a man. Gone were the childhood curls, the little boyish grin. Now, Raphael's hair was cut short, his blue eyes flashing in his tanned, desert face. He bore Mara's high cheekbones and her smile. But the rest... there was no doubting now he was Naftali's son.

"Imah, we have to go to Sebaste!" His words and his excited eyes surprised her.

"What do you mean, my son?"

Mara was an old woman of forty-five now – such a walk was no longer easy for her.

"You won't want to miss this, Imah! Philippos – a man from the church of Yeshua in Jerusalem. He has been preaching and teaching and doing signs in the city. Remember that wizard, Shim'on, the one they call the Great Power? Even he believes!" Raphael began to laugh his happy chuckle, excitement tangible.

"Imah, Yeshua's disciples, Shim'on Cephas and Yochanan are

coming to Sebaste. They've heard how the people here are accepting the message of Yeshua, the Messiah and are being baptised."

Raphael was right. There was nothing in the world that would make her want to miss being in Sebaste right now.

It was with all her dearest ones – with Dawid and Zimra, Eli and Avigayil, Shimrit and her darling daughter Rani, and their children, her precious son Raphael and Kerah, like a second daughter – that Mara was baptised in the river outside Sebaste, turtles swimming around them.

The disciple she remembered as a young boy – Yohanan – laid his hands on her head and she received the Holy Spirit of Yahweh – sent by Yeshua to comfort His people now He had left the earth.

Tears ran down the valleys of Mara's sun beaten cheeks. This was a moment to cherish. A perfectly beautiful moment. She knew the truth now. God knew what He was doing. She could see that now. He had beautiful plans for each of them. He was moulding and shaping as He saw fit. And He had planned it all out from the beginning of time.

Eyes raised to the skies – clear, brilliant blue – Mara whispered her thanks to her Creator. Thanks for the perfect life He had moulded just for her. For teaching her the only way to find true meaning in this world. For the water of life. And most of all – for Yeshua and that day at Ya'acov's Well.

About the author

Nina Peck

Nina Peck has been telling stories all her life through the written word and the performing arts. She is married to her high school sweetheart, Logan, and lives in the beautiful Manawatu, New Zealand. Together, they run The Genesis Revolution, an organisation dedicated to the telling of the stories of eternity.

DYAD

PETER OSWALD
SEAN BORODALE

Dyad

isinglass

First published in 2005 by Isinglass

Printed in England

A CIP record for this book is available from the British
Library

ISBN 0-9533273-3-7

CONTENTS

Dyad

[*Written under half a moon*]

There is a moon consoling, that to look
you'd say, I was not here before it, now I am
in fullness of its occupying, being
pitchered, with a handle of appearance,
it's as driving a car to walk, it's as walking a road to sit
in a chair to read its weight-banked fall
which so compresses space, it's like a shortness
of breath made long, a sigh brought short,
like saying, I'm certain, look
at who I am by who I'm not. This moon
has rolled down slopes of don't leave, leave,
lean forwards, back, change, stay,
each minute's muse's alternative, a clay-
slip moon out-sliding light, which fills your eyes.

(Sometimes a door slams in the earth,
sometimes a window shuts,
sometimes a man walks out of voice,
sometimes a chance to take grows closed
and some are kings who walk on radio steps
and some are keepers of small-mindedness
and some are dust who settle in low confidence
and some breathe well and some breathe ill,
sometimes a moon is nothing to a man
and when the outside earth's like pain, this large, that slight,
it certainly could be the moon is tricks,
sometimes that trickiness is looking up, saying, 'love,
this best-not-tampered-with, this wildness in flight,
this half-weight silence being, is most of us'.)

[*Because the moon is in my mind*]

In nights as lonely as the sun's
I live my second innocence,
dreaming about the moon's white thighs,
in dark asphyxiated skies.

The pricelessness of dawn demands
the heart and soul and resonance
of little birds with worlds to sell,
but I possess the still hour's owl.

When butterflies like pairs of hands
flit by me in a strobe lit dance,
gesturing in their ecstasy
that heaven is a shrubbery,

and breezes stagger drunkenly
into the slowdance of the sea,
I cannot feel the kiss of the wind,
because the moon is in my mind.

[*The man who rushed with nothing in his head*]

The man who rushed with nothing in his head
Out of his house, into the woods and in,
Over and over the mountains, up and up,
Left every valley like a golden cup,
And every wood a crowd of seraphim,
And every mountain top a marriage bed.

The emptiness of the future made him run,
He floods its channel as the present thaws,
And over his horizon farmlands rise.
The people see him with the same surprise
With which they see the autumn when it pours,
And with the awe in which they hold the sun.

He and this land, being each others' womb,
Love one another truly from afar,
Trees of one size across an equal stream,
Whose leaves are eyes but closed and in a dream,
In which they stroll and talk on a cold star,
Whilst the world smoulders in an orange gloom.

Following gravity through the tilted plough,
Stained by the faces of the self seeing souls
Only as long as they can meet his stare,
He hurries on and leaves them standing there,
As water leaves a bucket full of holes,
As rapidly as time is passing now.

Faster than darkness when the eyelids close,
Pressed by the thought of that which draws him on,
Nothing, until he runs against the mound
That makes the circle that he must run round,
In blinded rage, defending something gone,
Perhaps in penance but till when who knows.

[*Moon on Marldon*]

Danger, we thought as we walked up,
to our left a moon in elemental excess,
like a dog's cataract.

(The wind blew.
The moon shone like a peeled lychee.
The wind under the moon scratched.
It got up like the sound of a pig.)

And we kept pace
with death the footstep, death so we thought;
it sounded like a tip-tap kind of increment,
horrible to listen to.

The moon went down.
We stopped and listened
and our two hearts knocked.

We could go on or we could stop
but in the grass was a noise like
(swish-shish swish-swish)
a small knife being sharpened up.

[Poem to my daughter Io]

Sweetheart, while you were asleep I wheeled you
through the red sea into Jerusalem
where frogs lamented
the conquest of the insect kingdom,

past God on his gallows,
through the bogs of the Somme
where the red-haired angels,
work-numb, hung out their washing,

trucks smashing the hopes of puddles,
gamblers with stars in their hands,
dogs with their hearts in their mouths,
the sky on a brown hinge, turning;

famous paintings left out in the rain,
Mona Lisa hopelessly weeping,
and many other things I did not try to explain
to you since you were sleeping.

[*Copper beech*]

The copper beech is treacle-black
where the sun does not pass.
Our troubles gleam like the leaves' edges
with a stiffness set to disturb the air.
Our troubles are lying with last year's leaves
spread out flat as pennies. Up there, they permit
light by leaving gaps between themselves
and we soak up the remainder of the day.
We dip bread into the soup you have made.
The sun twitches behind the black effigy
of beech and slumps as swallows move.
They swerve, under brisk feathers
and piloted bodies, they slur spanned out
against leaves almost bat-winged as themselves.

'If you could see all the things
you've hurt in the world,
would you want to? You wouldn't have thought
there were so many dead for a start.'
You rise from the table like an evening star.
'It's too late,' I say, 'to show me that.'
Dark sky jogs the leaves,
the little eyes of stars between them.
'Where are the swallows?' The fields are sunken.
'Where are the swallows?' The shadows extend.
I clear the table of bowls and spoons and brush the crumbs.
'Where are the swallows?' The tarred beech
is full of tiny eyes and folded wings.

[Woman silently weeping]

How many times now have I watched the glass wall rising
between me and all sound,
and on the other side, cacophony,
rocks like cloths being wrung so the rivers run down,
but I'm standing
in increasing silence,
as if a great crack should spring
across the face of the moon
and then another and another one,
and I'm out in the garden imagining
the booms and the groans space is not carrying,
as the two halves of the moon
collapse into the chasm between them
with the roar of the red sea's corridor collapsing,
and me not hearing a whisper
of what I am seeing.

[*I fear the road*]

I fear the road
with its knived horns, the snake-heart
at ease with the earth's attitude of death,
I fear the dust.

I fear the thief,
I fear the gag of a gang,

I fear the treaties of hideouts,
hands invisibly touching my earth in broad daylight.

There is a voice along a certain road,
going to Bristol, somewhere along the dust
calling the blackbird out of the thorns,
it sings a song to whoever passes.

'I am your love, I am your love,' and you believe
in such a sweetness, it exorcises you
from any concentration
to a mellifluous love of everything.

And feeling generous, you give blessing
to the hand that feeds on your pocket.
Sing it again, sing it again
and so it sings

and you are helpless on the melodious shifting of dust,
so helpless your shadow is magicked away
by the trick of a thief
easing a noose over the road.

And when you bob up on the roughness
out of the spell
you see ten or so skeletons disappearing
over the brow of your nakedness

pulling houses out of their jaws,
sweethearts out of their pelvic bones,
observations out of their eye sockets
and you feel just this

wisdom of experience
and the weather of nudity
recalling something by a blackbird
in the fire of a thorn tree.

[*The blackbird replies*]

He cocks his head on one side,
an old man listening to a child.

Or a terrier tensed for the rabbit
to leap into daylight
just ahead of the ferret.

Silent as a cheese-taster
listening to the taste of the cheese.

Or the off-duty seismologist
in the roar of Los Angeles,
gauging his underground feeling.

A GP listening again to the body
articulating its complex pathology
in baby language.

Not an anthropologist
interrogating a shaman,
but the shaman
replacing his ears with the wind.

Mozart on a visit to Leipzig,
listening to Bach for the first time.

Thin from the larynx
of exhausted mines,
the seed of a sound,
'Passchendaele, Auschwitz, Soham,'
the earth sighs.

And
'Peace! Peace! Peace! Peace! Peace! Peace!'
the blackbird replies.

[*Pruner*]

Rooks comb the air of the day's first hour
with the stickle blackness of their song and chat,
each hacking a sound herringbone.

A noise lit from a single wrench
tears over sharp throats an aggregate.
They fly, netting sleepers in wires of flight.

They charge the slowness of an orchard.
A pruner turns through the shock of hearing
in the apple of his sleep, unwieldy harmonics bitching.

Parings shine like meteors in the new sunlight.

He can see them winking.

Young cocksure birds drill holes:
mouth ear eye womb
and suck the life out of every one of them.

They slice into the wet flesh of fruit like slates
and small rivers of juice well up on the glossy skins
and slip over into the earth

and disappear.

                    'Oh my simple-minded Eden!

My pruned workatrees with their coin-bright
twig ends snipped for love and profit.'
All a blind pruner's words.

A sleeve of shade pulls down on every branch.

Rooks regain the dark
in the massive order of their sleep.

18]

[Rainsong after rain]

Rain is gloating on the glairy moon
dull as the bruise.

Glaucous leaves get plucked
as the rain roars.

This stipple
step–step glissando of raindrops,
this lightning glitching the woman in her eye
looking up to God.

Rain drowning the beautiful to a crisis of beauty,
loosening its lady locks.
Bean flowers, wheat stalks
smashed into shanties.

The town in half an hour escapes into drains,
the violence of dust annihilates
and every heart sits in its shelter,
biding its four chambers.

oh, God the blinding noise
oh, God the staring eyes
oh, God the red and matted wheat
and all the petals dashed to death.

Around, around, the treacherous gangling eels
confused and mingling sadness,
alone, and rain, and rain and flooding rain,
the moonrise sinking on the mirrored wheat.

oh, Moon, oh, God, grey god and moon,
the grey and empty heaven,
the boiled moon and the sodden houses,
the horns in the dreadful mud.

God, lonely this time,
looked,
I think,
and gave the horizon another sun to suck.

[*In the garden*]

I am an orange fog
in the crab-apple tree in the garden.
I go out to get myself in.
I am refusing
in a stream of languages
and bird talk and moonsong
and genetic codes
and the cipher of viruses,
and the semaphore of accidents
and the dialect of Acts of God.
I am hissing and spitting,
I am hot iron in my head,
bending ash in my spine.
I am begging myself to come in,
to lie down out of the rain,
to leave the new moon alone
and the dreams of my neighbours under their roofs.
I change colour like the fog around traffic lights,
rage red, deep drowned green,
I change shape, I am giant redwood,
I am snail in can.
I am occult, I am terrifying,
juggling lightning
in the crab-apple tree in the garden.
I am threatening myself,
I say I will bite out my stomach,
crack my skull from within,
boil my bones soft with poisons.
I say I will crawl through worms,
join organisations.
I offer myself sweet prayers
wrapped in coloured paper,
rivers, woods, mountains,
possible changes of Government,
try songs from various stations –
can't find the right band –

I see I am feeding on the static
like an infant on sand.
I say I have jurisdiction,
the power of the death cell,
of solitary, of ritual humiliation,
have ratified no conventions,
and anyway no one will believe me;
have files and files of confessions,
say I will expose myself on National Television;
now I am climbing the tree like flame,
collapsing again
into the terrible cell of a thimble.
So I take myself in.
I lift myself to my ear, I hear
the tiniest, tinniest sobbing.

[*Lamb of death*]

I went through many human minds
till I reached a thorn
in a howling rage,
wind sang like eels through its black cage.

a lamb in me

In every human mind I passed
I felt a tundra's icy blast

and saw no sun but weeping sores
of light on a dark sky.

a lamb in me

A lamb of death stood in each brain,
its wool was matted ash,
its bleat charred to a cry's stump,
its eyes were hollowed to black fires.

a lamb in me

Stood like granite on a hill,
I could not move or turn my eyes.
A lamb of death was crying for milk.
I offered none.

a lamb in me

Grief-logged, weeping-gagged,
flames grew from my eyes.
A vision danced like feet on coals.
The lamb of death led me to its grave.

a lamb in me

fell to a heap, front legs buckled,
eyes wept, sorry sight.
Its death drank from my heart,
drank dry.

a lamb in me

Fleece clutching bones
rafted down to a black sea,
burning lightning shook the plains
around the brain.

[*The death of the young woman*]

All down the golden edge of everything
the people creep, in blue and green,
in country colours.
Children dance, fling balls into the air,
drop them, run laughing after them.
Seeds float, miniature armadas,
all down the summer breeze,
get hooked up in grass stems,
crash full tilt into wing mirrors.
A terrier, smiling gangster,
squashes a pork pie in the angle of his jaws,
just under the exhaust pipe,
ready if caught to look guilty.
The snakejaw boots are wide open,
bubbles are rising in cider and champagne,
the weather is warm, all is amphitheatred
in a circle of heaped-up clouds, electric, smothering,
enormous soft drums, not yet beating.
People are recklessly betting, they are happy
on this upward floating day, dropping paper cups
safe in the knowledge that they will rise eventually to heaven.
Now the dry djembe thuddering
of the hooves comes round again,
they leap, and brush dust off the fences,
each fence a gasp of mothers.
Here come the straining geldings,
leaping - thuddering - leaping -
young women are balancing
on the elastic animals
that reach for the ground
and push it away from them.
Now one, clutching for the green, misses, and pitches,
rolls right over,
ton of thumping blood.
Something lies crooked. The beast heaves up again
and off, into the race, stiffly.

This was the death of the young woman.
And now an old man walks over, looks at her, falls down,
and crawls off on all fours. Young men start shouting.
At last the ambulance comes,
spills a circle of helpless people, dangling their hands.
Now they are bringing her mother, here she comes,
over the turf. Now they are supporting her
under her arms, her legs are empty.
Tannoys announce the end of the celebrations.
Thunder begins, heavy rain.
The day has collapsed like a tent.
All the people go home,
steering their many-coloured caravan
along the golden edge of everything.

[*Song for an orchard singing its death*]

Once a land was an orchard
where I stood in all my crumbs,
all scattered, all left about.
I could not sing gladness to a god of crumbs.
I was so strewn, pecked,
dabbled in bits and pieces,
a death over the ground.

The whole sky ran through me as I was thrown.
What will love me? I thought,

laying down my heads to be taken.
And once, I was an apple's woman
who loved the roundness of perfection.
I heard her singing in my heads when I was apples,
her voice was dark.

Once a woman was an orchard and I tried
but a fox of wind killed the bird of desire
and lit a fire of angriness which burnt us
to flecks of grubby ash. She said, 'Love,
we have not twinkled out, a strapping giant
of silence has put our hands together
and given us some lambs.'

Once an orchard was my world
and I hid, biding my tongue in a curly acid,
rounding my greenness with experience.
I fell into the lap of autumn in the grasses,
shook as a wasp burrowed
and stole my sweetness.
'Gentleness is forgiveness,' she said.

Once I was an orchard feeding lambs.
They curdled together in their games.
Their god was simple infants' milk,
would become the whiteness of age.
But their first lesson was crimson
and slipped through their bellies
to their bleats. Their heads hung in grace.

Lost little creatures, little cleaned skulls
wrecked in the hag-rag branches in the froth
rapids of a storm flood. Their ribs shook with water.
'Choke.' 'Choke.'
Clean little caves in the treetops
fell like apples in the dry summer,
the land could not be an orchard.

[*B'bye*]

Went to Berlin with my friend
in 1989,
danced with Swedish girls
till six in the morning.
Made friends with an American guy
and a GI lady;
no addresses exchanged;
Goodbye Berlin,
Goodbye! B'bye!

Went outside with my love
arm in arm lots of times
to see the comet Hale-Bopp
high-tailing it over the sky.
Took six weeks to leave,
two hundred years to arrive.
Hail to thee, Hale-Bopp,
hail and goodbye!
Goodbye! B'bye!

Left home aged seven.
Left school lots of times.
Keep going back in my dreams,
over and over again,
tumbling around like washing,
like the sun's son flashing by
in his dad's chariot yelling
Hello! Goodbye!
Hi! B'bye!

Here comes the fish roving
round in a glass eye,
tasting the fading trail
of his seven-second memory.
Sees God, sees heaven,
sees all his past lives;

can't hold onto them!
Goodbye! Goodbye!
Bye! B'bye!

Stood on a mountain
with my brother in the wind,
ancient faces of stone
gathered like friends all around.
Here come the clouds now,
stop here and we die!
Better be getting down.
Goodbye! Goodbye!
Bye! B'bye!

[*Wine tasting*]

Gentlemen. Put your lips gentlemen
to the black strawberry
laid up in her blood.
This is the black tooth pulled from the sun's garrotte.

I spit. I spit I spit I spit.

Put your lips gentlemen
to the black forgetfulness,
pause, the galantine colour of the sky on the tongue.
This is the other black tooth pulled from the sun's garrotte.

I spit. I spit I spit I spit.

Put your lips gentlemen
to the gagging fixed eye of a star,
the Universe flowing into its dog's nose.
This gall-wine of the heart is out of its depth.

I spit. I spit I spit I spit.

Put your lips gentlemen
to this dead man in his glass goblet.
We are pouring from his gourd's night into vertigo,
this dysphoric hymn of the gentle blood.

I spit. I spit I spit I spit.

Gentlemen. Your last lips
to the hepatic grimace,
a toast to the heart in the gristly acid of its pains
to this rising of the moon's red falcate.

[*A spirit watches its body being devoured by lions*]

I cling to the air,
peering for a better view.
I now have no weight,
diver without leads
forever leaking upwards
with my own bubbles,
I have to catch myself,
holiday helium balloon,
haul myself down hand over hand,
a ship rigged with sails lighter than air,
impossible to handle in even the slightest breeze.
I am more metaphor than anything,
I can bring myself down to the ground
by thinking of rocks, disappointments,
shipwrecks, jokes badly told, and betrayal.

I have to imagine the smell of them,
even the most recent memories are now fables,
that is why I have to watch them,
just to make sure.
Yes. I am utterly done. Do not send
for paramedics with hunting guns,
one of them is prancing off
with my head in its fangs.
The head of one of them
is stuffed right into my stomach.

Now the air is loose with dark birds,
and the shadows of the jackals
shoot out from between the thorn trees.

I am satisfied. I leave
the red fog of slaughter beneath me.
All night the full fed,
fighting off sleep, will do battle
with the scuttling desperate,

who dash to outflank them,
while the earth, from beneath, picks me apart
by means of minuteness.

Whilst, in new rooms, I am encountering,
briefly, the saddest possible music.
And that is it – that is all my mourning
for myself and those stranded behind.
I have the capacity for grief of an infant,
as I descend into the guts of the Infinite –
rampant, heraldic
or invisible stalker of spirits
through the grass of the commonplace.

[*St. Cuthbert's tongue*]

I am this man to myself.
Then how should I respond.
I am old already to my friends.
I am here on the basis of my history.
They say I will be gone by four.
And when four o'clock arrives
like a doctor at the house
I am ill in Greek to them.
I am inconclusive at four-thirty.
My dust will creep into the corners,
coat the backs of drawers
and sleep on books.
They rearrange my dust.
At five o'clock they all agree,
'He is fairly gone by now'.
I will creep like treacle through their shadows.
When a man declares
I no longer exist, it will suffice.
At seven there are tears.
They are drowned in this belief.
I am dead not quite correctly.
One will claim not to forget me.
One will reassure his shadows,
'of course he's still among us'.
One will talk with shadow in his eyes.
I am a picture of myself.
I am a technique of grieving.
I am lighter.
I am in writing between two others.

[Sonnet]

Often I've tried to settle in this place,
And searching for a more-than-granite base
For my foundations, seized a line of music
Which by its loveliness - or else a face -
Might make perpetual repetition easy;
As if a man should snatch a dragonfly
Out of the air and on its back construct
A palace for his endless residence,
Or find a sea with breakers but no beach,
Where he could surf forever and not reach
Anything, carried on an inheld breath,
As on the awe of a vast audience,
Balancing on their not wanting to cough,
Without the need to rest by falling off.

[*Man among many*]

If you know him, the man who suffers well
With head stubborn quiet – was born to do so –
Continue, he is less likely to fall
Perhaps for striding on intent he knows you

As friend or awkward associate; though
Moves easily without the weight of love,
Or so it seems. At odds still with the rough
First stumble of affection, will not touch

A heart for long, fearing involvement.
He is just one whose nature is woven
Shifting against all odds alive, like shadows,
Since meeting on his terms is an obstinate

Disaster, and he cannot be loved for striving
Against the gentleness of others,
Or folding friendships in the middle, eagerly.
Never a homecoming for him, but he

Is long loved by those who cannot die.

[Description of a prostitute seen through a window in Amsterdam]

There has been a murder.
There is an investigation.
She admits everything.
She holds back nothing.

She has submitted her own body
as evidence. It has been frozen.
She accepts the jurisdiction
of everyone.

She has been locked
in a glass prison.
There is no limitation
to visiting times.

Neutrons turn in her nuclei,
but she is not moving.
She has promised not to try to escape.
Here she sits till death comes!

The poet who tried
to compose a sonnet to her,
sobs in a crab's stomach
weak jokes about the weather.

Of her three Magi,
one died a leper,
one was killed by the other,
who lives in a skyscraper.

Famous explorers
who have pierced her interior,
amazed, have discovered there
the ruins of their own civilisations.

She has established peace
where there was war,
she has achieved agreement
among the philosophers.

No one has ever done
anything against her.
A crime is no longer a crime
when it has been paid for.

She has lent to the kind of friends
who will not return them,
everything she has ever done,
everything she has ever seen.

Only what is hidden is wrong,
only what is denied grows inhuman.
She has done so much good
you can see straight through her skin.

Hatred, forgiveness, rage,
bitterness, have all bled out of her.
All that remains is the pure
clear certainty of murder.

Over the burned dunes,
through the grey acid streams,
under the green sky of Venus
she runs and she runs.

[*A definition*]

Lamb the grey blood of Jonah
Lamb the murder of somebody the grief
Lamb the Moses stuck on his commandments
banging his head against the rock
Lamb the skeleton of a car,
the warship's skeleton grounded at sea,
skull of a bomb flying into bits after its eyes and ears
have collided barking 'Come back Come back'
its tongue into shrapnel,
ghost of a bomb at the flashpoint, too much critical mass
Lamb the bone at the crunching impact of car and body
Lamb the monocle on the sun seeing the moon flogged
Lamb the spermatozoa made out of nothing
God the egg of creation laying itself,
the blood without any red, Lamb for the worse,
Lamb the Titanic's maiden voyage,
Lamb the tantrum dragging its mother like a kicking sack
Lamb the runt, the years of it,
Lamb the tin can of self
in dregs, wasted.

[*Deathsong for a lamb*]

Lamb put his head to the hill
listening to the day driving the heat.
Tongues and teeth of fire were in the stones.

Lamb slept through the sun. It was holy.
Walked from the wool and skull of his mirage
into the desert of the ravens.

Only his own belongings packed into the shape of him,
the one suitcase of his life,
its little legs and neck, the lungs, the brain, the teeth, the tongue.

The sea bled like a fire on the big side of the planet,
the sun passed the god of its hand like a skin graft.
Lamb saw the shiver of big waves crash.

'You,' said the rock, 'Blood is the prophecy in the cave.
Blood is the keeper of this prophecy.'
Lamb breathed the complete musical score of the horizon,

saw the semi-quavers of the big trees,
the chords of tors weighing tons,
the cymbal heatwave of the silent moor.

And the ligament of his tongue
tied the knot of its lamb's bleat.
And the stones drank the slow rivers from their lambs.

[*HMP*]

This one
having escaped all education,
struggles to study
among the prodigies of truancy

This one
fights for the rights to his teapot

This one
will not take part in the Easter play
unless he can be Jesus Christ

This one
once woke up just in time in a morgue

This one
suddenly remembers
shaking his daughter to death

This one
once looked down at himself from the ceiling

This one
says that he eats children

This one
is cured of himself
twenty years into his sentence

This one
is a policeman

This one
is diagnosed 'a political prisoner'
by the psychiatrist

This one
works out

This one
refuses to feel remorse

This one
cannot read
but holds the keys to the chapel

Here all the plots break down,
entirely discredited stories are hawked round
like boxes of wet matches.
Here all the failed disguises
are hung up to rot on gibbets,
beside a rubbish heap of alibis.

Here the stars won't float
but must be propped up, every one,
the trees kept green by your grin,
the walls white by your smiling.

[*The air*]

Now I will go up into the air,
and twist my mind into the wind's weave.

Much more is rising than falling –
steeples reaching a certain height
break open releasing
seeds that gyrate in the vane-spinning
north to south stepping,
bright blue eyed twelve league booted
invisible hurrying
that will turn, at the absolute limit of all things,
and stream back to the beginning.
Listen to them, hatching on the wing,
bubbles of music bursting,
high up above the leads and the flagstones,
instantaneous rainbows of sound.
As the congregation
drop like sacks to their knees,
blue flames are flickering
from their nostrils and mouths.
Much more is rising than falling,
even my own wings,
shedding what is wrongly called down –
it curls away up very quickly.
The surface of the earth now
is sweating rivers of steam.
Someone flicks a match into a rick
and the whole thing is leaping
up like a demon,
shuddering and rolling, pulling
itself up by its own skin,
shaking out in all directions,
raping the pale clouds,
rushing off into nothing.
Much more is rising than falling.
Here come the thoughts of old men,
wrapped in brown tissue paper,
unwrapping, revealing – nothing.
Hearts like hot air balloons
clutter the air lanes,
flare-off of opinions,

confused updrift from colleges
and hospitals, turbulent fog over prisons,
repetitive hours sloughed off
as gossamer skins,
shop window reflections,
abstractions, girl magazines,
blueprints, cancelled plans, missed meetings
of eyes, all insubstantial things,
limp in the updraught
of the inverse autumn,
swift in the slipstreams,
extinctions, abortions,
Earth's onion skins,
in endless perpendicular procession,
kites without strings
and rice paper paintings.
And the pre-speech of infants,
blown about husk-winged
and jewel-eyed,
with legs dangling.
Not one word falls to the ground.
All rise, a good haul
for the wind's fishing,
letters decoupling, tangling,
paragraphs pulled apart by the crosswinds,
where the swallows dive like dolphins
in the sardine run,
and schools of starlings flash turning
through the radio waves,
chat chopped by the chinook.
I flinch through crowds of sighs,
the daily trade of small deaths,
lives lighter than air
floating out of the flesh,
shrews, fleas, field mice, lacewings, soldiers,
plummeting upwards
through the transparent webwork
of shifting hexagons,

a beehive construction,
turned inside out and
inside in
at the speed of breathing;
seven mile high shafts of
invisible steel
bending and twisting,
plates of air
like oceans on end,
tilting, colliding, smashing, with no debris,
except the strings of gulls, dangling.
Emerald and topaz crystals
crash straight through me.
Now the earth breathes in her sleep,
odour of seeds, odour of cities.
Entire seas rise
with a yawn, half asleep,
climbing the stairs of the sky
in the furnace of dawn,
to the bathroom.
Cobras of smoke uncoil
from the baskets of cities.
Much more is rising than falling,
all things desire to be cloud,
and will have their turn
in the centrifugal machine,
joy riding,
all the heavy mourners by the grave,
will shoot up like rockets one day!
Now the whole earth is rising,
lifting her head from the pillow
to me bending,
the far lines drawn together
as if by a string's tugging,
the grand reach and scale of fences and woodlands
collapsing and vastly expanding
to this one damp green field
in which I am standing.

[*November walk*]

I watch crowflight in unintelligible rain,
fleets of weather,
a slagheap and clitter of wind screewalking,
a gunport of a sun prying into death's wind and rain.
I watch very much alive all over the moor's emptying of me.
What is this black crow, and then it's gone,
like a whimper corkscrewing to nothing,
and that is it, no other way of saying how a crow
glided off the map of itself.

I walk under beeches hassled close to the rain's crying,
like anorexics trying out skinny arms to each other,
one downy copper-skinned leaf falls
and then a hundred falling undress a cage's inner locked
statue of frames.
I stand in space being with just the atom of a small factory
of the weather producing the weather;
near to goddesses of whisper,
thighs and shoulders of lace leafwork on teabreak,
doing the emaciated needlework of whatever roars,
and I tip delicately swung about this.

A branch breaks like a teacup's handle,
but how do you consider a broken branch
when it lies in your next footstep. So I smile
going uphill in raindark sploshes of footsteps,
going around that broken mast of the ship of a tree
in wind mania smiling the automaton smile a man makes alone.
The wind is like sorrow - just listen -
hunkering into its headfill weight, then it pushes
a louder crisis gale, a sheet of the sky flapped loose
across twenty miles.

And what do I see next
but a collision of road accident woodland,
it's a tree motorway pile up under the crows,
where another branch cracks, and another
wheels through the air
like a man believing he can fly
and the crows are bent back like umbrellas
by a twelve hours force of wind per second
and the face down is a skin-only of expression
without the head behind it, holding an umbrella crow before it.

All last night the wind shoved in a land
and made hills dents and pushed up a frowning moor
and flattened it
and each crow shivered as it shivers now

strewn backwards through its stationary
flying forwards weight,
shrugged to the wing's shoulder.
I put my eyes out through the rain
in blindness like an eyeless man
as the wind-dough proves into an almighty loaf
of rain war drums
of everywhere beating through everywhere else.
'I am dead,' cries the air. And so I believe it.

Walking by a larch seeing Chinese bronze dragons
of splinters, a terrace of spines
a back so twisted, crippled beyond repair
but what are they now (as I look back) they are:
a blackbird, philosopher in a Chinese poem,
questioning open the white sun.
And there it goes, with a leap and a jump,
walking the gangplank of its step
and I, put simply, am made poor and rich
by the rainwater Atlantic dropped on me.

I am seeing the desert yellow of the sunrise turban
and a willow in streamwater paying its dues,
its leaf tax levied against its takings,
its source becoming its curtailing.
And there I go through the clatter of water
no longer with myself but like a shadow at a loose end
through industrious mills of transparence I go
through cathedral smell and machines of waste rain
gliding off in a series of downhills
onto the still bog pan of where I find my corpse
drifted out like a log, across ten bedrooms

with two eyes like fungal brackets
staring up from the anguish the pounding of the heart
charting the gloom's deep underwater,
seeing all the sub-diseases of all the unable to sing further
as the sun gone red dances itself pink and then frailer

than the gauze of the mantle of a cold
hurricane light's mantle without the clown's hair
of the gas flame's brightness to hide under.
Gone into the black tent of the night,
I'm suddenly pulling the snakeskin world
of a moment off the face of the Earth I've known.

I was the skin in one of its acts
going over November, making the notes
of a wandering leaf on a river
when the wind crashed and the moor shouted,
'Do not dance like a plane crashing please,
if your intuition is a monstrous burial
to which I'll become memorial'. The air –
and I am witness to this – the air cried back,
'Your wreck is the monstrous ghost of my most beloved'.
I listen away, I walk, and what do I meet but a sheep in bits.

I touch the dinosaur fish of its spine,
the relic of its head's downhill
wearing the tackle of Viking, a beautiful mottle
to every bone of it,
a trout's belly of a bone's rainsmudge,
big caves like opened tin cans
containing the rose remainder of its eyes
pawned to the wind birds, the rain godsends, the maggot
choosing and cutting jewels into itself,
the unsaleable brain tipped out
into mouths and the ground, and tufts of wool
pulled across the rough hill's stones.

It must look psychotic, all this weather round a man,
this man in the windscatter blowing the wind back
through a throat,
playing his bones like a cello just to walk straight
the virtuoso of a ridge, and this is the fretboard of his steps
and that, the string bowed out across its tautness, is the link
he makes between two points, singing to Grimspound

while the valleys are strickened in piano concerto
tenfinger hammered out by ten parts of a storm
and I listen away more than I can follow
creeping flat against my soundboard, the ground hollows,
and I'm smiling inside out to breathe back.

Then out pops the sun, and it's big as a fist,
walking the moor like a firewalker walks,
something strange with lizard legs,
the bracken is rigid as old warmonger's iron,
and the grassland's gone copper electroplate
conducting me and every lone walker to horizons
till I'm no longer one spot moving over others
but a liquor of voltage sweeping off
through the wind flickerage of grasses flapping over and over
and I fall through the barrow of my seeings
into the dark kingland of single burials
where I lie stonebroken
under the rain from the world's East and West,
shouting – that is all I can do beneath –
'Take back your sunrise, sun,
your cobra-hiss pollutants, sky,
your dust the scorpion colour of painfulness, innards,
the yellow cirrus of your fuming breath, all cars'.

And lying here, under my own walk
I truly know, love is a fence I crossed
whose stakes are driven through my buried stomach,
and I somehow am balancing on it,
being either in love with the moor or hating it,
across bogland unheavenly to cross,
but there's a mirror in which I hear
tightening exits of noise
like a galaxy played backwards through a fear.

Backwards over iron pans, over ghosts of crowds
on sliding abacus fingers made of water's entrances,
the rain strums out the sun,

the sun strums out the moon,
and no more skull of the drowned sheep, not a whisper,
no more landscape put up for sale
in the eyehole of the skull,
no more siphoning the planet for its black sun
to burn a car about on roads of oil.

I'm just a body with legs held up under the arms
by two kind old bits of air
clutching in my ears the baby cry no one answers,
the nightsweat of the hills,
the lightfear the darkfear the leftover surface
shaking its last coin in the space reserved for it in space,
croaking, 'a bit for the old star please'.
I shake my head together, sticking the final steps of my walk
to the cold red last ray of the boiling sun.

[*By the sea*]

As I was walking to the sea
through the tall bracken, still bright green
and filling me above the eyes
with memories of glens, I blinked

as from the corner of my eye
a moth got up, or so it seemed,
and flew away in front of me,
like a child ducking through a crowd

or a cork bobbing on the sea.
Wings like two white hands powdering
the face of air in a great hurry.
But when I looked more carefully

and touched my face, I saw for certain
that it was not a moth, but my
right eyelids flickering away.
And then – it was astonishing –

the other pair unclipped, disengaged –
peeled off and took flight (I felt no pain)
to join the first ones fluttering
in freedom to the sun – I saw them

black in the bright disc. Now the sea
was sniffing at my feet, far down,
and I was standing at the end
where no plank, no path, no rope, no pier

crosses the air. And then my skin
slipped off and floated to the sand,
and the waves washed it out and in,
and it turned over in the foam

and stretched out, white, to the horizon.

Breathe – I breathed out, and in the air
my lungs stood tendrilled like a cloud,
and then a V of geese, my bones,

and they crashed straight into the sea,
and my eyes followed. No more need
to dream what happens in the sea.
Lastly my heart sank down the sky

and slid, bright red, into the sea.

[*Cat's love*]

Cat's love has not a word but shadows streak
the child's heart, that love is glinting in the dark.
Quick to change the cat draws back,
the child's cry is dark and prowled upon.

A bleat in the child fears the cat.
The bleat runs to an abattoir,
crying, 'Cut me to the very heart
and cut my heartbeat into two.'

Then half will thunder through the universe,
then half will hurricane this curse
of being child fixed by a cat's rage
rising like a planet of sharp fire.

[*Technical manual to a moon*]

Once, there was this moon it flew up
among cows fields pylons.
When it's a night like this,
the moon cuts a guitar on the land,
all the ditches are its strings
over the sound boards the holes into the ground.
When it's a night like this,
the moon's wired to its skeleton.
It's so bright it's beguiling,
up there, not a name to disturb it,
a stillness invisible as a buzzard's routemap.
Like a shout to a hope for an answer, but no echo hangs
because no rocks, only the moon, only the silence of the
      opened jaw.
The moon sends back seriousness of light
like a woman at the full uncalm of her mind, and so on,
a chasm of gaunt moon like a sudden crack in a glass.
Or the sun just got smaller and made a shudder to itself
or did it wink or did it vanish
or imprint its emptiness as a footstep from a gland of walks.
She entered my bones on a night like this,
clouds roamed mottling like mould on cheese the dark
when mountainous crags, when dogs'-barks appeared and fled
through cows calling their calfless-milk's heaviness
over moors, and sighs (the air sighed to hold that noise
of nothing, emptied over the bent, the beard, the field's tresses).
Grasses shake like tassels on hems of Space,
like a dress, not yet with stars but near to coldness.
On a road alone shadows leer
in the headlights of a rushing car
like tongs handling a walker, still
hearing the billowy silence of the curious stars
like a dress warped out and magnetic everywhere.
Each star's a dog's eye in a dog's head called Space
wielding the horizon's bark to its echo's edge.

[*Dog*]

Dog of three masters, in the armchair,
lord of your laws, ignoring ours,
running upstairs, too old to care,
thistledown blowing here and there,
lion in your imagination,
which we deny but which you claim
by terrifying absences.

Over the arm I meet your stare,
hard under soft brows raised and lowered
according to the atmosphere.
You would do better to be kinder,
there is no need for cunning here,
but you are honour-bound to copy
Jackal, your famous ancestor.

All your conclusions are misguided.
We are defeated by the stars,
but you can't even cope with cars –
and off you slope into the forest
of fumes and hoots, but soon return,
proud of that stolen rag of time.
Dog of the heart, where will you lie,

dog of three masters, if you wander
out of the world? Then you and I
will be as flummoxed as each other.
Come when I call, then, keep within
the orbit of a stick well-thrown,
that spins a while into the sky
then kicks back down to the green ground.

[*Notes on Moon Farm*]

The lamb of the blind moon has no name,
drowned in the moonwater dripping from its wool,
as the snowman melting on the matted field,
the woman who is the farmer's wife
shouldering a big bale smudges the cobbles
of hoof prints pressed in the wettest mud of the year
hearing the lamb's cough
in the black barn
of her head
but listen, in the black barn
what is the lamb of the blind moon seeing
as the short grass flown from the sun
burns in the hoofprint of the blind moon.

The lamb's moon-bleat smashes it,
the good of it, the mess of it
sinks in the black moon of the barn,
but listen,
when the washed sheep's skull holds for its brain the wind
and the wind is hungover from its draught of spill
leaked from the body like a room running
by the light of its fire to the fire-exit,
the good of it is the farmer's smile, clean as the sun rise.
Somehow he smiles in eyes
shiny from looking at the frettish wind
fettling fieldtops and the sparrow's wing.
The tractor kicks up mud

and chugs singing its pistons loud
dragging the song of oil from the pool of the black sump,
the pink diesel curls in the pump
like a cat by the fire
dreaming claw flames pounced on the shouting night
huffing
exhausts oily as black crow wing,
gravelly as their mob

bashing earth bits for blood,
crowds the lane's lungs like hounds at ears,
the stickle-thresh of its sound
chasing the murmur of the man in his pulse who steers
swinging over the moon in a shadow tractor

his bones rattle on blood tyres,
teeth gold as the grass ears broaden,
the pig stands in the tin shadows
shouldering the high mud,
the long spine of the pig's back hangs like a line
with the heavy curled toes of its meat's clothes
grunty in the music of its eye-dark,
the hovel of its head set in the frown and jowls,
and piglets flash trotters like babies' hands
on the grey thistles fingered by the moon,
prance their games long moved from the silent sun,
the muckspreader stands quiet as a tomb,
stuck as a seaside donkey on troubling sand,

the horse sways in its deep box like a reader
glancing over notes all winter,
no words gleam
but the beacons of its breath steam
and report that the land of its long head
has somehow arrived
at this end of the worst wet lane under the speaking trees
where the road in the dip floods to the stable
as rivers rise through the netted ground
silencing the car, sodden in the valve and piston,
the engine-block fat as a head slumped on a plate
gluttoned in the bowels of its brain cannot think
whose driver damns in the milling rain

hissing in trees, black and wet thorns,
twigs splayed on the winds as combs through moving hair,
crooked light smiles, then the thundering
laughs in the ditch, under the stairs, in the plumbing

and the few houses scattered like wheat on yards
have closed all windows and the world is unplugged from wires,
aerials whisper, 'do not come here',
boys rush to the windows up the stairs
bumped by the scrum of the rugby wind and they stare
with hands at their eyes,
mouths from their stomachs gawp
and tongues rabble like moths to stars of cold
sparked from the winter turning its rough wheel

and the fleas jump like cats,
the nit bites in shoals through forested hairs
quiet as sorrel,
the smile of the farmer pours through the moonlit drain,
toads sit in the rain
listening to the row of dogs whose barks
clash sword to shield shielding fears
brightening the wide dark
and the weak fly teeters on its badgered wing
dulled in the battery of its buzzing,
slips from the gate latch thumbed as old coins,
it could be the ash leaves sighing
as the midnight begins

the tractor swings from the black lane,
the house pulls the farmer from his boots and coat
like a root from the earth, he is shook
and washed in the blind moonlight,
the house holds him up like a child,
his wife steps from the field
of her hips, the earth's mouth on legs lies,
he climbs with the strong body of love
between sheets cold as the winter wind,
the moon's pieces in the window
hang scoured as pigs, stripped and clean,
and these two loves are set to sleep
in the black moonlight.

[*Dairy farmer*]

Dazed dairy farmer racing round,
stepping and bowing, cow to cow,
in your hosed parlour, shit-sluiced now,
unlocking suckers, two by two,
on without looking to the next one –
hemmed in by quotas, sleep-starved, working
all weekend long despite believing,
sweeping your fields above the sea
in arcs of light like scythes laid down,
to keep so many slow mouths moving
to the dull pulse of the machine's
multiple sucking – in your dreams
slow hands in Africa pull down
the endless vine with tugs that send
the warm jet straight into the bucket
that quickly brims – you walk at dawn –
a cow is lying on the sun
and won't get up for all your banging
with a light stick on a long spine,
but now your dung-caked cow-dog's barking
uplifts the obstacle, and streams
of diamonds dive into your brain –
sweet daylight! From their parlour beams
others, strung up by numbers, hang
but you move on – and here's my question –
father of all your calves, begun
by your sheathed arm's inseminations,
selling for leather and for hounds
all your old brides when they run dry,
what's this bright outcome of a nightmare,
these rocks that breathe where rainbows bend
in the black hands of the east wind,
seventy-nine ships of the line
drifting in here and there formation
on a sea far from wars or storms?

[*About a dejection*]

When my tongue sat down and would not
shape even a stone's smallness or mouse
and I against, or some say with, adventure
with interested demeanour
took what was ours up as my jug
and poured a little into my ego's cup
being a self-confessed new farmer,
nothing grew. I took the subsidies
and thought, if this should keep me for long
I would grow desolate by resolution.
So I quarried under, but not a good stone in sight.
I put stone back, finding no plan fit for its use,
nor could I afford to build a big house.
By my bedside lit and dark
I resolved to kill to sell, I asked
for no miracle, but giant in hope through trial
I laid up nights to stalk, then shot our rabbits
and hung them up by their back legs on nails
and this, my love, seemed unilateral –
all our day's corpses brought to one another's deaths.
With high interest, with less subsidies
and more in need, my eyes projected out
the lean field fox ghost of pure ideals,
which haunted me across each field I'd failed with.

[*Foundryman lost*]

He wore wages to a pint's dreg,
he strutted black tigers from his mouth,
raged, 'Life! Life!' 'kill create, kill create'
till he couldn't decide which was his fate.

And if apprentice got up strength to confront
his awful edifice of face grunting extant
with foul patina under factory strip light,
or went upwind of the joker to put joke

like nutcracker about nut, squeezed tight
the bassoon would tremble at lip's quivery plight
and yell brass through each head's mountain
before sucking the foundry's

entire music into his diaphragm to assault,
as roar, as convulse continental fault,
chatter into millions upon millions
of bits flung as uncharted sparks in space.

Men absorbed at benches would not turn
or reflect from work to watch him burn.
While another wrought as lamb among lambs
so not to attract, he tore into and marked.

No grief veined his brainstone.
His hand of anger put him to the block,
thrashing the image of an inner lamb,
sharpening its bleat on fear as on a whetstone

till the bleat leapt up razor thin and fell
clean through the throat to the dulled apple.
The lamb groped its wound-grimace at the neck
and felt death smile more. But no one saw.

[*At rush hour, or a head's taking on another form*]

Say a man's head is a mountain
and a blood red evening lights
the dark horizon of the cave inside
where a hermit's shadow crouches.

Say his eye fails to attract a stranger's,
so he lowers his head to the ground
heavy with a mind as a rock dragging
while his body works its own way home.

Say his heart murmurs in the tightrope arena
of his chest, clenched at the moment
a foot slips in the dark mid–air
and balance is jeopardised close to falling.

Then say his deadly act requires a little miss
and bold mister to master the ring, tame lions,
or carry whip and whistle at the horses.
He sets his trap, waits. They come as lambs.

Say he is wolf dressed as shepherd
and the crowds flock to see him.
Say in each act are lambs running a field
towards the jaws of night.

Say the field is a desert of thorns
shredding their feet as they run,
piercing their flesh so they never lie down.
And in each act is a cry of love, pulling them down.

[*Childrens' lamb-ballad*]

The ravens took Lamb's eyes.
The ravens left Lamb opened.
The raven's mouths were death's keys.
The air was sharp with choking.

Tell me about the raven,
cried the voice at bedtime.
So I told about the raven
to the ears at bedtime.

The raven stooping

was the earth's short circuit.
The raven taking off
was the ground understanding itself.

The dead raven's beak lying like a dropped pencil lead
was the winter pondering.
The raven in winter
was in love with the black trees.

The mouth gagged by the raven's ear
was the stag on the moor.
The red moon
was the slavery of the car.

The car screwed up like a paper ball
was the drunk messing
buckled to the wheel
drowned in the mouldy ditch.

The raven kept him like a wine
in the gourd of its heart.
The red moon was the tongue of the man
calling, 'Woman. Woman. Can you do anything.'

On the ground
Lamb was like a sundown.
The colder sun went down
cutting with its beams.

Lamb was like a battle scene,
crossed with shadows
like a carcass crossed with crows,
like a hand with black coins.

The sun crashed its signal,
barred by wind and mountains
and formed a creeping shade
across the Universe.

And every star shone deadly.

Tell me a dream,
cried the voice at bedtime,
so I told the dream,
listen; listen;

red, the dark rose of Lamb's tongue
spoke no word,
but God, it was a living silence
prolonged in pain.

What grew in Lamb
so dark he could not know
were weird voices in his head
falling like a snow.

Lamb stepped, an engine
of fierce footsteps rose
and shuffled back to him
like wind and blinding hail.

Out of the ice it came,
out of the ice it came.
Out of ice it chattered
like voices on the verge.

A million mouths in armour,
a million mouths which champed and reared
and clattered over the air
and yet there was a beauty.

A low sound like a winter rain
passed through the bones of Lamb,
a low sound like a blessing,
turning in and out of sound.

Eyes and sun and mouth,

it choked Lamb's heart to see
so many swords and tongues and shields
heraldic as a currency.

An army like loose change
jangled through Lamb's brain,
gambling and promising
well beyond their means.

On they flowed on like monsters
breathing adventure fire
beating sticks and spurs
to make their voices higher.

All in the name of God,
all in the name of Name,
all in the name of Love.
Lamb heard those troubadours.

And listened to them fade,
and then heard in a silence,
the breath of men fell like a death
into the endless air.

Tell me the end,
cried the voice at bedtime,
tell me the end.
So I told the end.

The Universe flowed sighing.

Once there was a woman
in a pit of shade,
and she touched a child
and put it to her head.

Her legs ran into wheels,
her wheels ran into blowouts,

her heart grew mad
and with a whistle-mind she ran.

But just too much was sinking.
She rammed across a stream.
She splattered up her mountains
in a whistle-mind.

She reached a widespread scene,
and crossed and crossed
undigested canyons.
She found a cave of nothing.

And in it lived a man,
a keeper of the mountain echo,
who sheltered sounds
he found across the snow.

'This,' he hushed, 'is the mountain's home,
nothing will know you here,
and through the emptying of your mind
distance will consume you.'

She looked into horizons.
Her eyes flowed North.
And through the dark cold light she went
searching the raven's blood.

The Echo-Keeper closed his eyes.
And mists were passing on all sides
like shoppers in a dream.
And she went on from rock to rock

into the ice-melt's drip drip drip
and with a cold tongue drank the cold stream source
and all the shortness of her life's endurance went
and she flowed sighing and folded into emptiness.

[*Helen*]

I went out with this decent bloke
for fifteen years. I almost choke
with sobs now when I think of how
I left him. What a stupid cow
I am at times. I had it all,
servants at my beck and call,
security, security,
and all, if I was good, for free.

Alas! But doesn't every lass
with looks that sexually harass
the passers-by - like me I mean -
who could confuse a TV screen
by winking at it, sometimes dream?
Security was an ice-cream
on top of mints and Quality Streets
and trolley-fulls of other sweets.

A foreigner who owned a boat
came visiting. I liked his coat,
especially when he laid it down
on puddles. 'If a toe should drown,'
he said, 'may all my tankers sink.'
I really should have stopped to think,
but all my canniness went slack,
seeing my footprints on his back.

'I've seen them all, Venus, Diana,'
he said, and jingled the piano,
'and Juno too, but you're the best.'
The sun was crisping in the west.
The world that he described to me
was like an undiscovered sea,
and I was like a sunken treasure,
imprisoned at Poseidon's pleasure.

Desperate, enterprising man!
He was a bowshot of his own
into my dark, when I was sick
of walking in the daylight. Quick
as a shark he kissed me radically.
Do all disasters happen so quickly?
I'd need to tell you all I am
to tell you why I ran from home.

And that, young man, I don't intend.
Go and find yourself a friend
with friends, and you will shortly find
how much you can unload your mind,
and how to whom. Do not look here
for eloquence inspired by fear
of being misunderstood or forgotten:
all but my wit is dead and rotten.

'His place' was an ancient city,
well defended if not very pretty.
Everyone there was very refined,
slightly on edge but terribly kind
to me. I was what the black sheep had brought home,
and they struggled to think that some good would come
of his blunder. Until, with a tightening of lips,
they saw the horizon covered with ships.

They certainly rallied, you can't say they didn't,
they never asked whether they should or they shouldn't.
I walked wide-eyed on the castle wall,
watching them charge and ripple and fall,
and come back to me, some cutting and bloody,
but most of them thankful and quiet and moody.
My lover changed. He became a dedicated
bridegroom of battle, which was something I hated.

I might as well have been a duster
freshening the King's bedchamber.

Out on the plain, broad and divided,
the knights, like flying snails, collided,
forming one oozing, splintered animal,
now shuddering and huge, now smaller, now small,
as each side extricates - and then,
a shadow on the ground, of men.

The sound of bugles in the air,
and coloured plumes are flying. Fair
is the only word that comes to mind
to those made tired and almost blind
by the singularly single sun
at noon, that does what it has done
for aeons, shines. Let us not go
to watch them riding out below.

I was a duster loved by dust
for ten years. And it seems I must
draw them out here, if only because
then I was a sieve to the cause,
unable to hold their about-to-die eyes
with calm and a blessing, banish surprise
and fill my heart with a sacrificed life -
well look at me, how did I do as a wife?

Or did I do well? They continued to die
for a decade for the look in my eye.
My reasonable husband became a villain,
a monster lashing the walls in vain.
My lover took to poetry
and called civilisation a pollarded tree
that weeps its many gashes dry.
I gave confusion back to the sky

and left one night, in the seventh year
of the siege, when like a steel tear
the thin moon hung, and skipped across
the battlefield, not at a loss

though no one was there to appreciate me.
I knew the shadows would agree
with the way I felt, the violent shapes
like murderers hidden in sable capes.

And danced before the Grecian fires,
catching their eyes between the spires
of flame, and letting them go,
and looking where the moon burned slow
or wrinkled in the rising heat,
remaining, while my feathered feet
courted like doves, and heard the men groan
and belch, and wandered home alone.

'Doll, do you love me?' my partner said,
one afternoon as we lay in bed.
To do this enormous question justice,
I thought at length. A single kiss
might have sufficed. But with a creak
of springs he left before I could speak.
Gradually the monstrously sane
man outside seemed the better man.

Not long ago but far too late
your rich protector said to me
(I won't call him your father yet,
to keep the sense of mystery,)
'Helen, the monument to us
is us. Who gives a tinker's cuss
for what they say, if what they see
is unimaginable matrimony?

'But Helen, are your children mine?
What will men say when we have gone?
If your answer is just 'Yes',
then let us die and let them guess
by looking at our double tomb
that I was doubled in your womb.

But if it is forever 'No',
then Helen, Helen, please say so.

'Nothing will change. United by
hiding our knowledge of this lie,
we two will live until we die
forgiving, you my question, I
your answer, until loss of speech
makes each eternally trust each.'
Nothing is whole. There is no ear
for my reply to hide in here.

Thank God we cannot see what might
have been. Our foresight would take fright
and shelter in a smaller shell
than it already does. Oh well.
Perhaps I might have seen the eyes
that might have given me replies
to questions of the heart. I remain
the tomb of many unburied men.

One more lie before you sleep
to gild your minds and make them shine,
my darlings, as the countless sheep
of sleepless sinners pass in line.
At noon the clinkered horse's tail
was to the sea, as the last sail
fell brightly out of sight. Goodbye!
Our bravest met the horse's eye

from dunetops, while the tearful tide
entered the shapes the ships had made
in the sand, and a million crabs
were suddenly no longer like scabs
but shuffled rejoicing, and the stars
invisibly sang, if anyone cares.
If anyone cares, the sea's not deep,
and after sunset people sleep.

'The longer silence lasts, the more
important when it ends,' the bore
my lover whispered pleadingly.
I listened carefully to the sea.
'Now we have time and peace, our breath
not daily bargained for by death,
no opportunity for hate
to enter into our debate

'no more. Let's have the argument
heaven sends to reinforce content.'
Foam querulously shook the shells.
'We all must make our homes our hells,
so vibrant are our minds, but outward
loss is dwarfed by its reward
within – enormous heavens, free
of physical necessity.'

Those artful white wind-lovers skimmed
the waves and climbed and climbed and climbed.
Oh could you know it, I must cross
once more before my final loss.
And certainly the way they fly
suggests good sailing weather. High
birds obviate the sacrifice.
A handy tiller will suffice.

Cold dawn. A quick decision. Nothing
is dazzling in the early morning.
Old love for new. My deed disproved
that I have ever newly loved –
to those who live. A hyena crept
back over a hill. The heroes slept.
Now, as the proper day begins,
the bristles creep out over their chins.

For me to open the gate, I wind
the winch and scarcely look behind.

The horse has dropped, it has begun,
in shadow I can see the sun
is up enough to paint the tall
pale citadel, higher than the wall.
As the gap widens daylight creeps
on me and then the whole sun leaps

over me into the city. My shadow
falls like a tower, and there, below,
the sea, the plain, all in white heat,
and the tread of ten thousand armoured feet.
Troy dangles from the fingertip,
a crisping corpse upon a ship,
a fly-blown baby, as obscene
as vows of love from a machine.

Its image on the water runs
to meet the gently falling leaf
exactly. Similes and puns
evoke an echo of belief.
The imperfect moon the ripples make
and the reeds break is yet not fake.
Me metaphors of myself bombard,
but mostly miss, and I am hard.

Noon again. The exhausted plain
is covered in men covered in men.
My husband's shadow and my own
are one, as we walk out of town
past metal intertwined with bone
of animal and man, all one,
all burnt. I look up into his eyes,
and sincerely apologize.

[From the chaos when I looked up]

If God has sides ... inside, outside ...
then I am watching one side turned from one
(getting the fag-end of a glimpse)
and I have found it like a flower closing in
but since I'm close enough, it is like entering
a two-way tryst, in that I lean a little
on the turning side of things and feel,
when two glances spook the looking eye
they do not meet but almost miss.
Everything just moves a bit in the paranoid
second of checking at the door of things
that glance by odd intended shyings,
as one small snatch of me is handed on.

[*Clay slope story*]

For thirty odd years
I've been slipping down a slope,
going helpless stone-riddled as
heart lights liver throat

preening my colloids of the iron magnitude of blood
running a skin river in my side
near to not much but footsteps and difficulty
up to the ankles in dragged old beard old surface in-rolled

sifted over sort of lifestuff
when sometimes thirsty rubble over inner water
and luck's eeriness, some things turn up
I clean forgot.

[*Love song to a young woman*]

And what are we,
two linnets in a gale
or sound of air freezing,
two sides of one woodland

or the doubling up of knees together,
or the twin rocking blades of a cradle,
as the song of our rhyme
drowns us asleep?

[Bayleaf boat]

Love, to creatures bright and small
like us, offers no trials at all.
We flitted to it like two fleas
on a match and wire trapeze.
A castle in a goldfish bowl
tested the mettle of my soul,
and your hair could pull me up the tower
when trimmed to just below the ear.

But sighs in empty concert halls
and passion whispered in cathedrals
where echoes seem to grow forever
through chambers of unchanging weather,
made me vainer than the thrush
who knows that when his lovesongs hush
the risen sun will sink again.
Morning came and you were gone:

Fleeing in a bayleaf boat
as dawn broke mighty from my throat.

INDEX OF FIRST LINES